DIVISIBLE MAN™
TEN KEYS WEST

by

Howard Seaborne

ALSO BY HOWARD SEABORNE

DIVISIBLE MAN
A Novel – September 2017
DIVISIBLE MAN - THE SIXTH PAWN
A Novel – June 2018
DIVISIBLE MAN - THE SECOND GHOST
ANGEL FLIGHT
A Novel & Story – September 2018
DIVISIBLE MAN - THE SEVENTH STAR
A Novel – June 2019
DIVISIBLE MAN - TEN MAN CREW
A Novel – November 2019
DIVISIBLE MAN - THE THIRD LIE
A Novel – May 2020
DIVISIBLE MAN - THREE NINES FINE
A Novel – November 2020
DIVISIBLE MAN - EIGHT BALL
A Novel – September 2021
DIVISIBLE MAN - ENGINE OUT
AND OTHER SHORT FLIGHTS
A Story Collection – June 2022
DIVISIBLE MAN - NINE LIVES LOST
A Novel – June 2022
DIVISIBLE MAN - TEN KEYS WEST
A Novel – May 2023
DIVISIBLE MAN - THE ELEVENTH HOURGLASS
A Novel – October 2023

PRAISE FOR HOWARD SEABORNE

DIVISIBLE MAN - THE ELEVENTH HOURGLASS [DM11]

A *BookLife from Publishers Weekly* Editor's Pick - "A book of outstanding quality."

"A lean, fast-paced, and unpredictable story…An accomplished supernatural thriller from a series that keeps on delivering…Will Stewart is one of the most believable unbelievable characters currently running in fiction." — *Kirkus Reviews*

"…thrilling…an effervescent pace…littered with slabs of wicket humor…relentless action…full of fun…truly compelling." — *The BookLife Prize from Publishers Weekly*

DIVISIBLE MAN - TEN KEYS WEST [DM10]

"The best possible combination of the Odd Thomas novels of Dean Koontz and the Jack Reacher novels of Lee Child." — *Kirkus Reviews*

"The soaring 10th entry in this thriller series is as exciting as the first… Seaborne keeps the chatter fun, the pacing fleet, and the tension urgent. His secret weapon is a tight focus on Will and Andy, a married couple whose love—and bantering dialogue—proves as buoyant as ever." — *BookLife*

"The author effectively fleshes out even minor walk-on characters, and his portrayal of the loving relationship between his two heroes continues to be the most satisfying aspect of the series, the kind of three-dimensional adult relationship remarkably rare in thrillers like this one. The author's skill at pacing is razor-sharp—the book is a compulsive page-turner…" — *Kirkus Reviews*

DIVISIBLE MAN - NINE LIVES LOST [DM9]

"Seaborne's latest series entry packs a good deal of mystery. Everything Will stumbles on, it seems, dredges up more questions…All this shady stuff in Montana and unrest in Wisconsin make for a tense narrative…Will's periodic sarcasm is welcome, as it's good-natured and never overwhelming…A smart, diverting tale of an audacious aviator with an extraordinary ability." — *Kirkus Reviews*

DIVISIBLE MAN - ENGINE OUT & OTHER SHORT FLIGHTS

"This engaging compendium will surely pique new readers' interest in earlier series installments. A captivating, altruistic hero and appealing cast propel this enjoyable collection…" — *Kirkus Reviews*

DIVISIBLE MAN - EIGHT BALL [DM8]

"Any reader of this series knows that they're in good hands with Seaborne, who's a natural storyteller. His descriptions and dialogue are crisp, and his characters deftly sketched…The book keeps readers tied into its complex and exciting thriller plot with lucid and graceful exposition, laying out clues with cleverness and subtlety…and the protagonist is always a relatable character with plenty of humanity and humor…Another riveting, taut, and timely adventure with engaging characters and a great premise." — *Kirkus Reviews*

DIVISIBLE MAN - THREE NINES FINE [DM7]

"Seaborne is never less than a spellbinding storyteller, keeping his complicated but clearly explicated plot moving smoothly from one nail-biting scenario to another…The author's grasp of global politics gives depth to the book's thriller elements…Even minor characters come across in three dimensions, and Will himself is an endearing narrator. He's lovestruck by his gorgeous, intelligent, and strong-willed wife; has his heart and social conscience in the right place; and is boyishly thrilled by the other thing. A solid series entry that is, as usual, exciting, intricately plotted, and thoroughly entertaining." —*Kirkus Reviews*

DIVISIBLE MAN - THE THIRD LIE [DM6]

"Seaborne shows himself to be a reliably splendid storyteller in this latest outing. The plot is intricate and could have been confusing in lesser hands, but the author manages it well, keeping readers oriented amid unexpected developments…His crisp writing about complex scenes and concepts is another strong suit…The fantasy of self-powered flight remains absolutely compelling…Will is heroic and daring, as one would expect, but he's also funny, compassionate, and affectionate… A gripping, timely, and twisty thriller." —*Kirkus Reviews*

DIVISIBLE MAN - TEN MAN CREW [DM5]

"Seaborne…continues his winning streak in this series, offering another page-turner. By having Will's knowledge of and control over his powers continue to expand while the questions over how he should best deploy his abilities grow, Seaborne keeps the concept fresh and readers guessing…The conspiracy is highly dramatic yet not implausible given today's political events, and the action sequences are excitingly cinematic…Another compelling and hugely fun adventure that delivers a thrill ride." —*Kirkus Reviews*

DIVISIBLE MAN - THE SEVENTH STAR [DM4]

"Seaborne…proves he's a natural born storyteller, serving up an exciting, well-written thriller. He makes even minor moments in the story memorable with his sharp, evocative prose…Will's smart, humane and humorous narrative voice is appealing, as is his sincere appreciation for Andy—not just for her considerable beauty, but also for her dedication and intelligence. An intensely satisfying thriller—another winner from Seaborne." —*Kirkus Reviews*

DIVISIBLE MAN - THE SECOND GHOST [DM3]

"Seaborne…delivers a solid, well-written tale that taps into the near-universal dream of personal flight. Will's narrative voice is engaging and crisp, clearly explaining technical matters while never losing sight of humane, emotional concerns. Another intelligent and exciting superpowered thriller." —*Kirkus Reviews*

DIVISIBLE MAN - THE SIXTH PAWN [DM2]

A *Booklife from Publishers Weekly* Editor's Pick: **"A book of outstanding quality."**

"Seaborne…once again gives readers a crisply written thriller. Self-powered flight is a potent fantasy, and Seaborne explores its joys and difficulties engagingly. Will's narrative voice is amusing, intelligent and humane; he draws readers in with his wit, appreciation for his wife, and his flight-drunk joy…Even more entertaining than its predecessor—a great read." —*Kirkus Reviews*

DIVISIBLE MAN [DM1]

"Seaborne's crisp prose, playful dialogue, and mastery of technical details of flight distinguish the story…this is a striking and original start to a series, buoyed by fresh and vivid depictions of extra-human powers and a clutch of memorably drawn characters…" —*BookLife*

"This book is a strong start to a series…Well-written and engaging, with memorable characters and an intriguing hero." —*Kirkus Reviews*

"Even more than flight, (Will's relationship with Andy)—and that crack prose—powers this thriller to a satisfying climax that sets up more to come." —*BookLife*

THE SERIES

While each DIVISIBLE MAN ^{TM} novel tells its own tale and can be read on its own, many elements carry forward. The novels are best enjoyed in sequence. The pivotal short story "Angel Flight" bridges the third and fourth novels and is included with the third novel, DIVISIBLE MAN - THE SECOND GHOST. "Angel Flight" is also published in the ENGINE OUT short story collection along with eleven other stories offering additional insights into the cadre of characters residing in Essex County.

SUPPORT YOUR LOCAL BOOKSELLER

The entire DIVISIBLE MAN ^{TM} series is available from major online retailers as well as the many local independent booksellers who offer online ordering for in-store pickup or home delivery.

Search: "DIVISIBLE MAN Howard Seaborne"

For advance notice of new releases and exclusive material available only to Email Members, join the DIVISIBLE MAN ^{TM} Email List at **HowardSeaborne.com**.

Sign up today and get a FREE DOWNLOAD.

ACKNOWLEDGMENTS

When the words hit the page, I have no one to bless or blame but myself. Writing is a solitary endeavor. Inversely, delivering the words in final form to dear readers requires a team deserving sincere thanks. They are: My wife, first and foremost, for always believing. My friends and family for invaluable help at EAA's AirVenture (thank you, Robin, Rich, and Ariana!) My incredible editor, Stephen Parolini, whose occasional "nice" puts me over the moon. The TWD team including David, Carol, April, Claire, Kristie, Rebecca and Steve for making this passion possible. The infinitely generous Rebecca Schlei for invaluable bookselling advice, and Daniel Goldin for letting your beloved friend drag you to my aid. Rich Sorensen, for lifelong friendship, travel and trivia, and for unabashed cheerleading. The indispensable Robin Ann Schlei, my beta reader and re-reader and re-re-reader. The incomparable English woman, teacher, friend and beta reader, Judethe (Judy) Johnson for her cherished support. And for my sharp-eyed Copy Editor, the same ever-patient Robin Ann, who now threatens to glue the hyphen key on my laptop. This is the Divisible Man's tenth mission. As before it and ever after, this novel never reaches the runway without these many loving and supportive hands.

Thank you.

*For Judy and Robin and every other teacher
who ever answered an alarm clock,
because that was the day a life was changed forever.*

PREFACE

THE OTHER THING

It's like this: I wake up nearly every morning in the bed I share with my wife. After devoting a religious moment to appreciating the stunning, loving woman beside me, I ease off the mattress and pick my way across the minefield of creaks and groans in the old farmhouse's wooden floor. I slip into the hall and head for the guest bathroom two doors down—the one with the quietest toilet flush. I take care of essential business, then pull up to the mirror. The face offers no surprises. I give it a moment, then picture a set of levers in my head—part of the throttle-prop-mixture quadrant on a twin-engine Piper Navajo. The levers I imagine are to the right of the standard controls, a fourth set not found on any airplane, topped with classic round balls. I see them fully retracted, pulled toward me, the pilot. My eyes are open—it makes no difference—I can see the levers either way. I close my hand over them. I push. They move smoothly and swiftly to the forward stops. Balls to the wall.

For a split second I wonder, as I did the day before, and the day before that, if this trick will work again. Then—

Fwooomp!

—I hear it. A deep and breathy sound—like the air being sucked out of a room. I've learned that the sound is audible only in my head.

A cool sensation flashes over my skin. The first dip in a farm pond after a hot, dusty day. The shift of an evening breeze after sunset.

I vanish.

Bleary eyes and tossed hair wink out of the mirror and the shower curtain behind me—the one with the frogs on it— fills in where my head had been. The instant I see those frogs, my feet leave the cold tile floor. My body remains solid, but gravity and I are no longer on speaking terms. A stiff breeze will send me on my way if I don't hang on to something.

The routine never varies. I've tested it nearly every morning since I piloted an air charter flight down the RNAV 31 approach to Essex County Airport but never made the field. The airplane wound up in pieces and I wound up sitting on the pilot's seat in a marsh. I have no memory of the crash. The running theory is that I collided with something—something I recently found in a winter woods under a crush of broken trees. I believe that object—whatever it was—saved me and left me this way. I may never know how or why. The object is long gone. As time passes, the memory of its discovery plays like a dream.

Since the night of the crash, whenever I picture those levers in my mind and I push them fully forward, I vanish. Pull them back, and I reappear. It applies to things I wear, things I hold, and even other people in my grasp.

A gimmick? A party trick? A useful tool for espionage—assuming I knew anything about espionage? I don't know.

There's one aspect of this *thing* that I may never understand. On a fogbound Christmas Eve I held a dying child in my arms and made us both vanish. I found out later that the child stopped dying. That when this *thing* envelops a child stricken by cancer sometimes—often—it leaves the child whole and healthy.

Don't ask. I have no idea.

This *thing*—what I call *the other thing*—saved my life. It allows me to disappear. It defies gravity. It cures where there is no cure.

Those things don't scare me.

Far scarier things greet the dawn every day.

Lillian faced me.

"Do it."

"What?"

"Do it. That thing. Do it."

Andy's eyes met mine. We speak at times without words. This was one of those times.

I steadied myself and focused. I envisioned the aircraft cockpit I had constructed in my mind after the accident. The instruments. The control levers. I pictured my hand closing on that phantom set of levers.

I closed my eyes. I took and released a solemn breath.

After a moment, I opened my eyes to find Lillian fixing cold assessment on me, arms folded.

"I can't. It's gone."

PART I

April. Louisiana.

F *wooomp!*

2

I misjudged. Too high, too fast. Gravity grabbed me, demanding payback for my defiance. My bootheels hit the rooftop's loose pea gravel. Both feet shot out from under me. I dropped on my butt and issued a pathetic *Oomph!* amplified by the breath punched from my lungs. I slapped both hands down to stabilize. Gravel rubbed my palms raw.

I skidded to an unceremonious stop.

Special Agent Leslie Carson-Pelham glanced back at me from her yoga-posture perch at the edge of the roof. She held a straight face, but amusement bloomed in her dark eyes.

"You know, the guys in the movies do a really cool landing. You should work on that."

"Shut up."

"It's a kind of a three-point, kneeling pose. They stick one arm out." She showed me the arm bit.

Having demolished my dignity, I scooted forward on my butt to where she sat cross-legged behind a telescope mounted on a tripod. The telescope tube rested on a low parapet at the edge of a roof that smelled of tar and mildew. Leslie had placed a row of discarded liquor bottles on either side to camouflage reflection from the lens.

My palms burned. I rubbed them together to dislodge embedded grit.

A quarter of a mile away, a rundown service station slumped in the moonlight beside an empty highway. The gas pumps were long gone. Old plastic letters hung on the side of the cinder block building spelling out SIN

LAIR. Earl Jackson once told me that those stations gave away free inflatable green dinosaurs with any gas fill-up. Dinosaurs. Because that's what gasoline is made of—at least according to the marketing department of the Sinclair Oil Company. I told him he was full of crap. Nobody gives away freebies to persuade people to buy gas.

"Number six just showed up," I reported.

"They do this head down thing," Leslie put her arm out a second time and bowed her head. "Like this."

I forged ahead. Somebody had to tend to business.

One. Gun. "First to arrive was the one you called Randall. He carried a rifle case into the office. He's showing off his pet AR-15. It's desert tan. They're all ga-ga over the red dot optics."

Leslie held the pose, squinting heroically.

Two. Shoe. "Second guy wasn't in your photo lineup. He's wearing work boots, work clothes, a work shirt with an embroidered logo. I couldn't see it. Might be a power company lineman. Utility guy. Or cable." I closed my eyes for a second. "Thirties or forties. Curly black hair. Five ten-ish…maybe two hundred, two-twenty. Beer gut."

Leslie slowly shifted her gaze to me.

Three. Tree. "Third guy is short, heavy, a tree trunk. Too much maple syrup. Might be the oldest of the group. Long, stringy gray hair in an old-guy ponytail."

Leslie stopped posing.

Four. Door. "The fourth guy was in your photo lineup. Osterman, I think you said. Nervous type. He came in late but stayed by the door the whole time, looking outside, like he expected trouble and might bolt. You said he was one of the shooters in Essex."

I had Leslie's attention.

"Might be."

Five. Hive. "The fifth guy is Mr. Busy Bee. Buzzing around all the others. A little too enthusiastic. Irritates number six. Late twenties. Baby face. No tattoos that I could see."

Bemusement morphed into mild admiration on the FBI agent's face.

Six. Sticks. "The last guy looks like a trustee from Cell Block D. Buzz cut. Mean-looking with a lot of gang ink. Quiet. Something about him is not like the others. He looks like he's in it for the blood sport—the guy who shoves toothpicks up under your fingernails."

"Graphic. Not bad recon. The average eyewitness can't get past 'the guy was black.'"

"I read a book on memory. And none of them are black."

"As if. Any of them armed?"

"Except for the rifle, not that I could see, but we're in Second Amendment country."

"Dollars to donuts, none of these morons have ever read the Second Amendment, let alone the Constitution."

Leslie leaned down and eased her eye to the telescope's eyepiece, careful not to touch. A light breeze ruffled her short black hair. Dressed in dark tactical clothing, facing away from me, she all but disappeared on the unlit rooftop. Be it tactical or office chic, I could not remember ever seeing her in anything but black.

"How long do you want to do this?" I checked my watch. Almost two in the morning.

She did not look up.

"I don't think he's coming." I squinted at the distant target. Half a mile was too far to make out the sort of detail I had seen while floating outside the dusty service station windows. Pale light angled through the glass and painted the weedy asphalt. The illumination might as well have been a beacon; the gas station office showed the only light on a dark stretch of narrow highway. That seemed odd to me, but the men meeting in the empty building at this hour didn't seem concerned.

My gaze wandered to hazy stars hung in the moonlit night sky. For the twentieth time I marveled at being outdoors in shirtsleeves. Louisiana's spring air carried heavy humidity; the temperature was not expected to drop below seventy degrees overnight. When I spoke to Andy earlier in the evening, she said the temperature had plunged into the twenties in Essex. Winter's last gasp threatened ice for the coming Easter holiday. During the call, I pictured her in a flannel nightgown and buried in thick comforters, stubbornly refusing to tick the farmhouse thermostat a couple degrees higher.

A minute pretending to be an hour passed in silence.

"Seems like he would have been there by now," I said.

Leslie leaned away from the telescope and looked at me.

"I'm going to make the wild guess that you have not done many stake-outs with your wife."

"What makes you say that?"

She returned to the eyepiece. "Because you're still married."

3

———————

Shortly before Thanksgiving, a mob gathered in front of the house that Andy and I rent. The mob carried signs demanding the recall of three members of the Essex City Council, specifically the members who serve on the Fire and Police Commission. The gambit openly pursued a path to summary dismissal of my wife from her job as a detective for the City of Essex Police Department.

Recall and Replace, the signs read. *Replace* referred to Andy.

The recall movement was propelled by a lie that could have and should have been dismissed with a simple statement from The White House. Andy had been mistakenly accused of an attempt to assassinate the President of the United States when in fact she almost single-handedly prevented his death. The incident ignited social media fury among the President's loyal followers. Their misapprehension painted a target on my wife's back. Repeated statements of fact by the FBI and the Department of Justice only fueled deeper and more bizarre conspiracy theories. Fringe media sites fanned the flames, treating the lies as gospel.

Tom Ceeves and City of Essex snowplows broke up the recall demonstration, but before the snowplows deployed, a self-proclaimed and decidedly unregulated militia marched onto the scene brandishing semiautomatic weapons. Photographs taken by a police dispatch trainee captured fourteen men wearing mashup military clothing. At the time, I saw the trainee cheering the men on and I marked her as a traitor to the police department she aspired to join. Later I learned that she'd been tasked to take photos by my wife. Cute and clever, Ashley the Trainee flirted her way past the militia's suspicions. She played to their hero fantasies, toyed with their egos, and traded phone numbers with a few of the younger men. For several weeks afterward the dispatch desk phone at the Essex Police Department rang to connect bewildered, amorous young men with Mae Earnhardt, the past-retirement-age night dispatcher.

At the height of the demonstration, Ashley persuaded several of the men to pull down their face masks for selfies with her. Identification by the FBI followed, even of some who did not unmask. The facial recognition software employed by the Bureau, Leslie later told me, was that good.

The men belonged to a right-wing militia that calls itself Company W. The W stands for White and the military grade high-capacity semiautomatic rifles they carry promise supremacy of arms, if not intellect. Several hours after the Chief broke up the demonstration, some or all the men in home-made uniforms returned to my house and loosed a fusillade of rifle fire through my walls and windows. The gunfire made a mess of the house and everything in it. Andy and I escaped harm by throwing ourselves down the basement steps.

Outrage over the attack put the last coffin nails in the faltering recall effort—that and the arrest of the recall organizers after the police and FBI (in the persons of Andy and Leslie) confiscated a laptop used to coordinate the attack. The arrests and a stunning outpouring of support from our friends and neighbors ended the episode, at least in Essex.

I wasn't satisfied. I wanted justice to rain down on the men who pulled the triggers; heroic freedom fighters who bravely opened fire in the middle of the night without warning, shot up everything from the rain gutters to the kitchen sink, and then scurried away in the dark.

I wanted payback.

Leslie assured me that the wheels of a deep and far-reaching investigation were turning at the FBI, and that prosecutors at the United States Department of Justice were on the case. If they were, they hid it well.

November slipped into December. No arrests were made. Yard signs demanding the recall of stout and earnest city council members and the dismissal of my wife from the police force disappeared as quietly as late afternoon daylight. Andy did not speak about the case, even when I ranted about it over end-of-duty-day beer. Andy listened, agreed, and then deftly shifted subjects.

Leslie ghosted us. I chalked that up to learning that I could no longer vanish at will. I sold her the story the night of an epic party thrown by friends, neighbors, and complete strangers who rebuilt our home and erased any evidence of gunfire. I waited until Leslie had downed a few drinks, then told her the same thing I told Dr. Lillian Farris—that my ability to wink out of sight was gone, and the only flying I'd be doing would be with one hand on an aircraft yoke and the other on a pair of throttles.

In that awkward moment, Leslie said nothing. She flexed a Solo cup in her hand and stared at me with those near-black eyes of hers. I braced for a barrage of questions. For protest. Disappointment. Something. Instead, she shrugged. "Easy come, easy go." She went for a refill.

AFTER THE SHOOTING incident and the home reconstruction, Andy threw herself into her detective work for the Essex Police Department, tearing into our small middle-American town's raging crime wave. Missing practice dummies at the high school football field. A string of graffiti attacks expressing a Dungeons and Dragons theme. A robbery at the BP station on Highway 34 (during which the maskless would-be felon, whom Andy recognized from half a dozen previous encounters, paused to stick out his tongue at the security camera). Andy charged after these and other criminal enterprises with the same intensity she applied to preventing the assassination of the President of the United States. My wife is an equal opportunity juggernaut of justice.

I concentrated on flying for the Christine and Paulette Paulesky Education Foundation, although the flight schedule dropped off to nothing when public schools closed for winter break. Rosemary II let me fill in as needed on Essex County Air Service charter trips. I flew a few runs in the company's E-55 Baron, a sweet machine, and one or two trips as an unnecessary FO for Dave Peterson in Earl Jackson's King Air turboprop. The fill-in flights kept me current. The turbine time looked good in my logbook.

A pre-Thanksgiving snowfall raised hopes for a white Christmas, but a few days before the clock wound down on holiday shopping, low pressure pulled warm wet air up from the south. Most of the snow disappeared under gray skies and steady drizzle.

Fog shrouded Christmas for the second year in a row.

After grabbing a holiday beer with Dave, Andy and I celebrated the holy eve at her sister's house on Leander Lake. I enjoyed distracting my perpetual motion nieces, Elise and Harriet. Andy spent more than her share of the day fussing over the two infants in the family—Grace, Lydia's daughter and our new niece, and the Infant King Alex, the baby boy born to Lydia's teenaged nanny. Alex had been sired by Lydia's cheating late ex-husband and had the distinction of being the only male in a house full of females. Throughout the evening, someone, usually Andy's mother or her sister, always seemed to be handing Andy a baby, campaigning with obvious intent, nudging my wife's biological clock. I knew something the women didn't. Andy's alarm had already gone off.

Not long ago, during the recent rescue of a young mother and her child on a North Dakota highway, Andy abruptly declared to me that she wanted a baby. We had already discussed becoming parents many times in sunset light on our porch or over chips and salsa at the Mexican restaurant attached to the other bowling alley in Essex. Until that intense moment on a stretch of interstate highway in North Dakota, our conversations always ended with a firm and unanimous "Nah."

It didn't take a medical degree to see that biology had caught up with my twenty-seven-year-old wife.

Just as the notion took hold, Andy's unexpected admission to the FBI Training Academy postponed our parenting plans. I didn't mind, but I had the good sense not to express relief. Andy's career opportunity offered me a reprieve to learn which side of a diaper gets the baby.

Andy's FBI dream blew up thanks to politics and "optics" I did not understand. She took the reversal stoically, and returned to her post with Essex PD. I did a slow burn on behalf of my wife. Instead of an automatic reboot, our childbearing plans slipped into limbo. Andy gave off no signals. I gingerly broached the subject a few times, but Andy dismissed me with an evasive, "Can we talk about this later?" I did not believe that she had changed her mind on the subject. She just needed to renegotiate terms with herself. I held my tongue. Sometimes it's better to read the signals than to ask the question.

At Lydia's family Christmas gathering, I watched Andy cradle the smiling little Alex against her lovely bosom.

"Be careful," I warned her. "He's going to think you're lunch."

She teased me with a smile and mischievous glance from beneath long lashes. "You do."

"Not lunch, darling. Dessert." She knew what I was thinking.

I had no idea what she was thinking.

THE FLIGHT SCHEDULE picked up after Christmas. Winter and busy weeks peeled away pages of the calendar. Arun Dewar, the assistant Sandy Stone had hired to sort out paperwork for the Education Foundation, and who proved so adept that she maneuvered him into taking over for her as Director, kept me busy with a flurry of trips around the Midwest, doing my part to help the Foundation give away a corrupt dead billionaire's money.

I wouldn't say that I'd forgotten about the men who blew holes in my home, and nearly in my wife and me, but the episode slid onto the back burner. The DOJ and FBI remained mute on the subject.

Leslie popped up just after Valentine's Day. Andy texted me during a day trip to southern Illinois. Short and to the point. *Come straight home tonight. Leslie.*

I walked into my kitchen to find the FBI at my kitchen table with my wife, chatting and laughing over steaming mugs.

"You're a terrible liar," Leslie announced without preamble or greeting.

"Is that tea?" I asked.

"Yes," Andy replied.

"Good. I'll take mine with beer, hold the tea." I went to the refrigerator and pulled out a Corona. We were out of limes again.

Leslie looked across the rim of her mug at Andy. "I'm not wrong. He's a terrible liar. Seriously. Isn't he?"

"He is," Andy admitted, more amused than I thought she ought to be.

I gaped at my turncoat wife. We both knew what Leslie meant. Still, I thought at least token resistance was warranted.

Andy shrugged.

Leslie said, "I knew you were lying at the party. That BS about some object in the woods and—what did you call it? A life jacket?" Leslie paid out the lopsided smile she deploys with annoying superiority. "It's a good thing you can disappear because you wouldn't last ten minutes as an under-cover operative."

"I wasn't lying," I lied. "I can't—"

"Yes, you were. And you can."

"You're really not going to back me up here?" I asked Andy.

"You should have let me tell her. I might have gotten away with it. You. Not so much."

"Fine." I tried to sound sullen. I don't do that well either.

Leslie asked, "Your *thing*—it still works?"

"Yes. My *thing* still—" I caught her smirking. "I mean, no. *The other thing* is not gone. But you can't tell anyone because we also lied to the Chief and to a few of our friends."

Leslie looked at my wife.

Andy said, "It felt right—safer—for everyone. And for Will."

"Are you worried about Lewko?" Leslie asked Andy. She seemed to have no problem leaving me out of the conversation.

My wife nodded. "Lewko. Sebastian Manor. That Brogan woman. Too many voices tell the same story and sooner or later somebody is going to listen. Mostly Lewko, though. We knew he wouldn't believe it if denial came directly from us. But he will take Lillian's word for it."

Leslie seemed surprised. "You think Dr. Farris is feeding Lewko intel—gossip—whatever you want to call it? About you guys?"

"I think she'd rather chew on razor blades, but she'd also relish giving him bad news. Telling him that Will has returned to normal would not be good news to Spiro Lewko."

"You think he's a threat?"

"I think he's an opportunist who obeys billionaire law."

Leslie shifted her gaze to me.

"So…you never believed me?" I asked.

"Nope."

"I assume that's why you're here. You want something."

"I do."

"Good. Me, too. I want in."

"On what?" Leslie exaggerated innocence.

"You know damn well what. You've been chasing domestic terrorists since we met. You're on the hunt for those Company W assholes who shot up our house. I want in on that."

"Darling," Andy stroked my arm, "we've talked about this. Let the DOJ do its job. This isn't one of your silly action movies where all the clues line up in the third reel. It's hundreds of hours of boring investigative work, connecting dots, scouring phone records, scraping through emails and texts, building cases. Cases required to stand up in court and withstand assaults by defense attorneys."

"DOJ isn't doing anything."

"Not true. They just don't do their work on Twitter or cable news."

"Listen to your wife," Leslie said. "I'm part of a substantial team with serious backing. I can't discuss ninety percent of what we have uncovered, but trust me, people with a lot more juice than me recognize a growing threat. They're committing resources. The shooting here in Essex rattled people. Top people."

"Join the club. I vaguely remember feeling rattled when my wife pulled me down the basement steps. So what do you need?"

"Discretion, for starters. I can't just show up with an unexplained civilian—unless you want to discuss *the other thing* with the FBI's senior bureaucracy. I assume you don't."

"Affirmative." Andy spoke for me.

"Bear in mind, Will," Leslie said, "that what you do is a square peg to the FBI's round hole. Why do you think Director Lindsay kept you off book? In the FBI's button-down investigative world, what you do doesn't fit. Frankly, it is almost never needed."

"Never needed?"

"Never needed. You heard me. Think about it. We build cases. We investigate what happened, not what's *happening*. The chances of catching criminals in the act are slim and none. We catch them by uncovering what they did—past tense. Sending you in sounds like a great idea—but when? When the bad guys are planning the robbery? When would that be? How long are you willing to hover in some lousy bar? Or some double-wide?"

"I thought that's what undercover agents did."

She laughed. "Undercover agents spend months, years working in crap jobs, drinking with assholes, and going to barbecues with best friends they hate, living entire false lives to gain access and build a case. Are we supposed to have you just vanish and float around in some bad guy's day job until he lays out his plan for revolution? It's ridiculous."

Andy chimed in. "It's also inadmissible. Will, if the people who shot up our house are to be taken down, it can't be because you dangled someone over a water tower or humiliated a suspect in public. Cases need to be built and sustainable arrests made."

"Good luck with that," I muttered. "You arrest them and then they hire a sharp lawyer, delay the trial three years, and ultimately negotiate a reduced sentence."

"Darling, that's not—"

"Really? Not true? Parks has his case tangled up in motions from his lawyers citing mental incompetency. Those guys working for Clayton Johns are filing to have your testimony thrown out. *Your testimony, Dee.* Christ, you were the one that found him passed out next to the naked girl with his pants down."

Andy waved a dismissive hand. "Their motion won't fly."

"Probably not, but it's another six weeks of hearings and filings and rebuttals and motions." I tipped back the Corona and finished it. "The system sucks." I gaveled that into the record with the empty bottle.

"Maybe," Leslie said. "Maybe we don't always get convictions, but in the process these clowns will be buried in a mountain of legal burden, strung out in court cases, and at the very least tied up so badly that they don't dare make a move. Or they make dumb moves that net greater results for us."

"These *guys* are preaching revolution. Government overthrow."

"I'm not arguing with you, Will. But that's a high bar for prosecution. And you make a lousy witness."

"It's weird, Leslie, how you're arguing against my help when that's what you came here for."

Leslie's lopsided smile told me I was right. She pulled out her phone, scrolled through the gallery, then held up a familiar image.

"Louis Blaze. Remember him?"

"I do. Last time I saw that tub of guts he was painted with Derrick Spellman's brains. He's the Company W commandant, isn't he?"

"No." Leslie handed the phone to Andy who studied the image. "And yes. When you saw him in Idaho, he was the head of the American Bloodline Coalition, but he was engineering a merger with Company W, which was led by Spellman before Mrs. Palmer gave him a brief but fatal headache."

"Right. Blaze was Father of the Bride." I turned to Andy. "This asshat was bartering his daughter to close a merger deal with Spellman." The image of a bloodied wedding dress and the young bride's shock came to mind in cinematic color and scope. I didn't know which was sadder—the humiliation on the girl's face before her fiancé was shot, or the horror afterward.

"I remember."

Leslie continued. "Blaze did a disappearing act immediately after that shit show in Utah. With Spellman out of the picture, Blaze consolidated his group with Company W despite the *nuptia interruptus*."

"Has he turned up again?" Andy asked.

"Nope."

"Probably figured he was next on the hit list," I said.

"In point of fact, yes. In that sense, Mrs. Palmer did some damage. The militias glommed onto the theory that Spellman's assassin worked for the U.S. Government. In typical paranoid goofball fashion, they fever-dreamed an elite black ops assassination program intended to eliminate the leadership of—their word—*the resistance*. A preemptive strike ahead of the coming '*Civil War.*'" She fingered air quotes, twice. "It's nonsense, of course, but in their fantasy world nonsense is reality."

Andy asked, "Do they at least acknowledge that Mrs. Palmer was the shooter?"

Leslie shook her head. "Of course not. They deny that Mrs. Palmer ever existed. Their top theory is that she's a fictional character created by the CIA —honestly, I don't know why those guys always get the credit. Bureau legends are way better. Anyway, these misogynist assholes share Mrs. Palmer's photo in chat rooms to laugh at the idea that someone like her

—*physically like her*—could operate a firearm. Bunch of fat-shaming idiots. They've turned her into a cartoon construct planted by the evil government to smoke screen the *Real Truth*."

I felt anger rising. "Right, and part of their *Real Truth* is that Andy is the assassin."

"Of course. She's a member of an elite hit squad of assassins run by the Illuminati. Or she's the leader of a group of Ninja assassins hired by a cabal of radical leftist commie progressive pedophiles."

Andy nudged me. "I'm a ninja, dear. Fear me." She handed back Leslie's phone. "I don't know how you do it. I mean—closing in on a ring of bank robbers, that's one thing. But chasing these delusions…?"

"It's like swimming in molasses and playing Whack-A-Mole at the same time," Leslie said. "The looney stuff has always existed on the fringes. It used to be confined to pamphlets printed on mimeograph machines by people in tinfoil hats. The internet turned it into a bonfire. Online fringe media outlets posing as news networks have turned it into a California wild-fire. Josiah James. AFN. And because they put some glitz and polish on the turd, the craziness is leeching into the mainstream water supply. Into politics. Into institutions. Into Congress. It has grown legs on cable news because nothing gooses ratings and sells advertising like dark conspiracies."

"Meanwhile, the militias drinking this Kool-Aid become more and more dangerous," Andy said.

Leslie sighed. "Closed loop. Echo chamber. Call it whatever you like, it's insidious."

I pointed at Leslie's phone. "Getting back to that bucket of hate…you said he took over Company W? Does that make him the one who sent the shooters after us?"

"After your wife. I think so, yes." She assessed the darkness flooding my expression. "Before you get ideas, Will, keep in mind the bigger picture. And the larger threat."

"Andy and I dove down the basement stairs while point two-two-three rounds were drilling the walls. What's a larger threat than that?"

"You already know."

I didn't. I looked at Andy who said, "She's talking about the political movement underpinning all this."

Leslie pointed at me. "You've already tangled with that movement."

"You mean Pemmick?" The retired Marine Corps general who worked for Josiah James had tried to unite a collection of hate groups. Louis Blaze and his American Bloodline Coalition made the list. "Pemmick and that oozing open sore Josiah James are both dead."

"As a doornail. The Bureau hoped it meant Pemmick's project had fallen apart. But these guys are volatile. Their world changes daily. Power grabs. New conspiracy theories. The Q thing sucked away a lot of their hardcore believers. We saw that as a good thing at first, but then it reversed the wave and flooded us with new crazies. Ebb and flow."

"Leslie," Andy said, "it's one thing to trade conspiracies in chat rooms. It's another to take action—I mean *real* action."

"Like shooting up your house?"

"No. Shooting up our house was an act of ideological vandalism. Bombing the federal building in Oklahoma City is *action*. That's what I'm talking about. What's the Bureau's threat assessment on serious seditious action?"

"One day, everyone is gung-ho for battle. The next day, they wake up and realize that The New Civil War conflicts with their weekend fishing plans. Groups grow and decline. Leadership changes. But like clockwork, when we think the threat is fading, someone new comes along jockeying for leadership and that restores the momentum. Just because many parts and players make up this alpha-turd soup doesn't mean they're working in harmony. Pemmick failed to unite the hate groups. Mrs. Palmer drove people to ground. The movement lost cohesion."

"Good." I put up a one-finger salue. "Screw them."

"But that's the problem. They're foundering. They need momentum back. And what's the best way to achieve cohesion, Will?"

"A bake sale?"

"Create a common enemy."

"Essex." Andy took and squeezed my hand. We both glanced around our kitchen, remembering glass and wood splinters filling the air.

Leslie said, "The recall in Essex was supposed to be the start of a grass roots assault on local government. Yours wasn't the only recall they attempted. School boards. County commissioners. A slew of them nationwide. When the strategy failed—at least here in Essex—they resorted to a pseudo-military strike. Andy made the perfect target. Company W got the assignment, but don't think of them as the leadership. Think of them as the action directorate for the larger political movement that pushed the recall in Essex in the first place."

"So, let's go after them." I reeled us back to my original request.

Leslie frowned. "It's not an organization with a headquarters. It's like a fog moving across the landscape. Arch conservativism. Racism. White supremacy. Grievance. Fascism by a dozen different names. There are hundreds of individual groups on the Bureau's radar. Some have thousands of members. Some hold weekend drills, stockpile weapons, and draft military orders of battle. Some are nothing but internet trolls batting hate back and forth in chat rooms. It's not homogeneous or organized. If they ever come to power—God forbid—it will look like an Italian government."

"Which would suggest that they're not likely to get their act together any time soon," Andy offered.

"Not likely. In fact, on their own, they would probably die on the vine. But the political landscape has changed. Mainstream opportunists see potential power to be tapped. Pemmick tried. Legit political conservatives have been trying to harness this base for years. Mainstream candidates who claim they are not the crazies are scrambling over each other to win the crazies' votes."

"Jesus, Leslie," I said, "you sound like you're arguing against yourself. They're fragmented. They're cohesive. Which is it? Is Blaze the head of the snake? Is he the one who put out the order to try and kill us? Or just the errand boy?"

"You're looking for an easy answer, Will. There isn't one. Blaze may have issued the orders or accepted the orders—we don't know. What's more important is that an act of overt violence was connected to a political recall. The recall didn't originate in some encrypted chatroom. We think it came from something larger."

"We?" Andy asked. "The Bureau?"

"The Bureau. DOJ. The intelligence community."

"CIA?" I asked.

Leslie lifted her eyebrows. "There are overseas influences seasoning this soup. And before you ask, I can't tell you any more than that."

"Crap."

Leslie sighed. "Will, I get that you want to round up the guys with the guns. I do, too. But I also want to unmask the people in Georgetown bars sipping single malt scotch and gaming ways to make the guys with the guns their bitch in the next election. Or worse—if the next election doesn't go their way."

"Fine. Let's go get this guy, Blaze. You and your colleagues can haul him off to a black site and peel the rotting onion."

Leslie turned to Andy. "He watches a lot of movies." Andy nodded. To me, Leslie said, "Yes. I want your help, but not to 'go get' this guy. Blaze has dropped off the radar and off the grid. Rumor has it he won't go near anything electronic. He's probably using carrier pigeons. But in the investigation of the men who perforated your house I think I may have tipped to a series of meetings. Usually, we only hear about them after the fact, but I have intel suggesting Blaze might surface for one that's coming up."

"Is your intel solid?" Andy asked.

"Oh, hell no." Leslie laughed. "My bosses call it 'Leslie's Bag of Bones.' They claim I shake out some fossils and read voodoo signs. Nine out of ten times the higher-ups dismiss me."

"And this is the tenth time?" I asked.

"No. This is one of the nine. Nobody's on board with me on this."

"Ah…" I leaned back. "Which is why you're asking for help that they can't know about. You want me to get close to see if it's real, and if Blaze shows up, grab the asshat."

"Absolutely not."

"Put a tracker on him?"

"Out of the question."

"Jesus, Leslie, what the hell?" My frustration earned a gentle stroke down the back of my neck from my wife.

Leslie gave me a beat to cool off. "All I want is to get close, to record what's said—*strictly for my personal use*—and *maybe*—and I cannot stress that enough—figure out Blaze's methods of communication. His location isn't all that important because he's probably moving constantly. Like Saddam. Never sleep in the same bed twice. I want to know how he connects with his subordinates. And if we get lucky, how he communicates with whoever is higher up. That's IF the guy shows up. Big if."

"I want him wearing orange."

"As do I. But not yet Grabbing Blaze would burn sources, destroy intel channels, and send people fomenting more dangerous ideas to ground. And again—never lose sight of those assholes sipping single malt scotch."

I looked at Andy for support. She may wear my ring on her third finger, but in a room with other law enforcement, she's married to her profession. My hunger for vengeance got no sympathy.

"Will," Leslie continued, "I know what you want. You want to kick ass and take names. Be patient. If we get what I think we might from this meeting, Blaze is worth a lot more as a free man than he is in handcuffs."

"Fine." I silently reminded myself that every plan falls apart eventually, at which point the door to improvisation cracks open. "When and where does this confab take place?"

4

———————

P oint Coupee Parish, Louisiana.

Leslie met me just after sunset at the False River Airport near the town of New Roads.

The first question I asked after closing the Navajo cabin door was, "Any idea why it's called a Parish?"

"This all belonged to the French and Spanish at one time. Roman Catholic rule. In those days, settlements centered around churches. The state adopted the term officially at some point. The Point Coupee Parish Police Department is just down that road. We'll pass it on the way. Please don't wave. Get in."

Forty-five minutes later she parked her rental car behind the slab backside of an abandoned dog food factory. A rusting metal ladder took us to the roof where she established her observation post. During my approach to Runway 18 at False River, the final leg of which passed over the Mississippi River, I was impressed by the flatness of the landscape. South Dakota flatness. The dominant presence of the Mighty Mississippi in such tabletop terrain made it easier to understand the ever-present specter of flooding.

The flat landscape enhanced observing an abandoned gas station from a distance, but it did nothing to accelerate the clock. Sitting for hours bored me senseless. I didn't like to admit it, but Leslie had a point about using *the other thing* in an investigation.

When headlights finally appeared on the narrow country road, it felt like fireworks had been launched.

"Go," Leslie tapped her ear to affirm that I wore my Bluetooth earpiece. I gave her a thumbs up.

I pictured a set of aircraft control levers in my mind, gripped them with an imaginary hand, and pushed two levers full forward the same way I advance takeoff power in the Navajo.

Fwooomp!

The sound in my head seemed extra loud after several hours of silence on the dog food factory rooftop. A cool sensation touched my skin. My stomach wiggled as gravity ceased to rule my body. I vanished, head to toe, body, clothes, and everything I carried, including the earpiece. I'd been sitting cross-legged like Leslie, but almost instantly began to unfold my legs because my weight no longer compressed them. I pressed my chafed palms against the rooftop gravel and pushed.

I lifted into the night air and untangled my legs. Leslie and her telescope fell away. The dark landscape spread around me. Our business here remained serious, but I could not suppress a giddy wave that lifted my lips in a smile. *The Peter Pan moment.* Flight. Whether it comes in an airplane at eighty knots on an open runway or pushing off a tar and gravel roof, the sensation never ceases to touch my soul. The slow change of perspective that most people can only experience in a glass elevator—seeing horizons extend and surrounding flat surfaces fall—there is nothing else like it. Not long ago I shared this experience with an autistic eight-year-old boy unbound by decorum. His giggles spoke volumes and became my new soundtrack for every launch.

I understood Leslie's *square peg…round hole* comment. Nothing in my exhilaration conformed to the serious law enforcement business at hand.

Leslie wore tactical clothing for this outing. My gear consisted of an old fishing vest valued for its collection of useful pockets. From one of those pockets, I pulled a stubby flashlight tube with a slide control mounted one third of the way back from the end that once contained a light. The light was gone, replaced by a small electric motor, the kind found in a radio-controlled model airplane. From the same pocket, I extracted a six-inch carbon fiber model airplane propeller. I snapped the blade onto the motor's shaft. I wiggled the prop to ensure a solid connection.

The hardware had vanished along with me. Unseen, the tube/motor/prop combination made its presence known when I slid the control switch forward of the neutral position. The prop spun and the device muttered a low growl. Air blew back across my wrist.

Lane Franklin, the brilliant teenaged daughter of Essex County Air Service's office manager, was the first person aware of my ability to vanish.

She explained to me that the absence of gravity doesn't erase mass or suspend the laws of physics that govern attraction and inertia. But *the other thing* does. I can't explain it as eloquently as she does, but the result is that a handheld, battery-operated device with a swinging 6-inch prop pulls my one hundred eighty-four pounds of mass forward like I was nothing.

I've tested a variety of names for the device on Andy. Nothing has snagged her approval, but my favorite remains *Basic Linear Aerial System for Transport, Electric Rechargeable.*

BLASTER.

A name worthy of the exhilarating sensation engulfing me as I sailed over the edge of the roof and accelerated above an unlit country highway.

My earpiece chimed. I touched a button on the Bluetooth device.

"Divisible Man Airways. Don't bother with your tray table because we can't see it."

"Hit record and make sure the camera lens is clear."

I touched the electronic device she had clipped to the upper left pocket of my vest—a variation of the camera she had originally used to capture Derrick Spellman's demise. This one had a single button on top and a three-eyed lens cluster above a clip that locked the device in place and guaranteed that the camera eyes remain uncovered. She said something about gyro stabilization while she was attaching it.

I pressed the button. Brief red LED flashes told me recording had begun. "Clear."

"This is recon only, Will," Leslie warned me for the umpteenth time.

"What…sorry…you're breaking up. Say again."

"Don't screw with me."

I picked up speed to match my arrival at the gas station to the approaching headlights. Just before vanishing, my watch said it was twenty after three in the morning. There had been no traffic on this road for over an hour. This was our guy. I was sure of it.

I tracked a path above the center of the road to guarantee obstacle avoidance in the dark. Poles with wires passed on my left. I stayed above the tops of the poles. If any of the wires crossed the road, I would clear them. At the gas station, a set of power lines angled to the pole supporting the oval signage. I avoided the wires and steered into the station lot on a line that automobiles once followed to the pumps. I descended and reversed the BLASTER. A near-silent pull became a push, gradually bringing me to a halt.

A few yards away the second of the six waiting men—the cable guy— leaned on the door frame. Like me, he watched the approaching headlights.

Floating just above the weed tops, I waited. A moment later SUV headlight beams swept through me. I couldn't help but feel startled; the hairs on my arm rose. The same thing happens whenever people look directly through me.

The SUV parked beside the building.

Behind dusty office glass, the men inside showed no sign of interest or concern. Four members of the group dealt cards across what had been the sales counter. The scary guy, Number Six (*sticks*), lounged on a low shelf beneath the window, watching through the glass. He squinted when the headlights caught him. The SUV driver stepped out, closed the driver's door and double-feeped the lock. The vehicle lights winked out, leaving only the bare bulb in the office.

I wondered if it would be enough to capture Louis Blaze's face. He would have to enter the office, which meant I had to do the same if I expected to be able to record not only his face but his voice. I took for granted that Leslie's lenses adapted to darkness.

I pulsed the BLASTER for a slow glide toward the office door. Centered in the peeling paint frame, Number Two came to attention. I rotated to catch the vehicle driver in the camera lens. Leslie remained silent on the open connection between us.

The driver rounded the SUV tailgate and entered the light cast by the office window. My heart sank.

It wasn't Louis Blaze. It wasn't a *him*.

Louis Blaze's daughter, the sacrificial bride, stepped into the light. I tried to remember her name or remember if I ever knew her name.

"Howdy! Not a bad night for—" Number Two greeted her. She cut him off with a sharp gesture across her throat, then pressed a raised index finger to her lips. *Silence!*

This was not the same young woman I'd seen months ago with her hands folded on her lap and her sad flowered dress betraying secret hopes and dreams for a special day. Nor was it the nearly catatonic young woman covered in the blood and brains of her husband-to-never-be. The brown-blonde hair was gone, dyed a light-absorbing jet black. She wore no makeup, ditching the pink accents and blush she had applied for her wedding. She would not be considered attractive; she had too much of her father in her face. She had shed weight and gained fitness. Hard edges etched her cheeks and block chin with maturity.

Ms. Blaze commanded silence with both her gesture and a cold expression powered by intense eyes. She walked a direct line confidently into the office, not pausing or even acknowledging Number Two when he swept an awkward *ladies first* hand for her, then half stumbled out of her way.

Inside the office, Number Six sat upright on his shelf but didn't rise. The rest, clustered around the counter that once hosted a cash register and maybe a glass jar full of Slim Jims, shuffled to their feet in the presence of command. Before any could speak, she repeated her quick gesture for silence.

I pulled up to the door frame and stopped. The office didn't offer enough room to get safely inside without potentially bumping into someone. A low ceiling with a single bare bulb dismissed the idea of recording the meeting from overhead. No hand holds. I locked a grip on the door frame and aimed my chest—and the camera—at the proceedings within, prepared to shove off if anyone abruptly left.

Blaze regarded the men for a moment. She examined the space. She ignored pantomimed questions from one or two of the men, all of whom obeyed her command for silence.

She moved past the counter and searched the dark doorway that led to the empty garage bays. She searched behind the counter. She looked up, then pointed at the light fixture and then at her ear. She pointedly faced each of the men in turn to confirm that they understood her message.

Someone is listening.

We were, of course, but not in the way she asserted.

Confirming acknowledgment from each of the men, she lifted a shoulder bag against her abdomen and opened it. From within she extracted a candy bar. She examined the label. Oh Henry. She glanced around until settling on Number Two, the man in the work shirt now trying to blend into a corner of the office. She handed it to him. He took it hesitantly then pinched one end to tear it open. She threw up her hand and shook it. *No. Do not open it.* He froze.

She lifted another from her bag. Hershey's. This went to Number One, the man who brought in his gun for show and tell. He took it and made no move to open it.

Kit Kat went to Number Three.

Mars went to Number Four.

Snickers went to Number Five.

Number Six got a Bit-O-Honey.

All six men held treats in hand and wore blank expressions on their faces. She took one last look around then nodded, spun, and marched directly at me. I pulled myself to one side of the door frame just in time. She passed leaving a scented trail. Coconut shampoo. A moment later she unlocked her SUV, ignited the engine, and backed away. She didn't chirp the tires, but she was gone quickly.

I rotated back to face the doorway and almost collided with Number Six who departed without a word. The rest followed. The last one, Number Three, scooped the scattered playing cards off the scarred countertop, killed the light, and closed the door when he left. Everyone hiked around to the back of the old station and mounted up in vehicles they had hidden on arrival.

Covered by the noise of started engines, I used the BLASTER to position myself so that the camera could record their passing, the vehicles they drove, and maybe catch a license plate or two.

One by one, their taillights bobbed onto the highway. When the last one roared away, I stopped the recording and spoke.

"It wasn't Blaze. It was his daughter."

"What did she say?"

"Nothing. Not a word. She handed out candy bars."

I thought Leslie might ask me to repeat that, but she didn't. She said nothing. I guessed that she had seen the bullet points of the scene through the telescope.

"Do you want me to follow?" I estimated that with a quick launch, I could rise high enough to find taillights belonging to the daughter's SUV a mile or two down the road, well ahead of the other vehicles.

"No. We're done here."

"That's it? That's all?"

"Yup."

Well, this was a giant waste of time. I had expected my official return to using *the other thing* for the FBI would be a little more fruitful.

I zoomed my way back to find Leslie packing up her rooftop observatory. I landed—this time without falling on my ass—and reappeared. She stepped close to me and unclipped her recording device.

"She didn't say a word."

"Carrier pigeon. Let's go."

LESLIE DROVE me back to the airport in near silence. She dropped me off at the Navajo and promised to be in touch. I watched her drive off in darkness.

You're a square peg, buddy.

I pulled the wheels up just as the sun cracked the eastern horizon, wondering how smug my wife would be, having made her point about the pace of investigations.

5

____

I had barely landed at Essex County Airport when my phone rang in my pocket. I ignored it, obeying a personal rule that a phone in a cockpit is dead weight.

The phone rang again as I pushed the Navajo into the Foundation hangar. This time I stopped the tug and checked the screen to make sure it wasn't Andy. It was Leslie. Rules are rules. I don't answer the phone on the ramp either.

It rang a third time as the descending hangar door groaned to a stop.

"What?"

"You know I can tell if you're lying. Even over the phone."

"Oh…kay…?" I had no idea what that meant. I also had no difficulty hearing the seriousness in Leslie's tone. "What's this about?"

"Was it you?"

"Sure. It was me. I did it. Whatever this is, I'm sure I'd look guilty if you were standing here in front of me, so yes, I confess. It was me. Does that get us any closer to you telling me what the hell you're talking about?"

I credited the silence that followed to her detecting the lie in my confession. I waited, listening to the cables on the big hangar door tick. If she planned to hold out for me to speak first, she was in for a wait.

After a moment, she said, "They're dead."

"Who's dead?"

"All six. All of them. Shot. Point blank. Execution. They were found on a boat on a river slip not too damned far from that airport."

"Jesus. I take it back. It wasn't me. What the hell? When?"

"About an hour ago, but it looks like they've been dead since early this morning."

Right around the time I was leaving False River Regional.

I wanted to feel insulted that Leslie thought I might be responsible, but I could not muster the indignation. She knew I wanted payback. It wasn't a stretch from that to wanting them dead.

I have it in me. Something cold and dark resides in my heart. It has stirred in the past. Leslie, whatever else she may be, possesses a sharp investigative mind, and sharper instincts. Regardless of any personal connection she may have with Andy and me, those instincts would not fail her.

I spoke slowly, evenly. "You dropped me at the airport. I had no car. We agreed that I wasn't going to file a flight plan that could be traced. I was airborne fifteen minutes after you showed me your taillights—just enough time to preflight, startup, taxi, take off. I kept the transponder off all the way to the fuel stop at Cape Girardeau. After that I filed. Add up the flight time and I think I've got a solid alibi if it ever comes to that."

"Probably."

I ignored Leslie's weak vote of confidence.

"What about Blaze? The daughter? Was she also…dead?"

"Damn near. Someone beat her badly. Assumed she was finished and didn't waste the bullet."

"Jesus."

Leslie said nothing. Her silence sounded accusatory.

"Look," I told her, "I'm sorry, but I'm not going to shed a tear for these assholes. Behind bars or six feet under, I don't honestly have a preference. And the daughter's hard luck started at birth."

"You don't understand, Will. One of them was one of ours."

6

———————

"Navajo two one tango whiskey, hold your position."

Ground control's transmission caught me by surprise. Open taxiway lay ahead of me. Wichita's Dwight D. Eisenhower Airport sprawled with next to nothing for midday traffic. My toes pressed the brakes and brought the big twin-engine airplane to a stop. I touched the transmit button on the control yoke and replied into the boom mic.

"Tango Whiskey."

I didn't ask for an explanation. The cause of the stop would either become apparent—or the controller would explain—or she was busy with something I couldn't see in which case she didn't need me cluttering the frequency. The engines rumbled at idle on either side of me. I popped the pilot-side window to induce fresh air flow. The cabin retained a pleasant cool temperature acquired at cruise altitude, but that wouldn't last. The high Kansas sun was less than an hour from noon on a clear spring day—a day that TV forecasters called unseasonably warm.

I checked on my passengers.

Sandy Stone and Arun Dewar generally don't wear the headsets required to hear radio transmissions. They can converse in the cabin without the intercom, and rarely chat with me. Neither wore them now. Arun hustled to secure the paperwork he and Sandy had been trading during the flight. Sandy gazed out the window at the flat airport, prepping herself to meet and greet strangers, a task she did not relish.

Sandy Stone did not want to be here. She did not seek the duties imposed on her when one hundred million dollars fell under her control. She preferred to wrangle kindergarteners at James Madison Elementary School. For that reason, Sandy had successfully delegated Education Foundation business to Arun. Arun confided in me that he scheduled this Easter Monday trip during Sandy's spring break because he didn't wish to handle it alone. This trip tallied the largest Foundation grant to date—almost eight million dollars—and the young man sincerely wanted Sandy, still the Director of the Foundation, involved.

It made no difference to me. I get them to their meetings, but never go along.

Ground control remained silent. A flicker of uncertainty gnawed at me.

Did I screw up? I read the nearest taxiway marker. Alpha 7.

After rolling off at the end of runway 19 Left, ground control had asked my parking intentions. I requested Signature Flight Services and received quick and clear instructions to taxi via Echo, Bravo, then left on Alpha to Alpha 5. Simple enough.

I double-checked the taxi chart on the iPad. The blue airplane icon confirmed my position, dead center on Alpha just short of Alpha 7, exactly as instructed.

It wasn't me. Must be something else.

I searched the ramp ahead and to my left. Half a dozen pristine white executive jets lined up wingtip to wingtip on the Signature ramp. Nothing moved. Nothing rolled urgently in my direction.

Over my left shoulder and behind the left wing, the sterile air carrier ramp hosted a pair of Southwest Airlines 737s—early morning flights reaching out to Wichita to pick up a load and return them to Chicago or Atlanta or Denver. The big orange and blue fuselages nuzzled the terminal. Nothing appeared out of the ordinary where the big busses parked.

I waited.

Give them another minute. They'll explain.

I repeated my after-landing routine. Flaps up (*don't touch the landing gear*). Cowl flaps open. Transponder set to standby. I tweaked the mixture controls for taxiing and to account for the Wichita heat. I unnecessarily ran my fingers across the panel switches to check the position of accessory switches. All correct. All good.

"Is there a problem?" Arun's voice queried from somewhere in the middle of my head, an effect rendered by my Bose headset.

I glanced into the cabin. Arun held one cup of his headset against his ear and positioned the boom mic at his lips. The kid was going pro on me. I shrugged and said, "You've got me. They asked us to hold here."

A sleek TBM turboprop passed on our right and completed its landing roll on Runway 19 Left. I anticipated the pilot would get the same taxi clearance I received. A moment later the pilot's voice came up on the frequency and confirmed my expectation.

"Ground, TBM Two Seven Papa, clear of 19 Left at Bravo, taxi to Signature."

"TBM Two Seven Papa, taxi to Signature via Bravo, Alpha, left at Alpha 5. Hold behind the Navajo."

"Bravo to Alpha, hold behind the Navajo. Seven Papa," the pilot affirmed. "What's going on?"

I was glad he asked instead of me.

"Stand by Two Seven Papa."

And now there were two of us burning fuel and collecting solar heat without being told why. I noted that the TBM pilot had exited the runway at Bravo. He must have stood on the brakes. Money—and brake pads—to burn.

Another minute passed.

"Ground is there a problem?" the TBM pilot wanted to know.

"Stand by." A terse note joined the woman's voice.

"Never be the squeaky wheel," I told Arun who had donned the headset and slipped out of his seat. He crouched behind the two front seats to obtain a view out the windshield.

"Why?"

"You might wind up with instructions to taxi to the ramp via Canada."

He lifted his hand and pointed. "I bet that informs the situation."

Four SUVs decaled with law enforcement stripes and badges I could not make out wheeled across the TSA ramp. Red and blue lights on roof bars signaled urgency, as if high speed and tight turns weren't enough. They charged past us. When they angled onto the Signature Flight Services ramp, I felt our chances of being cleared to parking sink.

"What do you suppose that's about?" Arun asked.

"Some TSA excitement, no doubt."

Airports with Part 121 commercial air traffic can be touchy when things like fences are breached, or vehicles wander where they shouldn't. TSA complications are foreign to county airports like Essex where anyone with the gate access code can drive onto the ramp and motor off to a hangar. I would have preferred landing at one of Wichita's satellite airports, but Arun had been asked to meet the Wichita Public School administrative ambassadors at Eisenhower. Maybe they took pride in their international airport— that or they were unaware that their city had more than one airport.

I doubted that whatever had stirred the pot this morning would amount to anything significant. Someone with the wrong badge opened a terminal door. A vehicle wandered onto a ramp. A gate was left open. Any of a dozen benign events came to mind. Insignificant or not, we were in for some government-issue inconvenience.

"Can you text the folks meeting us?" I asked Arun. "We might have a delay. I expect they're about to route us somewhere we didn't intend to go. Your reception party may have to come and find you."

Arun slipped into the British accent that made his twenty-something sound like sixty to my ear. "I'll get it sorted." He backed into the cabin, removed his headset, and returned to his seat. Sandy lifted an eyebrow while he explained with words lost to the engine noise and my noise-cancelling headset.

I swiveled my attention back out the windshield and considered the path to alternate parking.

"All aircraft, all aircraft," a new controller voice broke the frequency silence, "operations at Wichita Airport are now shut down. Repeat. Operations at Wichita Airport are now shut down. Aircraft on approach, return to approach control for instructions. Aircraft in movement areas on the field, hold your position, remain on ground control, and stand by for further instructions."

And just like that we were bugs caught in the amber of a TSA security action. That the announcement addressed both airborne and ground movements told me it had been broadcast simultaneously on tower and ground control frequencies. I wasn't concerned about the fuel being sucked into the Navajo's engines; she doesn't drink much at idle. The TBM driver behind me might have an issue with his turbine engine draining the tanks, but he seemed to have the good sense to remain silent.

I hoped they didn't plan to shut us down where we sat. Hot starting the big fuel injected six-cylinder engines on the Navajo is more art than science, and while I have a deft touch, it doesn't take much to end up flooded or experience vapor lock. I preferred to let the motors rumble.

For the third time, I tweaked the mixture control, ensuring that the idling engines were not fouling their spark plugs.

The law enforcement SUVs stopped between a line of parked aircraft on the Signature ramp. Their lights sparkled among bright executive jets. Whatever hit the fan, it happened exactly where we would have been unloading if we'd arrived a few minutes sooner. The school administrators and teachers waiting for Sandy and Arun probably had a front-row seat to the action.

Odd, though, that this was an incident on the general aviation ramp and not the air carrier ramp.

We idled in place for six more minutes before ground control asked us if we would accept alternate parking. I had anticipated the question and requested taxi to the Textron Aviation Service Center. If nothing else, we could park and borrow their reception lounge while Arun arranged for our hosts to find their way over from the opposite side of the field.

We were told to stand by. Four more minutes passed before we were released. As usually happens, about thirty seconds after being issued a taxi clearance to alternate parking, ground control came back on the frequency and said we were now cleared to Signature if we wished to return to our original plans.

I responded in the affirmative and soon rolled to a stop at our original destination facing a ramp rat with crossed orange wands.

7
____

Sandy and Arun tidied themselves and walked across the ramp. They skirted two Sheriff's Department SUVs and entered the highline fixed base operation. Heavily tinted glass swallowed them as soon as the door slid shut.

I left the airstair door open and strolled to the front of the Navajo. Two of the four Sheriff's vehicles remained parked on the ramp near the building, their go-lights still flickering. A third had rolled back the way it came while we were taxiing to park. I saw no sign of the fourth.

More interesting was the cluster of people standing across the ramp from me in front of a Cessna Citation jet. Several deputies in light blue uniform shirts joined a group focusing attention on the jet's nose. A man in an expensive-looking suit pointed and sent harsh words flying among the onlookers. At one point he threw his arms up. Loud f-bombs carried across the ramp until a passing King Air turboprop drowned him out. He shook his head vigorously, spun and made a dramatic march to the building. One of the deputies and a young woman in business attire hurried after him. The rest closed in around the jet's nose. Two of the onlookers wore black ties over white shirts with stripes on the epaulets. The Citation's crew. I could not see what held their attention. A moment later the fuel truck rolled up between me and the odd scene. The driver caught my eye and I nodded. Yes. Fill her up.

The driver stopped the truck and hopped out of the cab. Before attending to my needs, he stepped to the front fender of the truck. He stole a look at the situation from behind cover.

"I don't blame you for hiding." I pointed. "Sounds like somebody over there is pissed."

"Yeah. At me." He ducked away from the fender and turned to the business at hand.

Embroidery on his shirt introduced him to me as Mike. Mike fit the mold of the typical young ramp rat—maybe working on his license or ratings, making minimum wage at the airport just to be near airplanes, chasing a passion he hoped to make a profession. Spring had come early to Kansas and the sun had already bronzed the kid's face and arms.

"Hey, I didn't mean…" I trailed off, not sure what I meant or what he thought I meant.

He shrugged off the apology. "I 'bout got my head taken off. Best if I keep a low profile."

"Head taken off…figuratively? Or by a prop?"

"By the guy that owns that Citation." He opened the rear panels of the fuel truck and drew out the ground line. The reel whirred until he had enough slack to clip it to the nose gear.

"Wouldn't have anything to do with all the cops, would it?"

"If you mean, are they going to arrest my ass? I guess that's still up for debate."

I gave him a minute to jot down the tail number, then reel out the fuel hose. I followed him to the right wing. I wasn't worried. If this kid had damaged that jet's nose, he probably wouldn't still be trusted to operate the fuel truck. But it was clear he had been rattled. I double-checked to confirm that he wasn't about to inadvertently dispense Jet-A into my tanks.

"Fill it up," I told him. He popped the fuel cap and squeezed the nozzle trigger. 100LL avgas flowed into the wing tank. I leaned on the leading edge of the wing. "So, what happened?"

Mike took a moment to determine whether he wanted to share with a stranger or not.

"Wasn't my fault." He did not look up. "Maryanne at the desk, she ran to the bathroom. That whole crowd came through to load up. I buzzed 'em out the door, no big deal. Then this last guy came dashing up, you know, like he was tail end Charlie. Happens all the time. I swear he said 'Wait up' or 'Hold the door' or some shit like that. I'm not the damned TSA, you know." Early twenties and fit or not, his voice was tight and close to breaking. He fought it off with an abrupt, "Fuck!" He tossed an apologetic glance in my direction and added, "Sorry."

"I think I've heard that word before. Seems like a lousy reason to be calling the cops."

He gingerly topped off the tank, then carefully twisted the nozzle to avoid dropping fuel on the paint. He capped the tank then backed away and maneuvered the hose to the other wing.

When he didn't respond, I added, "It can't be that bad."

"You didn't see what he did. Take a peek at that Citation."

I strolled to the fender of the fuel truck and leaned against it; just a customer supervising a simple gas-up. Fifty feet away, the pilots of the private jet had boarded, leaving two people to examine the aircraft's nose cone under the supervision of a single remaining deputy. One wore coveralls. The other wore work pants under a blue denim shirt. Both carried mechanical authority. With the extra bodies out of the way, I could see what the excitement was all about. There were marks on the jet's white paint. Had it been scratched? Did the kid hit it with the fuel truck? I squinted against the bright sunlight. Not marks. Gouges. A random pattern of thin gouges peppered the left side of the jet's nose.

"Whoa! What the hell?"

The kid snorted. "Guy got through the door but then he went for the back of the truck here. We keep a fire ax—you know—just in case. Before anybody knew what was happening, he grabbed the ax and went for the people loading up the Citation. I 'bout crapped my pants. I thought he was going to go full ax murderer right there on the ramp."

I know better than to think I've heard it all. This dropped my jaw. "You've got to be kidding me. Anybody get hurt?" The instant I asked the question I realized that no ambulances had joined the melee.

"No, thank Christ. He didn't go after the people, you know—like, *go after them*. He followed them, all mad and shouting. They scattered. Before anybody could stop him, he starts wailing on the jet. Like full swings. Like Alex Gordon going after a fastball. Wham! Wham! Wham!"

I had no idea who Alex Gordon was, but with the people out of the way I saw the damage to the aircraft. Just ahead of the cockpit windscreen the smooth skin of the jet looked like a dog's chew toy.

That's not going to be cheap. It doesn't take much to damage an aircraft, and it doesn't take much damage to add zeros to the repair bill.

"Holy crap. I take it the cops grabbed him?"

"Nope. Guy finished his business, threw down the ax, and walked back through the FBO like he was going to pick up doughnuts. Walked right past me. Maryanne was on the phone with the Sheriff's Department."

"Cops didn't grab him?"

Mike shook his head. "He was long gone by the time they got here. I sure as hell wasn't going to get in his way. Big mother. Like a pro wrestler."

"Man, you gotta be pretty pissed at somebody to do something like that." I returned to the Navajo and leaned on the engine nacelle, stealing an involuntary look at the airplane's undamaged nose skin.

"They'll get him. I heard somebody say they know who he is—one of the people from the jet, you know—before the boss told me to get my ass out here and don't come back until they send someone to question me— which doesn't sound at all good."

"Ah." I watched Mike carefully top the tank. "That's the head amputation part."

"Uh-huh."

"Wasn't your fault."

He didn't respond. He seemed like the responsible type, and they always find a way to blame themselves. He wrapped up the fueling, told me to pay at the desk inside, and drove off.

8

———————

"Check this out," I tugged on Arun's sleeve. "Look!"

We congregated over a late dinner at the bar at the Courtyard by Marriott Wichita. Sandy had declined the invitation to dine at the bar. I understood. She tends to attract unwanted attention in a hotel dominated by male business travelers. I pointed at the television screen tucked in a nook above the array of bottles shelved behind the bar. Arun suspended a French fry between his plate and his mouth.

"What?"

"That's it. The thing. On the news. That's the thing that caused all the ruckus at the airport today."

Stock news footage showed airliners on the ramp at Eisenhower Airport. A banner beneath the picture succinctly stated *Man Attacks Airplane*, giving the entirely erroneous impression that something happened on a passenger jet. From an inset frame, the local news anchor mouthed the story, looking alternately grim and astonished.

"Can we turn that up?" I asked the young woman hovering behind the bar. She looked up from her cell phone too late. The newscast moved on to the weather.

"Sorry? What?"

"Never mind."

"Did they get the guy?" Arun asked.

"Doesn't look like it. They know who did it."

"How do you know?"

36

"The crawl. Under the picture and banner. Didn't you see it? *Cancer Dad Attacks Corporate Jet.*"

"Cancer Dad? What's that supposed to mean?" Arun's attention returned to the plate of French fries and the double bacon cheeseburger that anchored it.

"Dunno."

"Perhaps he has cancer…and he's a dad. That would be unfortunate."

I didn't reply. I had my own monster cheeseburger to conquer while a voice in my head asked why a man with cancer attacks a multi-million-dollar corporate jet.

9

———————

Hoda Kotb and Savannah Guthrie answered the question on the *Today Show* the next morning. I might have missed it, except Andy woke me early.

"Hey, lover, how's—where are you?" she asked after I fumbled the phone to my ear.

"Wichita. Mecca of general aviation. Home to the greats. Beechcraft. Cessna. Stearman. Part of The Arsenal of Democracy in World War Two. I may never return."

"Does that mean I can finally clean out the garage and park both cars inside?"

"Absolutely not. Do not disturb my workbench. Historians would compare that to the burning of the library at Alexandria. You could disrupt the invention of the next BLARN."

"The next what?"

"Bidirectional Locomotion for Aerial and Relational Navigation."

"Relational?"

"I needed a word that starts with 'r.'"

"No. You honestly didn't."

"I see. You prefer to stick with BLASTER." *Gotcha.*

She changed the subject.

"Leslie called."

I scooched up on the mattress and propped a pillow behind my back.

"And…? Any word on that thing in Louisiana?"

"She wants to talk to us. Both of us."

I said nothing.

"She didn't say," Andy answered my unspoken question. "Sounded like she preferred not to discuss it over the phone. She asked when you'd be back. I told her this afternoon. Was I right?"

"As rain."

"Try to be on time. I bet she will literally be at our door when you roll in."

"I will not take that bet. This must be about Blaze and Louisiana. About finding whoever shot those six guys."

It had been two weeks since our stakeout. Leslie had practiced radio silence ever since.

"She didn't say, and I didn't ask. Don't dawdle at the airport tonight, okay?"

"My dawdle has been revoked."

That ended the Leslie discussion. Andy apologized for calling at this early hour; she had to leave soon to prepare for a deposition at the county DA's office, one of the continuing aftershocks of arresting the Connelly couple who coordinated the shooting at our home. She told me that the hardware store had called. Our gas-powered weed trimmer was ready for pickup. I do not like our weed trimmer and it does not like me. I sincerely doubted that Mel at the hardware store had persuaded the demon device to accept a truce. I told Andy I would pick it up tomorrow.

We finished the call with exchanges of love and no further mention of the FBI flitting in and out of our lives.

I dropped my phone on the sheets and found the TV remote on the nightstand. During the call, the muted *Today Show* opener flashed what looked like handheld amateur video of a man swinging an ax against the nose of a corporate jet—the very same Citation I'd seen. Someone shot video of the attack from a distance.

The clip returned as a teaser, adjacent commercial breaks, but the story didn't reach the screen until nearly forty minutes into the hour. Delaying a shower and shave didn't bother me. I had time. Arun's itinerary listed us as wheels up at 2:30 p.m. I laid back on the bed until the story aired.

"Wichita police and federal authorities are engaged in a manhunt for the perpetrator of an alleged assault on a Learjet yesterday. Bystander video shows the assailant, now being identified as Reuben Calbert of Kingman, Kansas, attacking the jet at Wichita International Airport." Hoda Kotb delivered the story introduction with the usual error identifying every corporate jet as a Learjet. A smile tugged at the corners of her lips. "Davis Halloran of NBC affiliate KSN-TV has more."

The screen cut to a young man wearing a polo shirt and holding a bulky microphone for a remote report. The airport sign hovered over his left shoulder.

"That's right, Hota," he began. "Operations at Wichita International came to an abrupt halt yesterday when a fight broke out between man and airplane," the video jumped to a shot of a Southwest Airlines jet taxiing, "It all happened when a man broke through airport security wielding an ax—"

"No, he didn't," I said aloud, editing for accuracy. "And that's not the jet."

"—which he then used to attack a jet parked on the ramp." The video jumped back to vertical format cellphone video, flanked by blurry duplicates of the same wiggling image. The would-be cinematographer caught up to the crime in progress after the man had already begun hammering the Citation's nose. "The incident took place late yesterday morning. Airport police and federal agents quickly raced to the scene—" The video showed Calbert land a final swing and then toss the ax aside before stalking back into the Signature building. "—but not before the assailant ran from the scene."

"No, he didn't." Looked to me like he walked. Details.

The screen cut back to the on-camera reporter whose expression betrayed high pride in his 'man versus airplane' bit. I took him for a local news reporter thrilled to be tapped for a *Today Show* bit.

"We now know that Reuben Calbert, the alleged assailant, has a connection to the company that owns the jet. That company is Amphitriton Pharmaceutical Laboratories, who has been in the news for the past several weeks amid rumors of a breakthrough in cancer research." Stock video of scientists in lab coats replaced the reporter. A tight shot showed glass droppers putting blue liquid into Petri dishes. "Unconfirmed reports suggest that Calbert's daughter took part in recent Amphitriton drug trials. The company, citing HIPAA laws, declined to comment." The scene switched back to the reporter, who for some reason now stood inside the airport passenger terminal. "Although several flights were delayed, normal airport operations quickly resumed after authorities confirmed that the alleged assailant left the scene. Police are now actively seeking Calbert in the greater Wichita area. We spoke briefly with Terrance Remington, President and CEO of Amphitriton, who was present during the attack." The man who flapped his arms and shouted Pidge's favorite word at people on the ramp appeared on camera against an indistinct office background. He wore an expensive suit over a dazzling white shirt and crisp silk tie. His hair was perfect, and he had applied makeup for the interview. He spoke softly and eloquently, considerably calmer than when I'd seen him at the airport. "Families that suffer from the tragedy that is childhood cancer are under immense emotional, mental, and financial strain. It is understandable when that strain reaches a breaking point. The violent act of one individual, however, in no way represents the brave families we have been working with for years in our effort to relieve suffering and find a cure for this devastating disease—*and I believe we are very close.*" He articulated the last bit for emphasis. Someone off camera shouted a question. Remington shook his head thoughtfully. "No. No, we do not plan to press charges. This individual clearly needs help. We do not condone his actions and we frankly fear for his state of mind. But we can forgive. We wish him and his family well."

The cellphone video got another play. Hoda and Savannah returned to the screen and offered words of shock while the video played two more times in an inset box. They closed with words of condolence for those dealing with childhood cancer. Savannah added a dash of praise for Remington's corporate compassion.

I hit the power button on the TV. The screen went to black. I stared. In that deep, glossy black, I saw night…and children. Children sleeping. Children attached to transparent tubes. A few emaciated and nearly all of them bald.

Matter in an altered state.

The words of an autistic eight-year-old rang in my head. Lillian Farris's young ward spoke those words when I made him vanish and took him flying over a woodland landscape of dead trees. We were, he declared, matter in an altered state.

I've thought a lot about Boyd Farris's declaration since that day. Taken in isolation, I might have chalked his comment up to—I don't know—nonsense from a child. Except that Boyd possesses an exceptional mind. He is also entirely unaware of one of *the other thing's* inexplicable attributes.

The other thing doesn't just make me vanish. *Matter in an altered state.*

On a fogbound Angel Flight more than a year ago, I made a girl vanish, a girl losing a fight with leukemia. I did it because it was the only way to get her out of an airplane that could not land and onto the ground where treatment waited for her. I didn't know it at the time but if I believe Boyd, I altered the state of her matter. The girl wound up in remission. Inexplicably and unmistakably. The discovery was revealed to me by the oncology nurse on that Angel Flight, a woman named Christine Watkins.

Watkins came at me hard about the effect *the other thing* had on her tiny patient. She was convinced that what I had done made the difference. I wasn't, but I couldn't ignore her. Since then, I've visited more than a dozen hospitals in the dead of night. I've vanished and slipped into scores of hospital rooms unseen. While cancer-stricken children slept, I closed a grip on a wrist or ankle and made them vanish, too.

I altered the state of their matter.

Dr. Douglas Stephenson, the neurologist who helped me regain my pilot's license after my accident, knows this. His credentials give him access to data that suggests whatever I'm doing works. Stephenson estimates I have close to ninety percent success. He, like Christine Watkins, encourages me to do more and has gingerly suggested making myself available to medical experts.

Therein lies the problem.

The single factor making me desperate to keep this secret is the ten percent failure rate. It doesn't *always* work—a point I carry as the memory of a young woman's face and the forgiveness she wore on it. I altered Angeline Landry's matter, and it didn't matter.

The notion of bringing this added dimension of *the other thing* into the light of day scares the hell out of me. The expectation of perfection would spotlight every failure. Whatever I'm doing, whatever this altered state of matter does to those tiny bodies, it simply isn't perfect.

That doesn't mean I plan to stop. I won't. If *the other thing* can help one kid, one family, I have no right to stop. But if I ever doubted my decision, this airport incident erased those doubts.

A man goes berserk and attacks a jet belonging to a pharmaceutical company out of rage over the terrible throw of the dice given his daughter—or in anger over the company's failure to deliver something promised. A father's fury made sense to me. His expectation of perfection collided with pharmaceutical failure. He dealt with his pain by swinging an ax.

If people knew what I did, disclaimers would make no difference. The expectation of perfection would be inherent.

What would that man do if I failed his child? What if someone lost a child and decided that I also deserved to lose a loved one?

I don't know how many children I've visited. I don't count. I don't record names—only the places I've been. I don't track results. I leave that to Stephenson, and I've asked him never to be specific, never to share.

But now I had to think.

I've been to a hospital in Wichita, one that specializes in cancer treatment. This was not the first Foundation trip to central Kansas, and it's on these trips that I slip in and out during the night. I don't remember the name, or even what the building looks like, but I know I've visited hospital rooms containing suffering children in this city.

Did I cross paths with this man's daughter?

Did I already fail her?

Was that why this man was driven to attack a jet with a fire ax?

I told myself there was no way to know if I met or missed this man's kid. And if I did fail, logic argued that the child's condition (or worse, death) was not my fault.

Logic.

The badly focused and wiggling cellphone video on *The Today Show* showed a big man, a powerful man, a dangerous man making bad choices. The video was shot too far away to show his face. I suspected that his face would soon be all over the news anyway, whether he was caught or not in the days to come.

I didn't want to see his face.

I told myself it was not my fault. That there was nothing I could do.

Logic.

I tossed the TV remote on the bed and hit the shower.

10

Arun's wheels up prediction of 2:30 p.m. proved perfect as always.
The ride home from Wichita took us through a cold front that curled down from central Ontario, across Lake Michigan and into the central plains. A line of spring thunderstorms marched into Detroit in time to mess with rush hour at Detroit Metro. Behind the line, tabletop layers of wet cloud stretched into the Dakotas. Cool, stable air made the layers soft and smooth, painted my windscreens white, and let me ride through the opaque sky with only my instruments and engines for company.

I chose the RNAV 31 approach into Essex County airport and let the autopilot navigate to the initial approach fix while I adjusted throttles and used the vertical speed function to nail the assigned altitudes. At the Final Approach Fix, the glide slope and lateral navigation bugs aligned on cue. When the green dots on the scales centered, I dropped the gear, set the flaps for approach, and hit the red autopilot disconnect button on the yoke to hand fly the approach.

Like magic, seven hundred feet above the ground, the veil ahead of the nose thinned and shades of brown earth materialized. I tweaked the power to slow from one-twenty to one hundred knots. Runway 31 appeared over the nose, exactly as promised by the publishers of the RNAV 31 approach procedure. Well above minimum descent height, I called Approach Control and reported the runway in sight.

"Final gear check," I recited aloud, confirming the three green lights on the panel along with visual check of a convex mirror mounted on the left engine nacelle.

I rolled back the throttles and dropped full flaps. The Navajo coasted down a three-degree slope to the asphalt where painted runway numbers waited. I flared out and landed with a gentle squeak of the mains, then held off the nose until it overcame backpressure on the yoke and settled of its own accord.

To save the brakes, I rolled out to the last turnoff and exited the runway for the ramp. A short taxi took me past the Essex County Air Service hangar and office, then left onto the wide middle ramp between two rows of hangars, the largest of which housed the Education Foundation.

Home.

The warm feeling got a boost when I spotted something I had never seen before. The ECAS propane-powered tug idled near the corner of the Foundation hangar. Like something out of my adolescent fantasies, two women lounged on the stubby machine. One—cute, petite, and blonde—occupied the driver's seat with her wrists hanging languidly through the steering wheel. She wore a black ball cap and Ray Ban Aviators. The other, a long-legged beauty crowned with locks of deep auburn hair, leaned back on the fender of the vehicle, striking a pose that some low part of my brain filed among glossy images from a tool calendar circa 1942. Tasteful. Clothed. And yet breathtaking.

The women watched me roll past the hangar. I cut a tight circle to place the Navajo in front of the door facing away from the hangar. For a bit of bravado, I killed the engines on the roll.

You fly the airplane until the wheels are chocked. It's an old saw I heard applied to the venerable Beechcraft D-18, but the rule applies to any airplane. Even with the props stopped, I had duties in the cockpit. I fought off the distraction caused when Pidge started up the tug and wheeled it in a tight arc that ended up facing me. Andy gripped the edges of the fender, looking fine and laughing like a girl on a county fair ride.

Damn.

I ran through the shutdown checklist. Pidge nudged the tug closer to the Navajo's nose. Andy waved at me. I shook my head and waved back. Behind me, Arun popped the cabin door. The airplane rocked when he and Sandy disembarked. I squeezed the garage-door style remote that launched the ponderous rise of the big hangar door. After securing my headset and giving the panel switches a final inspection, I followed my passengers to the ramp.

Sandy Stone trotted to the back of the left wing and waved at Andy.

"Pidge is teaching me how to park airplanes," Andy called out.

"Fucking A!" Pidge confirmed, then slapped her hand across her mouth. She searched for Arun to reassure herself that he was well out of earshot.

Arun and Pidge have been engaged in a strangely formal courtship, a secret known to everyone at Essex County Airport, and probably a few transients, too. In his presence, she is girlish and charming. Unrecognizable. I'm not sure he's ever heard her curse. I'm not sure I've ever heard her *not* curse. I couldn't even be certain he knew we all call her Pidge, a shortening of Pigeon which she earned as a young student pilot for her flying skill and foul language. Our smitten Arun uses her birth name, Cassidy.

Pidge cringed but Arun had already started for the hangar, pretending that he was still on the clock and not at all distracted by the young woman driving the tug. Sandy issued a hasty second wave at Andy and followed Arun into the hangar.

"Nice to see you expanding your skill set." I strolled around the wingtip. My wife blew me a kiss. "Then I guess the first thing you have to do is hop down here and hook up the tow bar." I pointed at the bar mounted on a rack above the hitch.

Pidge intervened. "No-no-no-no! That's what we have lowly ramp rats for. Hook us up, my man." Pidge gestured like someone brushing away a fly.

"Me? No way. I'm the hotshot pilot."

Pidge leaned toward Andy. "He's cute but delusional."

Andy giggled.

I hooked the tow bar to the nose gear.

Pidge fired up the tug and inched forward until the tow bar dropped into the latch. I hopped clear. She powered up and pushed the Navajo into the hangar. Inside, she killed the tug engine and left it attached to the airplane, which told me she planned to hang around until Arun finished post-trip business with Sandy.

I gave Andy a hand and helped her down off the fender. She kept the hand and planted a kiss, pressing herself close. I liked her touch and the suggestions it implied. I tried for seconds but she leaned back.

"Let me say hi and goodbye to Sandy, and then I need you for something." She planted a quick one on my lips, then pulled away. I watched her hurry across the hangar floor toward the office.

Pidge joined me. "Jesus, Stewart, get your tongue up off the floor. This is why I keep telling her to blink twice if she's being held against her will."

"She is held. Against her...Will..." I tapped my chest. "Get it?"

"Oh, shut the fuck up."

11

Andy drove the six-year-old Subaru Outback we purchased used shortly after New Year's. Al Raymond, who maintained a large used car lot in Essex, had been pestering Andy about selling her a new ride ever since her car wound up in Leander Lake. Andy insists she would commit grand theft auto before buying a car from Raymond. For as long as she could, she used a police department vehicle, which doubled as a symbol of security at the farmhouse. With the steam released from the recall effort and a general agreement that once our house had been shot up it didn't matter if we had a police cruiser in the yard or not, we decided the time had come to replace her car. The insurance settlement, per usual, didn't come close to providing the cash we needed, but Tom Ceeves steered us to a reputable dealer in Sturgeon Bay, and we were able to finance the shortfall.

I liked the little green Outback. Andy rocked the six-speed manual transmission, which colluded with her heavy right foot to make each ride a thrill. She promised that if I behaved, she might let me drive it one day.

"Where are we going?" I asked after she told me to leave my car at the hangar and ride shotgun in the Subaru.

"One quick stop, then I thought we'd get tacos for dinner." She pulled onto Highway 34 and quickly shifted up through the gears.

It's probably sexist of me, but I couldn't help but steal glances at a beautiful woman throwing that shifter up and down. The car windows were closed, but I always imagine wind sweeping back her hair when Andy drives. My libido wandered. Tacos meant dinner out, which meant time alone over drinks, which meant…

"What's the quick stop? Is this about Leslie?"

"No. Leslie texted. She's delayed."

"Delayed, as in…?"

"No idea."

"Did she give up anything new about the six guys?"

"Not a word."

I expected as much.

"So, what's the quick stop?"

"Something from work. Won't take long."

I did not ask for details, but that didn't prevent me from guessing. A chat with a witness. A knock on a door that probably wouldn't be answered. An ambush interview with someone who had been reluctant to speak to a uniformed officer. Andy carried both a loaded weapon and a load of charm. She used the latter with a marksman's skill.

Andy asked me about the trip. I told her the weird story of the man attacking the airplane, and how it showed up on television.

"Those people will put anything onscreen if they have video." *Those people* referred to journalists. Andy is not a fan of most media crime coverage. "God forbid video catches a cop doing something. Did they arrest the guy?"

"I haven't heard. Doesn't seem to be much doubt about who he is, though, so I'd say it's only a matter of time."

"True. The fantasy of 'going on the run' doesn't play well in a world full of cell phones and surveillance cameras."

"I don't know." I thought of our short-lived status as fugitives last fall. "We did alright."

She laughed. "For what? A few days?"

"You looked good as a blonde." I offered the compliment carefully, recognizing the potential for backlash.

"You're saying I don't look good with my natural color?" There it was.

"Let me rephrase…you made being blonde look good."

"Nice save." She laughed. "Hair color doesn't influence facial recognition software. We weren't going to get very far. From the description of your airplane ax murderer, I give him another forty-eight hours. He sounds like he stands out in a crowd."

"He's a big fellow. Not Tom Ceeves big, but I wouldn't want to meet him in a dark alley."

Andy executed a few turns and jogs. She drove into an older neighborhood in Essex where the home foundations were dug during the post-war building boom. Small cookie-cutter homes lined quiet streets. My curiosity simultaneously ceased and grew when she stopped at a familiar address.

"We're here to see Lane?"

Andy nodded. "There's a girl from her class. Possible missing. Most likely a runaway, given that she's done so half a dozen times before. The parents—who are not exactly sterling citizens—want us to declare her Missing. I'd like to get a better handle on things before we push the panic button. We were at school today nosing around and learning a lot of nothing to suggest anything nefarious. I saw Lane but I didn't want to put a spotlight on her. She's had enough of that. I texted to ask if I could stop by. This won't take long."

"Are you kidding? She'll talk your ear off." Lane Franklin finds a big sister in my wife. Lane visits the farmhouse often to nurture a female connection critical to a girl well on her way to becoming a young woman.

"I'll wait here."

"You'll do no such thing. It would break her heart. She still has a mad crush on you. C'mon."

I didn't buy the crush story as much anymore. There's no question that Lane and I are irrevocably linked after I extracted her from an abduction and the two of us from a burning building, but Lane has grown up and entered that part of life when childish things and feelings get tucked in a velvet-lined memory box. Lane's emotional connection to me had more of a father figure chemistry than a crush.

I wasn't sure which made me less comfortable.

She answered the door before Andy had a chance to touch the digital camera doorbell, something new that reflected Rosemary II's unease regarding her daughter's security.

I hung back to let the girl fly into a hug with Andy.

"Hi, Andy! Hi, Will!" Use of our first names had become a badge of maturity for the girl and a point of irritation for her mother.

I waved from a safe distance. "Lane! Who you gonna fly for?"

"Endeavor. Regionals for eighteen months, then upgrade to captain, then two years in the left seat until Delta calls me up as an FO in an Airbus!" The girl parted from her embrace with Andy and grinned at me. She made no move to hug, which suited me. We've been doing a bit less hugging—I've noticed—since she has physically developed the way young women do. I detected a hint of eye makeup against her soft milk chocolate complexion. And was that lip gloss?

"You've been doing your homework. But you still need college on your resume, kiddo." I added that last bit in case Rosemary II was inside listening.

"Ugh. You sound like Mom. Come in!"

Lane led us into the small house.

"Is your mom home?" Andy asked.

"Delivering meals."

Lane and her mother account for a fair percentage of the people of color in Essex. A part of me smiled at the idea of some of our older population greeting a black woman delivering meals to seniors. Volunteering and serving the community ran in Rosemary II's DNA, but I wasn't sure she didn't enjoy making an impression with a few locals who, as she generously put it, are "set in their ways."

Lane led us into a tiny sitting room. A small desk with a large Mac dominated one corner. School books and a backpack littered the floor. "I was doing homework. Mom's bringing home pizza later. Is this about Corrine? I saw you at school today. Everybody knew why you were there."

"I wanted to talk to you, but I didn't want to be too obvious." Andy and I sat on a small sofa.

Lane dropped onto the chair at her desk. "That's what I thought. Can't be seen talking to five-oh and all that. You know I don't care about that, right?"

"I know. I wish more kids felt that way. But since they don't, it's better for you if we chat privately."

"You mean kids will still trust me and say things around me." Andy started to protest but Lane continued. "It's okay. I totally get it."

"Lane, sweetie, I will *never* use you—use our friendship—that way. You know that."

"Totally! And I want to help. It's not being a snitch to help someone who needs help. But I don't know much. Is she really missing? Corrine runs off, you know. Everybody knows that."

Andy turned to me. "Usual disclaimer? Both of you?"

"Usual disclaimer." Lane and I spoke in unison. I was surprised. I didn't know that Andy had introduced Lane to the workaround for her policy of never discussing police work with civilians. More of the girl talk that I had been excluded from, I guessed.

"Corrine Hawley," Andy said for my benefit. "Sixteen last month. Like Lane said, she has a reputation of running off. Can't hardly blame her. Her parents are—and not a word of this to anyone, Lane—"

"Lips sealed."

"Her parents are a disaster. They've both been busted for possession of oxy.

They're both users. We suspect him of dealing both oxy and meth. He's definitely a user of the latter. He's been in and out, and he's on supervision right now, but that's not going to last. Corrine is the oldest of three kids in the family. The two younger kids are already in foster care. Mom has cycled in and out of rehab several times. And, yes, Corrine has run away half a dozen times. Last Sunday night the parents called to report her missing since Saturday afternoon."

"Must have been a tough sell," I said. "Do you know her, Lane?"

Lane nodded. "She's been in my class the last couple years. She gets in trouble a lot. But sometimes she can be really nice. Some of the other kids are...hard on her. She gives it right back, and that's mostly how she gets in trouble, so it's not fair. I hate that she has the family she has. I think she would be a lot better off, you know, maybe a different person if...I don't know. I guess you can't change that."

Andy slid to the edge of the sofa cushion. "That's what the foster care was supposed to do, and despite the rap it gets, most of the foster parents in this county are good, solid people giving clean, orderly homes to kids who really need the help. The system gets nonstop stereotyped criticism—" Andy caught herself. "Sorry. Soap box. Lane, some of the kids mentioned a party last Saturday night. And that she might have gone with some senior boys. Have you heard anything like that?"

"She hangs out with senior boys all the time. I don't know if she went with them or not, but I did hear that there was a party. Do you know Jason Anderson?"

"I know most of the kids in the senior class through police liaison."

"Jason is a junior. He's like this super loner kid. I mean, he's not in with the kids that she always hangs with, you know? He's not really *in* with anybody."

"This Jason...is he like...?" I tried to ask.

"Like Corey Braddock?" Lane picked up the thread without hesitation. "No. I mean, no he's not like what everyone thought Corey was like, you know? I don't think it's that kind of thing."

We were all wrong about Corey Braddock. Mention of him carried weight and pain. Both were evident in Lane's eyes.

Andy nudged the topic in a new direction. "Luke Dray, Cody Thompson, the Lewandowski brothers—are those some of the seniors Corrine hung out with?"

"I guess. I think Luke and Cody are on the baseball team so maybe not so much her type, but the jocks go after all the girls. They party a lot, so I guess she might have been part of that. Did you talk to those boys?"

Andy avoided answering. "We're still investigating. You brought up Jason Anderson. His name hasn't come up with the others."

"It probably wouldn't. He's not material for their crowd, you know? I mean, he's in band. Um…I can't think of anything else he's involved in."

"Is he in any of your classes?"

"No."

"I don't understand, Lane. What made you mention him?"

"Rumors. I just…I heard there was a party, you know, that kind of thing, it gets around. Nothing specific. It's you have to know the code, be in with the right people—like people don't actually say who's throwing it or where it is, but it gets around. Does that make sense? It's weird."

"And you think Jason Anderson was involved in the party?"

"Maybe. I don't know. Some people were saying that, but when I heard it I thought *that's got to be a code* because he's just not that type, you know?"

"And you didn't catch any specifics…any details?"

"I'll be honest, a lot of that social scene, I just tune out. Except one thing. I guess the party wasn't in town. Not at any of the usual spots, you know? Like the River Park, or the old fairgrounds."

"Somebody's house?"

Lane scrunched up her face. "No…I got the impression it was out in the sticks."

"Did you check the quarry?" I asked Andy, thinking of the swimming hole on the James Rankin property. It was too early in the season for swimming, but that didn't mean the location wasn't suited for a bonfire and other shenanigans.

"We did."

Lane said, "I'm sorry, I really don't know much more than that. I hope you find her."

"Oh, I think we will. She's done this before. Once we nail down who she was with, we will have a pretty good idea of where she would go. I wouldn't worry."

"I feel bad just the same. I mean—for someone who doesn't have friends, or maybe has the wrong friends. I feel bad that she doesn't have a good family. That's sad."

"Is this a case?" I asked when Andy and I returned to the Subaru. I feared we had other stops to make. I was getting hungry for dinner and for other possibilities the evening promised. Going off on an investigation did not make the top of my wish list.

We waved goodbye to Lane from the car and motored off.

Andy said, "There are currently six teenaged girls listed as Missing in Essex. Five of the six are known runaways and have had contact with friends or family and have actively posted on social media. Corrine Hawley has done this before. We have no reason to suspect that it's anything more than a runaway situation."

"Has she posted?"

"No. Not yet."

"Any evidence of foul play?"

Andy threw me a cocked eyebrow as she upshifted from second to third. "Who are you? Inspector Poirot?"

"More like Inspector Gadget. It just seems like there's a pattern here and what have you always told me?"

"If it walks like a duck and talks like a duck you still have to go with what the evidence suggests it is. Let's eat."

12

————————

"I have something…" I told Andy after our tacos landed on the table between us. We occupied a booth at our favorite Mexican restaurant, the one attached to the other bowling alley in Essex. Salsa music from cheap speakers hung at the corners of the dining room lent the air a pulse. A week ago, the place still displayed Christmas pepper lights and decorations. The same lights still hung from the ceiling, but pastel bunnies and chicks replaced cutouts of Santa.

"Mmmm?" Andy nipped off one end of a taco, careful not to crush the shell or let it drip at the other end.

I leaned back in my chair and rotated my half-empty bottle of Corona on its condensation circle. Andy sipped a Diet Coke and studied me with narrowed gold-flecked green eyes and a hint of amusement.

"You've got something?" she asked. "A rash? A cold?"

"Funny. No. Although you're welcome to examine me if you're concerned. In fact, I insist. Safety first."

She smiled. "I may take you up on that. But I don't think it's either of those. You have something on your mind. You have a tell."

"Do tell."

"That." She nodded at my hand and the Corona. "You spin the bottle around like that when the hamsters stampede on the wheel in your head."

I grabbed the bottle and took a slug.

"Ah. I was afraid the wheel needed grease and you could hear squeaking coming from my ears."

54

"Spill it, Pilot."

"It's about that guy."

"What guy?"

"The airplane ax murderer."

"Can I stop you there?" She held up a hand. "Did he—I mean, what he did—did he destroy that jet?"

"Hell no."

"I wasn't sure. Based on what you described. I wasn't sure if a person could successfully do that."

"The ax blade cut into the aircraft skin ahead of the cockpit. There might be some avionics up there, and he may have damaged some. Mostly it looked like skin damage. Probably a six-figure repair, but no, he didn't destroy it. If none of the avionics were damaged, the airplane might even be flyable. Throw a little duct tape on it. What he should have done, if he wanted to really cause havoc, was go at the wings. Bust up the leading edges. Puncture the fuel tanks. Now you're talking about one seriously grounded airplane and damage heading into seven figures."

"Good thing you weren't there to offer advice."

"The guy. I've been thinking about him. He sounds like a real piece of work. I found a couple online articles that said he had a record for assault and that he's made threats before. His ex-wife has a restraining order."

"If it walks like a duck..." She lopped off another bite.

"Here's the thing...they said his child has cancer."

Andy looked at me and lifted her eyebrows.

I offered a confirming nod and used the dramatic pause to grab a bite of taco. Andy swallowed, took a hit from her soft drink to wash it down, and fixed a stare in my direction.

"Let me see...may I?"

"I insist."

"You're thinking that, a) you want to do something for his kid, or b) that you may have already crossed paths with his kid and the treatment didn't work, or c) I'm not sure what c is. What are you thinking?"

"All of the above, I guess. Dee, how desperate do you have to be to track down the CEO of a pharmaceutical company and attack his jet?"

"Desperate. Or crazy, Will. Misinformed or underinformed people do all kinds of crazy things propelled by half-baked notions. I give you our shot-up house as evidence."

"Maybe. Probably. I don't know..."

"Will, you can't take responsibility for this. That is a wild, wild, *wild* stretch of the imagination, darling. You don't know anything at this point. Was the child being treated with drugs from…what's the company…?

"Amphitriton."

"Never heard of them. Was the child in a drug trial of theirs? Was the child treated with a new test drug? Or did he or she get the placebo? Is this a recent test? Or did it happen years ago? Were there side effects? Darling, those trials take forever, you know. And they're not done in some basement, for heaven's sake. Most of these studies are farmed out to university labs. And even that has been subject to scandal. Universities get huge sums of money and produce test results that bias toward the money source. Or drug companies publish the positive results but bury negative side effects. I don't mean to question your desire to do all that you can with the gift you've been given, but you simply do not have anything resembling a complete picture or a complete set of facts here. You can't lay this on yourself. And if you did, where would you start? If the cops are looking for this guy, you are not going to find him first."

"I wasn't…"

She reached across the table and pulled my hand away from the beer bottle I had begun rotating again. She closed her hand over mine and squeezed.

"I know you. Don't indict yourself for something that has nothing to do with you."

I gave it a moment and then asked, "How long have we been married? A week? Two?"

She fluttered her lashes. "Has it been that long?"

"I was just wondering when you'll be wrong about something."

"Don't hold your breath, love."

SOMETIME, hours later, in darkness, perspiring in each other's arms, drawing deep breaths scented with her perfume and dizzying narcotic effect of energetically loving this incredible woman, I realized that this was the first time she ever referred to *the other thing* as a gift.

13

"So…what aren't you telling me?"

Andy tented her elegant fingers and stared across the breakfast table at me. She wore a white cashmere sweater I desperately wished to touch, and the way she tied up her hair this morning looked more like date night than workday. I had attributed both to the lingering aftereffect of a passionate evening together. She had a glow about her.

I sensed an ambush. My wife can hold a straight face and did so now, however a light in her eyes betrayed amusement while I helplessly turned red.

"I have no idea what you're talking about," I protested, cursing the heat in my cheeks.

It's bad enough that I cannot keep a secret from this woman. It is absolute torture when she implies that I have, and I have neither a clue nor a confession with which to save myself.

"Stop it. You promised not to do this. Okay. Fine. I did it. Whatever it was." I realized I'd recently made the same universal confession to Leslie. This was getting out of hand. "Seriously, you're going to have to be more specific."

I slipped off my chair and went to the refrigerator for an orange juice refill I didn't need. The ploy removed me from the heat of my wife's interrogation lamp.

"I noticed something yesterday." Andy notices everything. I still had no idea what. I poured the orange juice and then lingered at the open refrigerator, contemplating a way to crawl in.

"And…?"

"Our young friend Lane did not hug you."

I popped up from behind the open door. Andy looked over her shoulder at me from the table.

"That's it? That's what I did? Or didn't do?" She remained silent. I felt relief. This had an explanation. "Our young friend doesn't hug me so much anymore since she's grown big-girl parts. And when she does, she kinda turns sideways, you know? Or she leans in. Like she's not sure she wants me to notice them."

I sat down again, relieved.

"That's not it."

"Okay, now you're just messing with me."

She smiled. "It is fun to watch you blush, but no, that's not it. I noticed that she didn't hug you the way she did right after we told her you could not disappear anymore. Remember? Telling her made her so sad. Like she was in mourning. She hugged you like she was trying to comfort you."

"Understandable. It was kinda our thing…" I now knew where this was going and the heat in my face bloomed again. "It really affected her, Dee. You know she and I have a deep connection over all that. Christ, she was the first person who knew—even before you. It broke her heart when she found out it was gone."

"You told her."

There it was. No denying it. Andy had me dead to rights.

"When did you tell her?"

Dammit.

I leaned back in my chair. My cheeks burned.

"I didn't lie to you. I might have forgotten to mention…"

"When?" A faint dimple appeared at the corner of Andy's lips, signaling that there was hope for me.

"New Year's Eve," I confessed. Andy blinked.

"New Year's Eve? Really?" The dimples pulled her lips into a smile. "Wow. I'm impressed that you made it this long."

"Thanks!"

She laughed. "Don't be so proud, darling. I think yesterday was the first time we've seen her since the holidays. So, basically you made it one day. But hey…" she reached over and patted my hand, "…A for effort. Spill it."

"Remember when we had everybody over? And Lane rode her bike out early to help you with cooking and to hang out?"

"I was supposed to take off at noon, but that was the day the Johns attorneys filed one of those stupid last-minute motions. Tom and I had to meet with the DA. We all ended up getting home late to our families because of those—"

She didn't say it. I did. Then I explained.

"Lane showed up on her bike, half frozen. I told her she should have called, and I would have picked her up. So, I got her in here and made her some hot chocolate and she was just sitting here warming up and the next thing I know she's bawling, and I don't know if it's me or if the whole thing with Braddock is popping up again, because that was almost exactly a year ago, remember? At the Freshman Freeze? And, well, crap, how was I supposed to know what this was about? I mean, the girl stuff, that's your department."

"Whoa. Take a breath." Andy wasn't wrong. I'd been blurting. I did as she instructed, twice.

"Anyway, she launched some serious waterworks, and I didn't know what it was about, and she's blubbering and all snotty and I gave her a hug, which I have to tell you, is not comfortable territory for me, especially being alone in the house with her like that—"

"Oh, stop. You're not some damned headline, Will. You would lay down your life for that girl. You already tried."

"Point is, I wasn't sure what was going on, and then she confessed that when we told her that *the other thing* was gone it was like losing a part of her soul, a part of what made us *us*. She pointed out it was literally the reason she was alive. I had no idea it meant so much to her. She went on and on about the times I took her flying, and how I was there for her after—you know—that whole Braddock ordeal, and she could *not* stop bawling, and—dammit, I just couldn't see any other way to make it better."

Andy stared at me for a moment. Her smile grew first as a glow in her eyes, then as sprouting dimples. She leaned over and placed both hands on the side of my face and pulled me into a kiss. When we parted, she said, "You are such a softie."

"I'm sorry I didn't tell you. You texted that you were going to be late, so I took her flying. Just around the back field a couple times. Honest to God, it was like raising her from the dead. She couldn't stop laughing or crying. I'm surprised she got her act together before you got home."

Andy delivered another kiss, then we settled down to our not-so-warm breakfast.

"Sorry I didn't say anything. But yeah…one more person back in the Circle of Trust."

She chuckled.

"What?" I asked.

"Pidge knows, too."

"Get outta town!"

Andy nodded. "She came to me right after you told her, I guess it was about a week after the big party."

"That's because I didn't tell her at the party. She was too wasted. She stopped over at the hangar a few days later, and I let her know. What the hell? She believed me."

"Nope. She said you're a mother-effing bad liar."

"God damn it." This genuinely disappointed me.

"Oh, don't take it so hard. It was a nice try. Besides, I think I'll be telling Tom, too. We may need your help with this Corrine Hawley business. And I really do need to get moving here, love. Do you mind cleaning up breakfast?"

"Jesus," I said, thinking what an utter failure I had on my hands. "At least Lillian bought it…"

Andy stood up and delivered her dishes to the countertop by the sink. She hurried back to me and gave me a squeeze and a peck on the cheek.

"No, she totally didn't believe you either. Love you. Gotta go!"

14

Pidge poked her head into the Foundation hangar lounge where I had set up camp with a laptop and plans to update the SD card navigation databases for the Navajo. She didn't enter. Her eyes shot to Arun's office. His door stood open with the light on. She flicked her head in a 'Come here' gesture.

"What's up?" I followed her out the office door into spring sunshine.

"I got a freight run to Frankfort."

"Germany?"

She made a face. "No human cargo to fuck with. Just over and back. You available for some safety pilot? I need it for currency."

I found that hard to believe. The FAA requirement to legally fly on an instrument flight plan in instrument meteorological conditions calls for six approaches plus some tracking and hold stuff under actual or simulated conditions within the last six months. For the average general aviation pilot, that can be a challenge. For a working pilot like Pidge in the American Midwest it shouldn't have required a logbook check.

Pidge read my skepticism. "I've had a stupid run of bad luck with nothing but good weather. You don't do anything useful here. Come with me and you can pencil whip my logbook."

I checked my watch, which had nothing to do with anything. Shortly after Andy left for work, a text message from Leslie popped up on my phone asking if Andy and I were available "today"—whatever that meant.

"That FBI agent is supposed to get in touch. I really should st—"

"Fuck that. We'll be back by lunch time. C'mon!"

TEN MINUTES later I joined her on the main ramp beside the Beechcraft Baron 58 model Earl uses for light cargo runs. It has a handy rear door. The seats were already out of the airplane, but I didn't see any cargo.

"We're picking up the package in Escanaba."

"Good. You can do the DME arc to the ILS."

She laughed. "Piece of cake."

We mounted up. Pidge took the pilot's seat. I took the right seat. We were halfway to the departure end of 31 when I realized we didn't have a hood, the plastic visor used to restrict a pilot's view out the windows as a means of simulating instrument flight. I told Pidge.

"Relax. I got it covered."

PIDGE EXECUTED a smooth takeoff and rapid climb to five thousand feet for the short run from Essex County to Escanaba, Michigan. She trimmed the airplane and punched the right buttons on the autopilot. After setting the power and closing the cowl flaps, she tinkered briefly with the mixture controls. Satisfied with the engine management system readings, she settled back and let me know the real reason for riding shotgun on this cargo run.

"Arun wants me to meet his parents. What the hell is that all about?"

"Why are you asking me?"

"Because, in case you didn't notice when you took your morning whiz, you're a guy. What's the deal when a guy wants a girl to meet his parents? I mean—I know what it means—but does it mean he's getting, like, serious? Or is he just covering bases?"

Chicago Center handed us a frequency change, which gave me a moment to think. Pidge dialed in the new frequency and reported level at five thousand direct Escanaba, which Center acknowledged.

"First off, you said 'parents.' His parents are divorced. From what I picked up, it was about as amicable as the Boer War. Are you sure he meant both parents?"

"His mother. He wants me to meet his mother."

"Ah. That's different. Mothers and sons. That's a different dynamic. If I were you, I'd be scared shitless."

"C'mon! I'm serious here! I really want to know."

"How the hell should I know? Are you guys just trading spit or are you talking about trading rings?"

"Fuck! No! Nothing like that. Is that what you think this is? Do you think he's thinking about proposing?"

I looked across the cockpit at her, but she stared dead ahead with a look I'd never seen on her face in an airplane.

"First off, I have no idea. Second…are you scared?"

"Fucking terrified! Wouldn't you be? Has he told you anything about his mother? She's like British royalty or something."

"She's not. She's wealthy, but she's not royalty."

"What's the difference?" She shot a quick glare at me through her Ray Bans. "I can NOT meet his mother. She's rich. She's smart. She's going to take one look at me and arrange for her son to marry some goddamned Indian princess or some department store heiress to save her son from the American trailer trash."

"Why would that bother you? You don't sound like you would touch a committed relationship with a ten-foot pole."

I shouldn't have said that. She punched me in the upper arm. It hurt.

"Look," I rubbed my bicep, "the kid is beyond smitten with you."

"He kinda is…"

"And I believe he has a strong bond with his mother. Dad's pretty much out of the picture, but from what I've picked up, Arun and his mother are close. She's important to him. You're important to him. I think he just wants to establish a connection between the two women in his life who are most important to him."

"Gak! You sound like daytime TV. Goddamned relationship bullshit. I mean—okay, that's the one thing about him—he's all touchy feely that way."

"Like he's the girl in the relationship?"

"Kind of…"

Pidge said nothing for a few minutes. She stared over the high curve of the instrument panel.

Chicago Center handed us off to Green Bay Approach who cleared us down to four thousand. Pidge dropped out of her fugue state and handled the calls and the transition to initial descent. Her hands darted around the cockpit, performing a rapid GUMPS check. Gas (main tanks). Undercarriage (to go). Mixture (set). Props (set). Seatbelts (on).

"You don't really need a safety pilot," I said. "You just didn't want to talk about this at the office."

"And people say you're slow."

"Joke's on you. We're doing this anyway. Ask them for the ILS Runway 9 via MAARC." She made the call. "What are you using for a hood?"

She turned her head and winked at me, then scooted to one side of the seat, lifted her right thigh, and pulled out the cushion she used to look like a grownup at the controls. She tossed the cushion in the back and dropped down into the seat.

"Are you kidding me?"

"What? I can't see a fucking thing from down here!"

I laughed most of the way down the approach, then took over for the landing.

Pidge had the last laugh. The "package" waiting for us in Escanaba was a twenty-two-inch diameter cast iron sprocket weighing a hundred and fifteen pounds. It arrived in a pickup bed. The driver and I horsed the sharp-edged monster to the rear door of the Baron, and then we tried hard to injure ourselves sliding it onto a plywood panel that had been placed on the carpeted cargo floor. Pidge supervised, grinning.

15

"I think I hurt my back."

"Oh, grow a pair." Pidge killed the Baron's engines in front of the Essex County Air Service hangar. Silence flooded the cockpit. I cracked the door and contemplated the gymnastics of rising from the copilot's seat, rotating, and exiting onto the wing in one smooth move.

"Bring your logbook over to the hangar later and I'll sign off the safety pilot time."

"Fuck that. I got plenty of currency. I just wanted someone else to handle that chunk of iron." She laughed, but it sounded forced.

"What are you going to tell Arun?"

"I don't have a lot of choices. I suppose I can stall, but that's an obvious answer all by itself. He's a delicate flower but he's no dummy. I don't know…"

"Hey, kiddo." I patted her knee and looked her in the eye, summoning every ounce of sincerity I could mount with a straight face. "You know that any time you want to talk to someone about deep emotional issues just come to me…and I'll give you Andy's number."

Exiting the cockpit wasn't a challenge after all.

Andy called during my walk back to the Foundation hangar.

"Leslie wants to do a Zoom call with us."

My pulse quickened.

65

"'Bout time."

"Are you free in about an hour?"

"Sure." I congratulated myself on impeccable timing.

I'd been expecting Leslie to simply appear. Lately, that had been her style. However, it made sense that Leslie wasn't traveling to Essex, Wisconsin. If I had to guess her location, I'd drop a pin on Point Coupee Parish, Louisiana.

"FaceTime or Zoom?"

"Zoom."

"Huh."

"Yeah. I know. That means she's on a computer, probably in an office. I think we need to prepare for the possibility that others may be involved in the call."

"Don't you think she'd give us a heads-up?"

"I'm not sure she's able. We need to be ready for anything."

"Like what?"

"If I were investigating those killings, I'd want to know the whereabouts of two people who were targeted by the victims. Two people with a motive for revenge."

I stopped cold on the ramp.

"Seriously?"

"Will, we talked about this." We had. Andy's first instinct when I returned had been to determine what, if any, trace of my presence in Louisiana could be proven.

I repeated the highlights. "You were in Essex. I was in Cape Girardeau. Rock solid."

I didn't like having to lie. My prowess at deception seemed to be in doubt lately. Andy recites a simple rule that so many of her criminal suspects fail to obey. *Always tell the truth. It's easier to keep your story straight.*

If questions came, they wouldn't come from Leslie. Taking me to the gas station meeting had been her scheme, which very likely meant she was lying to someone.

"You want to come to the hangar?"

"No. Um…can you come here?"

"The department? You want to do this there?" That made no sense to me.

"Have to. The chief is on the call, too."

16

———

Parking in front of the Essex Police Department, I realized that I'd completely forgotten to stop at the hardware store to retrieve my arch enemy, the annoying and unstartable weed trimmer.

"It can wait," I declared aloud, thinking it wouldn't take a psychologist to identify blatant procrastination.

Mae Earnhardt buzzed me past the bulletproof public entrance and led me back to Andy's cubicle.

"Been on any good dates lately?" I asked the back of her gray head as we navigated between desks. Mae is taller than Pidge, but not by much.

She laughed. "I got invited to a Luke Bryan concert. I like Luke Bryan."

"The man has talent. Was it one of Ashley's gentlemen callers?"

"I have many admirers."

"Did you take him up on it?"

"I said I would go with him if I could bring six of my grandchildren."

We found Andy at her desk and on the phone as usual. She claims fifty percent of her work is by telephone, which she likes to conduct in her cubicle. She prefers the old school handset over the department-issue cellphone; she has trouble cradling the mobile device against her shoulder while she scribbles notes.

Mae pantomimed a handoff, touched my forearm with a smile, then headed back to the dispatch desk. Andy spoke warmly and with a hint of excitement in her voice.

"...sure...yes, that's no problem. I can stop after school lets out...no, *thank you.* I appreciate your help…right…see you then." Andy relaxed her shoulder and let the black plastic handset drop into her open palm. "Nice." She hung up the phone, jotted notes on her notepad, then lifted her smiling face in my direction.

"Progress?" I slid my butt onto the low filing cabinet just inside her cubicle. My usual seat.

"Little by little." She checked her watch. "That was the boy's mother. I've been playing phone tag with her for days. I was afraid she was avoiding me. Now she sounds positively delighted to talk with me. Let me tidy this up and then let's go to Tom's office."

I glanced around to ensure that no one was within earshot. "Tom's office? Why is he on this call, too?"

"Unknown."

"The plot thickens."

17

Andy ducked into the ladies room for a quick appearance check. She came out with her hair in an all-business bun. How she managed it so fast and so perfectly was a mystery to me.

Tom Ceeves dominated the space behind a desk almost large enough to make him look normal. He might have sustained the illusion except he struggled with a laptop that looked like a Speak & Spell in his massive hands. His expression warned that one of those hands was about to ball up and smash the laptop to plastic fragments.

"Goddammit!" He shoved a wireless mouse back and forth on his blotter. "I can see them, but I can't hear them."

Panic spread across Andy's face. "Are they on already?"

"I guess. Here. You try."

Andy hurried around the desk and leaned into the problem. She swept up the mouse and clicked. The laptop speaker came to life.

"—hear you just fine—"

"We can hear you now, sir," Andy said quickly. "I'm so sorry. Let me reposition this so we're all on."

Sir? My guard went up. Andy's instinct had been correct. Someone else was on this call. Her eyes flared in my direction. She gestured for me to come around the desk and stand on the other side of Tom, who remained seated. Andy pushed the laptop midway across the desktop to adjust our framing.

I tucked in beside Tom and saw myself join Andy and Tom in a small rectangle in the upper left corner of the screen. The body of the screen displayed Leslie dressed in black business wear beside a man in a white shirt and tie. I recognized him immediately, and just as quickly understood Andy's panic.

Leslie handled the introductions.

"Hello, Andrea. Hello, Will. Chief Ceeves. May I introduce you to FBI Director William Simmons? Director Simmons, this is Andrea and Will Stewart, and Chief Tom Ceeves of the City of Essex Police Department."

I glanced at Tom whose eyes bulged. Tom is a man of few words. At the moment, the count dropped to zero.

"Gotta tell you, Chief, I have all kinds of trouble with these Zoom calls," the Director of the FBI said through a warm smile. "Half the time I need to get my grandkids to set them up for me."

"Uh…sorry, you know, about the…" Tom stammered.

Andy dove to Tom's rescue. "I apologize for keeping you waiting, sir."

Leslie waved a hand in the air. "That's on us. We were early."

"I have a briefing in fifteen minutes," the Director said. "But I wanted to be on this call personally."

The Director, a man in his early fifties, could have been pulled out of Hollywood Central Casting for the role. Handsome, square-jawed, with traces of silver touching tight wavy black hair at his temples, he had no quarrel with a camera. He had been tapped to fill the post at the start of the current President's administration. I suddenly could not remember whether he'd been confirmed by the Senate or retained "Acting" in front of his title. Headlines suggested that Simmons did not see eye to eye with the President. Journalists credited Simmons, an up-through-the-ranks career Bureau man, with a rigid respect for and adherence to the law. Some said his attitude chafed with an administration priority for loyalty.

Even onscreen, Simmons had an intensity about him. Leslie, sitting beside him, looked like the proud coach who just put her best player on the field. My mind raced. Was this a rerun of meeting Assistant Director Mitchell Lindsay? Was Leslie about to reveal me to the top man in the FBI? And then what?

The FBI Director leaned closer to whatever they were using for a camera.

"Special Agent Carson-Pelham can fill you in on the details later. I wanted to connect with you on the broad strokes. You're aware, I'm sure, that we have an open investigation into the shooting at your home."

"We are," Andy said. "It's very much appreciated."

"At the same time, I'm sure you understand that your incident is part of a much larger and far-reaching investigation involving hundreds of agents and personnel from the Department of Justice—specific details of which I will not be sharing."

"We're well aware, sir."

"I'm sure you're also aware of a recent incident in Louisiana in which six alleged members of a white supremacist group were killed."

"Yes, sir."

"I'm going to share several things with you. This is completely confidential. Is that clear?"

"Perfectly," Andy said. I muttered an "Affirmative."

"What you do not know is that several of the victims have been confirmed as shooters in Essex."

I checked. Leslie kept a straight face. Andy, too.

The Director continued. "You also do not know that one of the people killed was one of our own." Simmons paused to let the weight of his pronouncement sink in.

"I'm so sorry, sir."

"A tragic loss for the Bureau. A fine man with a family. He is owed a great debt. Once again, I share that information with you in absolute confidence, Detective, Mr. Stewart, Chief."

"No question, sir," Andy said.

"Affirmative," I repeated.

"The murders in Louisiana shine a harsh new light on our investigation. An unwelcome light. Certain voices blame the Bureau, which is ironic considering that we were victims in the matter. It's nothing new for the Bureau to be under scrutiny. But it does add difficulty to one the most heavily resourced investigations in recent Bureau history."

"Understandable, sir."

"Now here's the tough part and the reason I asked Special Agent Carson-Pelham to arrange this call. There are political ramifications at hand. Nothing that will sway us in our work, but we also don't work in a vacuum. Social media employed by groups targeted in our investigation is running wild. It's driving some of the weaker-minded members of our esteemed Congress to say things well out of turn. About the FBI. About DOJ. And about you, Detective. Of course, this is nothing new. They've been batting your name around for some time now. The shooting at your house pulled away the veil. I wish I could tell you that things are going to get better. I cannot."

Leslie took the cue.

"Will, Andy, we have known for some time that the people associated with the victims in Louisiana believe that you were involved in the presidential assassination attempt. Signs now indicate that they are expanding that belief to the recent killings."

"That's nonsense," Tom growled.

"One hundred percent, grade-A pure bullshit," the Director agreed.

I said, "None of this would be happening if—" Andy cut me off with a squeeze of the arm.

"What my husband is saying is that it would be helpful if we could get a definitive statement from…well, perhaps DOJ? Perhaps The White House?"

"I understand your feelings. It might simplify matters for you, but I need you to understand the problem, Detective. At this stage of the investigation —any investigation—we simply don't go public. The press likes to say that the DOJ speaks in court filings. They treat it as a clever expression. I treat it as a rule. There will be no statement from the investigation."

"But sir—!"

"Mr. Stewart, off the record, I wholly agree with you," the Director said. "Off the record, we are negotiating with White House staff and the Attorney General's office as we speak. We're looking for the best way to counter the misinformation—"

"Outright lies," I muttered.

Simmons nodded. "Yes. Outright lies—in a way that does not source from or jeopardize the investigation. And this is where I repeat to you, this investigation is massive. That's a good thing, but it has its downsides. Any public statement can ripple down through dozens of threads we're pursuing, generating unforeseen consequences and potential harm."

Andy squeezed my arm again to head off a rude comment about to fall off the tip of my tongue.

"Detective, Mr. Stewart, I asked to be on this call to assure you that everyone, all the way to the top, is on your side. I've spoken with the President myself. I made him aware that you've been unfairly entangled in something that never should have happened."

"And did he agree?"

The Director hedged. "I believe he understands the situation. The misinformation adds insult to injury after what you did to prevent a tragedy. But while we embrace reality, we must acknowledge the existence of alternate realities. People have deluded beliefs about you, Detective. And now that they think a 'hit' has been carried out on members of their group, they're doubling down on those delusions. A statement is unlikely to change minds —those minds, anyway."

Anger warmed the sides of my neck.

Tom spoke. "What…exactly…are you saying here, sir?"

The Director took a theatrical breath.

"We're on this. We're working it. We will take every step we can. I will personally see to it. But watch your backs. Detective, you're an officer of the law and you know the realities of a situation like this."

"Is there a specific, actionable threat, sir?" Andy asked.

"Afraid not."

"It's tidal, Andrea," Leslie said. "We monitor so much more than they think. So much that sometimes we can form assumptions the way geologists read tectonic plates, you know what I mean? NSA aids us in macro analysis. I can't give you specifics except to say your name is flagged."

"Detective, I wanted you to hear this directly from me. I will never downplay the threat. It might be deadly and real, or it might be a lot of wind from a collection of losers and trolls. I'm here to tell you to take it seriously. We can offer you protection, but protection like that comes at a personal cost —and I can't make any promises about how long it will take for our work to bear fruit."

"Understood, sir."

The Director leaned toward the camera. "We *will* put this thing to rest. We must. Not just for you, but for the country. To the extent we are able, I've asked Special Agent Carson-Pelham to keep you posted on our progress, but only if you hold any information we provide in deepest confidence. Do I have your word on that?"

Andy and I both agreed.

"Good. I thank you for all you've done, and for abiding these difficulties."

"I'll call you this evening," Leslie added.

The Director glanced at Leslie, then nodded at us one more time. He reached for his keyboard and the connection winked out.

"Son…of…a…bitch," Tom muttered. "I did not expect that."

18

Tom closed the door to his office and over the next half hour threatened to fire my wife six times when she adamantly refused to seek protection or alter her work routine. Andy called both notions ridiculous. Tom pointed out that she had recently resigned, and he was now accepting that resignation. Andy countered that he had torn up her resignation. Tom attempted to enlist me in his cause. I told Tom I agreed and would happily side with him but that I could not afford the divorce. Andy insisted that leaving her job would validate everything the *recallistas* had attempted, including the violent assault on our home. Tom claimed a violent assault on our home validated his point of view. He added that when the Director of the Federal Bureau of Investigation warns you of a threat, you take the man seriously.

The contest was never in doubt. In the end, Andy folded her arms across her chest, clenched her jaw in a way that enriches her lower lip, and prevailed against two men who, combined, equaled four times her body weight.

Andy put the subject to rest with a glance at her watch.

"I have to go, Chief." She struck a businesslike tone after passions had raised voices. "I was able to get the boy's mother to agree to talk with me."

"What boy?" I asked. The two cops in the room ignored me.

Tom frowned. "I thought she was avoiding us."

"She was. Now she's suddenly helpful. I think I got through to her. I told her I was worried about her son. She swears he's not involved in any of this business. I've got a feeling he might be. The family owns farmland out near Cinnamon Hills. It's not active but some old sheds are still standing. Old barns and sheds make a good spot for partying. A few other kids I've talked to 'fessed up to partying in an old barn and said they saw Corrine Hawley. I plan to ask for permission to search."

"You're going up to the farm to talk to the mom?" Tom seemed uncomfortable with Andy herding the elephant out of the room and shifting focus to the missing girl.

"They don't live there. She and the kid live up on D. She said I could talk with him after school gets out. I want to have a word with her before the bus drops the kid off." Andy tapped her watch.

Tom stood up.

"Fine. Let's go."

"Sir? I've got this."

"Yup. And I got your back. Let's go."

19

———————

I rode with Andy. Tom drove his big SUV. Andy told Tom she would drop me off at the airport and meet him at the Anderson home. I waited until we rolled out of the department lot.

"Take me with you."

"First, yes, I already planned to. Second, please, not you, too."

"Dee, that was the friggin' Director of the FBI."

"You and the chief are not going to babysit me, Will."

"Remains to be seen."

"I mean it. We'll talk about that later. But let's be clear. I didn't want you along to protect me. I'd like your help finding this girl. If that's a problem…"

"It's not a problem. But we're not sweeping that video call under the rug."

She didn't answer.

"Fine. What do you want me to do?"

Andy gave it a beat to ensure that we were both focused on the business at hand. She said, "The girl is not going to be at this kid's house. I'm just going there to talk to the mother and get permission to search the farm. Then maybe catch the boy by surprise when he gets off the bus."

"Because of what Lane said?"

"Because of—and regardless of. I simply want to have a conversation with the kid. And I don't want to do it at school."

"You want a look at the farm property. You said you already drove by. Did you go in?"

"Not without permission."

"Ah. I get it now. Perfect. You chat with the mom. If she says, Sure, go ahead and look around it's all good. If she says no, you and I go up there and have a look around my way."

"A contingency. Strictly for this Corrine Hawley situation, okay? But I want it perfectly understood that bringing you along has nothing to do with that Zoom call. Understood?"

"Absolutely."

She looked sideways at me and caught me grinning.

"What?"

"See? I can lie."

20

April is not kind to Essex County. The days may grow longer, but incrementally increasing daylight is often blanketed by layers of gray cloud. Some years, ten inches of snow arrives; winter throwing a tantrum and clutching the calendar. Even when the snow has largely melted, piled remnants litter parking lots, roadsides, and driveway edges, growing dirty and black. Spring sunshine breaks through, as it had today, but the low angle of the sun makes the light feel weak. Trees without buds and muddy fields hold the landscape hostage. Frozen manure, spread during the winter, thaws and the farmlands of Essex County welcome spring with a scent that is anything but floral.

These sights and sensations dampened my enthusiasm for our mission as Andy drove a zigzag course into the northwest corner of the county where the lavish Cinnamon Hills golf resort once hosted Sandy Stone's wedding turned murder scene.

The Anderson home gave no hint of sharing the neighborhood with an icon of wealth. A simple two-story box with aluminum siding and asphalt shingles several years past their expiration date occupied a lone weedy lot on County Road D between acres of corn stubble. Wisconsin mechanical flora, the obligatory old pickup on blocks and a tractor knee deep in weeds, decorated the yard. Sun-faded children's toys littered the brown lawn. Dozens of similar residences sprinkle Essex County. Signs of citizens on the edge of poverty, Andy tells me. I wasn't sure that was true. A nearly new Dodge

Ram pickup truck dominated the gravel driveway. Last time I checked, those things ran to the mid five figures.

Andy cued me to vanish half a mile before she pulled into the driveway. I dropped my window first, then—

Fwooomp!

—disappeared from the front seat of the Subaru. She parked behind the pickup, the bumper of which hung at our eye level, adding to the ominous sense I had about this property.

Lane described the Anderson kid as a solo act. When I pressed her about him being the classic "loner" who makes headlines, she said no. I tried to understand the benefit of the doubt Lane gave him but growing up on the fringe of the county alone with his mother didn't inspire faith. A junior who rode the bus branded him as having no car in a high school full of kids with cars. One more sign of an outcast.

Andy said the farm property was less than two country miles to the east of the house. An empty barn and off-the-radar party isn't a bad way for a kid struggling to build a circle of friends to make himself welcome. Teens gravitate to territory hidden from parental view. Maybe it was his idea, or maybe he'd been talked into the scheme. Either way, the scheme had unraveled. His mother undoubtedly viewed her little boy as the obedient Cub Scout, incapable of deceiving her, incapable of hiding anything from her. I understood why Andy wanted me along. If the mother stood her ground and refused Andy access to the farm, I became Plan B.

Andy stepped out of the car and hooked her satchel over one shoulder. In a black leather jacket, white blouse, and jeans over calf-high designer boots, she projected a nice blend of business and chic casual. She described the phone call with Mrs. Anderson as friendly and put on a face to match that tone. After the call with Simmons, Andy released her hair from the conference call bun. It swept her shoulders and lifted in the breeze as she walked across buried limestone slabs that constituted a sidewalk to the front door.

Tom Ceeves pulled up behind the Subaru. I released my seatbelt and hooked my hands on the top of the window frame. As Tom crossed the lawn to join Andy, I heaved myself out the window, bumping the console and dash with clumsy feet. I came prepared. The BLASTER in my hand hummed and pulled me up and away from the car.

I prepared to fly a circuit around the house. The gravel driveway connected to a freestanding one-car garage in the back. It might pay to know what if anything the outbuilding contained. If I needed to open a door, having Andy and Tom distract the property owner helped.

I was about to split off from the Essex PD contingent climbing the front porch when I hesitated. Maybe it would be better to hear what the woman had to say. Andy would surely relate it to me, but it might not hurt to record my own impressions. Anderson's reaction to Andy might inform my next move.

I flicked my wrist to the left and cut the BLASTER power. Roughly ten feet above the dry, dead lawn, I coasted toward the open porch. I aimed for a post that offered an anchor point with a good view. Andy would ask to go inside—a friendly, neighborly request—maybe ask for a glass of water or accept a cup of offered coffee. Her charming approach might be dampened by the Chief's imposing presence, but he had his own way of being neighborly.

If they were both invited in, I'd break away for reconnaissance of the property. If not, I'd hang around to hear what was said.

Andy knocked. Tom moved off to the side, out of view. Tom knows he can be intimidating.

No one answered.

Andy rapped her knuckles on the faded paint of the inner door—there was no storm door. She exchanged a glance with Tom but neither spoke.

Andy brushed a lock of windblown hair from her face. The sound of footsteps inside refreshed the warm smile on her face. She adopted the disarming affect she carries along with the Glock in her satchel. I imagined her first words to the woman, light and pleasant, grateful for the chance to meet.

The deadbolt lock in the door rattled and snapped. The door seal broke. Andy drew a breath to power a friendly greeting.

Both barrels of an over-under shotgun swept up and stopped inches from Andy's gold flecked green eyes. The hand cradling the shotgun jerked a finger within the trigger guard.

Time stopped. The earth ceased spinning. Conscious and unconscious thought failed me.

Click!

The owner of the shotgun hesitated, then—

She pulled the second trigger.

The barrel end of the weapon exploded in light and fire.

21

Tom's giant paw slammed the shotgun barrels upward. His other hand swept Andy backward. The blast tore a hole in the roof of the porch. Splinters and dust showered Andy. She dropped, lost her balance, and tumbled down the porch steps. She landed on her back. Her head hit the concrete.

Tom jerked the weapon from the hands of the woman at the door. He reversed the move and slammed the butt of the shotgun into her face, crushing her nose. She dropped in a heap. Tom reversed the move a second time and hurled the shotgun onto the dead lawn. He called out to Andy who waved one hand at him. The woman on the floor wailed and clutched her bloodied face. Tom produced a pair of handcuffs from somewhere—Tom doesn't wear the standard police utility belt—and stomped into the house. He flipped the woman on her belly and clapped the cuffs on her wrists. She lay bawling and howling and spitting blood with her hands trapped in steel behind her back.

"Dee!"

Too far away, and too slow to react, it took forever for me to heave myself onto the porch, plant my feet, and—

Fwooomp!

—reappear. I dropped hard. Staggered. Stabilized. Dove to the concrete sidewalk where Andy lay. She lifted herself on her elbows and touched the back of her head, then examined her fingers for blood. Seeing none, she flipped open her satchel and produced her handgun. She aimed it at the still open doorway. Tom filled the frame and gently waved Andy's drawn weapon aside.

"You okay?"

She nodded. She glanced at me. Tom followed the glance.

"Jesus, Will."

"Jesus, Tom."

Tom swallowed.

I helped Andy to her feet. She stiffened at my solicitous touch and pushed past me, mounting the porch, weapon at the ready. Squeezing past Tom, she stood over the moaning mess on the floor. Tom studied his Detective, then blinked at me.

"I thought you couldn't…"

"I lied."

Andy stared down at the Anderson woman. The shock on Andy's face transformed into something cold and professional. She drew a breath, counted to four, then released it.

"Will, please wait for me by the car." Andy's words were flat and hollow. Emotionless. "Please. I'm okay. Please."

I could not move. My lungs tightened, which made no sense until I realized I'd stopped breathing. I wasn't sure my legs would keep me upright if I obeyed my wife's wishes and walked back to the car. I felt a need to do something, anything. I wanted to wrap my arms around my wife, vanish, and kick the earth harder than I've ever done. I wanted to take her and leave.

"Please, Will. Go. I'm fine."

22

Fifteen minutes later I sat on the Subaru passenger seat with the door open. I stared at the front of the house. An Essex PD unit arrived, then another, then a third. Each disgorged an angry, urgent officer. Andy's distressed colleagues rushed to her, each needing personal assurance that she was unhurt. Word spread quickly. The porch and sidewalk filled with uniformed officers. Two county deputies joined the cluster, men who played on the Essex PD softball team when the roster fell short.

An ambulance pulled in behind Tom's SUV. Paramedics hurried to the house. I knew them both. Billy Thorson and Todd Eggert manned the rescue squad crew that spirited me out of the hospital after my accident. The mix of worry and gratitude they had shown me now repeated for my wife.

Thorson spotted me. "Is Andy okay?"

"Yeah." I found it hard to push out words. "Inside."

Their relief was palpable. Thorson's eyes glittered and he hurried forward. Eggert stopped to squeeze my shoulder, then followed quickly.

"Hey, Egg!" I called out. He turned. "Check the back of her head. She took a knock on the sidewalk."

"You got it."

Andy's colleagues entered the house and walked the grounds. Del Sims took up station on the road, which I thought was superfluous since almost no traffic happened by the scene. Any that might would crawl past a yard full of sparkling emergency red and blue. Radios crackled with words and phrases incoherent to my ear. I heard Mae Earnhardt's voice.

Sims' assignment became apparent when the yellow school bus pulled up and a bewildered boy disembarked, bent by an overloaded backpack. Sims hustled Jason Anderson into the back of his squad car.

Tom and Andy remained inside the house forever. At least it seemed like forever. My time sense blew up with the second pull of the shotgun's trigger. I don't know how a weapon like that works. One barrel fired. The other didn't. The math in that equation made no sense except that Andy lived.

Andy lived.

She found me sitting in her car, running the numbers over and over. Hearing that *Click!* over and over. Hearing the deafening second trigger pull and resulting blast *over and over and over.*

She rounded the open Subaru door. I caught her in my arms just as her iron professional presence folded. Her knees buckled. I wrapped my arms around her. Her fingers dug into my back, then found my neck. She clutched me as if I were a buoy found by a drowning woman. Neither of us spoke. I pulled her harder and harder against my body hoping we might merge once and for all and never again be parted. Surely then some loony with a shotgun could not take her from me.

We stayed that way for hours. Or seconds. I don't know. I think she cried. I think I cried. We both wiped our faces when we dared part. She sniffled and I tried and failed to swallow the hot iron blockage in my throat.

She composed herself. More than I could say for me.

"I thought the worst," she whispered, and for an instant I imagined her looking down the barrel of a weapon and thinking she was finished, leaving behind all that she loved and all who love her—but then she said, "I thought we'd find Corrine Hawley inside. That they did something to her." Andy shook her head, sniffled, and wiped at her eyes. "She's not here."

"Christ, Dee, that's what you're worried about?"

"I'm here for that girl, Will. I came here for that girl." She brushed off my instant protest. "Please, don't. I know what happened, and we will deal with it, but for the moment I am *here*—here and now, okay? I need to be here for that girl. Try to understand."

I could not think of anything more insane. I opened my mouth to argue. She planted both hands on the side of my face and kissed away the words.

"What have you always told me, Pilot? You fly the plane all the way into the crash. You never stop flying the plane."

"Right." What else could I say?

"I love you."

"I love you, too."

She went back inside the house.

23

____

Shortly after Jenny Anderson was taken to the hospital in custody and her son was taken to the station, Andy instructed Del Sims to drive me home. I argued. She ignored the argument. I protested. She said she had work to do. I threatened to handcuff myself to Tom's SUV. She gave me a peck on the cheek, pointed out that I had no handcuffs, and told Del to get moving.

Andy arrived at home a little after nine. I waited for her on the front porch. We hadn't removed the storm windows yet. The crunch of her car's tires on the gravel driveway was muted, distant, barely audible over my thundering heart.

I'd been alone for nearly five hours. Thinking, but not drinking. Some of my thinking had been about drinking, but I knew that if I started, I would be hammered by the time Andy arrived. I wanted to be hammered. Anything to stop that *Click!* from repeating in my head like a demon earworm.

"I'm sorry," she said when she entered the house at the back door and crossed through the mudroom into the kitchen. "You know these things take time. Everything must be done properly, or some defense attorney will accuse me of attacking his client and then call what she did self-defense."

I said nothing. She dropped her satchel on the table and for an instant I feared she would adhere to her daily routine of removing her service weapon from the satchel and securing it while I stood there with arteries throbbing in my neck.

She didn't. She left the satchel and hurried to me. We fell into each other's arms. We didn't speak. We listened to each other breathe. She rested her head against me. I gingerly touched her hair.

"Does it hurt?"

"No. Didn't even break the skin."

"You should be examined for possible concussion. I'm serious."

Andy shook her head. "Already done. Tom made Billy and Todd come to the office."

I wanted to argue but settled for silence. She may have listened to my heart, still jackhammering my chest. We didn't turn on lights. Eventually I parted with her just enough to take her by the hand and lead her onto our darkened front porch. We crawled onto my old lounge chair and curled together, counting heartbeats.

Tom's headlights made us squint when he pulled in the driveway. At the sound of his door slamming, Andy sat up.

"I'll be right back." She kissed me full on the lips then hurried into the house. She turned on a light in the kitchen.

I called out to Tom as he crossed the lawn.

"We're in here."

He diverted to the porch instead of the kitchen door. He climbed the steps with something in his hand and let himself in.

"Andy's inside."

Tom sat down in the bigger of the two wicker chairs beside me. The object in his hand glittered. He twisted a cap off and lifted a bottle to his lips for a hard gulp. He handed the bottle to me. In the dim light I read the label.

Highland Park.

"This better be twenty-five." I took a swig. The scotch burned my mouth, seared my throat, and sent a bewildering and bewitching array of flavors back on my next breath.

"On my salary?" Tom took the bottle from me and pulled another swig. "Twelve does the job."

Andy reappeared, silhouetted against the distant kitchen light. She placed three glasses on the small table between my lounge chair and the wicker chairs. One was already filled with iced tea.

"We're not animals." She took the bottle. She poured and handed out two tumblers with golden liquid. Then she lifted the third for herself. Without a toast, we each took a somber drink. Tom finished his. Andy poured more.

Tom carefully lowered his glass to the table and then stood and wrapped his huge arms around my wife as if she were a child. He did not speak. I thought I heard him sniffle in the dark but could not be sure. My hearing may have still been affected by the shotgun blast.

After a moment he let her go, but she rose on her toes as high as she could and pulled him down for a kiss on the cheek. I wanted to kiss him, too, for what he had done. I let Andy's kiss speak for me.

We drank again, silent, in the dark. Andy sat down and leaned against my knees on the lounge chair.

Tom broke the silence. "Jack, over at the DA's office, wants to take your statement. I told him it would have to wait until Friday. You're taking tomorrow off."

I expected Andy to argue. She didn't.

Tom looked at Andy. "Didja tell him?"

"No."

Tom spoke softly in the dark.

"We found Corrine Hawley. I sent the boys over to the farm and told them we had probable cause to tear the place apart."

I imagined a nightmare. A mother gone insane. Her boy a murderer, a rapist. A ghoul. The girl's body found in gruesome pieces in the barn. Or buried. Or burned. A shallow grave.

I watch too many movies.

"She was camping in an old Airstream parked out back. Stoned. She's been there since the Anderson kid let half the class throw a party up in the old barn last weekend. The boy didn't even know she was there. She let herself in and has been cooking her brain since Saturday. She swiped mom and dad's stash. That's why they reported her."

"Parents of the Year." Andy sipped her drink.

The news sent me over the edge.

"God dammit! Then why the hell was that woman trying to shoot Andy? I mean, if she wasn't protecting Norman Bates or trying to hide a kidnapping or a murder—for Christ's sake, *what the hell?!*"

"Not sure," Tom said.

"Yes, you are," Andy corrected him.

"I 'spose." He sounded reluctant.

"Am I missing something here?" I asked. "Did you find evidence? Something to explain that bullshit with the shotgun?"

"No," Andy said, "not specifically."

"We grabbed up her phone and computer," Tom added. "Jack'll start the paperwork we need to give it over to the techs at county."

Silhouetted against the porch windows, it wasn't easy to read Andy, but she looked resigned—serene in counterpoint to the fury boiling over in me. I looked at both of them.

"Then what was not specific?" Tom answered.

"Jenny Anderson raved most of the way to the hospital and then again in the ER. She thought she killed Andy. She wasn't seeing too clear after I bopped her. Her eyes were all swelled shut. Thorson and Eggert hauled her off. All the way there and at the ER, once she got her yap working again, she wanted to be let go. Said we had no right. Said she had conducted a citizen's arrest. That she's a hero. That she should be given credit."

"Credit for what?"

Andy let Tom answer.

"Credit for saving America. For killing the assassin."

For the third or fourth time in a day of jolts, I sat stunned. Andy felt it and ran her hand up my thigh, across my abdomen until she rested it on my heart.

"That's why she was so welcoming to me on the phone. She wanted me there."

"*She planned this?*"

"Yeah," Tom said. "She saw an opportunity to be a hero."

"A hero?"

"Yeah." He sounded weary. "First glance at her social media—she's in pretty deep. Save America. Fight for America. Lots of deep state commie takeover shit. We found meds in her cabinet. The kid says she's bipolar and it gets bad when she stops taking her pills."

I said something coarse and rude, then added, "Simmons. He warned us. He must have had *something*. We need to talk to Leslie. The FBI must have known this was coming."

"Ease up there, Will. I don't think the Director of the FBI knew that a bipolar woman hearing voices was going to take a shot at Andy."

"This can't be coincidence."

"It actually can," Andy said, contradicting her own beliefs about coincidence. "Just…the worst kind."

Tom stood up and downed the rest of his scotch.

To Andy he said, "You don't show your face at the office tomorrow. I'll pick you up on Friday to meet with Jack. By then I'll have the paperwork done. Keep her here, Will."

"Roger that."

I felt Andy stiffen. "Paperwork for what?"

"Leave of absence. I'll try for paid but…" He let that hang and exited the porch. "Keep the bottle."

24

Tom's headlights barely cleared the driveway when a new set swung across the yard and pulled in. I recognized the car—an antique Buick Roadmaster wagon—but was mildly disoriented when Sandy Stone stepped out of the passenger seat. Earl Jackson slammed the driver's door and stomped across the lawn. He beat Sandy to the door but gave way as a gentleman. Sandy reached Andy first and closed a desperate embrace around her.

I hopped to my feet, a reflex in Earl's presence. To my surprise, he shoved a hand at me. I closed a grip on the rough rock that grabbed back. We shook. Firmly. Decisively. Without words, we acknowledged how close to the abyss we had stepped.

Sandy grasped my wife by the shoulders. "Sweetie, are you okay?"

"I'm fine. Sandy, Earl, please, you didn't have to come out here. Both of you. I'm really fine."

"The hell you are." Earl's arms shot out. "C'mere!"

Andy pulled away from her friend and into Earl's open arms.

"Boss, can I get you a glass of water?" I asked, feeling self-conscious about the open bottle of scotch. Earl doesn't drink.

"Yup."

"I'll get it, Will," Sandy scooted off toward the kitchen, still the only light on in the house. I reached for and flipped a switch, illuminating a small lamp.

"Word travels fast." Andy spoke from within Earl's rigid hug.

89

"Goddamned right, it does." Earl gave Andy another squeeze, then backed off and dropped into a chair. Sandy returned with two glasses, one containing water and ice for Earl. She poured a healthy dose of scotch for herself in the other, then refreshed my drink.

No one spoke. We drank.

"Siddown. You're all making me nervous," Earl snapped.

Andy and I returned to the lounge chair. Sandy settled in the other wicker chair and tucked her blue jean legs under her. The porch was cool. I offered her a jacket or blanket, but she tugged on her Wisconsin Badgers sweatshirt and declared she was fine.

"I hear the woman is a goddamned lunatic," Earl muttered. "Izzat right?"

Andy adopted a professional tone. "I really can't—"

"Certifiable," I announced.

It was all Earl needed to hear. He launched. While I cringed at some of his language, I simultaneously marveled at the extravagant and colorful phrases that rolled off his tongue in a minutes-long tirade indicting mental health in America, politics, liars, disinformation, extremists, left lane campers, porch pirates, the designated hitter rule, Congress, the useless United Nations Security Council, pastel M&Ms, and a host of other travesties committed against humanity as adjudicated by Earl Jackson. His speech elevated Andrea Katherine Taylor Stewart to sainthood while forgiving her a disappointing marital choice. He denounced a raging epidemic of stupidity and swore revenge on all forms of cowardice, duplicity, and con artists preying on idiots, for whom a place in hell had been reserved along with people who text while driving. He praised any deity that had the bald good sense to misfire the top chamber of a shotgun and cursed the same deity for creating a plague of weak wills and weaker minds capable of raising such a weapon against my wife.

"And I will goddamned for certain one hundred percent guaran-damn-tee you, young lady," he said taking to his feet and holding out his glass, which prompted the rest of us to do the same, "that this world would for sure be nothing but a piss pot two-bit cursed shadow of the worst degenerate dog shit crap hole whore shanty congregation of worthless floating turds if you EVER leave it! So say I and that undeserving husband of yours! EVER! Bottoms fucking up!"

The scotch shot down my throat like a flamethrower. Sandy toughed down the liquid and coughed after it seared a path. Earl slugged back a gulp of water, then joined us when we each pounded our empty glasses on the table twice.

"Amen and more power to you." I reached for the bottle.

"Thank you, Earl." Andy delivered a daughterly kiss to his cheek. "You're very kind."

"The hell I am." He held out one arm for Andy. "Now come with me."

A few minutes later we clustered on the front lawn. Earl slouched away to the back of his wagon and popped the tailgate. He pulled out a bag and a large, flat panel. Moving fast on his bowlegged stride, he crossed the lawn and dropped the bag at Andy's feet. Then he marched off twenty paces and stabbed the wire frame of a stolen *recallista* sign into the ground. It wobbled in place but remained upright.

RECALL & REPLACE

He took two steps past the sign and pulled his cell phone from his pocket. He poked at the screen until the flashlight app ignited. He laid the phone in the grass, backlighting the yard sign. I wondered why. Backlit like that, and in the dark yard, the face of the sign was unreadable.

"Not quite the political statement I think we want to make right now, Boss," I said. He ignored me. He marched back across the dry grass.

From a repurposed canvas tool bag, Earl extracted a silver .45 automatic with woodgrain grips. Turning his back to us, he dropped the magazine, examined it, then smacked it home again. He pulled back the slide, chambered a round, then held the gun out for Andy.

"Here."

Andy's unease was palpable. "No, really, I'm—"

"It ain't a request." Earl held out the gun.

"It's been a long day," Andy protested.

"Careful. She's got a kick."

Andy did what any living, breathing being would do when facing Earl Jackson. She took the weapon from him as ordered. He dropped and reached into his bag once more and produced a pair of ear protection headphones which he carefully placed over her head, and a pair of safety glasses which he gently landed on the bridge of her nose. To the rest of us he said, "Cover yer ears, children. Mr. Colt can bark."

Andy stepped forward. Sandy, Earl and I match-stepped back and pressed our palms to our ears. Andy glanced at me. Her expression transited uncertainty, then resignation, then cold determination.

A split second later the weapon came up and she fired. Earl wasn't kidding about the .45's bark.

A bright, backlit hole appeared dead center on the sign.

"Again," Earl ordered.

Andy squared her stance and raised her arms.

She fired.

A second hole appeared less than an inch from the first.

"Again."

She fired. The third hole appeared between the first two. Andy adjusted her stance.

She fired again. Again. Again. Then once more, emptying the magazine and locking the slide open. Not one shot strayed more than two inches from the first.

I uncovered my ears in time to hear her exhale as she lowered the weapon. She gazed at the ragged holes in the center of the sign.

Earl dipped into the bag and pulled out a second magazine. He held it out for Andy. She dropped the first, took the fresh magazine from his hand, and smacked it home.

"This time get angry," Earl instructed.

We covered our ears. Andy resumed her shooting stance. She emptied the magazine in seconds. A fist-sized hole of light showed through the sign. Fragments of plastic sign floated in the air.

For a moment, she remained frozen, statuesque. Steel infused her posture. She spread her long legs for balance, squared her shoulders, and held her head high. I had taken Earl's gesture as a statement, but now I saw it as medicine.

Andy handed the smoking gun to Earl.

Earl said, "Recall my shiny pale ass."

25

Sandy threw me an eye gesture that asked me to follow her to the kitchen. She gathered the empty tumblers on the way. Earl packed up his shooting gallery and engaged Andy in a technical discussion on the merits of the 1911 Colt .45 semiautomatic. Artfully distracted, Andy did not see me slip away to follow Sandy.

A beautiful woman in her own right, Sandy Stone looked no less so for the layer of concern darkening her expression. After depositing the glassware in the sink, she took my arm and pulled me toward her.

"Was it really that close?"

"Yeah. Tom said the first chamber misfired. Not sure why. If it hadn't… and if he hadn't been there …"

Sandy's chest rose and fell with a deep, contemplative breath. Fear and imagined loss flashed through her eyes. I'd seen similar pain on her face when she lost her father and nearly her own life. I wondered if such paths, once traveled, became worn and grooved, and too easy to tread again. I wondered if such things eventually cut permanent age lines into both outer and inner innocence and beauty.

I wondered if she saw the same on my face.

"You watch her, Will. I know her well enough to know that she'll brush this off. She'll say she's fine."

"That's our girl."

"Take her away. It's been a strain for her since that business with the FBI

Academy. Take her away from all this. Go somewhere. Take the airplane and the Foundation credit card and go. I'll see that Arun handles everything."

I worked up a polite refusal, but she cut me off.

"I already squared it with Earl. Arun will book regional charters with Rosemary II, and he will fly commercial for the rest. That or we'll simply postpone trips. This is not negotiable. I won't take no for an answer from you, and you can't take no for an answer from Andrea."

She squeezed my arm for emphasis.

"I can't take money from—"

"Oh, for God's sake, Will! Nobody cares how we spend that money. I've been telling you that for over a year. Bargo Litton is a corpse, not a shareholder. I know he didn't give that money willingly. We don't answer to anyone. If you're worried about the accounting—don't. Anything you take that constitutes taxable income to you, the Foundation will pay the taxes, and then pay the taxes on paying the taxes."

"Huh?"

"Never mind. Dewey Larmond will ensure that the books are perfect. Why am I standing here talking about tax liability with you? This is about Andy."

"There's your problem. She can be stubborn. She won't just walk away from a case, even if Tom puts her on leave—which, by the way, he plans to do."

"I know. Tom called me." She glanced over her shoulder as if Andy might walk in on us at any moment. "He thought she might need a friend tonight. I'm the one who pushed for paid leave. He agreed to force it if I agreed to get over here and help make it stick. I'm telling you to make it stick. She needs a break. You need a break. When's the last time you had a vacation together?"

Answering would only make her case. A weak shrug said as much.

"You know I'm right."

"Being right does not necessarily influence my darling wife. You know that as well as anyone."

"True. So, play dirty."

"How?"

Sandy released my arm and poked me in the chest. A wry smile broke through the veil of worry on her face.

"Take her somewhere with sand and palm trees and get her pregnant."

26

I vowed to stay awake all night. The scotch challenged that intention, but the anger and adrenaline still coursing through my system promised to back my play. After Earl and Sandy left, Andy and I engaged in a bizarrely pedestrian end of the day routine. She secured her work weapon and asked if a quick shower would be okay. I told her to take as much time as she needed while I washed the glassware in the kitchen sink and silently screamed.

After violently scrubbing out the tumblers and rubbing them dry as if removing paint, I put all but one back in the cabinet. The straggler got another dash of Tom's expensive scotch, along with a drop of water transported from the tap by the tip of my finger. A trick that somehow made this third (or fourth) drink smoother than the last.

I tipped the liquid down my throat to kill another *Click!* rising in my head.

God damn that woman and the worms in her brain. And the people who put those worms there.

I understood Earl's tirade. Con men, liars, opportunists deserved a place in hell for planting conspiracy theories and twisted beliefs in the head of a woman who didn't have the sense or the daylight to separate bald lies from simple truth.

Even if Jennifer Anderson allowed half-baked social media disinformation to substitute for reality and convict (without evidence) my wife of crimes invented by internet trolls, and she chose to carry out the sentence of death, some fragment of rational brain should have challenged her with a simple question.

And then what?

The whole thing lay beyond my comprehension. Worse, the whole thing was dominated by the loudest noise I've heard in my life, and that's saying something.

Click!

The scotch had grown remarkably smooth by the time I downed the last gulp at the kitchen sink. Warm and wondrous flavors carried on my breath. I'm not much of a scotch drinker. Andy's father doles it out to me now that I'm in his good graces, and he drinks only the finest. The few tastes I'd had in my life were clearly not well curated. I feared Tom may have opened a door.

If that damned sound kept creeping into my mind, I might have to go through that door. But not tonight. Tonight, I vowed to stay awake.

Andy finished in the shower and didn't say much when we climbed into bed. I propped up a couple pillows and let her lie down with her head on my chest while I reached up under her nightgown and stroked the smooth skin over her spine. She hummed appreciatively and I hoped that the effect would sedate her. As bad as my earworm demon had become, I could not imagine what terrifying image haunted her. The twin barrels of that shotgun had been less than a handspan from her eyes when Anderson pulled the trigger.

I intended to stroke her skin until she slipped into sleep. Then I would stay awake all night and hold her and be ready when nightmares booby-trapped her sleep.

A perfect plan, I decided. One carried out while the myriad mysterious aftertastes of twelve-year-old scotch and soothing scent of my wife's hair and skin worked to untangle my seriously taut nerves.

How she managed to disappear in the darkness under my watchful eyes and guardian touch, I could not begin to guess. I swear I never fell asleep, yet I found her side of the bed empty a little after two a.m.

27

———————

Andy stood alone in the center of the living room. She faced the French doors that opened onto the porch. A less than whole moon had taken to the clear sky. Earl's shooting gallery, our yard, adopted shape and shadow outside the windows. Andy had shape and shadow as well. She stood on the oriental rug with her hands behind her back, fingers intertwined loosely near the base of her spine. Her nightgown, not the shortest she owns but short enough to allow moonlight to highlight her long legs, radiated a ghostly glow beneath the dark waterfall of her hair.

Creaks and groans from the wooden stairs announce all comings and goings. She didn't flinch when I came up behind her and closed a grip on her shoulders. She lifted one hand and placed it over mine. With the other she reached back to stroke my thigh.

"We need to fast forward."

"Okay."

"I want to skip ahead, past the part where I tell you I'm fine. And you tell me I'm not fine. And then I break down and admit that you're right because that woman scared the living hell out of me. And then you tell me to let it all out, and I cry and—" Her voice broke. She squeezed my hand. I tightened the grip on her shoulders and closed the space between our bodies. "And I tell you that the last thing I saw, looking into those gun barrels, was everything we never got to do together. You and me. The places we've talked about—the trips we haven't taken—the people we haven't met—the chi—child we—" Her throat closed and cut her off and a sob shook her. She gulped and fought on. "We—we need to get all that out, Will, because I love you so much and there's no time to waste—it was—it was you that she meant to take from me when she killed me—not my life. You."

"I love you." I buried my face in her hair. "So much."

Her grip on my hand became painful, but it was life-affirming pain. Her sobs developed a rhythm and I put my other hand around her and pressed it to her chest to try and take those sobs from her. I don't know if those involuntary jolts released her pain or fear or anger, but they drew each of those things out of my tense nerves and tight muscles.

"Fast—f—for—forward," she whispered.

She released my hand and drew her other hand away from my thigh. She reached for the hem of her nightgown and lifted it over her head. Her skin glowed silver, painted by moonlight welcomed through our windows. I renewed my embrace, but now moved my hands over satin and silver and so much more.

By the time she turned to kiss me, I was all in.

We eventually made it back upstairs, but it took a while.

28

I know we slept, because sometime before dawn a loud *Click!* in my head startled me awake. Reflex tightened my arms, which remained around Andy. Thankfully, the jolt did not wake her. I listened in the dark for the steady rhythm of her breathing. A strand of her hair tickled my cheek. I brushed it aside, then stroked the long locks that found their way down her neck onto her back. My blood pressure eased. My heartbeat dropped from a techno throb to a slow ballad cadence. Eventually I drifted back into sleep and stayed there until light sneaking past the shades woke me. Alone.

I dressed and found Andy in the kitchen. She looked stunning. She had brushed and tied her hair in a complex do that flowed into a ponytail. She wore a black cashmere sweater that lured my fingers the way sirens lure sailors, and her snug jeans confirmed that the landscape of her legs last night had not been a dream.

God, I love this woman.

"Sandy wants us to go away. All expenses paid." I sat down at the kitchen table. Andy brought a mug of coffee, blessed angel.

"Good morning to you, too." She landed a kiss that I grabbed and held for longer than is considered a morning greeting or would have been acceptable in polite company. The smile she paid me afterward judged it acceptable to her.

"She said we should go where there is sand and palm trees and have sex."

"Beach sex?"

"I guess."

Andy shivered. "Ick. All that sand."

"Let's not judge until we can gather evidence, okay?"

"It's the gathering I want to avoid."

I sipped coffee. Scent and taste fired electric wakeup calls to parts of me that were still sleeping.

"Let's not get ahead of ourselves, dear."

"Oh, no. Here it comes. 'I need to work the case. So much paperwork. Meetings with the DA. Reports. Depositions.' I remember your boss telling you something about paid leave."

"Probably not paid. A prickly problem for the city administrator, I fear. I've already been accused of taking too much time away from the job, as you may recall."

"Pun intended? Then take it unpaid. Listen, Tom isn't—"

She planted a hand on my chest.

"Can you just hold your horses for a minute?"

She lowered her chin and weaponized her gold-flecked green eyes. I surrendered and sat back.

"I'll just work on this coffee." I lifted my mug.

"Good plan. I have something to say." She took a sip from her own mug and stared at me for a moment to confirm that I remained mute. "Okay. I told you last night I want to fast forward—"

"Again? Right here? On the kitchen table?"

She slapped my arm. "Not that. Oh my God, you're going to use fast forward as a term for sex from now on, aren't you."

"Pretty much."

"I want to jump ahead on a few things."

"If you want to jump my—"

"Stop it."

I pretended to behave. She began again.

"Will, yesterday was terrifying. I know it will haunt me. But I was serious about getting past it. I want to get past me falsely claiming I'm fine and you having to pull teeth to get me to admit I'm not and me arguing and hiding my feelings and you dragging them into the light—all that emotional dancing. It's tiresome."

"Okay…"

"I will wear my heart and my emotions and my fears and terrors on my sleeve for you, okay? I will cry without warning or provocation and push you away without reason and fold like a cheap tent when you push back and rescue me. Because I trust you to not go off the deep end. I trust you to listen, and take care of me when I need it, and not effing baby me when I don't. Got it?"

"Got it."

"And yes, you have me pegged. Jenny Anderson is a case, but it's open and shut. The woman is in the system. I'll make a statement to Jack tomorrow, and he'll schedule an arraignment, and she'll go to county and that poor kid will end up with relatives or in foster care. Corrine Hawley will go back to her awful parents who will pretend all is forgiven until she steals their stash again and next time heads for Venice Beach or—God forbid—winds up overdosing. The wheels are turning. There's nothing for me to contribute."

Surprise must have shown on my face.

She said, "You expected me to go on a tear, didn't you. To track down the influences that made that woman feel a need—a duty—to kill me."

I tried a weak shrug, entirely unconvincing.

"There's nothing there, Will. There's no one to blame—at least there's no one who can be blamed. Social media? Cable news? The White House? Will, we have no power over any of that. Director Simmons may take another shot, and God bless him, he's got a lot more juice than me. But there's nothing you or I can do about it. We will never persuade someone like Jenny Anderson not to listen to lies from asshats like Josiah James and then go to war over utter nonsense. Countless studies show that you can confront these true believers with hard, cold, irrefutable facts and it only reinforces their twisted faith. Every fact you present is a new lie. Every piece of evidence is manufactured. Every witness is a new enemy. It's hopeless. She's hopeless. There's nothing there to investigate, or solve, or bring to light."

I sipped coffee and thought about a cure Mrs. Palmer had for such people. A cure someone had applied to four Company W morons and Louis Blaze's daughter in Louisiana. A dark impulse deep inside me wondered, not for the first time, if Mrs. Palmer had been right.

"So…you're not all up and at 'em this morning to mount a fresh charge against Company W? Because that's what I was expecting. You're not going to call up Leslie and tell her ready or not, here we come?" I suddenly remembered. "Did she call last night?"

"She did. I blew her off. I'll call her today. And yes, I want her take on that call yesterday."

"Me, too. The freaking director of the FBI—Jesus, you don't think she's doing a Lindsay and telling him about *the other thing*, do you?"

Andy shook her head. "About you? No, but I think there's more to it. But I'm still not loading for extremist bear."

"Gotta say…this is not what I was expecting."

An outbreak of dimples told me that she took satisfaction in being unpredictable. I found the dimples nearly as alluring as that damned cashmere.

"I have something else in mind." She reached across the table and tugged her laptop into position between us. She opened it. The screen woke up. She turned the device to face me.

I confronted the dead eyes of a man with a head shaped like a shoe box, long and slab sided. He wore a coarse black beard and sported a nose that had seen too many bar fights. He stared at a police booking camera with open contempt. His corded neck spanned the same width as his head. It sloped into lumpy, gym-generated mounds of muscle at his shoulders and on his chest.

"Reuben Calbert." I looked at Andy. "Do I win a kiss?"

She delivered a peck to my cheek.

"And to what do I owe the pleasure of having his scary mug greet me over my morning mug?"

Andy got that look. The one she gets when she's about to propose an expansion to the vegetable garden that requires me to do the digging, or the purchase of a new artificial Christmas tree when the old one is perfectly green. A look that says she plans to ask me nicely, but the order is already in.

"This is the man that attacked that jet in Wichita."

"Allegedly, although his presumption of innocence won't make it past his first day in court. But, yes, I was there, remember?"

"He has a daughter."

I sensed land mines ahead. Andy knows that I have a weakness for protecting children.

"I'll take your word for that."

"He has a daughter who has cancer."

"Oh, boy."

"I haven't been able to confirm it, but I have reason to believe his daughter was part of an experimental treatment program developed by Amphitriton Pharmaceutical—owners of the jet. Rumors have been floating around Wall Street that a new treatment they have is wildly successful, and Amphitriton is on the verge of announcing a new and possibly game-changing cancer drug. Amphitriton is on the verge of an IPO process that experts expect to set records."

"You want to go and capture the guy that attacked the jet? In another jurisdiction in another state? Where every law enforcement agency is already hot on his trail? Hey, I'm all for punishing anyone who hurts an airplane—but seriously? Why this?"

"No. I don't want to go after that guy."

She abruptly left the table and went to the coffee pot and poured herself an entirely unnecessary top off. My wife can deny it, but she has a flair for drama.

I held out my mug.

"This is decaf." She returned with the pot and sat down facing me. "I told you…I want to fast forward. I want to heal what happened yesterday. I want to *heal something.* But I cannot heal that woman or the things that made her think that killing me would 'Save America.' And we both know it will take some work to heal what she did to me."

"I'm not sure I see where this is going."

She closed her hands on mine.

"I think Reuben Calbert, right or wrong, attacked that jet because Amphitriton Pharma failed his child. I think his daughter was part of their study but *didn't* get the new wonder medicine."

"Dee, I'm not sure that's how those things work—"

"It's the running theory with Wichita PD." Her long eyelashes dropped, shielding the guilt in her eyes.

"The what? What time did you get up this morning?"

"You were out cold. I looked into it. I talked to the detectives in Wichita."

I glanced at my watch. Barely past seven. "Yeah, but surely if this company has an effective medicine that they're taking public they'd give it to anybody in the study that got the placebo. I mean—come on."

"One would hope. But no one seems to have any information, at least none they're willing to share. Amphitriton isn't talking. The kid's dad is on the run. And Wichita PD isn't sharing anything about the kid or her mother. I read between the lines and the reason they're not sharing is because they don't know anything."

"Lemme see if I have this right. You don't care about this guy. About finding him or seeing him punished for what he did. What, then?"

"I want to find his child."

I studied her eyes. They sparkled with absolute sincerity.

"His sick child?"

"Yes. More accurately, I want *you* to find his sick child."

PART II

29

Andy obeyed orders and stayed away from the office on Thursday. I expected aftershocks and found excuses to hang around the house. When Andy asked if I planned to go to the hangar, I told her I wanted to be on hand for the call we both expected from Leslie. The call never came. The aftershocks never came.

On Friday, Andy did not wait for a summons. She bolted for the station early. I fired off a text to Tom to give him fair warning. He did not reply. I think we both knew she was unstoppable. I crossed my fingers that she would be okay, and that Tom would tolerate her obsessive attention to every detail of the Anderson arrest and booking. Maybe the busywork would prove therapeutic.

When Andy returned home, I detected a note of fatigue. I gave her space to execute the daily routines that mark her transition from duty to off-duty. After she let her hair down, changed from her blazer to a sweatshirt, and descended the stairs, I spent the next forty-five minutes carefully listening to every detail of her day including nearly verbatim the statement she delivered to the district attorney. I felt like a tightly wound clock spring sitting silently beside her at our kitchen table, wanting with every breath to put my arms around her and hold her and tell her she would be okay. Wanting to stifle the demonic *Click!* that came too easily to mind.

The gush of minutia she shared was healthy and she knew it. Toward the end, she reached for and took my hands.

"This is good. I needed this. The day. *This*…with you."

It's a lesson I've been slow to learn in our marriage, that sometimes the best thing I can do to fix a problem is nothing at all.

We engaged in housework on Saturday. Shortly after lunch I found her crying in the laundry room at the back of the kitchen. I said nothing. She said nothing. We held each other until it passed. She wiped away the moisture on her cheeks and gave me a thumbs up, then switched the darks from the washer to the dryer.

We went for tacos on Saturday evening and over dinner we checked off the topic of being ghosted by Leslie. Neither of us felt it would be wise to initiate a call, but both of us complained about her lack of explanation for the Zoom meeting with Director Simmons. We engaged in speculation about the Director's motives but came to no useful conclusions. Switching topics, Andy declared that the first stop in "our" search for Calbert's daughter should be Madison where a little over a year ago Dr. Doug Stephenson had scanned my brain and spinal cord and found traces of what I think of as car stereo wiring, but which accounts for my ability to vanish.

Andy's proposal surprised me.

"Why?"

"Because he has connections. At hospitals. He's been your secret partner in this…*thing*…this whole time, Will."

Andy is aware of the special effect *the other thing* renders on children victimized by cancer. She doesn't disapprove of my nighttime trips into hospitals. How could she? Yet, more than anything else about what has happened to me, this scares her. At the very least, it chafes her analytical mind. I've learned not to mention using Education Foundation trips for after-hours hospital visits. Initially, I elected not to tell her that Stephenson monitored the results of my efforts through his medical connections. I may not be able to lie to my wife, but occasionally I practice the delicate art of omission. She eventually figured it out. So much for omission.

"What makes you think Stephenson can find the kid?"

"Got a better idea?"

My better idea was not to go on this quest at all. Since that wasn't an option, I saw Stephenson as an opportunity to dissuade Andy. I briefly considered calling ahead to encourage the doctor to derail Andy but figured she would tip to such a clumsy conspiracy.

"I suppose it's as good a place to start as any." *And I'm just a float in the parade.*

Stephenson asked to meet us at the Jet Room at the Madison airport.

· · ·

ON SUNDAY MORNING, I greased the Navajo onto Runway 14 at Dane County Regional Truax Field in Madison. The assigned runway facilitated an easy taxi onto the Wisconsin Aviation ramp. A lineman with orange batons waved us into parking. The heavenly scent of jet exhaust and fried onions met me when I dropped the airstair door. I climbed out and lent Andy a hand. The lineman with the wands trotted to the side of the FBO building and retrieved a set of chocks, which he placed on the nose wheel.

"Need anything?" he asked.

"Thanks, we're good."

"Gorgeous day, huh?" He hovered near the wingtip. I've seen this act before. Greetings and small talk are standard, but the gorgeous he was referring to wasn't meteorological.

"Spring is the best." Andy dished out a smile as radiant as the blue April sky. He grinned back, utterly enchanted. For a split second I thought he might fall in step beside her. Never mind the husband playing tail end Charlie.

I caught up with Andy and took her hand.

"Best hold hands, dear. Dangerous out here, what with all the airplanes and zeppelins and whatnot."

"Right."

The Jet Room Restaurant shares space with the Wisconsin Aviation FBO at Madison airport. It's one of the best hundred-dollar hamburger stops in the Midwest. The food is superb, and the prices are reasonable. The hundred-dollar label refers to the aviation fuel pilots burn to fly somewhere for a hamburger. Stephenson's choice of venue, however, had nothing to do with the food. He prefers to minimize records of me visiting his office. The doctor nurtures a paranoia born in the anti-war sixties.

We found the tall neurologist at a booth with a view of the airport ramp and rows of parked aircraft. At the sight of us, he waved and slid to his feet.

"My goodness, Andrea, you grow more lovely each time I see you." He gave her a hug.

Doug Stephenson had been a teenaged orderly at a U.S. Air Force hospital in Thailand during the Vietnam War. That's where he met a Tasmanian Devil named Captain Earl Jackson. I pegged his age somewhere in the seventies, yet he had the look of a man twenty years younger. Tall, thin, and fit, with a full head of hair and a perpetual tan, he projected athleticism often exercised on a golf course.

"Will, good to see you." We traded hearty handshakes. "Please, let's sit. Let's talk."

Andy slid into the booth ahead of me.

"Business first." He fixed a piercing stare on me. "How are you doing?"

"Fabulous."

"Headaches? Dizziness?"

"Nope. Nada." We play out this routine every time we meet.

"Any loss of memory? Disconnects? Things where you know the word but can't get it off your tongue? Everyday objects you don't recognize?"

"I drank some scotch a few nights ago and couldn't remember my name."

"What about smells? Any unexplained smells?"

"Not after laundry day. No, Doc, it's all good."

He seemed satisfied but couldn't resist throwing Andy a glance to confirm. She verified my answers.

"Okay, then. Good lord, I haven't seen you since that business in Lake Superior."

"You know about that?" I instantly flagged it for a dumb question. Of course, he knew. Stephenson maintained a sexual relationship with Dr. Lillian Farris that I tried not to imagine.

"I owe you a thank you. For helping—*for saving* Lillian and Boyd. A terrible near thing. I mean it. Thank you."

"Believe me, Doc, I had a vested interest in our survival."

Stephenson struggled for something to say but faltered. After a few seconds, he cleared his throat and restored his professional affect. "Lillian told me what you found in that woods," he said. "She must have been over the moon. Something like that? For her? Incredible. It throws your condition into a whole new light, you know."

I didn't want to linger on Lillian's otherworldly assumptions about the object that caused my collision and crash. Not with Andy at my elbow, whose skepticism on the topic had been relinquished only grudgingly and showed signs of growing back over time.

"Did Lillian tell you that I can't—you know—do the *thing* anymore?"

"She said you were a terrible liar."

I slapped a hand on the table. "God dammit! Does everyone think that?"

Andy made a show of looking out the window.

"If Lillian's theories are remotely correct, Will, I renew my open request for more testing. A DNA panel would be intriguing."

"And I renew my firm No Thank You. I can't have my wife discovering that I'm not actually descended from Greek gods."

"What would DNA tell you?" Andy asked.

"Well…" Stephenson leaned back and folded his hands on the table, the physician's equivalent of putting his autopilot in lecture mode. "How much do you know about DNA?"

"It's all the rage in TV cop shows. Solves every crime. If only. But… scientifically? Not much beyond its properties as a unique identifier."

"DNA is a polymer composed of two polynucleotide chains—they coil around each other to form a double helix—and they carry genetic instructions. My instructions, my DNA, doesn't have an on/off switch for vanishing. Will's original instructions didn't either. Lillian suggests that during Will's collision, in a microsecond, the device deployed a life-saving system—"

"Allegedly," I cautioned. With each passing day, the episode felt more remote, and more farfetched.

"I'm not sure 'life-saving' is the right term, but—"

"A life support system."

"Yes! Well put, Will."

"I stole that from an eight-year-old."

"Of course. Boyd." The expression on Stephenson's face confessed to affection for the boy.

Andy reeled in Stephenson's focus.

"Doctor, how is DNA involved?"

"That's what I'd like to find out. For us regular seafarers, in an emergency we rely on buoyant material in an orange vest. Or a seat cushion that can act as a flotation device. In Will's collision, the life preserver deployed was more sophisticated. I'd like to find out if—"

"No testing," I repeated. "No pokes, prods, scans, scrapes or probes, Doc."

"Regular scans, dear," Andy reminded me. "We agreed."

"No probes."

Andy repeated her question. "How is DNA involved?"

"DNA can be damaged. There are any number of mutagens which change a DNA sequence. Oxidizing agents, alkylating agents, even high-energy electromagnetic radiation—x-rays and ultraviolet light."

"What kind of damage?" Andy's growing interest put me on alert.

"Depends on the mutagen. UV light produces thymine dimmers, which are cross-links between pyrimidine bases. Sorry, uh, strand breaks. Breaks in the DNA strands."

"Breaks?" She looked worried.

He shook his head. "Relax—a typical human cell contains about 150,000 damaged bases—oxidative damage. Nothing to fuss about. But this plays into a theory I have been mulling over regarding Will's effect on children with cancer. DNA damages are naturally occurring, but some of the muta-tions can cause cancer. We all have damaged strands, but we don't all have cancer because DNA has repair mechanisms. Those repair mechanisms develop limits over time. Some researchers theorize that if we managed to live long enough, we would all eventually develop cancer because of those limits. Anyway—I've been thinking about the effect of—what do you call it?"

"*The other thing*," I said.

"Yes. The thing. I've been thinking about what happens when Will vanishes. His body still exists on our plane of existence. But he becomes—"

"Matter in an altered state?"

Stephenson pointed. "That's good, Will."

"Boyd, again."

"I want to know if by altering the state of matter, Will is altering the cancerous cells. Or if he's altering the repair limits, accelerating the repair function within the strands."

Andy's voice tightened. "Altering the DNA?"

"Yes. In a good way," Stephenson hurried to point out. I guessed that he also read her growing concern.

"Would that explain why it doesn't always work?" I asked. "Or why it seems more effective in younger children?"

"Maybe. Damage accumulates with age. In fact, that accumulation appears to be an underlying cause of aging. I suppose it's possible that the beneficial effect Will generates may be limited or at some point unable to overcome the damage. Mutagens fit in the space between two adjacent base pairs. It's called intercalation. When that happens, the bases separate, distorting the DNA strand by unwinding the double helix. That's why inter-calators may be carcinogens. The flip side of that is the very ability to inhibit DNA transcription and replication allows us to use other toxins to inhibit rapidly growing cancer cells. Hence, chemotherapy."

I stopped following him at *Maybe*. Andy leaned in. "Is Will's DNA altered?"

"I'd like to find out. It would be great if—"

"Nope," I didn't like where this was going. "Maybe we could save the science lesson and get back to the subject at hand?"

Stephenson looked at Andy. She tipped her head. She may have agreed to close the conversation, but I knew better than to think the subject was closed.

"Of course." Stephenson took the cue. "Perhaps another time."

A young woman approached the table, passed out plastic-coated menus and asked what we wanted to drink. I asked for coffee. Andy and Stephenson asked for water. The server took mental notes and hurried away.

Stephenson lowered his voice and turned toward Andy. "When you called, you asked if I am able to find a child who may have cancer."

"Yes. Last name is Calbert."

"First name?"

"Unknown…for now."

"Age?"

"Unknown."

"Hospital?"

"Unknown. The child might not be in a hospital."

"Can I ask what this is about?"

I gave Stephenson the bullet points of the incident in Wichita. Andy added an overview of the law enforcement hunt for Reuben Calbert and the prevailing theory that Calbert had lashed out at the pharmaceutical CEO because he had a child with cancer.

"And you know this child?"

"No," Andy replied. "There are…other factors involved, Doctor."

I thought he might press the question. I had no doubt he wanted to ask, but I was equally certain she wouldn't answer. I wasn't sure Andy understood her own impulse to heal this child nor did I think she could explain it to Stephenson.

I jumped in. "We think that Calbert believes his child was not properly provided for and lashed out in desperation. Andy got the idea that I might—you know—do what I do to help."

He frowned. "Are you familiar with the Health Insurance Portability and Accountability Act?"

I shrugged. Andy poked me in the shoulder.

"HIPAA. You knew that."

"Sure." I shook my head, *No*.

"Is that going to be a problem?" Andy asked.

Yes. Tell her. I crossed my fingers that Stephenson would skillfully talk Andy down from this mission.

Stephenson smiled. "Most people think HIPAA means nobody can ask anything about your personal medical records, which would be a hindrance to what you're seeking. Not so. While HIPAA was designed to standardize how personally identifiable information is protected from fraud and theft—it was also meant to modernize the flow of healthcare information. Within the industry, it has been helpful for the sharing of critical information between authorized healthcare providers."

This did not sound like the barrier I hoped for. "Meaning?"

"Key word 'authorized.' It means that where I am authorized, certain information is easy for me to find. But did you say this child may not be in a hospital?"

"Unknown," Andy said. "She may have been in a program that tested treatments for Amphitriton Pharmaceutical. Are you familiar with them?"

"Yes. On two levels. First, they're a minor player in the field. Oncology is not my specialty, but I believe that's been their focus—which points to the second level. Financial rumor mills are working overtime on Amphitriton. Word is they're poised to announce a breakthrough. My analysts tell me they expect to shatter records for institutional investment in a coming IPO. We're talking billions. I don't typically invest in my own field, but it's hard to miss the buzz."

"Do you know anything about this breakthrough? Anything about the testing they've done?" I asked.

"Not my specialty, as I said. Stephenson looked at me warily.

Andy read the exchange. "It's okay. I know you've been monitoring Will's...activities."

Stephenson heaved a healthy sigh. "Oh, thank heavens! I was afraid, well, I just..."

Andy laughed. "You two are not good conspirators."

Visibly relieved, Stephenson said, "You have no idea how this eases my mind, Andrea. Your husband's obvious 'talent' is, in my opinion, vastly overshadowed by the curative effect he can deploy. It's the reason I would genuinely love to explore—"

"Whoa, Doc," I put up a hand. "Let's not go off the rails here. I mean, yes, I want to use it to help where I can but turning this into a science project is not in the cards. I hope I've been clear about that."

I glanced at Andy who nodded in agreement.

"You have been. Okay. You want me to find this child, and if the circumstances permit, you'd like to see if you can affect treatment of her using the thing."

"That's the idea."

"It won't be difficult if she's in a conventional treatment regimen. However, if she's part of a drug trial, that may pose problems. Especially if the rumors in the financial community are true."

"Why?" Andy asked.

Stephenson's eyebrows shot up. "A potential cure for cancer? I can't think of anything more explosive in medicine. Any such trials would be closely guarded secrets. Deeply shielded by legal and practical measures. My outreach cannot penetrate that kind of secrecy."

"Then you think you can't find her?"

"Within the bounds of a drug trial, it's unlikely. However—" He paused. His eyes searched a dim distance for a moment. When he rejoined us in the Jet Room booth, he said "A trial of that sort calls for test subjects meeting a narrow set of criteria. This child would not be someone randomly selected. It's a cancer drug trial. That means they need cancer victims. The child therefore has a prior history of diagnosis and treatment. I can start there. It might not give you a current location, but I may be able to provide a lead for you, Andrea."

"That would be great."

"One more thing comes to mind. It is common practice for pharmaceutical companies to farm out their research to independent laboratories. Often academic laboratories. Universities."

"What?" I feigned shock. "They farm it out? I thought the whole reason for charging a thousand dollars a pill was so that they could invest in research and advance the boundaries of science with new cures."

"An argument for another day, Will. My point is that it's unlikely that Amphitriton, who is not a major player, has the resources for a trial of this magnitude. Find out who performed the research. If you can penetrate their secrecy—and I suspect you have means I'd rather not know about—you may be able to find the child."

30

"It's Leslie." Andy tapped her phone and lifted it to her ear. "Hi, Leslie."

Lunch had ended and Stephenson had gone. We stood in the Wisconsin Aviation lobby. I poked my head into the pilot's lounge and found it empty. I gestured for Andy to join me there. We closed the door behind us. Andy lowered the phone and tapped the screen again.

"You're on speaker. Will's here."

I braced for the inevitable *Are you okay?* but she took the professional high road.

"I heard what happened. Bitch."

Andy smiled. "That's one way of putting it."

"I'm sorry for the phone tag and for ghosting you. I'm in New York. It's been—let me see if I can put this in professional terms—a fucked up fire drill ever since Louisiana. I had to fess up about my surveillance, which is why they called me back here. And no, Will, your name didn't come up. There's been a lot of heat on me for being there, though. If it gets out, it just pours gasoline on the conspiracy theories claiming the FBI did the hit."

"Did you know about the man on the inside?" Andy asked.

"Not until after. It was highly compartmentalized. Problem is, now the swinging dicks in the field office are pointing a finger at me for having knowledge I wasn't cleared to have. Screw them. Nobody wanted to listen to my ideas, and now they want to say I came by my intel illegitimately. Jerks."

I asked, "Leslie, why was the Director of the FBI talking to some schlub and his wife in Essex, Wisconsin?"

"For the record, he was talking to your wife, Will. She's the one on his radar—not you. Just so we're on the same page."

"We are." Andy's assurance carried a reproachful glance.

"I've been pushing for what you wanted. A firm statement disconnecting Andrea from the shot taken in Detroit. The Bureau feels it has spoken. The RCMP doesn't want to discuss it for obvious reasons. DOJ feels that any statement issued would constitute commenting on an active investigation, which is horseshit. The White House considers the matter closed. Their official position is that calling attention to an assassination attempt invites copycats. More horseshit. There's an election coming, and they don't want the President to look weak. Word from the press office is that mention of what they are officially calling 'past history' is now forbidden. Long story short, given the heat and the scope of the investigation at hand—getting the boss on Zoom with you two was the best I could do."

"We appreciate it."

"He meant it. He's a good man and he stands by every word. Meanwhile —holy shit! I asked Chief Ceeves to send me a copy of the incident report. I plan to forward it to the Director personally."

"Fat lot of good that will do," I said. "It's not like the crazy bitch was part of a conspiracy or even a member of Company W. Ordinarily, I'd call that good news, but it begs the question of how many other unhinged true believers are drinking the same Kool-Aid."

"I like Kool-Aid. I have ever since I was a kid. I hate Jim Jones," Leslie muttered. I pictured her crooked smile.

"I know the feeling," Andy said.

"You two need to stay away from me for a while, and vice versa. Stay away from this investigation. And please promise me you won't go charging after Company W. I don't want any more of those morons taking pot shots at you, Andrea. Hear me?"

Andy and I traded glances. She didn't look ready to swear on any Bibles —I know I wasn't—but present plans didn't include pursuit of Leslie's extremists.

"Sure," Andy said. "But can you answer a few questions?"

"No promises."

"Louis Blaze's daughter. She survived?"

"She was beaten and left for dead either before or after the others were shot."

"Has she spoken?"

"She regained consciousness, but she's refusing to speak to anyone with a badge. Last I heard, they're prepping her for reconstructive surgery. Somebody made a mess of her face."

"Do you think they didn't kill her to send a message? To Blaze?"

"I do."

"I take it there's no hope of finding her father after all this."

"We are no closer now than we were before the killings."

I leaned toward the phone in Andy's palm. "What was the deal with the candy bars?"

"No idea. There was no sign of them at the scene. Your guess is as good as mine. On second thought, my guess is probably better."

"Which is?"

"Carrier pigeon. A coded communication containing instructions. Possibly instructions to meet on the boat where they were all murdered. If they're intercepted…they're just candy bars. That's unconfirmed, BTW." The conversation lapsed for a moment before Leslie spoke again. "Look, you guys, I'm sorry. I'm sorry for all of it. Sorry for pulling you in. Sorry for pushing you out. Hell, I'm sorry for saying I'm sorry all the time. But promise me you'll stay away. Chief Ceeves said you're taking some time off, Andrea. That's a terrible idea, but better than every other idea."

Andy bit her tongue.

"And you didn't say anything to Director Simmons about me?"

"No. Will, you know better. Lending yourself and your talents to the FBI will always be your decision. No matter what happens. You have my word on that. Listen, I need to go. Don't call me. I won't call you."

The connection ended.

"You okay with all that?" I asked Andy.

"For now."

I glanced at the flight planning desk. "I need to update the weather for Wichita. Wasn't looking good earlier."

"Can we go out to the plane first? I want to get my laptop."

31

I escorted Andy onto the ramp and opened the Navajo cabin. Andy fetched her laptop. The flight to Madison from Essex County had been short, but I hate taking off with empty space in the fuel tanks, so while Andy returned to the FBO I flagged down a lineman and asked for the fuel truck. The spring sun rode high and felt warm while I waited for the truck to arrive. As is my custom, I supervised the fueling. The Navajo took a short fill, but I got no judgment from the lineman. Full tanks are full tanks.

I found Andy in the pilot's lounge curled up in a fat leather armchair, face locked on the screen of her laptop. So often when she works like this, she strikes the perfect pose of a college coed cramming for an exam or pounding out a paper. She absently fingered strands of hair at her temple while she nudged a wireless mouse on the arm of the chair. I don't think she noticed when I seated myself at the flight planning desk. Using the workstation and my iPad, I prepared for a flight to Wichita.

A challenge.

Spring weather had broken out in the Midwest. Fast moving air masses sent mountains of cold air crashing into valleys of warm southerly flow. Airmets and Sigmets—the warning flags of aviation—popped up in long scrolled lists in the ForeFlight briefing feature on my iPad. The Airmets warned of turbulence and icing. The Sigmets predicted powerful lines of convective activity across Oklahoma and Kansas. Severe thunderstorm and tornado watch boxes dotted the maps. The forecast for Kansas offered

Dorothy and Toto nonstop service to Oz and played havoc with Andy's desire to reach Wichita.

I toyed with a detour west into Nebraska, holding open the option to make a dash south from Omaha or Lincoln while keeping a back door open for escape if the path ahead became blocked. The problem nested in the behavior of the air masses. The initial collision of cold and warm threatened to lock in stalemate. The front could stall, and the day's pattern of storms would then repeat over the next forty-eight hours, hammering the Midwest before gradually moving across the Mississippi Valley to deliver more mayhem in Tennessee and Kentucky.

Sometimes the best flight plan is tying down the airplane where it sits.

Half an hour passed without a word between us. I read prog charts, a dozen terminal forecasts, and myriad station reports for three or four possible routes. Andy remained absorbed by her laptop, clicking the mouse, and twirling her hair. I reached the conclusion that we could either book a room in Madison or Lincoln, Nebraska. The Lincoln option offered a chance to make an early morning run to Wichita ahead of the buildup of dangerous convective air. A slim chance because some of the storm lines were expected to be active through the night.

I didn't want to break Andy's concentration and was about to forage for coffee when she lifted her head. She spent a minute gazing into infinity, thinking…then she spoke.

"Amphitriton," she said as if tasting the name on her tongue. She looked in my direction. "Amphitriton—Terrance Remington, the CEO—has been crying wolf for years."

"About what?"

"Cures. Treatments. Mostly for cancer. One notable exception for anxiety." She moved to a matching leather love seat and beckoned me to sit beside her. I expected to see the pharmaceutical company's website on her screen. Instead, she had pulled up an archived *Washington Post* article. The headline read:

Legal Wrist Slap
Court Reclassifies Xeniten Double-Cross

My curiosity stirred, but Andy did not call attention to the screen.

She said, "Amphitriton has existed under half a dozen different names. Remington started out pushing supplements and homeopathic concoctions. He pushed athletic supplements for a while, then sidestepped into the cancer cure market twenty or so years ago. Remington had a hand in pushing the cyanide in apricot seeds as a cure long after it was debunked back in the eighties."

"I read about that. The King of Cool."

She gave me a blank stare.

"Steve McQueen. The King of Cool."

"What are you talking about?"

"Steve McQueen. The actor. *The Getaway*? *Great Escape*? He opted for cancer treatment in Mexico because they offered that apricot pit cure. Didn't help." I sometimes forget that my wife was born twenty to thirty years after some of my favorite movies were made. Andy's silence prompted me to ask, "So, you're saying it's all a scam?"

"Not entirely. Around ten years ago, Amphitriton partnered with Belling Shore University."

"Never heard of them. Is this what Stephenson was talking about?"

"Yes. Another startup. One of the first online universities. They got rich and bought a failing private girls' school for brick-and-mortar legitimacy. A smart move right around the time online university scams were winding up in court. Belling Shore avoided the collapse of credibility most of those operations experienced by acquiring buildings with ivy. They also claimed to invest millions in a state-of-the-art research lab. Critics suggest the cash came from Amphitriton. Regardless, Belling Shore found new fortune by pulling in grants for the farmed-out research Big Pharma throws around."

"So, Belling Shore is where the Amphitriton research is done?"

Andy tapped her nose.

"Lemme guess…this is where you think we'll find the kid."

"Unlikely, but I think it's where we will find out *where* to find her."

"You don't want to wait for the doc to check his connections?"

"If he finds her first, problem solved. But if the girl was in a drug trial, the records will be hard for him to access."

I leaned against Andy's shoulder and pointed at the screen. "What's this?"

"Sidebar, but—" she scrolled down until a photo appeared. I recognized Terrance Remington from his bit on the *Today Show*. Andy pointed at a man standing beside Remington. "—this is the man running the research lab at Belling Shore—the man we need to talk to. This is Dr. Philip Barkley."

He looked more like the chairman of the country club membership committee than a Ph.D. accredited researcher. In designer label golf apparel, Barkley leaned against a golf cart driven by Remington and carrying a third man. The chummy photo had been taken on a golf course. "What was that headline about?"

"An old case Barkley and Amphitriton were involved in."

"And? What does it tell you?"

"Not to expect cooperation. The man is a snake." Andy closed the browser and initiated a shutdown sequence for her laptop. "So how does the weather look for Wichita?"

"Have I ever told you that it is better to be on the ground wishing you were in the air than the other way around?"

"That bad?"

"Yup."

"Then let's go in the other direction. How long will it take us to fly to Ithaca, New York?"

32

Andy intended to drive directly from the Ithaca Tompkins International airport to the Belling Shore University campus until I pointed out that upstate New York was an hour ahead of Essex. By the time we landed, unloaded, secured the airplane, and lined up the rental, car my watch—adjusted for the time zone change—read after five-thirty.

She looked tired from a day with two flights, so I suggested we check into a hotel, get a meal, a hot shower, and start fresh in the morning. I had made a phone call during Andy's preboarding visit to the restroom in Madison. I was ready for her when she jumped in the Ithaca rental car and she told me to open my iPad and search for a place to stay.

"Done."

Andy had just pulled away from the FBO building. Long shadows from trees not yet flush with buds painted black lines on the road departing the airport.

"Already?"

"Stay on this, then take the first left."

She threw me a look that carried no trust whatsoever. I repaid it with a smug grin.

The drive took us down a long tree-lined residential boulevard that morphed into a narrow street populated with quaint houses that could have used the term cottage without pretense. I had expected rolling terrain in this part of the state, but the landscape remained relatively flat.

Andy grew suspicious when we turned onto Campus Road, but she said nothing.

"Turn here."

She slowed to a crawl. "Here?"

"Yes. Turn right." I pointed. A stone building with a castle tower and battlement guarded the corner and for a moment I thought it was our destination. A pillar at the road read Statler Hotel. I checked the iPad which said to drive a bit farther. "Keep going. It's ahead on the left."

Andy followed the short street to a turnaround loop in front of a squarish stone building that looked more like a proper hotel.

"Will," she reluctantly made the turn, "we can't. This is way too expensive."

"No, it's not. The magic plastic card pays for it. Besides, the reservation is already made. We can't cancel. They'll charge us anyway." I wasn't sure that was true, but it ended the debate. Andy pulled up to the entrance where a uniformed bell captain hurried to open her door. I went to the back of the rented SUV and opened the liftgate to offload our bags before Andy had a chance to dig in.

"Will you be self-parking or valet?" the bellman asked.

"Valet." I plucked the keys from Andy's fingers and handed them over. An argument lingered on the tip of her tongue, but our bags were scooped up and our wheels were about to disappear. I offered her a gentlemanly elbow.

She jabbed my ribs before taking my arm.

"THEY TEACH HERE, you know. This is a teaching hotel. Cornell University is world famous for its School of Hotel Administration." I opened the door to the luxurious room. "Check out this view."

I had been offered and had accepted a Campus View room. From the fourth floor, we enjoyed a view of the buildings and residence halls surrounding the Cornell arts quad. On winding sidewalks below old growth trees, random students hiked between academic obligations. Oblivious to the ornate architecture, most were absorbed in their phones.

Andy stepped up beside me and took a long look.

"I don't mean to burst your bubble—I mean, this is really nice—but I've been here before."

"Here? This hotel?"

"Might have even been this room." Her expression suggested the memory was not pleasant. I worried that what I had intended as a romantic gesture was about to go down in flames.

"Sophomore year in high school. Most kids do the college visits junior year, but Daddy wasn't going to stand in line. He brought me here. Well—I made him bring me here. He took me to Harvard and threw in Princeton—I don't know why—all he did was complain the whole time we were in New Jersey. I didn't want to do any of it. My mind was already made up. But he insisted I have a vote, as he put it. Trying to maneuver me into picking something in the Ivy League."

"Why did you bring him here?"

She shrugged. "I wanted to see the gorges. They have one called George's Gorge."

"You're kidding. How was it?"

"Gorgeous."

I made a jab at her ribs, standard payment for a bad joke. She ducked away and laughed, and I felt pleased to see the smile.

"I'm starving. But we're not eating here."

"Why not? The restaurant is supposed to be superb."

"I'm sure it is. I'm sure it's also expensive. Come on, dear. It's a college campus. I can't believe there isn't a sub shop or pizza place around here somewhere."

She wasn't wrong. We ate superbly crafted subs elbow to elbow with half a dozen Cornell undergrads at a small shop six blocks away. I had hoped for candlelight, a nice wine, an extravagant dessert, and pursuit of amorous intentions, but Andy needed air and space and a long walk. On the return trip, we strolled a path across the campus. I announced that the staid architecture—the very definition of old school—and occasional statues of scholars were expanding my brain as we walked. I told her that if I simply wandered the campus for a few months, they'd have to give me some sort of degree. She countered that the university had an extensive agricultural school, and no doubt an abundance of manure for just such a purpose.

By the time we reached the room, I felt strain slip away from Andy, replaced by a calm surrender to fatigue. A warm shower and an hour of mindless television completed the tranquilizing effect, and she fell asleep in my arms.

33

Andy screamed.

I fought the twin assailants of deep sleep and situational confusion in an unfamiliar bed and unfamiliar room. I felt the mattress shake. Violent movement disturbed the shades of black beside me. The sheets tangled my legs. I lunged for Andy and simultaneously threw full force into the twin levers in my head.

FWOOOMP! The sound I hear when I vanish thundered between my ears. Cold swept the length of my body.

My outstretched arms closed on empty air. She was gone.

A struggle broke out beside the bed.

Andy fought someone in the space between the bed and the window. I heard limbs hit the wall.

As has happened before—never on command—I shot upward and off the bed propelled by subconscious thought. The move swung me upright and carried me into the space between the foot of the bed and the small desk where I had placed my overnight bag.

She cried out again. Unintelligible. Breathless.

"Dee!" I shouted.

I sensed movement on the floor. Someone was on her. Someone had pulled her off the bed, out of my reach. Someone was in the room.

A wild confusion of thoughts fired through my mind like aerial lightning. Light switch. Weapon. Get the intruder away from Andy. Drop to your feet *NOW.*

Fwooomp!

I hit the floor and stumbled into a solution to the most immediate problem. Light. I had no idea where to find a light switch, but my awkward landing threw me against the windows. I heaved the room-darkening curtains aside. Light from the broad campus and city beyond cut through the black.

Every muscle I had was coiled to fight and claw away whoever had attacked Andy.

She lay on the floor beside the bed, arms wildly thrusting at—

Nothing.

There was no one there.

She struggled. She pushed and scrambled backward until the wall stopped her. She threw her arms up and covered her head.

"Dee!" I dove toward her, mindful that her legs and feet had joined the fight. She kicked. She bit off a sharp scream then released it as a feral howl.

I wasn't going to get anywhere near her with her legs pumping. I rolled sideways onto the bed and crawled forward until I was able to close two hands on her arms. For a moment, I had her, but she broke the grasp and flailed. Her fist caught me at the left eye. Something burned the side of my face.

She drew back for another strike, but I regained a grip.

"DEE! It's me! It's Will!"

A last broken shriek slipped out and she froze. Her eyes, which had been clamped shut, burst open. Bright wet whites surrounded her irises, neon signs of unleashed panic in the darkness.

She pulled but I held her wrists tightly. The fight ended. Her legs stopped pumping. She stopped twisting in the narrow confines between the side of the bed and the wall.

She stared at me. Frozen.

Her body remained rigid, so I took advantage of the leverage and lifted her off the carpet. I rolled and pulled her on top of me on the bed, then rolled her to where I'd been sleeping. In the morning, I would look at the scene of the battle and have no idea how I managed to get her off the floor.

She breathed in ragged gasps. Her muscles remained rigid, corded, and inflexible. I felt safe enough to release her wrists, but immediately threw my arms around her and pulled her against my body—as much to hold and soothe her as to protect myself from further attack.

Between desperate windy breaths I heard my name, over and over.

"I'm here. I'm here." I spoke softly into her ear. "It's okay. I'm here."

Tears came in a cloudburst. She broke into uncontrolled sobs. Some she buried against my chest. Some she released into the room. Some she fought to hold in, a losing battle.

I stroked her back. I caressed her hair. I pressed her gradually softening body against mine. Except for my name, she said nothing.

The curtain I had swept aside flooded the room with campus light, for which I felt grateful. I wanted nothing to do with darkness for the rest of the night. Dawn would be welcome.

I didn't have an angle on the lighted clock on the nightstand. I had no idea what time the attack began or ended. We both found sleep again, but when? I have no clue. I did not ask what happened.

Sometime before we slept, I heard her whisper.

"She was here."

34

I'm not sure what causes it, but whenever I have a sleepless night, I eventually drop into a sound slumber ten minutes before the alarm goes off. I can toss and turn all night, but perverse physiology grants me relief just in time to be jerked awake.

Andy didn't jerk me awake. We had no alarm set. Instead, I became aware of light from the windows and a movement on the bed beside me. For a moment, I thought Andy was trying to slip out of my arms, but then I realized she was sitting beside me, leaning over me, looking down at me.

She wore a horrified look on her face. Her fingers pressed her lips.

"What?" I asked. "Are you just now realizing you married me?"

"I am so, so sorry," she said. More information flooded in. The light outside the window displayed intensity well past dawn. Andy was fully dressed. The television was on but the sound was low, a trick she uses to try and gently bring me back to life in a hotel room.

"You're sorry? Really? That's not going to play well when you toast our anniversary."

She reached out and gingerly touched the left side of my face. I got my first hint when her touch produced a sharp pain and I recoiled.

"Oooh!" she winced as if she was the one feeling the pain. "Did that hurt?"

"Uh…I guess so."

She wrinkled her nose. "And there's blood on the pillow. Just lie still. Let me get a washcloth."

I started to squint, crafting a questioning look, but that produced more pain. I touched the area near my left eye. No doubt about it.

She returned with a hand towel and a damp washcloth. She used the washcloth to wipe the side of my face. It was cold. She folded it and placed it over my left eye. She dabbed away water that leaked from the washcloth.

"Just hold that there. *Will, I am so sorry!*"

"You mind telling me what I'm not seeing here?"

She winced. "You have a bit of a shiner. And…it looks like a scratch near your eye socket. I'm so—"

"Okay, stop saying you're sorry."

"I am."

"Understood. But stop saying it. *What happened?*"

She cast her eyes downward. "One guess."

"Crazy lady showed up in your dreams."

She nodded. She reached up and gently touched the cloth on my face. "And now this! I hurt you! I'm just—"

"Uh! Uh! Nope. Not another word." I pulled myself up and scooted against the headboard, holding the cloth. "In fact, we're never going to speak of this ever again. To anyone. I can't go around telling people my wife beat me up. If anybody asks, I got it playing rugby."

"Will—"

"No. Saving a toddler from a rampaging gorilla. Or better yet, jumping in front of a runaway bus to save a toddler *and* a rampaging gor—"

She pressed her fingers to my lips to shut me up. I expected another apology, but instead she leaned in and kissed me.

It did the trick.

35

———————

Driving from the Ivy League university to the would-be university, I could not stop touching the swollen socket of my left eye and the Band-Aid stuck to the side of my face. Andy had landed a balled fist on the eye and either a fingernail or her wedding ring sliced the skin. By morning the contusion turned purple and yellow, and enough blood stained the pillow to suggest a crime had been committed. Andy could not look at me without wincing and attempting, over and over, to apologize. I argued that it looked cool. Thankfully, I detected no damage to the eye, and it wasn't swollen shut. My Ray Ban Aviators hid the worst of it.

"I know what you're going to say." Andy spoke as soon as the valet returned the car and we pulled away from the hotel. She had insisted we defer breakfast, but I managed to grab a cup of coffee in the lobby, although it was still too hot to sip.

"That's incredible, because I haven't had any of this coffee yet, so I have no clue what I'm going to say."

"You're going to say we need to talk about it. And you're right. We need to talk about it. I told you I wasn't going to play that game of pretending I'm okay when we both know I'm not." Andy made a tight turn and accelerated. I risked a sip of caffeine, a prerequisite to coherent conversation. She continued. "It was one of those awake dreams, Will. I dreamed I was awake, in the hotel room, that room, in the dark and she was there, standing right over me. I froze and I couldn't move, and she had that shotgun and she put it in my

131

face and kept saying, over and over, 'This is for America, this is for America,' and I tried to fight her, and Tom wasn't there and—"

"Whoa! Dee, take a breath. And slow down. It's forty-five in here." She had topped sixty. She eased off the accelerator and I downed a second blessed shot of coffee.

"I saw it coming. I couldn't move. I tried to fight, and I couldn't get my arms to work. I—I looked right into both barrels. And Tom wasn't there. And you weren't there. I couldn't stop her."

"That sounds completely effing awful. You have nothing to apologize for. You are *not* to blame for last night."

"I hate it. I hate losing control like that."

"Can I tell you something?"

A glance hinted that it was a stupid question. I ignored her. "I have this dream…it's an amalgam of the accident with Six Nine Tango and then that business in Chicago, the thing with the window, you remember."

"How could I not remember?"

"In the dream—this is hard to say out loud—you go out the window. Thirty-some floors up. You go out, and I dive out after you and—" I looked over at the woman I love who, in the dream, falls away from my straining fingertips. Every time, so far, I thank God that I jolt awake before she hits the pavement. "Anyway, it's a crappy dream."

"Chicago. That was a while ago. And you're still having the dream?"

"Yeah. Every now and then."

"I didn't know. I'm sor—" she pursed her lips against the phrase I had banned. "I mean—you know what I mean."

"My point is that it has been a while since the incident and my subconscious is still trying to dump the freaking tsunami of fear embedded in that moment. I'm betting it's the same for you. You've got a lot of dumping to do. It won't happen overnight. Poor word choice, but…"

"I think you're right." She gazed over the wheel. "God…I was so scared. Not when it happened, because it happened so fast. But now. Afterward. It hits me in waves, Will. I try to put it out of my mind, but that's like leaning against a door that won't latch. The pressure is there, and I need to hold it. All the time. Every moment."

"Don't. Don't hold it. It's going to get out. In your dreams. When you're awake. Maybe when you hear a loud noise—I don't know. Just don't fight it." I reached across the console and took her right hand. "What about now? Are you leaning into it right now? Right this moment?"

She considered. A wan smile creased her lips. "No. I think I'm not."

"Because we're talking it through. You're gaining control."

I squeezed her hand. She squeezed back.

"You know…you weren't wrong to want to fast forward past senseless denial, Dee. Smart. But then, you got the brains in the family. One of the top three reasons I married you."

"Top three?"

"Number three, to be precise."

She made a face that attempted reproach for the obvious innuendo, but it melted into another wince when she glanced at the damage to my face.

"Seriously, don't fight it. You had a nightmare. The whole thing was a nightmare. Think of last night as your first pass at dumping it. It won't be the last. But even in dreams you can fight for control. Next time, who knows, maybe it'll be less terrifying. Maybe you'll have more control."

"Maybe I won't beat you up in your sleep."

"This? I got this punching out a telemarketer."

"Oh? A telemarketer? You got clipped by a telemarketer?"

"He sucker-punched me with his phone." I waited a moment, then decided to take a shot of my own. "Listen, Dee, there's something else that needs to be said. This thing you're doing, this investigation. You know that I love you and I support you and—"

"And you're humoring me. I know that, Will." She gave me a long look. I wished she wouldn't.

"Eyes on the road, dear."

"I know that you think this is not the best idea. You're sweet to go along with it. I can't explain it, Will. I need this. I don't know why, but—I need this."

"I just don't want you to be disappointed. Finding the kid or not finding the kid. There's potential for disappointment either way. Eyes open, okay?"

"Both eyes wide open."

"Good. I only have one eye open…just saying… on account of getting punched during my championship MMA bout."

"Right. By your opponent, the telemarketer."

"The guy was a ringer."

I was glad she was driving.

36

W e found Belling Shore University halfway up the side of Cayuga Lake, the middle finger of the Finger Lakes, bodies of water that appear to have been clawed out of the land by the hand of a titan. Andy nearly missed the entrance to the former girl's academy. Even without budding foliage, the turnoff came up without warning. A brick marker beside Highway 90 bore a bronze plaque with the institution's name. The plaque had an antique appearance. Any other university would have added a "founded" date going back a century or two. This plaque had no date, with good reason. The façade of age and substance would not have worked as well with a date younger than most cars arriving at the gate.

A narrow road wound down a slope, doubled back through thick woods, then opened onto a campus that looked like Cornell University in miniature. A broad lawn hosted a large main building flanked by two smaller structures, all three of them stone, old and covered in ivy. Hiding behind the main building, an incongruous steel and glass structure kicked back bright morning sunshine. Beyond that, a broad lawn sloped to where the waters of Cayuga Lake glittered.

The road curved to a wrought iron gate. A guardhouse had been erected. It looked new. The roof sprouted several antennae and a small satellite dish. Behind the guardhouse, a small travel trailer rested on cinderblocks.

Andy pulled up and lowered her window. A uniformed guard stepped out of his shack. He wore a badge, but the patch on his shoulder said he was private security. The absence of a firearm confirmed it.

"Good morning, ma'am."

"Hi!" Andy said brightly. "We're here for a tour. Our daughter is thinking of enrolling in the fall."

Nothing about that landed well with the security guard. Younger than both of us, he looked at Andy, then at me. The college-aged daughter story was a stretch. It didn't matter. His doubts were embedded.

"Sorry, ma'am, but there are no tours on the manifest today. Visitors must be cleared in advance."

"But we thought we could enroll her today."

"Happy to help you with that. Enrollment is online. I can offer you a pamphlet." He made no move to offer us anything.

"Right." Andy pulled a wallet containing her badge from the satchel tucked in the footwell. She flipped it open for him to examine. "Detective Andrea Stewart, Essex Police. I'm here to see Dr. Philip Barkley. It's a police matter, so being cleared in advance is counterproductive. Now, I know you've got a job to do, but I sincerely doubt your compensation package covers legal fees for an obstruction charge." She made the point with a smile.

"Essex County? What brings you all the way down here?"

"I told you, it's a police matter. A matter that I will be discussing with Dr. Barkley. Can you confirm that he's in his office today?" This, she delivered without a smile.

"I can't disclose that information," he said. He stepped closer to the window and leaned down. "And I know a fake badge when I see one. Essex County is upstate. Yours has Wisconsin on it. So, I'm thinking the only police matter we have here is someone impersonating an officer."

"I'll spare you the geography lesson and the embarrassment of being proven wrong. Are you going to open this gate?"

"Can't. University policy. Active shooter mitigation measures. You know how it its. Keeping our campus safe. Now, I suggest you back up, turn around, and have a nice day."

The door to the trailer opened and a second officer appeared.

"'Sup, Jack?"

"These folks were just leaving." Both men adopted a folded arm pose. Conversation over.

"I said Essex Police, Jack. Not Essex County." Andy folded away her badge. "Look it up." She hit the power window button and dropped the rental in reverse, executing a tidy Y-turn.

"Now what?" I asked.

"Now Barkley knows we're coming. We do it your way."

37

F*wooomp!*

    I pulled Andy against my body. The instant the cool sensation enveloped us our feet broke ground. The bed of damp brown leaves ceased announcing our every step. We floated.

A few yards away, the rental sat on a narrow lane just off the highway. We hoped it looked innocent—someone stopping for a walk in the woods, someone with good reason and permission. Best case, nobody would notice or think twice about it. We were less than a mile from the campus and uncertain as to who owned the land. Andy speculated that Belling Shore owned the property, which touched the edge of Cayuga Lake, because the land showed no sign of expensive development.

I planned to use the lake to navigate back to the campus. I pulsed the BLASTER clutched vertically in my right hand. We rose through a gap in the leafless tree branches. Topping the trees, the colorless woods spread in three directions. In the fourth, stark blue waters stretched to the north and south. I estimated the opposite shore to be a mile away. Low humps of terrain rose on either side.

"Big lake."

Nothing disturbed the water's surface. Too early and too cool for pleasure boating. I imagined flotillas of triangular white sails navigating the waters all summer long.

"Not so high." Andy tightened her grip on my left arm.

I had just crested the treetops. We were less than sixty feet up. I

136

wondered if she knew that once you were past twenty or thirty feet, it really made no difference how far you fell.

"Okay. As soon as we clear these trees we'll drop down to just above the water. Sound good?"

"Don't go over the water."

"Why?"

"I don't want to fall in."

Forward motion generated a light breeze that tugged at our clothing and hair. We swept across the treetops. I hooked left and descended to a few feet above a gravel and grass tufted shore. Brown woods and an occasional toppled tree glided past us. The power unit hummed. The landscape had a breathless quality, a sense of spring wanting to burst with the next exhale. Green patches of moss peeked from the ground behind and beside tree trunks. In a sharp cut between humps of rising ground, a patch of snow hid in gully shadows like a fugitive from sunlight.

I caught a glimpse of a hiking trail that paralleled the shoreline. I became more convinced that the property on our immediate left belonged to the school. Perhaps the pamphlet offered by the gate guard featured effusive prose about nature and solitude, and leisure beside the lake. Passing over the sooty evidence of a bonfire, I imagined what such solitude and leisure meant to partying students.

Andy's request to stay low caused us to fly all the way to where the campus sloped down to the lake before seeing any of the university buildings. We burst into the open near a small boathouse. A boardwalk joined two piers that extended into the lake. Picnic tables dotted the lawn above the boardwalk. A sloped, paved path connected the waterfront to campus buildings.

I veered left and followed the path.

As if to signal us, the glass structure flashed reflected sunlight like a beacon. I homed in on it and gradually eased off the power, reducing the sound emitted by the prop and electric motor. The path curved left around an oversized ivy-walled cottage that I guessed to be an administrative building, given its prime location and view. Next in line came the lab. Modern walls of blue tinted glass rose to three stories above the manicured lawn. A parking lot spread out behind the building. I aimed for it.

The building had no loading docks to offer access, but a rear entrance looked viable until I saw a podium and security guard near the double glass doors.

"Take me around to the front. And then let me down."

"Down…as in visible?"

"Uh-huh. Just like we planned. I want to walk in the front door. You tag along out of sight."

I hardly considered Andy's hasty instructions, issued when we parked the car, to be a plan.

The front of the building had a looped driveway anchored by a dormant fountain. If the weird swirling sculpture at the center of the fountain made sense, it escaped me. I would have guessed *A Collapsed DNA Helix*, but maybe I had Stephenson's lecture on the brain.

I didn't like the layout. Too open. I saw no concealed spot to lower Andy to her feet and release her to reappear.

"Maybe we should go behind one of the other buildings, or the boathouse to drop you off?"

"No. Take me right to the front door. Close. If nobody's there, it's no big deal. Anybody looking in this direction from the other buildings will assume I just came out the door and then went back in."

I mentally patted my wife on the head. She was usually the one insisting on complete stealth while I tended to argue that even if we appeared out of thin air, people would dismiss the impossible with plausible explanations.

I maneuvered onto the broad concrete slab outside a rank of glass doors fronting a lobby. I saw no one inside which prompted me to worry that the doors might be locked. We touched down. Tight against me, Andy moved. She must have placed a grip on the door handle. I felt her tug our feet firmly against the concrete. I let her go and she released her grip on me.

Fwooomp!

She instantly appeared, close enough to kiss. I was tempted, but she turned and faced the glass. She paused at her reflection long enough to settle her windblown hair and tidy the leather jacket she wore over a white blouse and jeans.

"Grab my purse strap." She tugged the satchel at her side to make the strap tighter. I wrapped my fingers around the leather. I lifted my feet.

Andy pulled the door open and gave it an extra nudge to ensure I had room to glide in behind her. We entered a wide lobby. A few pieces of low leather furniture were arrayed geometrically near the windows. A long reception desk faced the doors. Clean and silent, the place looked abandoned. I saw the logic of a security guard on the other side of the building where visitors arriving would park and enter in the back. It seemed a little odd that they made no effort to secure the front doors, which faced the small campus quad. Maybe no one from the campus had business here.

Andy strolled directly to the desk and leaned over it. Nothing on the back side suggested it was being used. No computer. No monitors. No phone. She moved toward an elevator alcove. Between twin sets of elevator doors, a glass panel covered a directory with small, customizable lettering. The listings were sparse.

First Floor – Unit A
Second Floor – Unit B
Third Floor – Unit C, Dr. Barkley

I sensed an ego at work. Andy pushed the call button. The left set of doors opened immediately. She stepped into the elevator with me in tow. After swinging me around inside, she touched the button for Three.

"Camera." She stared straight ahead at the door. I looked up at the small black lens watching us—or rather, her—from the upper right corner. We stayed silent against the possibility, albeit illegal, of audio recording.

My feet hit the floor when the elevator rose. A moment later, a metallic female voice announced our arrival on the third floor. The car stopped, but I didn't. I had to reach up and straight-arm the ceiling to halt. The doors opened. Andy waited a second for me to tug myself back down behind her, then she strolled out, walked through the elevator alcove, and stopped.

The alcove extended to and ended at the windows on our right. To our left, the bulk of the building spread out, open all the way to the windows overlooking the parking lot at the back. I had expected a laboratory. Work-stations. Cabinets. Beakers and glass tubes with bubbling chemistry. People in white lab coats.

This looked more like a hive of cubicles in an insurance office. Near the elevator alcove, a cluster of floor-to-ceiling glass walls contained individual offices. Beyond that, channels ran between the low walls of cubicles. People at uniformly light gray desks wiggled mice and stared at screens. Inside the individual offices, dour-looking men and women did the same or talked into telephone handsets. One woman chatted with a man staring back at her from her computer monitor. A low buzz of conversation and some vague HVAC hum thickened the air.

All of this was guarded by a startled middle-aged woman seated behind a desk facing the elevator alcove. She carried weight that strained the small, armless desk chair beneath her. Except for a thin silver laptop and a telephone full of intercom buttons, her desktop lay bare.

"Can I help you?" Her tone did not sound helpful. Her double-wide desk blocked access to the maze of cubicles. A few of the occupants glanced up from their work, registered that a visitor had arrived, then returned to business.

We had agreed on a gambit before vanishing in the woods. Andy now played it out. She extracted her badge from her satchel and flipped it open.

"I'm Detective Stewart. I'm here to speak with Dr. Barkley."

"Dr. Barkley is in New York." The woman made a point of not offering an alternative.

"In that case, I'd like to speak with Evelynn Fitzgerald." Andy waved the badge a little higher than necessary for the benefit of anyone watching from the cubicles or the more immediate private offices.

I pulled my attention away from the cold stare coming from the gatekeeper and did as I was assigned: I watched the reaction in the expansive room. I didn't expect this to work, but carried out the assignment, nevertheless.

At the front desk, the woman who greeted Andy said nothing. She picked up her telephone and poked a single button on the keypad.

"Evelynn Fitzgerald?" Andy repeated. "Is she here?"

"One moment." The gatekeeper pressed the handset to her cheek. In a voice laden with indignation, she said, "I have a police detective here."

She stared at Andy while someone on the other end of the line chattered.

"Evelynn Fitzgerald?" Andy asked again. She took a step forward and addressed the broader room. "Evelynn Fitzgerald? Anyone?"

A few heads looked up. Each dismissed the inquiry.

Except one.

I must not be an optimist because I am shocked when a plan works. In a cubicle two rows over, a young woman stole repeated glances at Andy. She worked at looking when Andy's searching gaze swung to the other end of the open floor.

I released my grip on Andy's satchel strap and tapped my toes on the carpet, producing a rapid rise toward the acoustic tiles of a twelve-foot ceiling. My view improved. I watched the young woman. Slender. Mid-twenties. Short black hair in a stylish cut. She had attractive features behind glasses with thick black plastic frames. Her surreptitious glances at Andy shifted to something on her desk.

A quick pulse of the BLASTER pulled me over the guard desk blocking Andy's entrance. I sailed between two rows of private offices and crossed diagonally over cubicles which, from above, resembled honeycomb.

The young woman shrank slightly in her chair and turned away from the scene at the front desk. She reached for her purse on her desk. She maneuvered it so that the large black bag blocked her hand from her colleagues. I glided closer overhead, gaining full view of the woman's attempt at sleight of hand. She laid her phone flat on her desk and tapped the screen while pretending to look at a desktop monitor. At one point she paused and pretended to shift a stack of papers beside her keyboard.

Too high to see words on the screen, there was no mistaking a text app. She touched out a message then quickly pushed her phone behind her purse and returned to her work. From above, I saw a reply bubble pop up on the screen. She caught it out of the corner of her eye, checked to see if anyone was watching, touched out a second message, then slid the phone away and returned to busywork on her keyboard.

I gave the BLASTER the smallest possible shot of power, just enough to position myself above her eight-by-eight cell. A push against the ceiling initiated a trajectory that took me down to the empty cubicle beside her. The shared wall helped hide the phone from view, at least from the side.

The young woman now gave full attention to her keyboard and screen. Too much attention. She pointedly ignored the drama playing out at the front desk.

"Who gave you access to this building?" the gatekeeper demanded of Andy.

"Mmmm, no. I think you misunderstand how this works. I ask the questions. You answer. Unless you'd rather have this conversation in a more formal setting. Let's try again. Evelynn Fitzgerald. Is she here?"

"Ms. Fitzgerald is not an employee of this laboratory. Nor is she allowed on the grounds."

"Is that so?" Andy pretended surprise. "Then would you please tell Dr. Barkley that Detective Stewart is here to see him."

"About what?"

Andy smiled. "Didn't you mean to say that he's in New York?"

Caught in the lie, the gatekeeper dug herself deeper. "I—uh—he will want to know what it's about and who you are."

"Tell him it's an inquiry into the incident in Wichita."

"Well," Gatekeeper folded her arms, regaining composure. "As I said, Dr. Barkley is not here, and he is not expected to return today. If you have a card, I will forward it to him."

"Interesting."

I descended and grabbed the cubicle divider. I leaned over into the space occupied by the young woman. A stack of file folders had been placed on the corner of a narrow credenza. I slid the top two off the edge. They slapped the floor and spread papers onto the carpet. The young woman turned around, surprised, then flustered. She rotated her chair and bent to pick up the mess.

I finished my mission and pushed off for the ceiling again, rotating to face Andy as I rose. A shot of power pulled me back across the cubicle hive, into the hallway between private offices, and over the head of the human barrier facing Andy.

Gliding, I reached down and tapped a light touch on Andy's shoulder.

As if the woman barring entrance had ceased to exist, Andy placidly returned her badge to her satchel and walked back into the elevator alcove. She touched the call button.

I followed using minimal power. Progress was slow and I began to worry that the car would arrive before I could take up my position behind Andy, but she covered for me. When the door opened, she propped one hand in place to hold it. She leaned back. The woman at the desk had risen and walked to where she could watch Andy go.

Andy regarded her casually. "You really shouldn't lie to the police. Next time ask what it's about *after* you remember that the doctor is not in."

I caught up and hooked the strap on her satchel. Without another word, Andy stepped into the elevator car, pulling me in after her. The doors closed.

38

Our departure from the lab timed out perfectly. Andy stepped out of the glass door. I floated in her wake, tethered by her satchel strap. I checked for traffic and saw no one. I shifted sideways and hooked her right arm and—

Fwooomp!

—she vanished. At that moment, humming at full speed, a golf cart carrying our friendly uniformed security guard wheeled around the corner of the building. He raced to a halt beside the waterless fountain. Leaping from behind the wheel, he touched a small radio to his lips.

"Front clear. Nobody here." He hurried across the concrete to the door we had just exited. I kicked off. He passed under us as we rose along the glass front of the building. The security guard hurried inside.

"We should steal his golf cart. That would really mess with him."

"No," Andy said. "Straight back to the car please. They're going to be chasing their own tails trying to find the intruder."

Instead of retracing our flight route along the shoreline, I overflew the lab building and its companion parking lot, then cut across the tops of the trees. I executed some damned fine navigation, because the roof of our rented SUV soon appeared below us.

After loading up and driving out of our wooded hiding place, Andy backtracked on Highway 90 to the Belling Shore University entrance. She turned in and stopped a hundred yards from the road, parked with two wheels off the pavement. Angled sunlight laid tree shadows across the hood

143

of the rental. It wasn't camouflage, but the alternating light and dark lines might cause a careless observer to fail to see us at first glance. We waited.

"Here." I handed Andy the cell phone I had stolen from the young woman's desk.

"You're light fingered with other people's phones." She examined the device. "It's locked." She pocketed the phone. "She's going to panic and she'll want to make a call but she won't do it on a university phone. She will want to get off the property. She can't just take off, though. She'll use a lunch break, or she'll wait until the end of the day. We wait."

"Uh-huh. When are you going to tell me who the heck Evelynn Fitzgerald is? You told me to watch for a reaction when you call out a name. I thought you meant Barkley."

"I didn't."

"I noticed. And?"

"Evelynn Fitzgerald is a reporter for the *Boston Globe*. She wrote the article I showed you in Madison."

"Oh." I knew better than to ask *what article?* The question was on the tip of my tongue. Then I remembered the headline on Andy's laptop. "You said it was unrelated."

"I said it was 'sidebar.' It was about an anxiety medication. Fitzgerald wrote a series, but I looked at her recent work this morning while you were sleeping. She's been reporting on the rumors and buzz surrounding Amphitriton's new cancer drug. She questions the research. *This* research, at Belling Shore Labs."

"Okay. Now I get it." Andy tossed me a glance that said it was sweet of me to catch up. "Are you thinking we should talk to this reporter?"

"Not really. It's unlikely she would know if Calbert's daughter was in the treatment program."

I checked my watch. Just short of eleven. We had time to kill. I looked over at Andy.

"Want to make out?"

She paid out a pitying look. "It's just one track, isn't it?"

"Not my fault that I'm stuck in this tiny car with someone who looks like you."

She smiled. "And I would point out that this tiny car has a full-length console between these seats and I'm not about to get bruises jumping your lovely bones, dear."

"Your loss."

A delivery van came and went. Two cars rolled past us, both moved at a healthy clip. Each carried lone occupants absorbed in their own urgent business. Andy used a compact pair of Swarovski binoculars she carries in her satchel to examine the driver of each vehicle. Neither matched the young woman from the cubicle. As each vehicle passed our observation post, Andy held her phone up to her face and pretended to talk. I simply vanished.

I expected the golf cart cavalry to mount up and zip out to where we were parked, but they did not appear. They were probably doing as Andy predicted, chasing their own tails on a hunt for the police detective who breached their perimeter after having been refused entry.

By twelve-twenty I became convinced that our prey had opted for yogurt and some blueberries in the company cafeteria and would not be leaving work until the end of the day. I was about to suggest Andy and I find a road-house for a sandwich, having skipped breakfast, when a red and white Mini Cooper rounded the curve in the wooded road. Andy fixed her binoculars on the driver.

"That's her." She laid the spy glasses on the console and stepped out of the car. She stood in the middle of the narrow asphalt drive and held up the stolen cell phone. The Mini Cooper slowed to a halt beside her. The driver rolled down her window, glanced at me, then glared at Andy.

"Give me my phone." Panic electrified the words.

Andy returned the phone to her coat pocket. "Let's have a chat first."

The woman glanced at her mirrors and at the road behind her. "Are you really a cop?"

"Yes."

"Did Dr. Barkley call you? Or Fennick?"

"No."

Stress in the young woman's face caused me to think she might bolt. She searched her mirrors and the road behind her. Her grip tightened on the steering wheel. After a moment, resignation cracked the sheen of her fear and tension.

"Not here. Please. Not here."

39

"Who are you? And give me back my phone."

Andy slid into the booth after gesturing for me to slide in first; she wanted the quick exit seat. The young woman took the opposite seat and sat stiffly waiting for an answer. The roadside tavern had a small lunch crowd and what looked like a few regulars at the bar. The back corner booth offered isolation.

We had followed the red and white Mini at least six miles, passing two similar establishments before she chose this one. Putting distance between our meeting and Belling Shore indicated a degree of paranoia. I wondered if she had used this location for clandestine meetings before.

Andy laid the phone on the table but placed a firm hand over it. With her other hand, she produced her badge.

"Detective Andrea Stewart, and yes, this is a Wisconsin police badge and no, I have no jurisdiction here and no, Dr. Barkley did not send me to ferret out the press leak in his laboratory. What's your name?"

"You don't even know my name?" Stiff became angry. "Do you have any idea what you did back there? Saying that woman's name in that building?"

"It got your attention."

"Just give me my phone and I'm out of here." She reached. Andy slid the phone back into her lap.

"Two minutes. Give me two minutes and then I will hand you the phone and watch you walk out the door if that's what you want. And no one will ever know we spoke. Not Barkley. Not Fennick. Two minutes."

I had no idea who Fennick was. I didn't think Andy knew either.

The young woman stared daggers at Andy and ignored me. She had symmetrical features with enhanced long eyelashes and a little too much makeup for a face that was naturally attractive. Her black hair was cut short with the spiked look favored in Japanese graphic novels. Her hair contrasted a lightly tanned complexion, and the style gave her an edge that conflicted with the natural warmth in her brown eyes. When she lifted her left hand to make a show of looking at her watch, I examined her fingers for rings and found none.

"Two minutes. Go."

Andy extended her right hand.

"Andrea."

"Forget it. I'm not telling you my name if you don't already know it. You're down ten seconds."

Andy sighed and leaned back against the wooden backrest.

"Fine. I'm not here to out you for being a source for a *Boston Globe* reporter."

"Could've fooled me. Then why are you here?"

"A week ago, a man named Reuben Calbert attacked a private jet belonging to Terrance Remington, a name I'm sure you know. Calbert's attack may have been prompted by his daughter's involvement in an Amphitriton research study."

She shook her head. She tried to make it look firm, but I saw a hint of hesitation. "No. That's all wrong. I know about the attack, but there was no one named Calbert in the study. I ch—"

She stopped.

Andy tipped her head slightly. "You checked? That's interesting. What prompted you to check?"

"I don't know you. You come to the office calling out a toxic name and then my phone disappears and—" she looked at me "—how did you get my phone?"

"Magic," I said, instantly feeling heat from Andy's direction.

"How did you know about Reuben Calbert's daughter?" Andy asked.

"You know what? Screw your two minutes. I don't trust you. I don't know anything about this girl or any study. I want my phone. What's your interest anyway? Never mind. I don't want to know. Give me my phone or I'm calling the real police." She made a move to slide out of the booth but froze. Her skin blanched. Her eyes flashed wide. "Fuck!"

Andy and I turned to see a man enter the front door at the far end of the bar. My height and build, he had silver and red hair, a close-cropped reddish beard, and the kind of pale skin that invites sunburn. He wore jeans and an olive drab t-shirt under a tan fleece vest that did a poor job of concealing the bulge under his left armpit. From behind plastic sunglasses, he searched the bar, stool by stool, table by table. In a moment, his methodical search would find us.

A nearby hallway offered access to restrooms, but no exit. The only marked secondary exit went through the kitchen and required passage behind the bar near where the man now stood.

"Who is that?" Andy asked.

"Fennick! Remington's pit bull. I gotta get out of here."

Andy slid out of the booth. I thought she would pull the woman out and make a run for the Women's room, but instead she shoved herself onto the seat, pushing the woman sideways and locking her in the corner.

"What are you doing? I need to get out of here!"

"Will!" Andy whispered. She flicked her eyes at our panicking companion. "Yes." She said in answer to the question on my face.

"You sure?"

"Do it." Andy's eyes locked on the man. We had only seconds before he would spot us.

I reached across the table and grabbed the woman by the hands. She instinctively tugged to free herself. I tightened my grip which accelerated her panic.

"*What are you—?*" I shoved the levers in my head to the firewall.

FWOOOMP!

I vanished. She vanished. I heard a gasp. Andy leaned into her and closed a grip on what I assumed to be her right arm.

"Hush! Stay still and don't speak. And don't let go."

The fight in her hands turned rigid.

The man called Fennick stalked through the bar. He fixed a steady gaze on Andy. He crossed the floor, skirted tables, and stepped up to the booth.

Andy leaned back, lifted her legs, crossed her ankles, and planted both feet on the seat beside me.

Fennick stopped and spread a thin smile across his bearded lips.

"Detective Stewart. Mind if I join you?"

"Not without a resume." Andy did not move. "You seem to know me. Who are you?"

"Desmond Fennick." He said extended a hand. Andy let it hang until he dropped it. The rebuke only fed his smug grin.

"Have we met?"

He reached into his vest and pulled a cell phone from a pocket. After opening the screen and swiping at it, he held it out for Andy to examine. A security camera image portrayed my wife facing the gatekeeper on the third floor of the Belling Shore Laboratory.

"I thought we might discuss trespassing, improper use of police authority, and maybe talk about the Belling Shore employee you're here to meet. A woman. Dr. Bailey Maxwell."

Andy pulled a small note pad and pen from her satchel. She opened the pad and wrote. "Is that Desmond with an s?"

"Do you know the woman? She drives the Mini Cooper parked out front."

Andy held her pen poised over the notepad. "I know of her, but we haven't met. What do you do for Belling Shore University, Mr. Fennick? Are you on the faculty?"

He did not answer. The grin faded.

"Fine." Andy put away the pen. "Maybe you can help me. Mini Cooper notwithstanding, it appears I've been stood up. When you see Dr. Maxwell, tell her that her ex is up for parole in Wisconsin, and that the story he's now peddling about the sack of oxy that earned him two-to-four is that she used her position with Belling Shore Labs to act as his supplier. He's counting on gaining parole board sympathy by throwing her under the bus. It's obvious BS, but I asked to meet her so we can all get ahead of it before the hearing next week."

"You're meeting Dr. Maxwell about some ex-boyfriend? A second-rate pill pusher?" Fennick's face said he wasn't buying it.

"He's not second-rate if I can leverage a parole denial into getting the name of his real supplier."

"Then why were you asking for Evelynn Fitzgerald?"

"Evelynn Fitzgerald is a reporter for the *Boston Globe*, but you already know that. She wrote about Belling Shore. She also wrote a series on pharmaceutical research labs pipelining unprescribed oxy into rural communities."

"That doesn't answer my question."

Andy paused. She narrowed her gaze to a cold stare. "Dr. Maxwell has been avoiding my calls. Banking on avoiding me. I told her if she didn't meet with me, I'd start throwing around Fitzgerald's name—hinting that there might be something to the boyfriend's story. Maybe even suggesting she was connected to the reporter. It's not true, of course, but I think I made my point because she immediately texted me to meet here."

"You could have just asked for her."

"Maybe. But she said if I came to her work, she would have security throw me out. I decided to use a little leverage." Andy made a show of searching the interior of the pub. "I saw her car pull in, but it looks like she's given us both the slip. What's your interest in her?"

Fennick studied Andy. If he hoped to find a fissure in her tale, I wished him luck. Andy's poker face gave away nothing.

"Belling Shore Labs has nothing to do with oxy or any other narcotics," he said.

"I never said they did. I do my homework. I have no interest in Belling Shore. I have a lot of interest in denying parole to a three-time loser who pushed oxy in my county. I came here to nip a story about an ex-girlfriend who works for a pharma lab in the bud. Stories like that tend to grow legs and sow doubt. I came to get her statement in person, then I'm gone. Beyond that, Dr. Maxwell is of no interest to me. But I am now curious about you, Mr. Fennick. You seem like a fellow with something to hide—besides that weapon under your vest."

"Cute." He restored his grin. "You sure I can't join you?"

"Afraid not. And the truth is, whatever you're hiding is not my problem. I have a plane to catch this afternoon."

"Without seeing Miss Maxwell? Seems like you're giving up easily."

Andy shrugged. "Oh, she can think she won this round, but I'll pay a visit to the Ithaca PD before I depart. I had hoped to avoid enlisting local help, but some people don't know when to get out of their own way."

Andy extinguished her smile, signaling an end to the conversation.

Fennick paid out a slow nod, then turned and walked out of the bar.

I twisted in my seat and watched him go, then searched the room. When I felt certain there were no eyes aimed in my direction, I pulled back the levers in my head.

Fwooomp!

Bailey Maxwell locked frozen shock on me while her hands squeezed a death grip on mine.

40

Whiskey helped. Maxwell's hand trembled when she lifted the shot to her lips and downed it. Andy and I ordered coffee.

"*What the—?*" Maxwell asked for the tenth time after she planted the empty shot glass on the table. "*What was that?* How—what—I—?"

"Hi." I put out my hand. She stared at it as if it might be venomous. "I'm Tony Stark. The real Tony Stark, not the comic book guy. That was one of my inventions."

"This is my husband, Will. And yes, that was real. And no, we're not explaining it. And if you're helpful, he will show you one more time, but first you will talk to me about Reuben Calbert's daughter. You lied. She is on the list, isn't she?"

Maxwell held up the empty shot glass and waved at a passing server. "Can I get another?"

"Sure." The server angled toward the bar.

Maxwell couldn't take her eyes off me. I lifted my eyebrows to let her know she had the floor.

"I am so screwed. How did Fennick know I was here?"

"You might check your car for a tracking device, which is quite illegal, by the way. He knows there's a leak at Belling Shore Labs, so he's using active measures to plug it."

"Shit!"

Andy shook her head. "I don't think his interest is specific to you. He's probably tracking all the likely suspects to see whose path crosses with the press."

"You mean with Evelynn Fitzgerald. Jesus, I've only met her once."

"But you texted her. The minute I called out her name, you texted that a cop was asking for her. Not a good idea. You might want to clean that up." Andy slid the woman's phone across the plank-topped table.

"Yeah. Stupid of me. I freaked out." She dug her fingers into her spiked black hair. "Oh, God, I can't go back."

"Yes, you can. Fennick doesn't have proof of anything."

"Thanks to you he thinks I'm dealing oxy!"

"No. Thanks to me your behavior has a complex and plausible explanation. Dr. Maxwell, Bailey…" Andy leaned closer. "Fennick and Barkley and Remington are focused on one thing. They have a multi-billion-dollar IPO on the line. That's why Fennick is uptight about security. Any connection to a reporter poses a threat to them, whether there's a story or not."

Maxwell stared down at the scarred wooden tabletop.

"I am so screwed…"

Andy leaned closer. "Listen. I'll make a call and have someone from Wisconsin call your office to cement the parole hearing story. I'll make sure they say enough to turn it into office gossip. Okay?"

"Great. Instead of being a whistleblower, I'm dating a drug dealer. You could have stayed out of my life in the first place."

"I am not the enemy. I'm trying to find a little girl. This IPO doesn't matter to me except that in my experience, when that kind of money is flying around, people are not on their best behavior. Although now I must ask… Fitzgerald's source for the story she wrote on Xeniten…was it you?"

Maxwell shook her head. "It wasn't. I wasn't at Belling Shore when that happened. That's ten plus years ago. I wasn't the source. My stepmother was."

41

Maxwell sipped her second whiskey. She alternated between staring at me and watching the door.

She spoke slowly, quietly.

"My stepmother had a Ph.D. in biochemistry and in pharmacology. She worked for Dr. Barkley when Amphitriton contracted Belling Shore to do the studies for Xeniten during the heyday of the new anti-anxiety meds. She saw millions pumped into the university and Barkley's pocket, but next to nothing was allocated to the research. Barkley called it a slam dunk. Clinical trials were glowing. Results reported to the FDA were universally positive. And not just Belling Shore. The same was true for all the SSRI meds. The psychiatric community was thrilled."

Andy and I gave Maxwell the same blank stare.

"Selective serotonin reuptake inhibitor. SSRI."

"What was the problem?" Andy asked.

"Mom noticed that test subjects exhibiting side effects were excluded from final summaries. When she went to Barkley, he pretended to listen, but didn't do anything. She raised the question at peer conferences. No one in the scientific community would engage. The FDA was only interested in positive results. Mom pushed and things got ugly fast. People claiming to be from the government showed up at her home. She was sidelined, then shunned. Belling Shore didn't fire her. Too obvious. They parked her in a clerical job. But that was their mistake because she still had access to the study results. With nowhere else to turn, she reached out to Evelynn

Fitzgerald at *The Globe*. Even then, the story might not have gone anywhere except for William Edward Stone."

Andy turned to me. "That name was in an article I showed you—about the court case being reclassified."

Maxwell laughed.

"I didn't read it," I confessed. "What are we talking about?"

Maxwell sipped her whiskey. "You have to understand…when anti-anxiety wonder drugs hit the market, the money didn't flow, it gushed. Rivers of it. The drugs had *promise*. People—especially kids—were freed from a lifetime of stress and debilitating anxiety. Doctors prescribed them like candy. Xeniten didn't top the list, but it raked in its share. However, there were isolated reports of side effects. Patients—kids—having suicidal thoughts—precisely the side effect my stepmother noted. But nobody collated the data. Nobody pushed for answers. The opposite. Suicidal tendencies were called random or attributed to other causes—until William Edward Stone, a boy from Louisville. In middle school, he had such intense anxiety that he could not get out of bed. Along comes Xeniten, a miracle drug. In a matter of a day or two, he's his old self again. Until he isn't. Within a couple weeks, he became moody. Withdrawn. One day he went to his mother's office on the tenth floor of a building in downtown Louisville. He asked her to bring him a glass of water. When she stepped out, he smashed the window and climbed out. The parents blamed Xeniten and sued Amphitriton. Everyone expected Amphitriton to settle. That's how things were done. Deals get made and lips get sealed. But Amphitriton fought it."

"Because they had Dr. Philip Barkley in their pocket," I suggested.

"No. Barkley testified for the plaintiffs. For the parents. He grew a pair and sided with what my stepmother had been crying in the wilderness—or so it seemed. By that time all the major players were facing the same problematic data. All the SSRI studies were being reviewed. Momentum was with the parents. With Barkley on their side, they had it in the bag. Only Barkley botched it. He botched the testimony. The plaintiff's lawyers screwed up the submissions, missed deadlines. It was a shit show. The jury found in favor of Amphitriton, who—against all expectations—walked away with a win and avoided a payout—and more importantly preserved Xeniten's reputation. Turns out that was the point."

"I don't understand," Andy said.

"After the trial it was revealed that Amphitriton paid the plaintiffs and their attorney to throw the case. To lose. Barkley was probably in on it, but that was never proven. His deniability was plausible."

"That's insane," I said. "That's a huge ethics violation. The attorney should have been disbarred. Why wasn't there a retrial?"

"Why would they? The attorney acted on behalf of his client. The client was in on it all along. Nobody knows how much Amphitriton paid. The money didn't matter. Amphitriton knew that settling equaled losing in the eyes of the public. So, they settled secretly for a show trial win. How's that for messed up?"

"Holy crap," I muttered. "But this all came out."

Maxwell laughed. "So what? The court simply reclassified the verdict as invalid. The bar association refused to review the attorney's actions because everything he did was on behalf of his client. At worst, he wasted the court's time. The case got a footnote in the county clerk's record. Amphitriton still claimed the win and declared the drug exonerated. Xeniten stayed on the market. So did all the others…Paxil, Prozac, Zoloft, all of them. Eventually the FDA required warning labels, but Xeniten remains Amphitriton's biggest seller…but not for long."

Maxwell looked skyward. A damp glitter sparked in her eyes. She drew a long slow breath then let it slip between her lips. She said, "I loved Mom— my stepmother—yeah, I know, I'll never make it as a Disney princess because in my story the stepmother is the good guy. She was so smart, so talented. She was right, but they ruined her. Rumor. Innuendo. Lies. When she left Belling Shore, she couldn't get interviews and when she did, they came to nothing. Ghosting before that was the word for it. She never worked in research again. She—uh—she passed away two years ago. Breast cancer. Ironic, considering the path she put me on."

I said nothing.

Andy asked, "Why are you at Belling Shore? Why work for a guy like Barkley?"

"Mom encouraged me to get the job at Belling Shore precisely because of people like Barkley. She said, and I quote, 'Never let a dick fuck up good science.' The work I do in cancer research is solid work and it's obviously personal. I have faith in what we're doing."

"That doesn't track. After what they did to your stepmother, why would they hire you? Or trust you?"

Maxwell laughed. "Because Barkley thinks he's smarter than me. His ego lets him think he has control over me."

"Yet you've been feeding doubts to a reporter."

"No. Fitzgerald approached me because of the connection to Mom. She's the one with questions, doubts. I pushed back. I'm trying to set her straight. I believe in what we're doing. She challenged me to be the scientist my mother believed in, to look deeper. For my mother's sake. That's what I'm doing. But…"

"But what?"

"This IPO clouds things. Decisions are being made that—I don't know—they don't fit. Things like pulling this girl out of the study. She's not the only one. There are others. Never because of the meds or the tests. Always something external. And the minute they're extracted, all the data is pulled. That's how I get the names. When the data is pulled."

"Pulled?"

"Extracted."

"Erased?"

Maxwell tipped her head back and forth. "I don't think it's erased. Segregated might be a better word. It's stripped out of the study."

"To cleanse the positive results."

"Exactly."

"What happens to these kids? I mean, if this med can save them, surely Amphitriton doesn't just cut them off?"

"I don't know," Maxwell said. "I don't know if the kids who dropped out were on the med or in the control group. And if they were on the med, I don't know if they were allowed to continue or were cut off."

"I can guess," I said. "What would make a man attack the CEO of a pharmaceutical company if not the fact that they cut his child off from a life-saving medication?"

Andy's attention drifted. Her wheels turned. This had not been the easy answer she was seeking.

Andy spoke pensively after a moment. "Bailey, what's your role? Day to day?"

"Bio data analysis. I get feeds from all the test subjects. Vitals. Blood test results. Imaging. You name it. We follow hundreds of data points."

"You're not doing the treatments on site? These kids are not here in Ithaca?"

"God, no."

"Where does the data come from? I mean—physically. Where? What hospitals?"

"Half a dozen hospitals across the Midwest. The drug trials went to the subjects. The meds are administered on site. It's all carefully tracked and controlled by regional Amphitriton reps. We take on test subjects where they are found."

"Can you get me a list of hospitals?"

Maxwell grimaced. "Honestly? I don't think so. You're talking about nuclear code level secrecy."

"But you said you get data from all over."

"The data channels through a central server. It's all coded. No names for the subject or the hospital. I only have names of the dropouts because the data gets extracted from the study when the files are closed. I don't think anyone beyond Barkley has the test subject information. Even the supplement packs are unmarked…" Maxwell froze, staring into a blank distance.

"What?" Andy asked.

Maxwell didn't answer for a moment. She squinted, then muttered, "…the supplement packs…"

"What about them?"

Maxwell reeled in her distant gaze. "The supplement packs…I might be able to access the shipping records."

"What shipping records?"

"For the treatment support packages that are sent out. The meds originate at Amphitriton in Princeton, New Jersey, but they're bulk shipped here and then parceled out to the test sites."

"Can you get that to me?" Andy pulled out her notepad and wrote an email address. She tore off the sheet and handed it to Maxwell who folded it. Andy reached across the table and closed her hand over the slip. "No. Memorize it. And don't use your phone, or any device you own to send it to me. Find another way."

Maxwell nodded. She opened the slip and read the email address aloud several times. Then closed her eyes and repeated it. She handed back the slip.

Andy tucked the paper in her satchel and said, "This cancer med. Is it really all that?"

Maxwell's eyes flared. "I'll be honest, I've never seen anything as promising. The results posted in the last year—some of the cases are stunning. It was iffy for a while, and it's been a long road, but the data summaries I've seen show response patterns beyond definitive."

"Then why agree to talk to Fitzgerald?"

"Because this is good science. It's too important. This needs to be done right. No shortcuts. We can't repeat Xeniten. Despite the win, all the SSRI meds got bad press. If there are any negatives, they need to be part of the conversation, not the coverup."

"That's a powerful word. Do you think there is a coverup here?"

"I worry that something is being *handled* by segregating the dropouts. If there are negative results, they need to be brought to light. If not, the work is biased. Nothing is perfect. Hiding failure is the worst thing they could do."

"And you shared this with Fitzgerald?"

"Some of it. But only on condition that she be one hundred percent balanced. And if she uncovers nothing, she reports it that way."

"You're staying loyal to Belling Shore."

"I'm loyal to the science, Detective. Barkley is a turd who will cut corners because his ego drives him. Remington is consumed by the money—by this IPO. I don't care about that. I won't let them destroy good work. There are good people behind this. I want the data to be real. To speak for itself. These treatments have achieved amazing results. Even if it is not perfect, it promises to be—my God! It's what generations of researchers have been dreaming of."

Andy cast a glance at me. "We should go. Dr. Maxwell, I suggest you leave your car here. We'll drive you back to the Belling Shore entrance. You can walk in. Tell them you went for lunch, but your car wouldn't start so you got a ride back."

"Fennick will see right through that lie."

"Yes, he will. Let him. If he confronts you, confess to the ex-boyfriend story. Admit to being pestered by a cop from Wisconsin. Get angry and tell him you're sick of the whole thing and don't want to talk about it. Call it a bad chapter in your life. Then get angrier and tell him it's none of his damn business. Play the emotional woman card."

I chimed in. "While you're at it, tell him you're having your car towed to a shop to have it gone over bumper to bumper. That should ratchet up his pucker factor. If he planted a tracker, he'll want to pull it right quick."

Maxwell smiled. "Sounds like fun."

Andy waved at the server and hand signaled for the check.

"Hold up!" Maxwell pointed at me. "What about—*Jesus*—*what about what happened?* Are you going to tell me?"

I looked directly at her and smiled.

"Nope."

42

Thanks to the weather system pounding the Midwest, I advised staying a second night at the Statler Hotel on the Cornell University campus. Andy agreed because she wanted time to visit the university library. She suggested I go and see George's Gorge. I set off to explore and got the joke after asking some students for directions. When they finished laughing at me, they said my choices were the Fall Creek Gorge and Cascadilla Gorge. The latter of the two bordered the south edge of the campus not far from the hotel. A pleasant walk took me to the College Avenue Stone Arch Bridge over Cascadilla Creek. I strolled across the bridge beside its low stone wall. At the center, I stopped to absorb the stunning view into the gorge. Like tens of thousands who had crossed the bridge before me, and a handful who never completed the crossing, I considered the act of leaping over the wall. I wondered if the impulse to suicide—the permanent solution to temporary problems—gained a hypnotic charge from the natural beauty enshrined in stone and flowing water far below.

Leaning over the stone wall gave me a twinge that was equal parts fear and thrill. The daring view also showed me the solution local authorities had applied to the question of suicide prevention. Tightly drawn nets spanned the space just below the rim of the bridge. Anyone wishing to jump would experience a short flight followed by some lengthy explaining. I wondered if first responders practiced extracting failed suicides from the netting.

Nothing resembling a suicidal thought sprang to mind, but I felt an overwhelming urge to climb onto the stone wall with a BLASTER unit in hand

159

and launch, not leap. A steady stream of pedestrians with cell phones stymied the impulse. The last thing I wanted was to be caught on video, or to generate half a dozen 9-1-1 calls, a roadblock, and a fruitless search of the creek below for my body.

Still, the allure grew potent. I walked back to the campus end of the bridge and turned an immediate left onto a paved path that paralleled the gorge beside an old and English-looking building. Opposite the structure's wall, bare trees populated a short span before the terrain took a plunge. A few students hurried toward me on the same path. I waited until they passed, then checked my six, saw no one, and—

Fwooomp!

—vanished. I briefly considered the option to cut through the trees and reach the gorge. That simply would not do.

With a BLASTER in hand, I rotated and navigated back the way I had come, then turned right and flew a short path above the sidewalk and over the heads of several pedestrians until I reached the center of the bridge. The view from ten feet above the pavement was exponentially more thrilling. My chest tightened.

I lightly thumbed the controller on the BLASTER and lowered myself until my feet touched the stone wall. Bending my knees and pushing, I surged out over the gorge.

Was this what people had expected—people who made the jump? An instant indelibly fused by death? Since gravity had no jurisdiction over me, I possessed the unique ability to freeze the moment without paying the ultimate price. I didn't accelerate to the stone creek below. I hung in the air and owned the view.

William Edward Stone came to mind. A boy who needed to go out his mother's office window so badly that he had to "break glass in an emergency." His emergency. I could not begin to guess what passed through his mind in that moment. Relief? Resignation? Terror?

What demons, released by Amphitriton's money-making anti-anxiety med gave him a hand going out that window?

The other thing generates immeasurable joy. Flight. I've shamelessly taken that drug countless times, cruising fields and woods, chasing Sandhill Cranes or trailing spooked deer. Until shoving off the wall on Stone Arch Bridge, I never thought about people seeking the same sensation in their last moments on earth. I didn't know whether the notion dampened the experience for me or defined its value as priceless.

Either way, I did what the moment demanded as if I owed it to everyone who had tried and paid with their lives. I cranked the BLASTER to full power and dove. For the next half hour, I sailed between the walls of the gorge, under the bridges, past the trees, and just above the rippling spring water. I didn't care if the device in my hand screamed or if laughter escaped my throat.

If anyone heard me, screw them. They would never believe it anyway.

I RETURNED to the hotel thinking nothing could surpass the exhilaration of my Cornell gorge tour. I was proven wrong when Andy took me by the hand after a fantastic dinner at the hotel restaurant and led us back to our room.

43

We didn't fly to Wichita. Andy derailed the idea over a breakfast I devoured thanks to my wife's pursuit of passion—the woman left me spent and starving. Not that I was complaining, but I began to wonder if I had Andy's close encounter with a shotgun to thank for her sexual appetite.

I didn't ask. Instead, I asked, "Not Wichita? Where?"

"I'll show you." She lifted her laptop onto the white tablecloth. She turned the screen in my direction. "I did a little research at the library."

She browsed to a photographic image. A sign in the background read, *Jim Newell Christian Ministry Hospice for Children*. In the foreground, a handsome man dominated the photo with his open hands spread at his sides, flanked by children of varying ages, none of whom looked healthy, some of whom wore oxygen cannulas. For the viewer too dense to make the connection, a caption read, *Suffer the little children to come to me...*

"Look familiar?"

"I'm guessing somewhere in my misspent youth I came across a painting of Jesus in the same pose."

"Not that. Here." She clicked open another window. The headline she had shown me in Madison filled the screen.

Legal Wrist Slap
Court Reclassifies Xeniten Double-Cross

Andy scrolled down to the photo of three men and a golf cart. I recognized Remington and Barkley and said so. Andy pointed. "Him. The driver."

"Ah. The Jesus wannabe drives a golf cart."

"That's Jim Newell. Multi-millionaire televangelist, online preacher and the owner and operator of a *highly exclusive and apparently secretive* hospice for children."

"Preparing them to meet their maker after earthly cures fail them? Suffer the little children, indeed." I looked at Andy for whom dots had connected. "Let me guess. Amphitriton has been testing and pushing cancer cures and this is plan B for cases that prove unsuccessful." Andy nodded. "And now they're on the verge of announcing that one of their concoctions works." Andy made a spinning gesture with one hand, urging me to catch up. "Dr. Maxwell believes in the meds, but is troubled by a lack of transparency regarding participants that have dropped out of the drug trials, one being an angry ax-wielding Reuben Calbert. She asks the question 'Where have the failed cases gone?' while coincidentally, the CEO of the pharma company plays golf with a TV preacher who runs an exclusive hospice."

"A nearly hidden hospice. I only tripped over it—or rather its existence —while searching tangent medical stories. The photo originated with a local newspaper that's long gone. It's not on any of the church websites. And check this out." Andy tugged the laptop back into her possession. She clicked the mouse and tapped the keys. After a moment she spun the device my way for another look.

The screen showed a simple map—the kind printed on the back of a brochure or programmed on a web page. A network of roads connected a series of buildings curved around one large building labeled The Jim Newell Citadel of God. Andy rolled the top of her mouse and the map zoomed in. She pointed at the caption for an ancillary building.

"The Citadel of God campus. That's the Remington Religious Library."

"Is it now."

"Not only do they play golf together, but it appears the CEO of the pharma company is a significant doner to his golf partner's ministry."

"Okay." I sat back and folded my arms. "I see where you're making a connection here, darling. But what if they're just friends and what if they just share some religious beliefs and what if the hospice thing is just an attempt to do good works—you know, the whole Christian thing?"

"Will, The Newell Ministry positively trumpets its 'good works.' Youth ministries to spread the Word. Ministries to spread the Word among the homeless. Ministries that bring the True Word to business conventions, conservative political conventions, executive retreats. There's an overall tone here that's a bit more self-serving than selfless. Nowhere is there mention of this hospice. I had to dig."

"Maybe that's the point. Maybe it offers the wealthy a place to hide a family tragedy without disrupting the lifestyles of the rich and famous."

"That's a bit cold, dear."

"Sorry. Rich guys don't have a great track record. So, you think that when Barkley hits a snag and results don't come up rosy, he drops the test subject and uses this hidden hospice to sweep bad data under the rug?"

Andy gave me her best *sure looks that way to me* face.

"Wow. And you said I'm cold. Would this scheme pass your circumstantial sniff test?"

The police officer that is my wife is all kinds of skeptical when encountering coincidence and circumstantial connections.

Andy took command of her laptop again. The screen jumped to Facebook. She scrolled vigorously. I have no presence on or use for the social media platform, nor does Andy except for a profile she invented for work.

She pushed the screen back in my direction. She pointed at a posted message under the name Sarah Calbert.

I cannot begin to express the depth of my gratitude for the righteous intervention and prayers of the Reverend Jim Newell on behalf of our precious Gabby. My heart is full! Leading us in prayer today did more than you can ever imagine! Bless you! Bless you!

A string of emojis, some of them faces, many of them hands clasped in prayer, trailed off the message. A footnote linked to a GoFundMe page.

"Dated four weeks ago." Andy stroked back a lock of hair that had fallen across one eye.

"You think the mother placed her daughter in the holy hands of a TV preacher and her faith in prayer instead of medicine?"

"Possible."

"Isn't that easy enough to confirm with a few phone calls?"

"I can't find anything with an address or phone number. No web page. No email. I tried the ministry's main switchboard, but if navigating their phone menu is anything like getting into Heaven, we're all going to Hell. When I did get a human, I was stonewalled. They were either politely not familiar with any hospice for children or they wanted to know who I was and what my business with the ministry was. I'd say our best bet is visiting the Citadel of God."

I searched her face for signs that she'd gone off her normally well-grounded rails. If such signs existed, she hid them well.

"Okay. So, where is this place?"

44

____

The storms hammering the Mississippi Valley didn't come close to topping the Super Outbreak of 2011, which spawned 362 tornados. Nor did they approach the next worst outbreak in 1974 which kicked off 148 twisters. News reports on Andy's laptop reported 57 tornadoes over two days across nine states. Failing to make the record books probably did little to comfort people whose homes looked like spilled toothpicks when seen from news drones. Line after line of thunderstorms formed the vanguard of a cold front stretching from the Great Lakes to the Gulf of Mexico. The system had grown since I first began challenging it two days ago. Worse, the deep low-pressure center had slowed to a crawl, causing its deadly frontal arms to linger.

Our Ithaca departure point remained clear of the aerial violence, but a flight path to Mountain Home, Arkansas, drilled straight through the weather marching east. Ample danger lurked in the form of embedded thunderstorms laden with hail, icing, turbulence, and general nastiness. Heavy rains were predicted for towns already dealing with downed powerlines, demolished homes, and fraught searches for casualties. Damage had been recorded in Branson to the northwest of Mountain Home, and in West Plains to the northeast. I was not enthusiastic about landing at an airport where the locals might be prying collapsed hangars off damaged airplanes.

Making the trip required routing west to near Chicago, then turning south to fly behind the storm line. Such a route made a fuel stop mandatory. Being "practically in the neighborhood" of Wisconsin, I hatched a plot to divert home to Essex for a day or two to let two things settle down—the storms, and Andy's growing obsession with the Calbert child.

We returned to the room to pack before checkout. I worked on flight planning at the small desk and prepared to make my case when Andy stopped and stared at her phone.

The look on her face prompted me to ask, "What?"

"A Missouri State Trooper was assaulted during a highway stop near Springfield. Witnesses say it was Calbert. Authorities are widening the search."

"First airplanes. Now cops. My two favorite things. I do not like this guy."

"That's a direct line from Wichita to where we're going, Will. How soon do you think we can get there?"

"I'll be honest. I was about to suggest we go home. Give it a day."

"No." Her abrupt answer startled us both. She softened it. "Please."

"Okay…then plan B. We go as far as northern Illinois and park it for the night, then make a run to Arkansas in the morning. Plan C is to stay here another night and do the whole thing tomorrow. I prefer Plan B. If we get up at the butt crack of dawn, we can make the second leg to Mountain Home before things heat up."

"We can't get there today?"

"Not safely."

"Okay."

"Dee, what about calling to let someone know? About the hospice thing. Give the local authorities a heads up."

She frowned. "I can try. But it's only a theory and I'm a Monday morning quarterback. I've been on the other side of calls like that." The frank assessment carried a reminder of her temporary off-duty status.

"Better than nothing." I tried to sound encouraging.

"I'll make some calls. It's just…I feel like we really need to get there."

<h1 style="text-align:center">45</h1>

I would do anything for that woman. When Andy climbed the airstair into the Navajo, I felt *need* wafting off her like the sweet summer fruit scent of her perfume. Her need to reach Jim Newell's Citadel of God flashed in her gold flecked green eyes. Her need to find the Calbert girl, Gabby, radiated from graceful motion that camouflaged urgency and tension. If asked for an opinion, I would have rejected both ideas. Nothing about Andy's affect said she would ask, which gave me no choice but to move mountains to get her there.

Mountains notwithstanding, I will not put her life at risk.

Any attempt to fly south into the storm front was a high-risk proposition. Instead, we flew for close to two and a half hours from Ithaca International Airport to Purdue University Airport in Lafayette, Indiana. It was as close as I could get to the top end of the storm line. Even at that, the ride in was rough. Andy joins me in the cockpit when we fly together. I felt her tense up with each jolt and bump in the thick clouds. We flew the ILS Runway 10 approach in steady rain. As the wheels touched the runway, she reached over and squeezed my arm in gratitude for a safe return to Earth. I don't know if she realizes I have a vested interest in making a good landing, but her appreciation touched me.

We did the basics. Refuel. Tie down the airplane. Uber to a Fairfield Inn. Eat at a Subway next door. Sleep. Before hitting the unremarkable mattress in the unremarkable room, I spent time on the iPad planning for the run to Mountain Home.

"If you don't mind an early wakeup call, I see a window that can get us in before things get rough," I told Andy when she emerged from the bathroom in her plain, we're-not-fooling-around-tonight nightgown.

"How early?"

"A part of me wants to suggest we just stay up and watch movies until it's time to go."

"How early?"

I grimaced. "Three-thirty?"

She took it in stride. "I'll set the alarm on my phone."

I spent another fifteen minutes flight planning before I slapped the iPad cover closed, connected it to a charger, and joined Andy on the bed. She sat with her laptop on her thighs and gestured for me to slide in close beside her.

"Check this out." She tapped and stroked the touchpad.

Onscreen, Andy scrolled through a YouTube page dedicated to the sermons of the Reverend Jim Newell. Andy told me that Newell broadcasts his sermons twice each Sunday morning and once each Sunday evening from a building that served as church, auditorium, studio, and evangelical television network. She selected a recently uploaded recording and hit Play.

Half carnival show, half rock concert, half tent revival extravaganza, and all money-oozing enterprise, I gave Newell credit for professional level camera work, high-quality lighting, expert video and sound editing, and overall slick production. The man's charisma leaped from the screen. He pranced and prayed in front of a bank of robed singers who hit their cues perfectly against what sounded like a full symphony orchestra.

We fast-forwarded through most of it.

The lead-in and closing to the show portrayed a building I can only describe as a Mother Ship. The chapel of the Citadel of God sprawled beneath a radiant spread of support beams that reminded me of the hat the Statue of Liberty wears, except bigger, broader, more extravagant. Each sunray line in the vast arch contained stained glass windows. A link at the end of the video connected viewers to donation web pages. Another link took us to a virtual tour of the Citadel of God Campus. Andy clicked on the tour.

A camera glided through the most manicured landscape I have ever seen. Not a single leaf littered perfectly shaved lawns. Uniformly mulched gardens sprouted roses climbing white trellises. Shrubs cut in spherical shapes lay like pool balls on sprawling felt lawns. Smaller buildings fanned out beside a broad main avenue like supplicants to the giant chapel. The layout reminded me of the quad at Cornell, but without the scholarly atmosphere. The ancillary buildings looked like Las Vegas strip versions of classical architecture, as if gaudy defined good design. A marble panel above one building contained scripted engraving identifying the structure as the *Remington Religious Library* precisely where the map had predicted.

Something about all of it, a kingdom built on coin and single dollar donations from the desperate faithful, perhaps hoping their contribution bought favor from their Lord, made me sad. I wondered what all this money would do for Dr. Maxwell's cancer research.

"Enough." I took the laptop from her. I typed out a search and tapped the touchpad. A music video of Sharon Van Etten and Angel Olsen's *Like I Used To* popped up. I hit play and pumped up the volume to let the music cleanse the screen, the air, and my mind. Andy didn't object. She curled against me under my arm.

When the beautiful ballad ended, YouTube tried to lure me into its algorithmic idea of what I wanted to hear next. I closed the laptop and hit the room lights. Bold notions about staying awake in case nightmares assaulted Andy crossed my mind, but my eyelids sank. Eventually I released Andy from my embrace. She rolled away and slept. I laid the uninjured right side of my face on the pillow and slipped into darkness that remained pitch black until minutes later—it seemed—when Andy's travel alarm squalled at us.

If Andy had nightmares, she kept them to herself.

We were wheels up in the dark. We landed at Baxter County Airport under steady rain two hours and fifty-six minutes later.

46

I should have detected something amiss on the drive from the airport to the Citadel of God. My iPad laid out the route. We joined Arkansas Highway 5 and followed it north from the airport through tidy countryside populated by metal sheds and an armada of pickup trucks. A few miles into the drive, we passed a sign for *Liberty Church of Christ.* A small L-shaped building passed quickly, joined to the highway by a weedy gravel driveway. The all-white building looked boarded up. I wondered if the local ministries had seen their flocks tugged away by Newell's glitz and glamour.

There were almost no signs advertising for the Citadel of God. I expected neon. Billboards. At the turnoff from Highway 5, a single plywood panel mounted on two fence posts listed the name above an arrow. Neat and unpretentious, the sign bore only lettering. No flashy graphics. No leading-man image of Newell.

Andy drove and followed a narrower road that took us toward the vast snaking waterway listed as Bull Shoals Lake. Digital maps portrayed the body of water as something more likely seen under a microscope, a creature with twisted limbs and hairy tributaries.

Two more signs, equally unassuming, confirmed that the narrow road took us in the right direction. A third announced that we had arrived and pointed us into a gravel driveway. Not the broad avenue I had been expecting.

"Are you seeing this?"

We drove under a golden arch emblazoned with *Citadel of God* in Old

English lettering. Chips in the metal revealed that the lettering wasn't solid gold, it was painted.

Praise Jesus and pass the offering plate.

Andy leaned forward to watch the arch pass over our Nissan Sentra rental.

"Don't be judgmental."

"Have I mentioned that it bugs me when you read my mind, dear?"

She reached across the Nissan's console and patted my hand. "You don't need to mention it. I know what you're thinking."

Instead of the broad boulevard flanked by the campus buildings portrayed in the virtual tour, we drove on a gravel lane that cut through an uneven, less-than-healthy lawn. Patches of dirt spotted the acreage on either side. Tamarack trees bordered the lawn. No roses. No gardens. No cueball topiary.

Ahead, the largest metal shed I'd seen so far rose to mark the end of the drive. An open field beside it contained orange cones to guide parking. Several smaller buildings clustered around the shed. One stood out. A palatial Queen Anne style home done in wood with gables and gingerbread accents. The gardens bordering the home were better maintained than anything seen so far.

Several pickup trucks nosed up to the giant metal building. More sat parked in front of the house. A blazing red Ferrari nudged one of five garage doors.

"This looks more like gardening sheds for that Citadel of God campus we saw online. Are we in the wrong place?"

Andy rolled the rental to a stop in a spot near the side of the barn-like steel building.

"We need to find the admin office." Andy killed the engine. It had stopped raining, so we stepped out and locked the rental.

"I have a feeling we're about to be shown the way." I pointed.

A golf cart driven by a hefty young man wearing a blue polo shirt and khaki pants wheeled urgently toward us. Looking him over I felt self-conscious about my hair, which was overdue for a trim, and my black jeans and black t-shirt, which made me wary that the locals might misidentify me as a demon.

"Good morning!" He braked to a halt. "It's a blessed day!"

"It certainly is." Andy returned his good cheer.

"How can the Jim Newell Ministry be of service to you this fine day?" He displayed twin rows of perfect teeth.

"I'm Andrea Stewart. This is my husband, William. I don't really know how to ask this…" Andy prompted the young man.

"Peter. I'm called Peter."

I bit my lip.

"Peter, we're…we're here seeking help. May I?" She reached in her satchel and pulled out her phone. After opening the screen to a captured image, she held up the phone.

Suffer the little children to come to me.

Peter stared at it blankly and said nothing. Like showing a dog a bank statement.

"It's about our child, Peter."

Peter's eyes lit up. "Oh! You're here for a Prayer Circle!" He pointed at one of the smaller buildings. In any other setting it would have passed for a ranch-style home in a cookie-cutter subdivision. "That would be in the John the Baptist Meeting Hall."

"It's never the wrong time for prayer, Peter, but what we would really like to do is speak to Reverend Newell about his hospice for children."

Peter's blank stare returned. He reminded me of an animatronic that just got asked its favorite color. His programming hunted for the nearest search result.

"Then you're here to enroll your children in our Christ the Savior Bible School! You passed it on your way in. If you'll follow me, I can show you the way to Deacon Portman's office."

Andy stepped closer to the golf cart and placed her hand on the young man's forearm. Her move placed his eyes level with her chest.

"Peter, where can we find Reverend Newell?"

"Oh, that's not possible." Peter's response needed no search engine time. He struggled to look up at her. "The Reverend is engaged in the Lord's work. Today is rehearsal and run-through day. But I can provide you with passes to see him in person at Sunday's Celebration of His Kingdom. Would you prefer 9 a.m. or 11 a.m., or the evening celebration at 7 p.m.?" He lifted a small pouch from the golf cart's cupholder. The unzipped top of the pouch showed a roll of tickets, the kind they pass out for drinks and rides at the Essex Fall Festival. Andy shifted her hand to cover his hand holding the pouch.

"Peter," Andy drew closer, "you're obviously filled with the Holy Spirit. It glows in you. You're a young man dedicated to his job and his service to the Lord. May I share with you?" Andy didn't wait for a reply. "Our child has been diagnosed with an inoperable brain tumor—"

"Dear Lord, I will pray for her!"

"I know you will." Andy inched closer, "It would be ever so helpful if my husband and I could speak to Reverend Newell or someone about the wonderful hospice care he provides families like ours in this hour of need. Can you do that for us? In His name?"

"We don't have a hospital here, I'm so sorry to say."

"Not hospital. Hospice. Do you know what that is?"

Peter shook his head. Andy sighed, momentarily stumped.

I leaned over. "Peter, which building is the *Remington Religious Library?*"

His face brightened. This one, he knew the answer to.

"For the glory of God, that's going to be built right over there." He pointed. "You've seen the plans! Aren't they stupendous?"

Andy and I traded an enlightened glance. What we had seen online had been an expertly rendered CGI vision of the Citadel of God.

"To which we intend to contribute generously," Andy said, "just as soon as you can direct us to someone able to help us weather the terrible tragedy that is unfolding in our lives."

Peter's eyes had drifted again to the slice of cleavage Andy used to kill off half the neural connectors in his brain. He blinked as Andy's hand moved from his forearm to his shoulder.

"Will you help us, Peter? In His name?"

"Uh—maybe I—uh, I guess. Maybe I can take you over to the administration building and you can talk to someone there."

Andy beamed a smile at Peter, ruthlessly taking out a few more brain cells.

"Lead the way."

47

─────────

The administrative offices of the Jim Newell Ministry occupied the Queen Anne structure we'd seen on the way in. Set back from the gravel road, the building's wood siding and ornate trim looked freshly painted, the accents recently restored. Three stories tall and festooned with gables and a pair of turrets, it stood shoulder to shoulder with old oak, maple, and hickory hardwoods on a chemically enhanced green lawn. A single trellis nurtured a tangle of roses in front of the porch, the obvious inspiration for the digital fantasy of the Citadel of God that Andy and I had viewed online.

Peter shepherded us onto a loop driveway in front of the building. I braced myself for the inevitable encounter with the tough-guy gate guardian, but no one materialized to threaten us or chase us off the property or tell Andy she would never work in law enforcement again.

Peter cheerfully ushered us up the sidewalk, up three wooden steps, across the porch and through a beautiful front door filled with colored, leaded glass. The interior of the building matched the exterior, a showcase of woodwork. I saw dollar signs in the restoration and maintenance consumed by every varnished panel, sconce, and gleaming door.

"If you'll please wait right here, I'll fetch someone who can assist you," Peter said, waving a hand at a Victorian love seat upholstered in blue velvet. I preferred to stand, but Andy sat obediently and patted the cushion beside her. I did as she asked. She scooped up my hand and pressed it between hers on her lap. Peter hurried into a side room. When he returned, he smiled and said, "Miss Hampton will see you shortly. Have a blessed day!" He ducked out the front door and I heard his golf cart scoot away on the gravel.

We waited. We were not alone. Sliding wooden doors on either side of the foyer muted the sound of voices and the modern electronic ring of telephones. The house telegraphed movement on the second floor through creaks and groans, although I did not see anyone transit the landing at the top of the three-flight stairs ascending from the foyer.

I squirmed. The thin, buttoned cushions of the love seat were surprisingly uncomfortable. Built in an era when sight of a woman's ankle was considered scandalously arousing, it made sense to me that a piece of furniture designed for torture had been assigned to lovemaking.

My watch did us no favors. Each time I checked the hands barely moved. I wanted to lean close to Andy to ask how she intended to play this, but she clearly had something in mind, and I preferred not to expose my ignorance. Shortly after suppressing the impulse, I noticed the camera mounted in the upper corner of the room, aimed directly at us. I had no doubt that Andy registered it the moment we entered the building.

At one point a young woman hurried down the stairs and into the foyer. She stopped, startled by our presence. She blinked at us from behind wire-rimmed glasses.

"I'm sorry. Who are you waiting for?"

"Miss Hampton," Andy replied.

"Huh." Without a second glance, she darted across the foyer and disappeared into a side room.

The interminable duration of our wait was not my imagination. Twenty-five minutes passed before another young woman appeared. Like the first, she may have been in her mid-twenties, slender and fit, with long hair nicely styled. Both women, I noted, wore skirt and blouse combinations, with plenty of bare leg offered below a slightly high hemline.

The revered Reverend has a type, I mused.

"I'm so sorry to keep you waiting." She poured out compassion. "Who did you have an appointment to see?"

"We didn't have an appointment." Andy sustained a sweet tone that would have been a strain for me. "I hoped to meet with Reverend Newell."

"Oh, my. Reverend Newell has so many demands on his time. He would love to meet with every member of his flock, but there is so much to do in service to the Lord."

"The young man who brought us here, Peter, said we would be seeing Miss Hampton," I said.

"And may I ask the nature of your visit?"

Andy explained again, squeezing my hand at the appropriate moments to sell the sad story.

"I'm so sorry. Can I ask you to wait just a few minutes longer? Would you like some water?"

"We're fine," Andy said.

She disappeared almost as quickly as she appeared.

I reminded myself that we were on camera and tried to mirror the play-acting sigh that Andy issued.

Five more minutes passed before the girl appeared again clutching a clipboard to her bosom. She stopped in front of us and held out the clipboard. She lifted the top sheet and pointed at the second.

"This is an application for admission to The Newell Ministry Hospice for Children. Before you fill it out," she let the top sheet fall, "you must read and sign this Non-Disclosure Agreement. As I'm sure you are aware, this is a part of the ministry in which confidentiality is of supreme importance." She handed Andy the clipboard and pen.

"Miss," Andy handed them back, "you're moving a bit fast for us. Just glancing at this form, I can see it asks for a great deal of personal information. We're not quite sure this is the right path for our child. Isn't there someone we can talk to about the services you provide? The facilities? The location? Perhaps a tour? As you can imagine…" Andy swallowed theatrically "…this is a very difficult time for us."

The girl hesitated, caught by an unexpected reaction. She pressed the clipboard to her chest again.

"Uh…okay. Please, just a moment…" She hurried away.

Andy dabbed one eye with the back of her knuckle. She retook my hand and squeezed it.

"There, there, darling." I patted her hand. "It will be alright. I feel in my heart that we've come to the right place."

A flash and roll of Andy's eyes panned my performance.

A few more minutes passed during which I made plans to ask for a restroom, in which I intended to vanish and start prowling the place. In tandem with my growing frustration, I was getting hungry, which did not bolster my patience.

The girl appeared again. Andy stood, prompting me to do the same.

"I'm so sorry, but Miss Hampton is completely tied up. She said she understands your reticence regarding the paperwork, and she asked me to give you this." She handed Andy a sealed, plain white envelope. "Miss Hampton said you would find comfort in the materials inside, and guidance for your difficult decision. Can I offer you a visit to our Prayer Circle before you go?"

"We're comfortable seeking the Lord's guidance on our own, but thank you." Andy clutched the envelope to her chest. "Bless you."

"Have a blessed day."

A FEW MINUTES later Andy drove the rental back the way we came. I spoke as we reached the highway.

"Well, we're getting nowhere faster than usual."

Andy threw me a Cheshire Cat smile. "I wouldn't say that."

She reached into her satchel on the floorboards behind her legs and pulled out the envelope. She handed it to me.

"Open it."

I held it up to the windshield. Through the paper, I saw that the envelope contained a single business card. I tamped the card to one end and tore off the other, then fished out the card.

"Ramona Hampton, Executive Director, Newell Ministries. There's a phone number and an email address."

"Look at the back."

I flipped the card over to reveal the cause of Andy's satisfied smile.

"Hoopla Henry's. 9:00 p.m."

48

———————

Darkness descended early thanks to the heaving overcast that hung low in the sky. Rain fell intermittently all day, the damp remnants of the passing storm. Andy and I waited out the hours by driving into Mountain Home on Highway 5 and taking a long, late lunch at Skipper's Restaurant, a brick single story diner that satisfied our refueling needs. We passed the better part of the afternoon at the Donald W. Reynolds Library where Andy divided her time between her phone and her laptop while I found and started reading a biography of Chester Nimitz. At some point, around the time Nimitz arrived in a still-burning Pearl Harbor, I caught a catnap.

Andy researched Hoopla Henry's, a roadhouse, bar, dance hall set on a country road not too far from the Citadel of God, probably serving the same patrons, just on different nights of the week. She studied the layout and the roads around the bar via Google Maps. On the drive to our meeting with the Executive Director, Andy explained the building layout, noting entrances and exits that could be seen thanks to Google, and speculating about those not seen in the rear of the building. We traded theories about the card we'd been handed. Andy, always charitable, guessed that whoever watched us on the security camera connected her name and image to the fact that she was a police officer, suggesting that the viewer knew her pretenses were false, and that the card represented a desire to divulge information without being revealed as a source.

I was less trusting.

· · ·

AT 8:45 we pulled into parking that could have doubled as a used pickup truck lot. Vehicles that weren't pickups were SUVs, predominantly Jeeps. The only models that weren't trucks or SUVs were a set of Corvettes parked in twin handicap spots beside the entrance. I had a feeling that was considered a joke. Diamond raindrops coated all the sheet metal in the parking lot, reflecting red and blue neon from the Hoopla Henry's sign on a telephone pole near the road. In addition to lettering for the name, the neon rendered an animated cowboy who kicked up a booted heel every five seconds. A steady bass beat throbbed from the building's wooden walls.

Andy rolled slowly through the gravel lot. We were intentionally early. She parked at the fringe by backing into the last row in a spot with a view of the entrance.

"I don't like this place," I said. "Reminds me of that joint in Nebraska." It wasn't a pleasant memory.

"Limited possibilities. She's either already inside waiting for us. Or she's out here watching us right now. Or she hasn't arrived yet. If nothing changes and nine o'clock rolls around, we go in."

"As is?"

"Uh-huh. It's a public place. Probably the reason she picked it. Busy. Crowded. Noisy. Not someplace her co-workers frequent. We can scope it out and decide if it's best for you to…you know…"

"You think she's going to share some dirt on this hospice operation?"

Andy shrugged. She usually doesn't speculate.

"I guess we wait."

She looked at me from the driver's seat with an impish grin. "Want to make out?" For a moment I wasn't sure what I'd heard, but then she laughed. "Kidding! Keep your pants on, cowboy."

"I am surprised you didn't burst into flame at the Citadel of God, woman. You are the devil's spawn."

DURING THE NEXT fifteen minutes two more pickup trucks arrived, parked, and disembarked their passengers—couples who joined the party inside. One patron departed, tracking a serpentine path across the lot to his SUV and fumbling with his keys before gaining entrance. He drove away without hitting anything, but I know Andy bristled at having to watch a drunk take to the highway. Even out of her jurisdiction, I think she would have stopped the man, grabbed his keys, and thrown them into the weeds had we not been otherwise engaged.

A shiny new Dodge Ram crew cab with dual rear wheels pulled into the lot and followed the same slow path across the gravel as Andy. It stopped with its headlights glaring at us. There was no way to see whether the driver was a man or woman. Rain added glaze and reflections to our windshield. I felt stupidly vulnerable at eye level with the truck's front bumper until the truck turned as if to exit the lot. I dismissed the Dodge and took up watch of another set of headlights that pulled in, until I saw that the second vehicle was a full-sized Peterbilt dump truck—instantly launching a joke in my mind about the owner trying to one-up all the pickups in the lot.

The Dodge pickup stopped at the exit, then reversed. It backed into position in front of us. The driver's window hummed down. A woman turned her head and leaned out. She put her hand out and gestured for Andy to roll down her window.

"Follow me," she said, quickly leaning back in and raising her window.

Andy did the same and started the rental.

"I guess that's our mysterious contact." She dropped the car in gear and pulled out behind the pickup truck, which kicked up gravel as it accelerated out of Hoopla Henry's lot. So much for meeting in a noisy public place.

The Dodge hurried away, but if she planned to test Andy's pursuit skills, I gave her no chance. I tightened my seatbelt. Andy stomped on the pedal and asked the little Nissan for everything the four-cylinder engine had to offer. She kept pace with the truck's taillights.

"We need to start renting beefier vehicles," I said.

"Is anyone behind us?"

"What?"

"Is anyone following us?"

I twisted in my seat to watch the dark road play out in our wake. Hoopla Henry's neon sign floated above the ribbon of wet pavement. Undeveloped land spread on either side of the road, making Henry's shrinking neon moon the only light for at least a mile in either direction.

Andy navigated a curve. The sign slipped from view just as vehicle lights spread across the road from the roadhouse's parking lot exit.

"Somebody was pulling out, but I can't tell if they came this way or went the other way."

Andy held a two-handed grip on the wheel. The speedometer nudged seventy. She paced the pickup about a hundred yards back, letting spray from the dual rear wheels fly and dissipate. Even so, she switched on the wipers.

"I think you should be ready." I patted the BLASTER tucked in the pocket of a fleece vest I wore. I reached for it, but she added, "On second thought, don't hold that propeller thing in your hand. It looks too much like a weapon in the dark. Just be ready."

The road curved again. I questioned the wisdom of our speed on a road we didn't know. Andy riveted her focus on the back of the pickup, using its moves to telegraph twists in the road. The driver knew the road. I hoped.

I glanced at empty darkness behind us. No one followed.

The truck slowed. Andy braked. The truck cut sharply to the right. Andy followed, losing ground. She pushed the Nissan rental hard to catch up.

"She's not making this easy," I said.

Andy said nothing.

I turned to check our six again, but the road dipped and curved to the left, cutting off my view to the rear. We entered wooded terrain. Trees bereft of leaves loomed overhead looking skeletal in our headlight glow. The road weaved back and forth on smooth but narrow pavement, the kind of winding highway that roadster lovers chase on Sunday afternoons.

The absence of lights—any kind of lights—on either side of the road gnawed at me. We shot through dark terrain. We dipped and curved, then rose on a steady incline. As we crested a hill, I stole a look behind us and caught a fleeting glimpse of lights flickering through the trees half a mile back.

"We might have company."

"Hang on!" Andy stomped the brakes.

The pickup had abruptly decelerated. We caught up quickly, but before it became an issue, Hampton turned sharply right. The truck bobbed onto a single lane dirt track and passed through a fence row. Andy followed, slamming the front bumper into a hump in the process. Our headlights flashed skyward and back down.

"Jesus." I planted a firm hand on the dash. "Where the hell is she going?"

Andy didn't reply. She focused on chasing the truck on wet dirt and grass. I felt traction slip. She fought the steering as the Nissan's rear end slid from side to side.

Andy closed the gap with aggressive driving. Mud and spray spattered the rental. The wipers streaked the glass. Andy kept both hands firmly on the wheel, jerking it back and forth to counter the fishtailing rear end.

I pulled the BLASTER from my pocket and snapped the prop onto the shaft, then held it at the ready. I glanced up, mentally kicking myself for not checking this earlier. The car had a sunroof. I reached for the button but missed. Rugged ground caused the entire car to shake and shudder. Our speed seemed faster here than on the pavement, but it was an illusion. I caught a glimpse of the speedometer hovering just above forty.

Once more, the pickup made a hard right turn. Once more, Andy followed. It was a huge mistake. The effect was immediate. As if a giant hand had gripped the rear bumper, the Nissan became a plow on soft, dark earth. The engine fought and the front-wheel drive spun, but the car lost speed rapidly.

"Don't stop!" I knew exactly what would happen if we lost momentum. My teen years on the farm taught me that when you're sinking, the worst thing to do is stop. Keep moving, no matter where it takes you.

Andy tried. She twisted the wheel back and forth and rode the accelerator, but the car was not built to fight muddy earth. On whirring front wheels, we slowly ground to a halt. Andy deftly threw the shifter into reverse, but the lag caused by the automatic transmission robbed her of the ability to rock the vehicle backward. When reverse gear engaged, we bit into the dirt and sank deeper.

Andy stopped fighting.

"Dammit!" She smacked her palms on the wheel.

Through prisms of raindrops and streaks of mud on the windshield we watched the taillights of the pickup truck wiggle from side to side as it pulled steadily away in four-wheel drive. The truck surged ahead then curved left. It carved an arc in the dirt until it circled back. The headlights swept onto us. The vehicle stopped. The driver switched to her high beams, blinding us.

"I don't like this, Dee." I jabbed the sunroof button to gain an escape hatch. The plan formed in my mind. Grab Andy. Vanish. Squeeze out and fly. No. Squeeze out. Reach back. Grab Andy.

The sunroof opened six inches, then stopped.

"What the hell?" I reversed the switch and the sunroof closed. Hit it again. It opened. Stopped. "Dammit!"

We sat in near silence. The Nissan engine idled, daring us to put it in gear again and dig ourselves deeper into the mud.

Outside, vehicle doors thudded. Someone shouted. The words were muffled. Andy lowered her window.

"Detective Stewart! Hey! Step out of the car!"

Andy and I traded a glance. I said, "That voice…who is that?"

"I know who it is." It hit me the instant she said the name. "Fennick."

"Detective, please. Let's chat," Fennick called to us from behind the blinding truck headlights. "Just a chat. You wanted to speak to Ramona. She's here with me."

"Open your door," I commanded. I opened mine. "Give me your hand. We'll both go out this side." I held up the BLASTER to make the point.

Two sharp pops cut the air. Something metallic hit the front of the Nissan.

"Now, Detective!" Fennick shouted. "Show me your hands and get out of the car! Both of you!"

Andy glanced at the power unit. "Not yet. Put that away."

I slipped the BLASTER back in my pocket.

We both lifted our hands toward the windshield, then swung our legs out and climbed out of the car. Greasy dirt made the footing slick and uneven. Andy squinted. I held my left hand to shield my eyes from the headlights.

Two figures stood just beyond the glare, one on each side of the truck cab. In black silhouette against a black background, there was no chance of distinguishing which was Fennick, and which was Hampton. From their positioning on either side of the cab, I dismissed the idea of Hampton being present under duress.

Andy spoke calmly. "Hello, Desmond Fennick. Did you just shoot my rental car?"

"I hope you took the extra insurance."

"What are we doing here? Ms. Hampton, are you alright? Was there something you wanted to share with us?"

"Don't worry about Ramona, Detective," Fennick said. He muttered something neither of us could hear. Hampton climbed back in the pickup cab.

"Step out where I can see you," Andy said.

"And get my shoes all muddy? I don't think so. I want you to *very carefully* deposit that bag in the car. If you get creative, just know that my next shot goes through your husband's skull."

You can't shoot me if you can't see me, asshole. I closed an imagined grip on the imagined levers in my head. I planned the move. Duck down behind the door, vanish, then kick off as fast as possible. Fennick would be smart enough to know that a car door won't stop a bullet. The question was whether he would fire before I had time to launch.

Andy's mind reading kicked in because across the top of the Nissan she sent me the tiniest shake of the head. *Don't.* She lifted the strap over her head, hooked the strap on her open car door, then stepped aside.

"Hands back up where I can see them, please."

Andy complied.

Headlights crested the hill we had climbed. I counted four sets. They slowed, then one by one made the turn onto the dirt lane. The projector headlights flashed with each bump and bounce. Four more pickup trucks drove through the opening in the fence row and onto the dirt field. Like Hampton's, their four-wheel drive easily conquered the loose, muddy surface. Engines revving, they swung right, then curved left again to form up with two on each side of Hampton's Dodge.

A straggler with a bigger-sounding engine slowed and made the turn in from the road. It, too, bounced over the uneven ground toward us. The big vehicle made a heavy metal banging sound over the largest bumps.

"Friends of yours?" Andy asked.

"No, friends of yours. I did my homework, too, Detective. You're not very popular in certain circles. Some good old boys shot up your house last fall, so I hear. Sounds to me like you were lucky to get out of that alive."

"Lousy shots," I said. I sidestepped the open car door. If nothing else, I needed a clear path across the hood of the rental car. A dive to grab Andy might look so stupid that Fennick would not fire before I made us vanish.

"I guess," Fennick laughed. "Did you know that the Company W militia has chapters all around the country. I was pleasantly surprised to learn of a well-organized chapter right here in Mountain Home. Well-armed. Weekend drills. The whole schtick. I thought they might want to meet you. Word in their little coffee klatch is that you did some of their brethren harm over in Louisiana."

The four newcomers added their headlights to the glare. It grew impossible to see beyond the arc of light. I heard cab doors open and close but could make out nothing in the black beyond the lights.

The last vehicle joining the circle roared closer. Headlights backfilled the darkness and dimmed the shadows cast by the half-ring of pickups. I edged forward, closing the small distance between my legs and the car's right front fender.

"Dee." I spoke softly, hoping she would see the move and mirror it.

"That was some stacked bullshit back in Ithaca, Detective. I don't know when or how, but after you talked to Dr. Maxwell, I figured there was zero chance you were going anywhere but here. The folks at the airport confirmed it. Showing up at Jimmy's Citadel of God iced it. And now you've come all this way to have your Deep Throat moment. Turns out, this is as far as you go. Ramona and I are leaving, but your old friends will be sticking around. Seems they have a bone to pick with you."

Andy had not moved. Headlights from the last vehicle entering the field completed the circle. I assumed the intent was to block us in, until I heard the powerful engine behind gain RPM, hesitate for an upshift, then accelerate, growing louder and nearer.

Things happened fast.

Instead of stopping to seal our escape, the newcomer roared at us from behind.

"Dee!" I shouted, but she moved an instant ahead of me. She dove away from the car the moment the full-size Peterbilt that I'd seen at Hoopla Henry's plowed into the vehicle's rear end. Metal crunched and glass shattered. The dump truck rammed the Nissan forward. The open passenger door slammed shut, nearly hitting me.

Instead of diving away like Andy—

FWOOOMP!

—I vanished and shot upward on autopilot—tugged off my feet by a rigid core muscle running down my center and by a command from my subconscious. For a fraction of a second, I was unaware that I had vanished. Only that my perspective had changed.

Like a freight train passing under a bridge, the rental car and gravel truck roared forward. Hot exhaust from the truck's stacks buffeted me from below. Andy disappeared from my line of sight, stabbing sharp panic into my chest. An instant later, the empty box of the huge truck cleared. I spotted her prone on the dirt, twisting to see what had just happened.

The Peterbilt heaved left causing the rental to skid in the opposite direction off the truck's massive front bumper. The Nissan's front end slewed right. The truck bumper bit the rental's rear quarter, which tipped the car and sent it rolling into the grille of the parked Dodge, killing its headlights. The Nissan rolled up the grille and onto the hood. Metal screamed in protest. The rental crushed the Dodge windshield, hung there for a moment, then slid backward and crashed back to earth.

Without hesitating, the Peterbilt found a second victim. Headlights swung wildly through the air. The driver of the big truck clipped the leftmost pickup parked in the ark. The dump truck immediately heaved right and caved in the rear quarter of the next pickup in the line.

Frozen fifteen feet in the air, I watched the action across the beams of headlights that no longer blinded me. Men darted away from the two trucks that had been crushed. Several carried rifles. One flung his over his head before diving out of the marauding truck's path.

The Peterbilt driver upshifted, picking up speed. He cut behind the Dodge. A tight turn took him into the rear of the next pickup in the line. The severed bed of his victim spun off its chassis and skidded onto the dirt. The chassis jolted forward and then tipped when the dump truck's rear wheels caught the frame. The pickup did a slow roll onto its side, but not before the

Peterbilt slammed into the passenger side of the last pickup. It spun out of the way.

The big truck, still roaring at full power, bounded ahead, shaking the cab shell. He cut left, then circled back around the wreckage. He clipped the first pickup a second time, spinning it around. Wheeling tighter, he bore down on Andy, but before I could react, he turned and drove across the scars in the dirt where he had pushed the rental into the Dodge.

With jerks and grunts, the truck heaved to a sudden stop across the front of the Dodge. The lightweight cab jittered. Air brakes hissed.

The truck driver leaned across his front seat and threw open the passenger-side door and shouted at Andy. "Hampton! Get in!"

"Dee! Go! Go!" I shouted. I saw what she couldn't.

The men who had scrambled from the pickup trucks had run. They sprinted across a remarkable span of ground in an amazingly short span of time. A few staggered to a halt. One lifted his rifle.

Andy didn't wait. She scrambled up out of the dirt and climbed the cab steps. Even before she could enter, the driver threw the clutch and the truck leaped forward. Andy almost lost her grip. A hand flew out of the dark cab and pulled her in.

Hampton. *He thinks he rescued Hampton.*

Gears ground. The Peterbilt lurched forward, pumping up through low gear ratios.

The Dodge driver's door shot open.

The real Hampton tumbled out of the Dodge pickup. She screamed, staggered, and fell. I heard gunfire, the harsh crack of supersonic rounds in the air. Fennick's Company W friends had found their wits. Hampton sprawled in the mud and threw her arms over her head.

That truck driver thinks Hampton is the target, I thought.

Against every instinct that told me to hit the BLASTER and climb for altitude to clear the gunfire cutting the air, I dove. Full power. The BLASTER yanked me to the ground beside the Dodge cab. My feet hit, slid, and my knees folded into the mud. I collided with the woman pressing herself into the earth for protection. She cried in the dark, clutching her hands over her head.

I grabbed one arm and threw the levers in my head to the stops.

FWOOOMP!

The woman lying in the dirt vanished. I unfolded my legs and kicked hard against the ground, not just vertically, but on an angle that hurled us both in the direction of the gravel truck.

The cab lurched and jumped through the gears. The driver stomped the accelerator. The big engine roared. Pinging and plinking sounds came from the steel box behind the cab. At least one gunman of Company W took aim.

Hampton shrieked and fought. She clawed at the grip I had on her arm. She started to slip.

My angle shot me up and over the empty steel box. Clearing the rim, I let go of the woman for her own good. She reappeared and dropped. Her body made a dull gong sound when she hit the empty bottom of the dump box. As the truck lurched forward, she slid backward and collided with the tailgate.

More pinging. More gunshots. Either up or down—I needed to decide and fast.

Fwooomp!

I reappeared and let gravity grab me. From ten feet above the steel floor of the dump box, I dropped. My feet hit. A jolt shot up through my body. I stumbled and fell on the moving box bed. Not the worst idea. I heard bullets hit the steel side of the dump box. I dropped hard and hit the floor with my arms and chin. Stars burst into my vision. The bruised and sore left side of my face took a fresh shot when I bounced.

The driver roared up through the gears. Acceleration sent me sliding against the tailgate where Hampton's huddling lump screamed.

Gunfire cut the night. Bullets banged against the steel box. I wasn't sure if they were stopped or if they cut through the steel and sliced the air just above my head. Either way, I pressed myself down as hard as I could.

A new sound joined the angry roar of the engine. Hydraulic whine accompanied a sharp lurch by the box floor. I instantly understood what was happening.

Turning away from the mayhem toward the lane leading into the field, the driver of the truck hit the hydraulic lift to raise the cargo box, turning it into a bulletproof shield for the cab. Not so much for Hampton and me. A hydraulic ram pushed the box upward as if disgorging a load of gravel or dirt.

Hampton had not stopped screaming. I threw my arms around the woman and pressed her to the steel floor that continued to rise. The tailgate stood between us and bullets arriving now in steady bangs and pings. Most of the shots sliced the air above us, aimed at the truck cab now protected by the box floor. Was it enough? Would the fire penetrate? How thick was the tailgate that protected Hampton and me? I had no idea. I squeezed the woman and tried to make us both as flat as possible. The truck accelerated, pounding across the rough ground. The entire truck bed shook and thundered.

Distance eventually diminished the frequency of bullet strikes. The box reached its maximum height. The angle threw Hampton and me against the locked tailgate. I prayed nothing would release the tailgate or both of us would flip us out and onto the ground.

Well beyond the point at which the gunfire stopped, the driver continued to accelerate. The truck thundered over rough ground with the truck box at full tilt. I felt a sharp turn and a bone-jarring jolt when he hit the highway. I feared the high center of gravity might tip the truck. The tires skidded but the vehicle remained stable. It wasn't fast. On smooth pavement, he rammed his way up through the gears.

Eventually, he remembered the shield he had thrown up. The truck box suddenly jolted and dropped, slamming back down, giving my bones a crack.

Wind swirled in the truck bed. We roared down the highway.

"HEY, IT'S ME." I spoke into my phone.

"Where are you?" Andy cried out.

"Right behind you. I'm in the box of this monstrosity."

No sooner did I say it than the driver hit the brakes. The rear wheels locked. Tires skidded and shrieked. The truck jittered to a hard stop.

The driver's door opened. I rose on watery legs and walked to the left side of the truck box. I leaned over and saw a large man back awkwardly out of the cab and climb down. Reaching the pavement, he backed away holding his hands in the air.

Too high to jump down, I cast a glance at Hampton. The woman lay curled in a terrified knot on the truck box floor. She would keep.

Fwooomp!

I gripped the side of the box and levered myself over. When my feet hit the pavement—

Fwooomp!

—I reappeared. The man with his hands in the air startled, but kept his eyes on Andy, who now climbed down from the driver's seat holding her Glock with a bead on the man's face. Andy descended to the pavement and saw me. Without taking her eyes from the driver she asked, "Are you okay? Are you hit?"

"I'm good. You?"

"Yeah."

The large man who had driven a matching beast of a truck to our rescue glared at Andy. He looked angry and powerful enough to make his anger felt. Tall, with corded muscles under a tight shirt, his head was dark and narrow, adorned with a rough beard. Near-black eyes still seemed to have a light of their own, even in the darkness.

"Where's Hampton?" he demanded in a guttural bass register. "If you're not Hampton, where is she?"

"Who the hell is this?" I asked.

Andy didn't answer me. Instead, she said, "Reuben Calbert, you're under arrest."

49

"The hell I am. Where's Ramona Hampton?"

"The hell I will shoot you. Hands behind your head."

"No." Calbert slowly lowered his hands to his side. "Shoot me."

Andy adjusted her professional two-handed weapon grip and spread her feet to stabilize her stance. Calbert glanced up and down, assessing her.

"Do it. Or else get out of my way. I'm going back to get Ramona Hampton."

He took a step.

Andy took an equal step backward. "I'm looking for your daughter, Mr. Calbert." He stopped. He looked at Andy, then looked me over for the first time.

"So?"

"So, half the cops in two states are looking for you. I'm looking for your daughter."

"That doesn't make you my friend. Get outta my way." He took another step. Andy matched him, keeping her distance.

"Your daughter was in a drug trial, yes? An Amphitriton drug trial to treat her cancer, correct?"

"What would you know about it? Are you really a cop? Or some goddamned reporter?"

"Amphitriton dropped her from the trial. They cut her off from the medicine they're testing. Medicine that could save her. Medicine they're about to make billions with."

Hard cords rose in Calbert's thick neck. A vein snaked under the skin in the center of his forehead. Menace radiated from him like over-applied cologne. I didn't think making this man angrier was wise.

I stepped closer to Andy. Good intentions or not, Andy could easily find herself in his path. I made a guess that it would take more than one shot to stop him.

"My name is Detective Andrea Stewart. I'm with the Essex Police Department in Essex, Wisconsin. My badge is in my bag."

Andy had her bag at her side again. I wondered how she managed to pull it from our now crumpled rental car.

"What do I care? You're not arresting me. You're not stopping me. I'm going back to find that bitch Hampton."

"Because she knows where your daughter is," I said. Much louder, I called out toward the high side of the truck box, "Don't you Ms. Hampton?"

50

Andy insisted that we put some miles between us and the demolition derby Calbert had just created, citing equal chances that reinforcements or law enforcement might have been called. I volunteered to climb back in the truck box and keep Ramona Hampton company. Andy said she would ride in the cab with Calbert. My wife, always smarter than me, gave me her weapon and told Calbert that he now had no reason to try and overpower her. His best interest, she reminded him, was in not getting caught before he found his daughter.

"I thought you already caught me."

"I told you. I'm not interested in you. Besides. No jurisdiction."

It seemed to do the trick.

I tried sitting down in the truck box near Ramona Hampton. I thought it might be less menacing. She was a mess. Covered in mud and nearly catatonic, she backed into a corner and clutched her knees. Dressed in a business suit, she was a woman of medium build, light brown shoulder-length hair (now covered in mud and plastered against one side of her face) and features that were probably cute in the light of day. I put her age at thirty, max. Another of the Reverend Jim Newell's cookie-cutter types. She dressed the Executive Director part that her business card listed, except for being terrified, which was why I thought sitting down near her would have a calming effect.

I couldn't sustain it. The suspension for the rear wheels had been designed to adjust to tonnage, not passenger comfort. The box slammed and banged over each seam in the road. Jolts transmitted themselves up through my bones, reminding me of my once broken pelvis, and reaching into the bruised side of my face and eye. I couldn't take it. I had to stand.

This caused the woman to cringe and shrink away from me. It didn't help that I had Andy's gun in my hand and that the truck cab had yellow marker lights which gave everything a ghoulish tint.

Wind swirled in the box as we drove. I made no effort to understand our route. Andy had Calbert make seemingly random turns.

Eventually, we rolled onto another unpaved lane and through some trees. Calbert brought the truck to a jerky stop in a wooded area beside a small river. Picnic tables spaced out on wet grass identified the spot as a small park. Calbert brought the beast to a halt with a final hiss of the air brakes. He killed the clattering diesel engine and switched to parking lights. Against what had been the truck's steady roar, the silence became as thick as the humid air.

I contemplated the question of getting the woman over the high steel sides of the truck box and made a quick decision.

"Close your eyes." I waved the gun without pointing it at her. She shuddered and squeezed her eyes shut. I grabbed her upper arm. She flinched but didn't fight.

Fwooomp!

I made us both vanish, then tucked Andy's gun in my belt and used my free hand to grip the rim of the truck box. Up and over. I tugged us down onto the ground behind the truck. My feet landed.

Fwooomp!

Practice makes perfect. I planted my feet firmly with no trouble. I completely forgot that Hampton had no experience with this. Because she was still curled in a knot, she dropped to the ground when she reappeared. She cried out and sprawled just as Andy rounded the back of the truck.

"Will! What did you do?" She darted to the woman's aid.

"Nothing. It was a little awkward getting down, is all."

I wasn't Hampton's worst problem. She looked up and blanched at the sight of Calbert, who joined us.

"Please! Help me!" She pointed and tried to scramble away. "He threatened to kill me!"

"It wasn't a threat," Calbert said calmly.

"No one is going to kill you." Andy grabbed the woman's hands. "Listen to me. I'm a police officer. I'm here to protect you. No one is going to harm you."

Hampton diverted her wide-eyed stare from Calbert to Andy, from terror to hope. Andy pulled her badge from her bag and held it up in the taillight glow.

"See? You have my word. He will not harm you." She tucked away the badge then held out her hand to me. I surrendered her weapon. "See? I'm armed and dangerous. I will protect you."

Calbert loomed over them. "Where's my daughter, bitch?"

Andy shot a flat hand up at him along with a sharp look that had more stopping power than her nine-millimeter handgun. He froze.

To Hampton, Andy spoke in a soft, solicitous voice. "Let's get you up off the ground, ma'am. Come with me." I helped Andy lift the woman to her feet. We guided her to a picnic table. In the dim amber glow of the truck's parking lights, Andy knelt in front of her and brushed dried mud from the side of her face.

I walked back toward Calbert to give the women privacy and do what I could to keep the man away. Close up, he wasn't Tom Ceeves' size, but he had an inch or two on me and there was no questioning the muscle content of his body mass. In a close-fitting t-shirt, the man looked like a movie superhero. His narrow face matched the width of his thick neck. The nose that looked broken to me in Andy's mug shot was even worse in person. Thick black eyebrows shaded dark eyes in deep sockets. He wore a short, rough beard. I caught a deeper tint to his skin, a man who worked in the sun. Whether his behavior had earned it or not, the man wore the Bad Guy label like team apparel.

Thankfully, he made no move toward the women. Nor did he attempt to speak to me. He stared at Hampton.

"Do you want some water?" Andy asked Ramona Hampton.

"I want to go home," the woman replied in a tiny voice. "I didn't want any of this."

I leaned toward Calbert and asked, "Got any water in that cab?"

"How the hell would I know? The truck is stolen."

"Why don't you go and look. And see if there are any rags or some cloth you can take down by that river and soak for her to wash with."

Calbert glared at me. It was not comfortable. Nevertheless, he moved away in the darkness. When he had gone, I let go of the breath I held, thinking I'd look like a raccoon if the man decided to pop me in the other eye.

Andy picked dirt and mud from the woman's hair. "Ms. Hampton, why did you send me your business card? Why did you set up a meeting tonight?"

"He told me to."

"Fennick?"

"Who?"

"The man with you."

Hampton shook her head. "I don't know who that man is. I never saw him before he got in my truck tonight."

"Then who? Who told you to set up a meeting with me?"

The darkness and her bowed head obscured her face. I could not read her expression. She took a moment before answering.

"Reverend Jim."

"Personally?"

Her head bobbed. Andy lifted herself to the bench beside Hampton and put an arm around her shoulder.

"Can you walk me through it? Can you tell me everything leading up to…up to now?"

"It's Detective Stewart? They said your name was Stewart."

"Yes. Call me Andrea."

"Are you religious, Andrea? Do you believe in our savior, the Lord Jesus?"

"I sing in the church choir, Ramona. Every Sunday. Well…I had to miss last Sunday."

"He forgives you."

"And you. He forgives us all. Tell me."

Calbert materialized out of the darkness beside me. He held out a plastic bottle of Ice Mountain water and a dripping flannel shirt that he had soaked. I took both and gave them to Andy who dispensed the water and used the shirt to wipe more dirt from the woman's face.

"That man there. He called. Over and over. He threatened me, my staff. He said we had his daughter. We don't. I have nothing to do with the hospice—"

"Bullshit!" Calbert barked. "My ex told me you were the one in charge."

Andy fired a warning glare at Calbert.

Hampton continued. "I have nothing to do with the hospice. No one does. No one at the ministry. Not for over a year. It's been over a year since the former director transferred. We were told it had been closed."

"Liar! You're a goddamned liar!" Calbert snapped and stepped off. Hampton cringed. Andy stood and charged across the grass to the back of the truck. She intercepted Calbert. He towered a full head above her and came close to three times her weight, yet she jabbed a finger into the center of his chest that stopped him in his tracks. Through gritted teeth she all but hissed at him.

"Get—your—act—together!" She drove her finger in with each word. Calbert backed away. She followed. "Do you want to find your daughter or not? Yes or no."

Calbert didn't speak but heaved a loaded breath that answered in the affirmative. Andy jabbed him one more time.

"Now you either shut up and let me talk to her, or I will handcuff you to the front bumper of this truck. Got it?"

Calbert nodded. As Andy stalked back to the table and sat down, Calbert looked at me. I pointed at the bruise on my face and my swollen eye socket.

"She'll do it."

Andy returned to Hampton.

"The hospice. You say it closed?"

"That's what we were told. It was always a very private, very personal part of Reverend Jim's ministry. His own son died of cancer you know. When the boy was just eight. They said Mr. Remington's new medicine and the blessings it brought ended the need for hospice care for those poor suffering children."

"Are you sure it closed?"

"I don't know. I don't know anything about it. When he called," she pointed at Calbert, "he said that his little girl was in our care—we just didn't know how to answer. None of us at the ministry knew anything about his daughter. We said so. We answered him honestly. *We did!*" She spoke the last two words directly to Calbert.

"What about today? When I came calling?"

"It was…unusual…someone else asking in just a week. We went to Reverend Jim for guidance. That's what kept you waiting. We asked Reverend Jim. He—he—I don't know."

"He didn't confirm that it was closed, did he."

"He instructed me to give you that card. He said he would meet you personally, and that he would pray with you. But it was best done off campus."

"Why didn't he come tonight?"

"I don't know. He said he would. But that other man arrived at the office this evening and said he was going with me. I didn't want to go. But he said Reverend Jim sent him and that it was important for me to meet with you and that Reverend Jim would join us. The man—Fennick—said Reverend Jim wanted me to follow his instructions to the letter. That's all I know. I didn't know any of that was going to happen. *Those men with guns—I had no idea!*" She clutched Andy's hand. "*You have to believe me!*"

Andy stroked the woman's hand and arm. "It's alright. It's alright."

Tears came. Ramona Hampton cried in the darkness. Her body shook.

"I—d-don't know—anything abuh-about—your daughter, sir!" She stammered through an emotional downpour.

Calbert lifted one arm and ran his thick fingers through dark hair. He stared at his feet. I expected violence, but he looked like a weary man, a man who had run out of ideas. For all his size and power, something deflated.

Andy called out to Calbert. "Reuben."

He turned his head toward her.

"Reuben, I came here to find your daughter. To find Gabby. I mean that. But you have to turn yourself in."

"No."

"This has to end. Turning yourself in won't stop me. I won't stop looking. And I can get help."

"No."

Andy shifted a long look to me, transmitting frustration tinged with sadness.

Hampton took the flannel shirt from Andy and pressed it to her face, wiping away tears and dirt. She folded a corner over her nose and blew noisily.

"If—if you—d-don't believe me—just go there."

All three of us stared at her.

"Wait, Ramona, what did you say?" Andy asked.

She blew her nose again and gathered herself. She cleared her throat.

"The Healing Center. I'll show you where to find it."

51

M y flight bag, two overnight bags, and a plastic garbage bag of dirty laundry remained inside the crushed trunk of the Nissan rental. Problem.

The cab of the stolen Peterbilt had bucket seats for a driver and a passenger, and we were a party of four. Problem.

We were dirty, tired, and hurt, and fifteen miles from the site of the Jim Newell Ministries Hospice for Children—according to Ramona Hampton—who was justifiably capable of claiming she'd had been kidnapped. Problem.

And I'd had nothing to eat since grabbing a Reuben sandwich at lunch. The irony was not lost on me.

Andy told Calbert to take a walk. She informed him that she would get the hospice information from Hampton.

"To hell with that!"

"Fine. Then I'm calling 9-1-1 and we'll get this sorted out with the county sheriff."

"You know I can take all three of you," Calbert said. He wasn't wrong.

"Not before I shoot you," Andy replied. "Which gets none of us any closer to your daughter. Take a walk and catch your breath, Reuben."

Calbert hovered on the brink—of what, I wasn't sure. I tensed and prepared to vanish. After a few seconds, he turned away and muttered to me, "Tell me you're not married to this woman."

"She insisted."

He stomped off toward the river.

We huddled over maps on Andy's phone. Hampton reeled out directions. Andy located something called Bickler Beach. Hampton pointed and said that it had once been a camp, and that the Reverend Jim Newell purchased it and converted it into a place of comfort and closure for families with children in the last stages of terminal cancer. Andy marked the map point and gestured for me to follow her out of Hampton's earshot.

"I don't want to take her with us," Andy said quietly.

"You sure? She might be helpful. The place could be locked up, gated, who knows? She could pave the way at this crazy hour."

"No. We are on the wrong side of an abduction with her."

"Maybe. Or she's lying to cover up the fact that she led us to what was supposed to be your execution."

"That was Fennick, and I assume Remington and his pastor pal. Believe me, they are all on my list. I plan to reach out to Leslie about them, and to let her know what the patriots of Company W are up to here in Arkansas. It didn't take much to get them out for an evening of committing murder."

"You think Remington is partnering with the militia idiots?"

"Honestly? No. I think Fennick is a ruthless opportunist. And I believe him when he says he did his homework on me. Sharp guy that he is, he saw a way to dispose of a problem without having to handle it himself. What does he care if a bunch of racist gun nuts end up doing life for my murder?"

"But why?"

"He wants me out of the picture because we're obviously tugging a string he doesn't want pulled with a billion-dollar IPO on the line."

"Not real bright of him to bring a witness." I said gestured at Hampton.

Andy squinted at her. "Yeah…that's a good point. I've been wondering about that. I think he needed her because he couldn't show his face at Hoopla Henry's or we would have tipped to him. He needed a buffer, someone to get us out to that field."

"You think she was in on it? I mean—in on *all of it?*"

"Ninety-ten against. I have a feeling Fennick did not plan on letting Ms. Hampton see the dawn. Something to blame on me. Maybe shooting her with my weapon after I'm down."

"Another good reason to take her with us."

"No." Andy folded her arms across her chest. "No, Will, the situation is too volatile with Calbert. If we get in a tight spot, there's no predicting what either of them might do. I'm ninety percent certain she's innocent and was being used, but if I'm wrong and we take her with us, we have a whole new problem."

"We can't leave her here."

"Why not?" Andy looked around. "From what I saw coming in, the nearest residence is half a mile down the road. In the time it takes her to reach help and a phone, if she is on the devil's side of all this, we'll already be there. It's dark. She's dirty and wet. She might not get anyone to open a door."

"Wow. That's harsh."

"I'm sorry. The alternative could be a lot worse. We might not be done with Fennick and his militia friends. And if we see them again, I don't think we can count on the bulldozer cavalry to come to the rescue. Next chance they get, we won't hear the shot that kills us."

I turned to her in the dark and slid my arms around her waist. I pulled her close, caked mud and all. She returned the squeeze in kind.

"You're just a ball of good cheer tonight, Dee."

<h1 style="text-align:center">52</h1>

Andy sat down beside Ramona Hampton. She pressed a card into her hands. The drizzle in the air caused a wet drop to fall from the woman's nose when she looked down at it.

"That's my card. I'm going to have a very frank conversation with you. Some men tried to kill me and my husband tonight. You led us to them—"

"No, no, please! I had no idea—"

"Ramona, listen to me. I can choose to believe you on a human level, but as a police officer, I cannot afford to be deceived by you. Do you understand? My actions must account for the possibility that you were part of that ambush. I pray you weren't—"

"I wasn't! I swear!"

"Trust. But verify. Okay? I trust you. But I'm going to take steps to be sure. We're leaving. And we're leaving you here. Do you have a phone?"

"It's in my purse, in my truck. *Why are you leaving me here?*"

"It's safer. If you go back to the road and go to the right, about half a mile back there were houses. It's the middle of the night, but someone may let you in. What you do from that point is between you and your Savior. I will pray for you. Okay? When you get there, you can call for help. You can call the police. Or you can call Mr. Fennick and try to finish what he started."

"I would never—!"

"I hope that's true." Andy stood up. "I sincerely hope that's true. One more thing, Ramona. If you're a part of all this, you may think you're safe with your boss and Fennick—but you're not. If they don't harm you, I will still come for you. If you're not part of this, then you're a witness to what you saw in that field and I will expect you to testify. Fennick and Newell will not let that lie. Do you understand what I'm saying? It's not safe for you to go back to The Reverend or the ministry."

She either belonged on a stage, or the terror that washed across her face was genuine. "*What do I do?*"

"Go somewhere no one knows about. No one. Not family. Not friends. *No one.* No matter how much you trust them."

"For how long?"

"Until this is over."

Andy turned and gestured at the truck cab. Calbert went to the driver's side. I joined Andy on the passenger side.

"Detective!" Hampton called out. Andy paused. "I think I'll wait here. Until dawn. Until it's light. I think that will be safer."

Andy met her gaze and tipped her a gentle nod. Then to me she said, "Let's go."

53

"It's time for you to talk to me, Reuben." Andy adjusted herself on my lap in the high passenger seat of the truck cab. I watched over the long, muscular hood as Calbert shifted up through the gears. The ride in the cab surpassed the ride in the dump box, but not by much. I appreciated the warm dry air coming from the cab vents.

"Nope." He gripped the wheel and stared out the windshield.

"Your wife has a restraining order against you. I saw the court order. You're not allowed anywhere near your wife or daughter."

"Ex-wife."

"Why?"

Calbert said nothing. Andy matched his silence. He pretended to ignore her, but the way he flexed his grip on the wheel said she was winning. He caved abruptly.

"You know what, lady? I don't know you. You ask me why? Fuck that. Why do *you* want to find my daughter? It's time for you to talk to me. *Why do you want to find my daughter?*"

Andy settled in my arms. She looked at Calbert with something approaching serenity. I waited, more than a little curious about this myself.

"A few days ago, I knocked on a door and a woman opened it and put a shotgun in my face and pulled the trigger."

Calbert darted a glance at Andy.

"No shit?"

"No shit. The gun or the shell failed to fire. So, she pulled the trigger on the other barrel. That one went off. My Chief of Police got a hand on the weapon in time to deflect the shot."

Calbert stared straight ahead. We rolled down a long straight stretch of two-lane blacktop.

"All I have to do is close my eyes, Reuben, and I can see the barrels of that over-under right in my face. My hearing has had tinnitus ever since."

"That's a bitch…but that don't tell me nothing about you wanting to find my daughter."

"I was there," I said, "the day you took an ax to Remington's jet. I had just landed. You made me sit on the taxiway for close to half an hour for that stunt."

"Asshole deserved it. You still ain't telling me squat here."

"Well," I said, "you might have gotten lucky that day—because of me being there. I told my wife about it, and she thinks there's a chance we can help your girl. A chance. That's all I'm saying. And if we do, all the credit goes to my wife here. Because—" Dammit. A knot formed in my throat. I tried to clear it. "Because right now, don't ask why, the way she sees to getting that crazy bitch and her shotgun out of her head is by finding and helping your little girl."

Calbert rolled his eyes. "That is the dumbest thing I ever heard."

Andy shrugged and broke out a thin smile, which caused me to give her a squeeze.

Andy looked down at her phone, then at the road ahead. "There's a junction about a mile up. Silver Bay Road. Take that to the left. The point is, Reuben, you're going to have to trust us."

"All I want is for that sonofabitch Remington to give Gabby his goddamned medicine."

"That's all we want, too," Andy lied.

"I seen the stories online," Calbert said. "They all say he's got something that works. That it's worth billions. I don't give a shit if he makes billions or trillions. He said he was giving it to her but that was a lie. He was using her in his whatchacallit group—"

"Control group," Andy said.

"Whatever. It was wrong. She's sick and he has a cure and he refused to give it to her."

Andy gave him a minute to cool off before she asked, "What does the Newell Ministry have to do with it?"

"My goddamned ex has been thumping Newell's Bible for years. She watches all his sermons on the YouTube. When Gabby got dropped from the treatment program, Remington told Shelly he had an in with the famous preacher. He's the one got Newell to do prayer circles for Gabby. And then Newell convinced Shelly that God would fix Gabby, and he offered to put her in his damned hospital thing."

"Hospice. Remington brought Newell into the picture?"

"Yeah, and that was all it took. My ex is so damned star-struck by the guy and she's all about the power of prayer and the Citadel of God. Christ! Half her paycheck goes into that place!" Calbert slammed a fist on the wheel. "She thinks giving them money turbocharges her prayers."

"I need to understand, Reuben. You're saying that Gabby was in a treatment program for the new medicine, and you thought you were getting it, but when Gabby didn't respond, they told you she was in the Control Group?"

"Fuckers used her like a lab rat."

"And when she presented worse and worse, they refused to switch her over? Instead, Remington introduced your wife to Newell."

"Bastard."

"When was she moved to the hospice?"

"Couple days before I hammered the bastard's jet. My ex just up and took her. They don't let me see her. I couldn't find out nothing. I kept calling the hospital and all I got was that HIPAA bullshit from the nurses on account'a they knew about the restraining order. So, I went there. Nobody would tell me nothing. I called everybody. All the way up to Remington, 'cept you can never get past his secretaries. All I wanted was to know that she was getting the meds. That's all I cared about."

"Turn here." Andy pointed. Calbert downshifted and slowed the beast. "If nobody's telling you anything, how did you find out about Newell and the hospice?"

"I seen a post on Facebook from Shelly, my ex-. She was all ga-ga over meeting the preacher. Newell. I musta called Shelly a hunnert times before she picked up. She finally told me. And she was proud. She said that the Lord had our girl in his arms. She said Newell put his hands on our daughter. He said he could feel the cancer melt right out of her. I told her to make Remington give Gabby the medicine, but Newell said God's medicine was more powerful."

Calbert made the turn onto a narrow road that wound through scrubby woodland. He upshifted through the truck's gears.

"How did you find out about Hampton?"

"Shelly. We got to screaming at each other on the phone—that's mostly where we end up these days—and she threw that whole Newell Ministry crap in my face and told me she was working with their top people—organizing more prayer chains or circles or some nonsense. I called it all BS and she gave me Hampton's name and told me to call her if I didn't believe it."

"How did you end up in that field tonight?"

"Nobody at Newell's place would tell me diddly. I finally decided to go there and rattle some cages. 'Course, getting there got a little harder in the last few days."

"You mean, being wanted by the law and all?" I asked.

"Kinda puts a damper on getting around. I got most of the way here but ran into a statie at a truck stop in Springfield. Had to rough him up a little. And then I saw an opportunity to borrow this truck. It was in a maintenance yard next to the truck stop."

"You hot-wired this? I've always wanted to know how that works," I said.

"You got me. I walked in the office and told them I needed to get my log sheets outta the stash box. They handed me the keys."

I had to admit, his move was slick. Stolen but not noticeably gone, a work truck like this would be unlikely to attract the attention of law enforcement despite its size.

"And Hampton?" Andy prompted him.

"I waited for her to leave tonight. Simple as that."

"How did you know it was her?"

"Staff picture. On the website. I parked at the road and watched. She drove out with that other fella. I followed her. Figured I could catch up with her somewhere and have a few words. When I got to that field you were all silhouetted in those lights. I thought you was her—and it didn't seem like you were among friends. I needed to talk to you—her—before they got to their business. Simple as that." Calbert pitched a sharp glance at Andy. "You gonna tell me why there was a bunch of guys in that field shooting at a cop?"

"Thought you'd never ask. They're under the mistaken impression that I did them wrong."

"No shit. If I was you, I'd see about straightening that out."

He downshifted. A series of snaking curves called for a reduction in speed.

"I still don't get it," I said. "If your daughter wasn't getting the Amphitriton treatment and she was getting worse, why didn't they just switch her over?"

"All I know," Calbert said, "is that I need to find my baby girl and get her that medicine. I'll go through anybody that says otherwise."

54

A small wooden sign by the road read Bickley Beach. The sign portrayed a faded tableau of sunbathers. Nothing else identified the property as belonging to the Newell Ministries. Calbert maneuvered the big truck onto a gravel driveway and horsed it back up through the gears. Behind the cab, the exhaust stacks thundered. There was nothing stealthy about the vehicle. Our arrival was well announced.

Broad weedy fields spread on either side of the long driveway. Decaying soccer goals and a leaning baseball backstop confirmed Hampton's description of the property as a former summer camp, but it may have been decades since teams gathered on the fields.

The driveway passed into a stand of tall oaks. A light appeared ahead. Beyond it, I caught the glitter of water I took for a branch of Bull Shoals. Tucked under the trees were small cabins, uniformly dark. Calbert aimed for a long, low building dead ahead. A single vehicle nudged the building beside a set of steps that rose to a rustic porch.

Calbert focused on the vehicle. "That's my truck. Dammit! That's my truck!"

The black truck was a crew cab Ford F-250 on a jacked-up suspension. Like people with dogs, the muscular vehicle matched its owner. The front wore a heavy brush bar. The roof was topped with an extravagant rack of lights. Rust chewed the fringes of the tailgate and rear fenders. The truck looked rugged and well-worn.

"Stop." Andy tensed. Calbert hit the brakes. "Did your ex drive the truck here?"

"Hell, no. Shelly wouldn't know how, an' she doesn't have keys." Calbert opened his door.

"Wait!" Calbert ignored her. Andy looked up and down the length of the single-story building. Interior lights glowed at the center. The ends were dark. There was no sign of movement, but at this hour I didn't expect to see any. If anyone violated the peace and quiet, it was us. We stood a good chance of scaring the crap out of someone.

Calbert climbed down.

"Listen to me Reuben," Andy snapped. "You follow my lead here. Got it? I won't have you tearing into this place like a criminal."

"Hell with that."

"Reuben! Do you want to scare your daughter? Because charging in there and creating a scene is going to do more harm than good."

About to close the driver's door, he hesitated. Andy didn't wait to advance her argument. She popped open the passenger door and jumped from the cab, landing lightly on her feet. I saw her slip her hand into the satchel on her hip and rest it there.

"Follow me," she said without taking a vote.

I hopped down and fell in step behind her. Calbert didn't. He hurried to his parked pickup truck. He opened the door and leaned in, then reached for and pulled something from the dash. Keys jangled in his hand. He dropped them in his pocket and closed the door.

Andy climbed the steps to a broad porch. Old boards creaked. I understood the idea of a camp maintaining a rustic appeal, but as a medical facility the ambiance inspired zero confidence. The building was run down at the edges. Cedar siding showed signs of dry rot. The steps, porch, and porch rails needed refinishing. A metal gutter on the edge of the roof sprouted weeds, and moss frosted the shingles. Light came from a bare bulb in a fixture missing its housing. Spider webs draped the area around the bulb, trapping an abundance of food for the half dozen housekeeping spiders I counted. More flying spider food circled the bare bulb.

We crossed the porch and entered through a double screen door. Reuben's footsteps landed heavily behind mine. Andy pulled her hand from her bag and lifted her weapon to eye level in a two-handed grip.

"Stay behind me."

I saw why. Broken glass lay on a concrete floor inside the building. The heavier interior doors had been swung open and remained so.

We entered a bare bones space that had once been a dining hall or an activity space on rainy days. To our left, a counter fronted two offices, trying hard to look like a reception desk. The offices backing the counter were small rooms with a single glass panel beside an office door. To our right, a partition had been erected to shield the makeshift lobby from the long dining hall.

Andy saw the body first. She bolted ahead and cut around the end of the counter, quickly dropping to her knees. I followed and watched her touch one hand to the side of the neck of a man facedown on the concrete. I didn't need to guess that Andy failed to find a pulse. A gaping bloody hole in the center of the man's back said there were no vitals to be taken.

Reuben marched past Andy and shouted. "Gabby! GABBY!"

He turned left into a hallway just beyond the reception counter and disappeared, calling out his daughter's name.

I thought Andy might pursue him to get him to shut up, but she rose slowly and stepped over the body. She cleared the corners and cautiously poked her head into the first office. It must have been empty because she moved quickly past it to the second.

"Another one." I started toward her, but she waved me to stay back. "Don't touch anything, Will."

I held up my hands in compliance. Over Andy's shoulder I saw what looked like a woman catching a nap at a desk in the second office. Andy skirted the desk. She checked for life and found none.

Calbert continued shouting. Doors slammed. Andy worked her way back past the first body, hopped over it, and moved into the corridor. Using an elbow, she found and flipped up a light switch. Cold fluorescent lights winked and flickered on. One or two failed, leaving uneven dim spots in the hallway. The bluish light did no favors for pale yellow walls and a gray concrete floor.

Calbert emerged from the last of four side rooms.

"Fuck!" He slammed a fist against a wall.

Andy hurried down the hall, pausing for a cursory search of each darkened room. Of the four, two contained stacked boxes, unused chairs, and what looked like old medical equipment. The other two contained hospital beds. In the first, the bedding had been stripped and the mattress rolled up. Except for some children's artwork and a poster for the Disney movie *Pirates of the Caribbean*, the room showed no sign of occupancy.

In the second room, bedding on the thin mattresses looked recently used.

"Reuben," Andy said. He paid no attention. She snapped at him. "Reuben!"

"What?"

Andy pointed. A marker drawing attached to the door showed a child's impression of sunrise over an island landscape with palm trees. In the lower left corner, written in block letters, the name GABBY. The artist's hand matched that of the artwork in the first room.

Reuben pushed past Andy and reentered the room. He found a chest of drawers and jerked it open. With one huge hand he scooped up a ball of brightly colored clothing.

"These are hers. She was here."

Andy stepped beside him and picked up a yellow t-shirt with red lettering. She held it up in front of Reuben.

"Listen to me. Take this. *Take it!*" She dropped the wad in his hand. "Now go back the way you came and wipe down everything you touched. Got it? Everything."

He stared blankly at her.

"Reuben, that's your truck in front of the building."

"So?"

"There are two bodies here. Were you already here tonight? In the last six hours? Did you kill them?"

"No! Hell, no!"

"I didn't think so. But someone is working hard to make it look like you came here, committed murder, and abducted your daughter." Andy looked around. An overnight bag sat in one corner beside a narrow sofa. The sofa had pillows and a blanket neatly stacked at one end. "Would your wife have been here with her?"

"Yeah."

"Well, they're gone now. This was all made to look like you came here, killed two people, then abducted your wife and daughter—probably in your wife's vehicle. Go. Clean up after yourself. Go. And hurry. We're leaving."

He marched out. Andy picked up another shirt. She wiped the handles on the drawer, then dropped the shirt, leaned down, and shoved the drawer back in with her shoulder.

"Dee, check this." I gestured at a glass-fronted cabinet over a sink. Small boxes of medicine occupied two shelves inside. "Purinthol. Rituxan. I recognize some of these. From hospital visits. Stuff they give to kids with lymphoblastic leukemia. But nothing here says Amphitriton. This looks like conventional treatment stuff."

Andy tapped the glass with the tip of her weapon. "Diclofenac."

"Is that a cancer med?"

"No. It's a mild analgesic for treating pain in children. For acute pain, they would be combining it with an opioid. I'm not seeing any of that here, but they wouldn't leave opioids laying around."

"This place looks like a half-assed operation at best."

"Obviously not shut down. There are only two patient rooms here. We need to see if any of the cabins were occupied."

"I'm not sure that's smart. Somebody set all this up, which means they need for it to be discovered. We don't have a lot of time. What if they called this in already?"

Andy moved around the bed, studying details. She examined an IV stand with tubing draped on its hooks, but no empty bag. She looked at a rolling stand meant to hold a medical monitor.

"I don't think so… A call requires explanation. My bet…someone is due here in the morning. Staff. Janitor. Somebody. Whoever did this is counting on some innocent finding the bodies. Gives them a running start." She ran a knuckle through a thin coat of dust on the monitor stand. "Will, I feel like they were just waiting for this girl to die." Andy picked up a stack of child's drawings piled where the monitor would have been. "Look."

She held up a drawing that showed two children holding hands under a sky filled with hearts. The caption read *Gabby Loves Sonjay* and *Sonjay Loves Gabby.* Another drawing showed palm trees and a treasure chest under a pirate flag. Two pirate figures flanked the chest. I made a guess. Gabby and Sonjay. A caption below the tableau read *X marks the spot.*

"She had company."

"In the next room."

Andy stared at the empty bed. A white hospital blanket and companion sheet had been pushed aside. The fitted sheet over the mattress retained wrinkles in a pattern that suggested the size of the occupant.

"She's small." Andy touched the indentation in the mattress.

"We need to go."

Andy blinked and shook herself out of a moment of contemplation. We hurried out of the room.

Calbert waited for us in the small lobby. He stopped us in our tracks. A black semi-automatic rifle rested against his shoulder, aimed at Andy. One hand inserted a meaty finger inside the trigger guard, the other held the rifle steady. The hand bracing the weapon also gripped an oversized sheet of paper.

I sidestepped to position myself closer to Andy. She slowly slipped her weapon back into her satchel. "Reuben, where did you get that?"

"My truck. I'm not going to hurt you. I came back in to tell you not to follow me. Understand? I'm leaving. Don't follow me."

"Is that your gun?" Andy asked.

"What if it is?"

"Seriously, man," I said, "you've never seen the stupid movie where the wife finds the husband stabbed…and she picks up the knife?"

Andy shook her head. "Reuben, they used your gun to kill these people. You're being set up. Don't do this. Let us help you."

"Not happening." He backed toward the door.

"Please. If you take that weapon and they find it on you, that's an open and shut case. You might as well confess. At least leave the weapon."

"How is that better? Look, I still don't know what your deal is, but if you really want to help me, leave me the hell alone. They took Gabby and I'm going after her."

"Where?"

He reached the screen doors and bumped them open with his back. Without another word, he stepped into the yellow porch light. We watched him descend the steps, then turn and bolt into the darkness. A moment later his pickup truck roared to life. He churned the gravel when he pulled away. Headlights swept the building windows. Then he was gone.

Andy cursed softly.

"I can try and chase after him." I pulled the power unit from my pocket.

"No."

"Okay. Then we should leave."

"In a minute." Andy said it without urgency.

She slowly turned and scanned her surroundings. I tried to see what she saw, but my impressions were only surface deep. The paint on the walls needed touchup. The woodwork carried scars from summer after summer of campers. The partition wall opposite the counter was obviously temporary, more a divider than a wall, hiding the extended and unused dining hall beyond it. Two upholstered chairs pushed together in a corner testified to an attempt to create a small waiting area. A dry and dusty fake fern sat beside them.

Andy ran her eyes over all of it. She rested her hands on the small of her back. She spread her feet slightly.

While Andy studied the scene, I went outside and climbed into the cab of the Peterbilt. As I suspected, Calbert took the keys with him.

When I returned, Andy remained rooted to the same spot.

"What are you looking for?"

She didn't answer. I was not sure she heard me. She looked at the wall between the two office doors. Above a rank of filing cabinets, there were shelves. Mostly empty, the shelves contained three-ring binders, a stack of folders, a few personal photos, and a stuffed koala bear.

She moved around the end of the counter, carefully stepping over the body on the floor. She searched for and then found a clipboard. From where I stood, the top sheet looked like a grid, a schedule of some sort. Andy took out her phone and snapped a photo.

"He's going somewhere. Somewhere specific. Did you see?"

"See what?"

"He had a sheet of paper in his hand. He found something. He thinks he knows where he's going. Where to find Gabby."

"Whatever he found, he took it with him."

Andy returned the clip board, then faced the temporary partition wall.

The divider put up to shield the lobby from the dining area was made of modular carpeted walls, the type found in cubicles like the one occupied by Dr. Maxwell at Belling Shore Labs. Gray textured cloth covered lightweight panels. The panels rose from the floor to a height of about eight feet, leaving a gap of three or four feet below wooden rafters. A few pieces of children's artwork had been tacked up. In the center, a cork bulletin board hung at eye level. The bulletin board contained official-looking notices, printed workers' compensation rules, schedule sheets pinned one on top of the other, and a card with emergency phone numbers.

Dead center on the bulletin board, a gap matched the poster-sized sheet of paper Calbert had held in his hand. A torn corner of the poster remained pinned to the board.

"There." Andy stepped to the bulletin board and unpinned the remnant. Printed on glossy paper, several thin stripes ran through a field of sky blue. "This is what he took. I didn't get a good look, but I saw blue. Like this. And I saw the torn corner. I'm sure of it."

"You got a better look than I did. All I saw was that gun."

Andy stuffed the slip of paper into her bag. She hurried to the end of the counter where the first body sprawled in a spreading pool of dark red. I felt my gag reflex wake up when she lifted the man's shoulder. She reached under the body, feeling for something and not finding what she was looking for. She checked his trousers. Careful to avoid the blood, she searched the victim's hip pocket. She lifted a phone from his pants and stood up.

She pushed a button. "I love people who don't use screen lock." She tapped the screen.

"What are you looking for?"

"Photo gallery. Got it." Andy scrolled. Her head bobbed as she scanned through screen after screen of photos. "Jeepers, who takes this many pictures of such an ugly dog?"

"That's usually the point."

She kept going. When she stopped, it was sudden, and she had to reverse. She zeroed in on something, tapped the screen and then pinched her fingers to spread them and zoom the image. A smile creased her lips. She looked up at me and held up the phone.

"What is it?" I approached and squinted at the image.

The photo was a selfie of the murdered man standing beside a smiling brown-haired woman in a shoulder-to-shoulder pose.

"Is that...?" I gestured at the body in the second office, the one Andy asked me not to enter.

"No. Different woman."

I don't know why I felt relief. The girl in the photo was pretty, beaming a smile enhanced by sparkling eyes. The man had held his camera high, snapping the image on a downward angle. The girl was short. In the gap above her hair, the center of the bulletin board could be seen. The camera automatically focused on the faces, rendering them in sharp detail. The bulletin board background was fuzzy, but it was clear that a poster occupied the gap Andy found.

Andy pinched and zoomed again, expanding the poster.

"It's a collage of photos. Pictures of children on a boat. A yacht."

"Gabby?"

"I don't think so. Judging by the fact that the poster had to have been created and printed, I think these were all taken a while ago. Before they supposedly closed this place."

"Nice boat." The sleek and sculpted vessel in the photos had to be over a hundred and fifty feet long. Beneath the collection of photos, bold lettering spanned the page in two lines.

OUR HUNT FOR PIRATE TREASURE
TEN KEYS WEST

The topmost photo showed the yacht anchored on placid waters as seen from a beach. The lines we had seen in the torn corner piece were palm fronds, which dipped into both corners of the frame. The rest of the photos showed kids—some wrapped in blankets, some in wheelchairs—in various poses on the boat, on a beach, and in the sun. The lack of focus made it impossible to see faces.

"Wait right here." Andy hurried around the corner and down the hall. I watched her duck into the hospice room Gabby Calbert had occupied. A moment later she emerged holding the collection of artworks we had seen on the medical stand. Back at the front counter, she leafed through them.

"Here." She stopped and held up a sheet of copy paper covered in marker colors.

"It's a map. A treasure map."

The drawing showed a winding segmented line. At one end, a crude boat with sails and a pirate flag prepared to follow the drawn path. At the other end, the classic Maltese cross where "X" marked the spot. In between, dotting the journey, Gabby had drawn what looked like ten skeleton keys.

"So, what are the keys? Clues?"

Andy set the drawing aside, then picked up her phone and examined the poster image.

Andy poked the screen with her finger. "Calbert saw this. He connected it to something he already knew. This is where he's going. This is where he thinks they're taking Gabby."

"Right. So, where is this?"

"No idea." Andy put away her phone. She gathered, folded, and placed the drawings in her bag. "I need my laptop. And I need to talk to Leslie. And I need to get out of these muddy clothes."

55

We came in high to avoid wires. By the time we reached the site of Calbert's demolition derby, Andy and I were soaked. We flew through an unrelenting drizzle that dropped from ragged low clouds. The issue with wires sprang from the need to follow roads. Prior to takeoff, since we could not see the phone screen once we vanished, we studied the route we had traveled from the small park where we left Ramona Hampton to Bickler Beach. From that, and what Andy could remember of a few turns she had commanded during our escape from Fennick, we extrapolated a new route.

Neither of us was certain of where the muddy field was located. I wanted to climb higher, figuring that a field full of wrecked pickup trucks would be obvious from the air, but the cloud bases hung just a few hundred feet up. Absent a moon or stars, the night was black. Navigating above a rain-slicked road surface was easier and safer than peering down into dark patches of tilled earth or scrubby woods.

In the end it was not Andy's sense of direction and memory of the escape route that yielded success. From several miles away, flashing yellow lights from two tow trucks and a collection of headlights arrayed around the damaged trucks broke through the mist like a beacon.

The men of Company W had called for help.

Two of the pickup trucks were already gone, as was Hampton's Dodge Ram crew cab. I made a guess that Fennick had departed in the still drivable truck, despite the crushed windshield. The two remaining wrecks included the one that lost its truck bed and had been rolled on its side. As we descended on the scene, a tow truck winch pulled the wreck upright again. A circle of men supervised the recovery. One man cursed loudly after seeing the damaged truck back on its own wheels. He had good reason. The frame was twisted. Only three of the four wheels touched the earth.

A few of the onlookers shouldered rifles. Some wore camo clothing and bulky vests. I reduced power on the BLASTER to avoid drawing attention.

"Take us down to the car," Andy whispered in my ear. I squeezed her to signal affirmative.

The white Nissan lay on its side where it had rolled off the hood of the Dodge. The windows were gone. A pool of sparkling shattered glass spread out in the mud. The boys of Company W paid no attention to the smashed rental.

"Maybe we should wait," I whispered back. "Until they're gone."

Andy moved in a way that felt like a head shake. She forgets I can't see her.

"Let's have a look. If getting our stuff requires making noise, then we wait."

"Okay. By the way, this thing is getting low on power."

The BLASTER in hand had served to get us back to the field, but the batteries were running down. I carried spares in my flight bag. I crossed my fingers that the men recovering their pickup trucks would ignore the Nissan and its contents.

The rear of the rental was crushed. The trunk lid had accordion folds. I saw little chance of prying it open. We maneuvered above the vehicle and looked down through the broken windows. Despite all the lights in the field, it was hard to see in the dark interior. The rear seat was a jumble. The damage gave me hope that the seatback could be pulled away to access the trunk.

All of which entailed making noise. We decided to wait.

We floated with a light grip on the rental's roof until the tow trucks pulled the last two victims onto their flat beds. I had a moment of concern when one of the militiamen wandered over and aimed a flashlight inside the rental. Less than a meter from Andy and me, he sniffed around, perhaps looking for anything valuable, then strolled off to catch a ride out of the field after the last tow truck pulled away.

When the final set of taillights bounced onto the distant road, I moved into position beside the exposed belly of the car.

Fwooomp!

Andy and I reappeared and settled on our feet in the slippery mud surfacing the field. I leaned over and looked inside the vehicle. The interior was tar black.

"I think I can break away the rear seatback," I said, calculating access to the trunk.

Andy walked to the back of the car and used the key. I reached down and tugged on the seatback.

"Or we could just open the trunk." She released the latch and swung open the crushed lid.

"I don't know, Dee." I yanked on the rear seat. "I'm not sure something so simple is viable. Perhaps for leverage we could build a small tower from tree trunks and fashion blades of grass to form a rudimentary chai—"

"Shut up and get back here."

56

It took some effort. We traveled with two small roller bags plus my flight bag. Andy stuffed the garbage bag with dirty laundry into my roller bag, which always has more room than hers. It was still a lot to carry. I've successfully vanished with two adults and an eight-year-old boy, but we were all holding each other.

We started by hooking arms and then having Andy grip both roller bags while I used my free hand to hold the strap on my flight bag.

Fwooomp!

Andy and I disappeared. None of the luggage went with us.

We tried again. This time we awkwardly huddled around the bags and did our best to hug them between us.

Fwooomp!

My flight bag went with us, but both roller bags stayed visible.

"This isn't going to work," Andy declared after we reappeared. "We need to leave something. We can walk all this out to the road and find a safe place to hide the bags, and then come back for them."

"Hang on. I'm not ready to give up. I've been wanting to see how much I can carry. This is a good test."

"Will, we don't have time to fool around."

"Just one sec. Grab hold of me."

She hooked my left arm. I lifted one of the roller bags between us.

Fwooomp!

We vanished with the bag.

"What about the rest?" she asked.

"Take this one and hold it in your free hand." I passed the handle of the unseen and now weightless bag into her fingers. I felt her swing it away. I bent down and lifted the second roller bag and held it between us. In my mind, I pushed the control levers hard against the stops and concentrated on pushing *the other thing* over the visible bag.

Fwooomp!

"Whoa, I heard that," Andy said. The bag disappeared. "It worked!"

"Take this one, too."

Andy's fingers slid into the bag handle. Mine slid out. She now held both bags while keeping her right arm hooked in my left.

"One more." I repeated the experiment, focusing on pushing *the other thing* over my flight bag after I lifted it against my chest. The flight bag disappeared and became weightless. I transferred it to my left hand. "Bingo!"

"Nicely done."

"I live to impress my girlfriend. Should be no trouble holding on to all this stuff since it doesn't weigh anything. Ready?"

"Never."

We had already drifted off the muddy surface of the field. I lifted the fresh BLASTER I had taken from my flight bag and aimed it skyward.

"Fasten your seatbelts." We launched.

57

Mountain Home grew out of the low-hanging mist as a dull glow. We traveled above sparse traffic on Highway 5. Dots of individual lighting gave way to strings of streetlights, lighted business signs, and occasional vehicle headlights and taillights. I guessed the time to be somewhere around two a.m. and could come up with no excuse for vehicles to be moving at this hour, yet they did, whispering beneath us on the wet pavement.

We worried about Fennick. He knew we had escaped. We had no idea whether he knew that it was Reuben Calbert who had driven the Peterbilt into his Company W firing squad. Andy and I agreed, however, that the murders and the planted evidence at the hospice had been Fennick's work. He may not have identified Calbert at the wheel of the truck, but he knew all about Calbert. Staging the crime scene at the hospice would have been pointless otherwise.

The question Andy and I discussed on the low and relatively slow flight down Highway 5 was *What now?* What do we do? I was pumped full of adrenaline and felt no need for sleep, but that wasn't going to last and when it hit, it would hit us both hard. Andy wanted to get at her laptop and her phone. She had calls to make and questions demanding answers. Work best done from a hotel room.

The town had the usual strip of hotels. I suggested we simply drop into one of them, book it for the rest of the night, ask for a late checkout, grab some rest and some answers, and then head for the airport.

"Uh…I don't think that's a good idea."

"How so?"

"We should not underestimate Fennick's reach. Or Remington's reach. Or, for that matter, Newell's. This is a small community. Remington has a ton of money. That buys help. Fennick being here means Remington has interests here, and we have just made ourselves highly visible obstacles to his interests."

"So?"

"So, Fennick may be watching the hotels. I'm a mess. The two of us will stand out like a sore thumb. How hard would it be for Fennick to drive around to the local hotels and give the night clerks a few bucks with the promise of more if they call a certain number in the event two messed up people show?"

I felt the warm shower and dry sheets that had been teasing my thoughts slip through my fingertips.

"What do you have in mind?"

"Something criminal."

58

———————

"I just want to say that this is positively devious, and I have never been so hot for you."

Andy touched her hair. "Ugh! I'm a mess."

We reappeared inside the front door of a nice house on an isolated lot just outside the Mountain Home city limits. I switched on a lamp.

Andy stood in the soft yellow glow spattered from forehead to foot with dirt, caked mud, and soaked clothing. Her hair hung in strands. The white blouse she wore under her leather jacket was saturated and nearly transparent. It revealed everything beneath.

"Let's take a shower together."

"Let's get our luggage in here first." She lifted one leg at a time and unzipped the calf-length boots she favors, carefully removing them. "Shoes off. We're not messing up the carpets." She sidestepped both the suggestion I made and me and opened the front door to retrieve the bags we left on the porch.

This was the fourth house we tried. I thought it might take a dozen. The idea came from a case Andy worked two years ago. Essex County kids visited remote houses in the middle of the night. They banged on windows, threw branches against walls, and found other creative ways to wake people up in the middle of the night, but in a way that didn't prompt a call to the police. When a light came on, they took off—until they found a house where a light didn't come on. After more earnest banging, they affirmed that no one was home, and helped themselves in through a window. Not many homes in Essex have security systems. In at least one case, the kids figured out that the family was gone on vacation and stayed for the better part of a week. Andy was never sure how many times they pulled the stunt. They were such courteous guests that some victims only learned they'd been visited after the kids were caught and confessed to Andy. They might not have been caught at all except a homeowner had an argument with his wife at their lake cabin and returned in the middle of the second night to find Goldilocks and friends sleeping in their beds.

Andy's approach was methodical and tried to be kind. A single wrap on a window—the sound of a bird strike—did the trick for the first three. A light came on. A face cautiously peered out from behind shades or blinds. We moved on.

At the fourth house, nothing happened after a good rap on what we guessed to be the master bedroom window. We tried a second. Then a third. Each thump grew louder. Nothing. We tried the front door, hammering vigorously just in case the occupants were heavy sleepers. We rang the door-bell. Nothing moved inside. No lights illuminated.

We deposited our luggage at the front door. At a second-floor window lacking a screen, I did my trick of extending *the other thing* through the sash until the metal latch severed. Once inside, Andy insisted we take a quick tour while still in the vanished state. We looked for interior cameras belonging to a home security system, the kind people access from their phones. Andy searched for a security system keypad. Nothing.

Satisfied we were safe, I released us from *the other thing.*
Fwooomp!
"This is nice," I said. "Crime B 'n B."
"Check to see if they have pets." Andy retrieved our bags from the front porch. "Don't turn on too many lights. Don't touch anything if you can help it. Don't move anything. Don't take anything."
I threw her a perturbed look. "Except jewelry, right?"
She returned the look in kind.
I checked the kitchen for pet dishes, dog bowls, kitty toys. The presence of a pet might mean the absent owner had arranged for someone to dole out food and water twice daily. Someone might stop by first thing in the morning. I saw nothing to indicate the presence of furry friends.
Photos in the hallway leading from the front door to a rear kitchen displayed a middle-aged couple surrounded by grown children and a cluster of grandchildren. A pile of bills on a sideboard gave Riley as the name of the owner.
"We thank you, Mr. and Mrs. Riley," I tapped the top bill.

I rejoined Andy in the front foyer. She looked hesitant.

"What's wrong?"

"This is the worst thing I've ever done."

"Wow. Really? This is Pollyanna's worst? I'd hug you right now, but you're filthy. Go upstairs. Don't use the master bathroom. Use the second. Take a picture before you do anything so you can remember where everything was." I held out her bag. "Go. I'll guard the front door. If anyone shows up at…" I checked my watch "…two forty-seven a.m., I'll holler for you to dive out the bathroom window."

Off she went. At the top of the stairs, she called back to me. "We're leaving these people money."

59

"How are you connecting to the internet?"

Andy faced her laptop on the guest bedroom floor beside the bed. She wore fresh clothes. Her clean hair hung wet, looking nearly black, at the sides of her face. A small plug-in nightlight provided slightly more illumination than a candle. She lifted her phone, which she had attached to a charger. "Mrs. Riley has a Post-It with bananawhale787 taped inside a kitchen cabinet door. You get one guess."

"Wi-Fi password. Sheesh. And why are you on the floor?"

"I don't want to mess up the bed."

I held out a hand. "C'mon. We'll re-make the bed. Do you plan to stay fully dressed?"

"What if we have to leave in a hurry?"

"Dee, it's not like anyone would see us." I gestured at myself. After a quick shower, I bagged up my dirty clothes and donned a pair of boxers and a t-shirt, thinking we might get a couple hours of sleep.

"I'm not flying out a window in my underwear," she declared.

We settled onto the mattress side-by-side with her laptop resting on her thighs. Andy switched into what I call her Presentation Mode.

"Remington has a boat. Well, more of an ocean liner. Look at this thing." She brought up pictures of a sleek, sculpted yacht. He calls it *Amphitrite*, which is a minor Greek sea goddess, mother of Triton—hence the name of the company. Mother and son. Registry listings show it based in Ft. Lauderdale, but there are pictures in here of the thing all over the Caribbean."

"Any pictures of taking sick kids on a treasure hunt?"

"Yes and no." Andy clicked and scrolled. A new image filled the screen. "Two things of interest. There's this," she pointed, "which matches one of the fuzzy poster pictures on that man's phone—by the way, before we left Bickler Beach, I dialed 9-1-1 on his phone and left it on the counter with an open connection."

"With your fingerprints?" She rolled her eyes at me. "Sorry. Doesn't that mean they'll know someone was there after the fact?"

"I hope so. I plan to explain that in detail when the time comes. Will, I'm still a police officer. At this moment, however, I don't see a point in getting caught up in days of answering questions. We need to find Gabby Calbert. Now more than ever."

"You think they—and I mean Fennick and Remington—killed those two people? And plan to do something to Gabby?"

Andy didn't commit.

"Okay," I said. I pointed. "What are we looking at here?"

"So, like I said. Remington has a boat." She scrolled to a photo.

"That thing is huge. That's gotta be two hundred and fifty feet long," I said. "That's not the boat in the photos on that poster."

"You are correct. This is his second boat. Here's the first boat." She scrolled to another photo, this one of children boarding the smaller yacht. "Here they are, boarding *Amphitrite* to sail off on their treasure hunt. Look at the background."

A familiar-looking bridge spanned an expanse of water. Onshore, a round building shared the background. In the foreground, a brick boardwalk fronted grass and trees under quaint lantern-like lights. A line of frail children posed on a boarding ramp, waving at the camera. Jim Newell rested his hands on the shoulders of two flanking kids.

"Why does that look like something I've seen?"

"That's Woldenberg Park on the New Orleans waterfront. That bridge is a city icon. You probably saw it in photos after Katrina. I have a theory about where Reuben thinks he should go."

"New Orleans."

"Good guess, but no. Look at this." More scrolling. A few clicks. A new image appeared. The smaller yacht docked near what looked like a resort hotel fringed with palm trees and a beach. "The caption says this was taken in Key West, Florida. That's where Newell took the kids for their treasure hunt and a bit of sunshine before…you know…" she trailed off.

"Keys? Florida Keys? You think that's what Gabby meant? And Reuben is headed there?"

Andy snapped the laptop shut. She spun on the bedspread to face me. In the dim ambiance, her face was alight.

"I think that's the where. And I think I know the why." Her hands took flight the way they do when inspiration does a mashup with revelation. "I looked it up. SEC final approval for Amphitriton's IPO is locked in. Remington has his investment bank lined up. The S-1 Registration Statement —it's a prospectus—already received SEC approval. And Remington has been on his road show for weeks—that's where he meets with institutional investors and brokerage firms to set a stock price. That's why he was in Wichita. Wall Street is blowing up. Word is, the stock price will be through the roof, but the final price won't be revealed until the night before the stock goes live." Andy sat back and pressed her palms together as if in prayer. "That's Tuesday night. Five days from now. He plans to announce it at a private, invitation-only gala at—you ready for this?—the Met in New York."

"The Metropolitan Museum of Art? That Met?"

"Uh-huh."

"Fancy."

"Will, you don't understand. This is an IPO for a cure for cancer. That's what they're selling it as."

"I get all that. Billions. I get it."

"Remington will let nothing," Andy said, "and I mean *nothing* get in the way of pulling this off. And I think that includes any shred of evidence that the magic medicine is not all that magical."

I let her words sink in.

"You mean Gabby."

Andy nodded.

"I think she was on the medicine all along. I think they lied to Reuben and said she wasn't. And when he raised hell, I think they refused to give it to her to save her because they know it doesn't work for her."

60

─────────

"**L**eslie!" I greeted her too cheerfully via the speaker function on the phone that Andy placed between us. "How the hell are you?"

We heard what sounded like rustling cloth, and possibly lips smacking.

"Andy?" She spoke like someone with a mouth full of cotton.

"I'm here. Sorry about the hour."

"No, we're not." I laughed.

"What's wrong? Are you okay?" Her urgent query grew clearer, but quieter. "Wait. Hold on." We heard more rustling. Then silence. Then a door latch. "Just…hold on a sec." More silence. Then thumps, bare feet on a stair. She coughed twice and cleared her throat. "Okay, go. What's going on? Are you okay?"

"Except for a little run-in with a Company W firing squad, we're fine," I said.

"What?"

I let Andy explain. She brushed past the gunfire and segued quickly into essential points about Remington, Fennick, and Newell. Leslie listened without comment until Andy finished by asking if Leslie had any contacts with the U.S. Coast Guard.

Leslie didn't speak for a few seconds.

"Lemme see if I have this straight. I ask you not to mess with Company W and you're out there stirring up a bunch of them in—where did you say you were?"

"Mountain Home, Arkansas. And we did not stir them up. They came after us because of Fennick."

"Desmond Fennick?"

"Yes."

"And what was the thing about the kid? I'm sorry. It's butt-fuck o'clock here and I haven't had my coffee."

"We're trying to find a child who might have been in an Amphitriton drug trial. Her father is Reuben Calbert and—"

"The dude that attacked the airplane with a hatchet. I saw that."

Andy conducted a second recap of events, leading once again into her question about the Coast Guard.

"Why the Coast Guard?" Leslie asked.

"I want to know the location of Terrance Remington's yacht. It's called *Amphitrite*. Does the FBI have connections with the Coast Guard?"

"Sure, we do. But if you're looking for Remington, I can tell you where he's at. He's here in New York. He was on Bloomberg last night, and I think on CNN, too. And I believe he's doing Rachel Maddow Monday night. Love that woman. Point is, he's doing all the shows. His boat is probably parked at the New York Yacht Club, wherever they park. If what he's selling is real...holy shit. He's about to make Elon Musk and Spiro Lewko look like paupers."

Andy leaned into the phone. "Can you find that boat for us? And something else. Can you find out anything about a boy named Sonjay Chandira Nazim? Not sure what age. Possibly being treated for childhood cancer." Andy spelled out the name.

"Parents' names?"

"Unknown."

"Location?"

"Unknown."

"Ach! You two!" Leslie pushed an audible sigh across the cellular network. "Yes. I can find your yacht and I will see what I can find about the boy even though you've given me absolutely nothing to go on. Now rewind. Go back. Tell me more about this Company W crap."

61

———————

"**W**ill, wake up!" Andy shook my shoulders and simultaneously pressed her fingers to my lips. She leaned over me close enough to kiss and whispered in my ear. "*Someone's here. Downstairs.*"

I didn't need to be told twice. I jolted from a deep sleep to wide awake in the duration of a heartbeat. Andy backed away. I rolled off the bed. I'd no sooner planted my feet than Andy pushed me aside. She tugged the bedspread tight and fluffed the pillows we had been using. She grabbed the stuffed puppy that had been the bed's sole occupant before we arrived and planted him back in place.

A door opened and closed downstairs. Footsteps crossed from the back of the house to the front. I heard a male voice. The footsteps pounded up the stairs.

Andy whirled to face me. I hooked my arm around her waist.

Fwooomp!

We vanished. Both of us irrationally froze as if movement might give us away. Our feet slowly parted from the floor.

The voice from below spoke impatiently. "Where did you say you put it? Because it's not in the kitchen…no, I looked…You sure it's not upstairs?"

A young man appeared at the top of the stairs holding a phone against the side of his head. Panic joined the cool sensation wrapping my body. If he came into the guest bedroom, he would run right into us.

He passed by our open door. I pulled Andy closer and touched my lips to her ear.

231

"*Where are the bags?*"

"*Outside,*" she replied, barely above the sound of a breath.

"Mom, it's here. Told you it was in the bedroom." The young man trotted past the door again and rapidly descended the stairs. "Right. Call you when I get there. Love you, too."

We held our breath until we heard the front door open and slam shut.

Fwooomp!

We dropped the inch or two we had drifted off the floor. Andy looked up at me with astonished eyes. After holding it in for a moment, she burst out laughing.

"I am so *done* with a life of crime." She looked at me and something struck her as even funnier. "You should see your face."

"Nice way to wake me up." I fought a smile of my own.

"Let's go," Andy said, still giggling. "I'm putting a couple twenties under their mail in the kitchen. Hurry up."

She bounced out of the room leaving me appreciative of the bright smile and good cheer she left in her wake. It matched the sunlight leaking through closed blinds. I realized I hadn't seen her that way since the shotgun blast.

"Be right down."

Fwooomp!

I reappeared beside Andy at the back of a small yard. My feet settled into wet grass.

"Whoa! It's cold out here." The sky was a stark cloudless blue. The crystalline after-storm air couldn't have been much above fifty degrees. Shadow angles and a sun disk barely above the treetops confirmed what my sluggish body told me; that we had garnered less than three hours rest.

Andy, dressed and looking fully alive, gave no hint of exhaustion.

"Told you to stay dressed. The bags are behind this little garden shed."

I retrieved the luggage and unzipped mine. I found pants, a shirt, socks, and my boots and set about pulling them on.

"When did you bring them out here? And more importantly, why?"

"I put them out here after you dozed off. For exactly the reason we just saw. To be ready if somebody showed up. Did you think we could make all this disappear in a split second and cram it out the window?"

The bathroom window, the one we had used to enter the house, had been my exit from the house. Andy departed through the front door after requiring me to turn the deadbolt from the inside.

"Any word from Leslie?" I struggled to stand on one foot and pull a sock over my wet foot.

"Not yet."

I completed the miracle of dressing without falling on my ass, then closed and zipped the overnight bag.

"Got your laptop?"

"All packed."

"Everything accounted for? Toothbrush? Charging cord?" I pulled my Ray Bans from my flight bag and slid them on.

"Affirmative, captain."

"Any chance we could get some food on the way to the airport?" Andy had rejected the idea of raiding our host's pantry.

"I'm not sure appearing out of thin air at the local diner is a great idea. Especially with these bags."

My stomach argued, but I didn't.

We gathered ourselves, vanished, worked our way through the ritual of making the bags disappear, and then launched.

Ten minutes later I swept down on Baxter County Airport, careful to avoid the traffic pattern, even if there were no arrivals or departures in sight. We landed beside the Navajo on a nearly empty ramp. After clearing the area to confirm the absence of curious eyes, we reappeared and dropped the bags beside the fuselage. I opened the door to load the bags.

Andy's phone chirped.

"Message from Leslie." She scanned the screen. "Coast Guard reports the boat left New Orleans for Key West yesterday."

"Looks like you nailed it. Betcha that's where Calbert went."

"Calbert can't show his face at an airport, which means he has at least a twenty-two- maybe twenty-four-hour drive." Andy checked her watch and did the math. "Even if he goes straight through, he won't get there until the middle of the night tonight. How long for us to fly?"

"Guessing…four and a half, maybe five hours."

"I'm calling the Florida Highway Patrol."

"Dee, wait. Hold on. Is that necessary? I mean…you said it yourself, if they find him with that gun, he's toast."

"I'm off duty, Will. But I haven't forgotten my duty. I have no choice. He's armed. He's violent. He said he would go through anybody that tried to stop him. He already assaulted an officer. Don't tell me you're siding with him."

"He did save our butts."

"He didn't save our butts. He tried to kidnap Ramona Hampton. Our butts got lucky. Will, it's for his safety, too. I can't let this slide."

"I guess."

"With any luck, he'll be taken into custody, and we can sort it all out later. Worst case, he makes it to Key West but we get there ahead of him. I'm going to visit the restroom."

"Fine. I'll get her untied and do a quick walk-around."

"Don't leave without me." Andy started across the ramp. She hadn't gone more than halfway across the ramp when she heard me shout out a furious curse.

62

Andy sprinted back across the ramp.

"What is it?"

"SON OF A BITCH!"

I stood in front of the right engine, halfway through my walkaround. Blood burned in my face. My fists closed. I planted them on my hips and bent over, fighting rage.

"Will!" Andy closed her hand around my arm. "What's wrong?"

I wanted to scream.

I broke Andy's grasp and marched around the nose of the airplane to the left engine. I didn't have to stroke the length of one of the three prop blades as I had on the right side. I could see it.

"God damn him! Fennick!"

Andy followed me. I pointed. Her eyebrows squeezed together an expression that said she wasn't seeing what I saw.

"Here!" I snapped.

A thin line ran from the leading edge to the trailing edge of one of the three metal prop blades. As part of a preflight walk-around, I routinely run my hand along each blade to feel for nicks or damage. I might not have seen it, but my fingers found it. This wasn't damage. This was criminal sabotage.

"What is that?" Andy ran her fingernail through the groove.

"Guaranteed structural metal failure."

Someone had sliced into the prop blade. Not deep. Not obvious, but more than enough to weaken the metal. Once the full force of the engine

235

spun it, the damaged blade would snap off. Full force would happen during and just after takeoff. A single broken blade would immediately throw the three-bladed prop wildly out of balance. In seconds, perhaps faster than I could cut the throttle, the vibration could tear the engine from its mounts. One blade on each side had been cut, but there was no guarantee they would both break at the same time. Even if recovered from the first break, maximum power on the remaining engine guaranteed the second failure.

This was a fatal accident scheduled for seconds after takeoff with full fuel on board.

With Andy on board.

"Fennick." I spit out the name with venom on my tongue.

Andy examined the damage. She didn't ask the dumb question we both knew the answer to. This airplane wasn't going anywhere.

My thoughts went cinematic.

I saw us trapped in the cockpit just a few hundred feet in the air with both engines tearing themselves apart. Low, slow, stalling. Fighting controls that have nothing to offer. A vice closed on my chest. I saw our last seconds together.

In the same fatal flash, I saw two black barrels of a shotgun.

I froze and looked at Andy's angelic face and gold-flecked eyes. I looked at the beauty nearly lost in flaming wreckage.

She locked her eyes on mine and read the message there perfectly.

"I'm so sorry," I whispered. "I get it. I do. I get what you've been going through. I'm so sorry."

She drew close and reached for my face. She touched the yellowing bruise at the corner of my left eye.

Me, too. Her lips formed words without sound. After a moment she asked, "Now what?"

I walked a few paces away, then turned around and looked at my sleek, sad, stricken bird.

"Now I cool off, we call the cavalry, and then I kill someone."

PART III

63

The twin-engine Beechcraft Baron executed a smooth flare just above the runway. Like breathing a sigh. Or settling into a pillow. She steadily lifted her nose and eased the main wheels down until they kissed the concrete. From a distance, I could not hear the signature squeak of rubber tires on the runway. The nosewheel stayed high for a few more seconds, then gently dropped to join the other two on Earth.

After a long, casual rollout that preserved the brakes, the plane turned off the runway. The flaps rose. She taxied to the ramp and killed the engines on a roll that ended in front of the gas pumps.

Against an orange sunset, Pidge pulled herself up and out of the cockpit. She wore a leather flight jacket, jeans, and a black t-shirt. A light breeze fluffed her short blonde hair. She leaned an elbow on the top of the cabin and regarded me through her Ray Bans.

"What—the—fuck, Stewart."

She didn't wait for an answer. With two steps and a hop, she dropped off the wing and stalked to the parked Navajo where I stood with my arms folded.

"Are you fucking kidding me?" She ran her finger along the slice in the metal. "Jesus, Mother Mary, and Joseph! I give you about thirty seconds after takeoff before this blade comes through the cabin."

I hadn't thought of that.

"And then the engine tears itself off. You won't even have time to remove all external apparel, tuck your head between your knees, and kiss your pretty ass goodbye. Un-fucking-believable!"

"Huh." I considered this new information. "You think my ass is pretty?"

"I think it's just like you, Stewart," she said solemnly. "Full of—Jesus!" She walked up to me and touched the bruise on my face. "What happened? Andy finally whack you?"

"Got it saving a baby seal from a polar bear. Don't ask."

"Hi, Pidge!" Andy crossed the ramp on a line from the FBO office. "I didn't see you come in."

Andy and Pidge exchanged a quick hug.

"This is some fucked up shit, Andy."

Andy huffed an angry breath. "The person responsible for this has done a lot worse and is going to pay the price. Thank God Will caught this in time."

"Yeah," Pidge sighed. "Every once in a blue moon he does something right." She pointed at my face. "Is that your handy work? Because I get it. I'm sure he deserved it."

"Um," Andy showed us her watch. "We really need to go."

"No worries. Your secret's safe with me." Pidge rapped her knuckles on my chest. "Don't just stand there, Stewart. Gas her up and let's beat feet. I gotta hit the head." She trotted off in the direction Andy had just traveled. Halfway there, she called back, "Any idea where we're going?"

"Already filed."

64

———————

The weight of fatigue settled on my shoulders the way the weight of the Baron settled onto Runway 27 at Key West. Pidge and I both felt it. Her day started with my call for help and a drop-everything-and-go flight from Essex County to Mountain Home. My day started somewhere in New York, give or take. At least it felt that way. I caught a fitful catnap while Andy and I waited for Pidge to arrive at Baxter County Airport, but I can't say it helped.

A direct flight from Mountain Home to Key West was a non-starter. Too much of the flight would have been over the Gulf of Mexico, uncomfortably distant from the Florida coast in an airplane not equipped with survival gear. Worse, we didn't lift off in Arkansas until twilight. I've done night flights over water. It's like flying in a black bag.

I filed a two-part flight plan with the first leg to Tallahassee, and the second leg down the Gulf Coast of Florida to the Keys. The security of remaining within sight of land only added fifteen minutes to the flight time, but a total flight time of four hours and thirty-eight minutes exceeded the fuel in our tanks by roughly eight minutes. I planned for a fuel stop at Tallahassee, but as soon as we leveled off to cruise at nine thousand feet, I told Pidge to find a place to refuel just past the Florida capital. Someplace with 24-hour credit card fuel. Someplace without traffic and ATC and the delays that Class C airspace might impose. She picked Perry-Foley Airport two hours and forty-three minutes from Mountain Home, a municipal field with a triangle runway layout. A stop for self-serve gas and bladder relief at an airport with virtually no traffic saved time.

The final stretch of the second leg, cruising south from Fort Myers and Naples, was the hardest. Black and empty, the Gulf of Mexico lay on our right. Equally black and empty, the Everglades lay on our left. The night sky carried a full load of stars, but ahead and below we saw nothing. ATC cleared us to KARTR intersection, then arrow straight down an airway into Key West, carefully skirting the national air defense zones. Fifty miles out, the island lights crept over the horizon and hovered at the bottom of the windscreen the rest of the way. At times the lights crawled toward us so slowly that I began to wonder if the 194-knot groundspeed readout was lying.

Andy doesn't sleep in cars, on planes, or during any other form of transportation as far as I know. When we drive at night, I suspect her steady chatter is intended to keep me awake at the wheel. Sharing the intercom with me and Pidge, she put her habit to good use. She explained everything to Pidge. The part about Mrs. Anderson's shotgun riled my copilot into a fresh frenzy of F-bombs. Pidge did a reprise when Andy explained the appearance of Company W in the muddy field.

"Jesus," Pidge marveled, "you two need a hobby. I hear pickleball is a big deal with old guys like you, Will."

Despite severe clear night air and ATC's offer of a visual approach, I asked for clearance to fly to Runway 27 via the final approach fix designated for the RNAV 27 instrument approach. The added guidance helped me deal with the vast black hole to our left, and the imbalance created by the island lights on our right. My head developed a slight case of the leans on the way down the final approach course. Thanks to the open water void, I kept wanting to roll left. The instruments said otherwise, and as always, they were right.

After landing, we rolled to a stop at Signature Flight Services and parked in an open tiedown spot. My watch put us five hours past the FBO's published closing time. We were on our own.

A sign on the building provided instructions for getting off the ramp and through the airport fence. Andy worked some phone magic and summoned an Uber ride to the Hampton Inn Key West, which had an available room thanks to a no-show.

A little after two-forty a.m., a Tesla driven by a friendly woman with the longest dreadlocks I've ever seen pulled up to the hotel entrance. She helped us offload our bags. After receiving our assurances of a top rating, she drove off into the warm tropical night.

Andy took charge.

"Will, get us checked in. You two go ahead and crash." She pulled out her phone.

"You don't have to tell me twice," Pidge said.

"What are you doing?" I asked Andy.

She held up her phone. "Calling the cops."

"Dee…what? Hold on." I fished the Foundation credit card from my wallet and handed it to Pidge. "Go get us checked in. We'll be there in a minute."

"Minibar, here I come." Pidge planted a kiss on the credit card. She grabbed her bag and waved her way through the hotel's automatic front door.

I repeated my question to Andy.

"Whatever I can," she replied. "What did you think we were going to do here?"

I shrugged. "I don't know. Get some rest, then go find wherever Remington docks his boat. Maybe find Fennick."

She lifted her eyebrows. "Fennick? Really? To do what?"

"First thought that comes to mind is lift him about twenty feet in the air and drop him. See if two broken ankles evens the score for two ruined props. Oh, and there's that little thing about him trying to kill us. Minor detail."

Andy took a step closer to me and placed her hand on my arm.

"Darling, none of that is going to happen. You go in and get settled and get some sleep. I'm going to call the Key West PD and see if they'll send a squad to pick me up and take me to their shop to talk to a supervisor about all this. About Calbert. About Fennick. About the boat. And I hope, about Gabby. If the boat is here, and we can sort it all out, then I'll call you."

"Take me with you."

She smiled. "One too many variables, love. I need to flash a badge and get someone to take me seriously. I've been in their shoes. Bringing along 'the husband' only diverts interest and attention. I need them to focus. I want to see if Florida Highway Patrol picked up Calbert. Maybe call Leslie. Maybe call the Coast Guard. It's a lot to ask and I'm here with zero authority. I love you, but that's best done on my own. This is a tourist town with more than its share of entitled rich people. These guys have heard it all. I need to break through some justifiable skepticism by being as professional as possible, okay? Having you there…"

"I get it."

"Go." She popped a kiss on my cheek. "Get some rest. I'll be fine. This was never going to be one of your action movie scenarios, love."

I pulled her in for a more substantial kiss. It produced a smile that only thinly masked determination.

"Listen." I held her tight. "I'm dead on my feet, so I won't argue about sleep, but that goes for you, too."

"I'll be fine."

"Something else, Dee. This little girl. Finding her. I know you made it a 'thing' because of what happened. I get that. And I'm all in with you. If what I do helps her where the new drug failed, hoorah. But making her better doesn't make *it* better. It doesn't make what happened to you better. Do you understand what I'm saying?"

"I know."

She looked up at me. Gold in the green of her eyes dared me to question her.

"I know."

It doesn't happen often, but I met her gaze and knew she was lying. If not to me, then to herself.

65

Light sliced past the room-darkening curtains. I had to think for a moment to gain my bearings. Key West. Hampton Inn. The queen-size bed tried to pull me down into sleep again, but a tightening in my chest fought it off. I reached. The span of smooth sheets beside me lay empty.

I shot upright. Time check. Almost nine. I pulled on the pants I had dropped by the side of the bed, then my boots. My phone lay on the night-stand. Too tired to dig out a charger last night, now I feared that the battery had died.

Fifteen percent. The screen showed multiple text messages from Andy.

I swiped and opened them.

At 3:12 a.m. she wrote, *No sign of Calbert.*

At 3:48 a.m. she wrote, *Boat in KW.*

At 5:07 a.m. she wrote, *CG and PD won't search. No PC.*

At 5:27 a.m. she wrote, *Opal Key Marina. Call you soon.*

At 5:44 a.m. she wrote, *Ru*

I texted, *Call me,* then hit the phone button for her contact. The phone rang. Six times. The voice that finally answered was not Andy's. *The person you are calling...* I didn't wait for the rest.

A tuft of blonde hair topped a petite lump under the sheets on the other queen bed. Pidge left a pile of clothes on the floor at the foot of the bed. The sheet rose and fell with her deep sleep breathing.

I checked the in-room phone. The red message light did not blink. A placard on the phone listed hotel and local numbers. At the bottom of the list, I found the number I was looking for.

"Key West Police Department," a woman's voice answered.

"Hi." I tried hard to sound calm. "My name is Will Stewart. My wife, Andrea Stewart, visited your offices last night. She's a detective with the City of Essex Police in Wisconsin. She stopped in to speak to a supervisor. Can you tell me…is she still there?"

"Hold, please."

I waited. Frozen. Counting breaths and suppressing a gathering sense of panic. It may have been less than a minute, but it took forever.

"Who's this?" The voice that came back was male.

"My name is Will Stewart. I'm the husband of Detective Andrea Stewart. She was in your offices last night."

"What can I do for you, Mr. Stewart?"

"Can you connect me with Detective Stewart? Is she still there?"

"Lemme check."

Seriously? I bit back impatience that threatened to morph into anger. Another long minute passed.

"Nope. Nobody by that name here."

"She was there this morning around three. She talked to one of your supervisors."

"I'm sure she did. Do you know what this is about?"

"Yes. It's about a fugitive named Reuben Calbert. He's on his way here, to Key West, to find a yacht belonging to a man named Terrance Remington."

"What's the name of the yacht?"

"*Amphitrite.*"

"You mean *Amphitrit-ee*? Like the Greek goddess? I think that's how it's pronounced. You make it sound like a mineral."

Andy has taught me, over and over, that the caller who loses their cool loses their credibility. I bit down hard on the curses threatening to boil over.

"You're saying that Detective Stewart is not there? Is that correct?"

"That is correct, sir."

"Can you tell me when she left?"

"I'd have to ask the night supervisor. And he's gone."

I bit my lip.

"Okay. Thank you for your help." I tapped the End Call button and hurried around the bed. I jarred the lump under the sheets on the other bed. "Wake it and shake it, Pidge. We gotta go! Now!"

66

"Whoa! Whoa! Pull up here, please," I tapped the back of the front seat. Julio, the Uber driver, maneuvered his Chevy Traverse to a stop. "This will do it. Thanks!"

I hopped out. I was halfway across the street before Pidge concluded business with the driver and jumped out to follow.

"What was that?"

"This truck." I jogged to the vehicle. Black. Brush bar. Jacked suspension. Bits of rust. "It's Calbert's."

The pickup sat between lamp posts at the side of a narrow street. It had been parked in a hurry. One tire had climbed a low yellow No Parking curb, intruding on the edge of a sidewalk that bordered a well-aged, white wooden building. A parking ticket fluttered under one wiper blade. I pulled it out.

"7:33 this morning," I told Pidge when she caught up. "It's made out to a Leonard Solling from Tampa."

"That's not your guy."

There was no mistaking the vehicle. I walked to the front of the truck.

I pointed at the Florida license plates. "This guy is from Kansas. He must have stolen plates from a nearly identical truck. Explains how he got all the way here."

A quick look in the cab revealed nothing. I saw no sign of the weapon. If he'd been smart, he would have tossed the rifle in Florida Bay on his way down Highway 1. I was beginning to think Calbert was smarter than the rough, violent man he exhibited.

The side street called Rose Lane turned to cobblestone and cut a narrow path between shops in a busy tourist district. Ahead, an awning advertised the Key West Aquarium in turquoise lettering. Colorful tour trams idled at the side of the street, collecting passengers. This had been Julio's best guess when I asked him where the super-rich parked their super yachts.

"Where's the damned marina?" I searched the street. Ocean scent carries everywhere on Key West, but it seemed stronger here.

"This way." Pidge darted ahead. At the corner, she turned right and angled across the street. Reaching the sidewalk, she continued to the next corner beside something called The Island Welcome Center. Under a jungle of overhanging palm leaves, she hooked left.

An alley led us to a broad plaza, and to the sea beyond. The plaza ended at open water. Pilings designed to secure cruise ship mooring lines dotted the waterfront, which was empty. Empty of cruise ships. Empty of multi-million-dollar yachts. We crossed the geometric brick inlay pattern of the plaza and surveyed the Gulf of Mexico.

"I'm not seeing this boat you were talking about. Or any boat. Well, there's that little one," Pidge said, pointing at a sailboat catching an early morning breeze on the tabletop turquoise sea. "If it was here, it's gone."

I pulled out my phone and dialed again. Same response.

"Did you try Where's My Phone?" Pidge asked.

"My phone is right here."

"Gimme." She snatched my phone and went to work on the screen. I searched the plaza. Early morning tourists wandered toward the water's edge. A few shot pictures. Some held coffee cups.

A middle-aged couple near the edge finished having their picture taken by a young woman. The young woman handed a phone back to the man just as I approached.

"Excuse me." I smiled and tried to look like a tourist. "I wonder…did you happen to see a yacht out here this morning? Big one? White?"

The young woman shook her head and walked away.

"Got a bunch over there." The gentleman pointed at the boxed in slips at the side of the plaza a few hundred feet away. A few private boats occupied spaces between short piers, none larger than a cabin cruiser.

"Bigger." I pointed. "Out there."

"Sorry." The gentleman followed my gesture. "Not seeing much on the water this morning."

The lady shook her head in agreement, but then said, "Our friends are staying at the Opal. They might have seen it."

Her husband brightened. "Yeah, they been bragging about their waterfront view. Paid double for it."

"Not double." She frowned at the exaggeration.

"Are they here?" I asked.

He pointed. Another couple strolled toward the waterfront holding coffee cups. They passed under a brick structure comprised of three arches.

"Lou!" The man shouted. "Lou!" He waved for his friend to come. "This fella wants to know if you seen any fancy yachts parked here."

"Big one." The friend held his hands out as if sizing the fish that got away. "Big bucks."

"When?" I asked.

"This morning. Probably five. I'm up early." The friend looked at his wife. "Was it there last night?" She issued an exaggerated shrug. "I'm pretty sure it was there last night."

I thanked them and turned around in time to see Pidge bolt across the plaza. Thinking she had seen Andy, I took off after her. Pidge moved quickly, thanks to sparse morning tourist traffic. Where the plaza ended, she jogged across a wooden bridge, then onto another waterfront esplanade, this one fronting the Opal Key Resort. She sprinted along the water's edge. Her path led to where another small harbor cut into the waterfront.

Halfway there, I caught up. "Did you see her?"

She lifted my phone. A screen showed a map with a pin planted in what looked like the spot where we were standing.

"She's here." Pidge looked around. A few people walked either toward or from the waterfront. All were tourists. None were my wife.

"Let me have that." I held out my hand for the phone. I expanded and contracted the map. It seemed correctly detailed. I backed out of the application and brought up the phone function. I dialed Andy's phone again.

The call rang in my ear followed by the words *The person you are calling...*

"Hey!" Pidge alerted. "Hear that?"

I pulled the phone away from my ear and listened. Faint, somewhere nearby, I heard it. Andy's jangling all-business ring tone. I searched and tried to pinpoint a direction.

Pidge took off along the brick walkway where it dropped off to a wooden pier on the marina side. In the opposite direction a string of tourist shops occupied a single-story building, part of a district designed for passengers visiting Key West from cruise ships parked beside the larger plaza we had just crossed. I scanned the shop fronts absurdly thinking I'd find my wife shopping for a *conch critter* or a t-shirt souvenir.

"Dammit, Dee" I muttered. "Where are you?"

The ringing in my phone stopped, replaced by *The person you are calling...*

Pidge abruptly halted at a stone cylinder set in the pavement. A circular plastic top covered the cylinder. Pidge flipped the top off. It clattered onto the pavement. She reached down and tugged out a large, partially filled plastic garbage bag which she dumped on the bricks. Coffee cups, food bags, and bits of garbage spread at her feet.

She bent down and lifted Andy's phone from the heap using two fingers to avoid whatever dripped from the side of the device.

My heart sank.

67

───────

My phone rang. I swiped the accept button under the caller's name onscreen.

"Leslie, I need your help."

"I live to serve."

"Andy's missing. We think she may have run into either Desmond Fennick or Reuben Calbert. Neither one is good news. She might be on that damned boat."

"Remington's yacht? That's on its way to Key West."

"We're in Key West. It was here. Now it's gone, and I think Andy found a way to get on it. Or was forced onto it."

Leslie said nothing.

Pidge and I rode in the back of a dark gray minivan emblazoned with Florida Keys Taxi on the side and a checkered stripe below the doors. I attempted to use body language to get the driver to go faster. It had no effect, except to make my abdomen sore.

"We found Andy's phone in a trash bin at the marina," I added. I recounted the text messages I had received.

"Are you...what?" I didn't understand. She added, "The last message, Will. Are you...are you what?"

"No. It was the letters. R. U. Andy doesn't do the texting abbreviation thing. I think she meant to type Reuben but got rushed and interrupted. Maybe tried to shortcut it. I think she ran into him, or he ran into her."

"How long has she been missing?"

251

I filled her in on what I knew. She peppered me with questions about the Key West police, about Andy's intentions, about our present location. At the end of the exchange, I asked, "Can you go back to the Coast Guard and see if they have a location for that goddamned boat?"

"Do you believe she's in imminent danger?"

"Hell, yes. If Fennick's involved, he already tried to kill us twice. If she found what I think she found on that boat, he's not going to bring her back from wherever they're going."

"You mean the girl? Calbert's daughter?"

"Yes."

"Any idea where the boat is going?"

I'd been thinking about that since Pidge discovered the phone. I gave Leslie my best guess.

"West."

"West…from Key West? Isn't that the Gulf of Mexico?"

"There are more islands. There's a wildlife refuge called the Dry Tortugas."

"Sounds like a haven for pirates."

"Exactly. Can you call? The Coast Guard? There's a big station here on the island, but I don't think I'd get too far if I just drove up to the gate and asked them to launch a search. Can you see about getting a helicopter out there?"

Her hesitation only lasted a fraction of a second, but it was enough. "Will, you're not giving me a lot to go on. There's nothing in the way of probable cause here. Just hear me out…are you sure you and Andy shouldn't take a step back?"

"Or…maybe you should just hear me out…kidnapping? Murder? Jesus, Leslie, what more do you need?" She didn't answer. I plowed ahead. "These ships—don't they have transponders with GPS datalinks?"

"How the hell would I—never mind. I'll find out. Where are you?"

"On our way to the airport. I'm going to gas up and go after her."

"How do you plan to land on the boat?"

"I'll figure something out. That, or I'll find the damned boat and guide in the Coast Guard. I don't know."

I caught Pidge throwing me a cold look.

"Okay, okay. I'll do what I can." The line fell into silence or what I considered to be the inaudible hum of Leslie's skepticism.

I waited. After a moment, I said, "You called."

"What?"

"You called me. What were you calling about?"

"Oh. Did you personally know the boy? Sonjay?"

"No. Why?"

She sighed. "There's a notice online. He passed a few days ago. There's a memorial service at the Citadel of God. It's today. Newell himself."

"Cancer?" I asked.

"Lymphoma. He was only ten."

Hearts in the sky. *Gabby loves Sonjay. Sonjay loves Gabby.*

"Leslie? Can you find out what they're doing—the family? Are they doing a burial or cremation?"

"Is this that cancer drug trial thing you two have been chasing after?"

"Something like. Find the damned boat first. After that, if you have a chance…"

"Got it."

We ended the call. I resumed silently urging the driver to bend the speed limit, but my thoughts bounced back to the shabby hospice room. Was Gabby at the boy's side when he died? Was his family there? When the tears and the agony consumed Sonjay's mother or father or a sibling, did Gabby hang back or slip away? Was it all too much, knowing that she walked the same path? Did she realize that she and her shipmate Sonjay would never hunt for buried treasure together?

Pidge rode beside me without comment. Pointedly so.

"What?" I read criticism in her silence.

"The Baron isn't a Navajo." A mild glare suggested I should know what that meant beyond the obvious.

"So?"

"So, I don't care what we try to do to slow down, you're not going to get the door open to do that stupid thing you do and climb out. And even if you were to manage it, I'm not sure I can maintain control."

My phone pinged a familiar tone alerting me to an incoming message. To avoid admitting to Pidge that she was correct, I checked the screen. The notification displayed a text with an attachment from Doug Stephenson. Just as I aimed a finger at the screen to open it, the phone rang, and the screen changed to display an incoming call. The 305 area code made me hesitate, but just for a moment because only seven percent of the phone's battery power remained. I touched Answer.

"Will Stewart."

"Mr. Stewart, this is Sergeant Ellison at the Key West Police Department. You called earlier about your wife. Have you contacted her?"

"Not yet. Have you?"

"No, sir. But we did speak to the crew of the *Amphitrite.* I thought you would want to know. We reached them by radio."

"And?"

"They say they did not take on any passengers in Key West. They swapped out the crew at the Opal Key Marina, but that's all. They said they were not aware of any passengers coming down from New Orleans."

"The girl? A little kid? Possibly quite sick?"

"Nothing like that."

Liars.

"Can you locate the yacht? Don't they have transponders?"

"You mean AIS? It's not required but I'm sure they do on a high-end boat like that, however AIS works mainly for ship-to-ship traffic monitoring, and that's assuming they turn it on. Plus, those systems are only good for seven or eight miles. It's not like air traffic control. Some skippers leave it off because the frequency gets too cluttered around Key West. And the weather here—well, you know. It's not like we get Nova Scotia fog."

I took a moment.

Thinking.

"Sir?" Ellison prompted me.

"Sorry," I said.

"There's a lot to do in Key West. It's possible your wife just got busy, lost track of time. Can I ask where you're staying?"

I explained that technically we weren't staying at the Hampton Inn. The room had been available for a single night only. The manager agreed to store our bags until we found new accommodations.

"Just the same, it's possible she will go back there to look for you. You may want to wait for her at the hotel."

"Look, Sergeant, I don't want to cry wolf here, but there's something else you should know. There's a pickup truck, a black Ford F-250, jacked up, parked on—dammit, I can't remember the street—it's near the Key West Aquarium. One of your patrol officers issued a parking citation on it this morning. The plates are stolen. Check the VIN. The truck belongs to Reuben Calbert. That's the fugitive my wife talked to your night supervisor about. He's in Key West. I believe Calbert was determined to get on that yacht and I think he may have coerced my wife. I also think the crew of that ship lied to you. You should talk to the crew that got off here. Ask them if they picked up passengers in New Orleans."

Ellison said nothing. I waited a moment.

"Sergeant?"

No response. I looked at the phone screen.

Dead.

At that moment, the taxi turned off the highway. The Key West International Airport control tower popped into view. The driver followed a path past the tower into a lot for Signature Flight Support. I dug out the credit card and took care of the fare.

"Now what?" Pidge asked.

I thought about asking Pidge for her phone so I could finish my call with Ellison, but I felt a much stronger tug in the direction of the Baron parked out on the ramp. Getting into the air felt a lot more productive than talking to a Key West police sergeant whose primary theory about Andy was that she had lost herself shopping.

"We gas up and go."

68

———

P idge stopped at the service desk to arrange for the fuel truck. I hurried out the door and onto the ramp. Late morning sunshine heated my arms and the back of my neck. The bleached asphalt ramp would have been blinding without my Ray Bans. An omnipresent offshore breeze kissed and cooled the sweat on my skin. I hiked across the hot pavement toward the far corner of transient parking. The Baron sat against a fence separating general aviation aircraft from the constant comings and goings of the Part 121 air carriers. First and foremost, I needed to open the cockpit and air it out. It would be sweltering inside and would remain so until speed and altitude provided air conditioning.

I climbed onto the wing and opened the cabin door.

Pidge wasn't wrong about the difficulty of exiting the Baron's cockpit in flight. I've leaped from a Navajo twice, but that's a cabin class twin with a rear airstair door. The Navajo door shouldn't be opened in flight, and it's a handful on the controls if it happens, but it can be done. The door of the Baron is flush against the cabin where the front seat passenger sits. It swings into the wind like a car door—a hundred-mile-per-hour wind. The passenger seat is below the bottom edge of the door. I might be able to shove the door a few inches with my shoulder, maybe half a foot, but holding it open and getting up and out of the seat, reversing myself, and somehow crawling through the opening might prove impossible. Worse, pushing the door into the slipstream was the equivalent of stomping right rudder. The yaw induced on the airplane would be significant. Finally, the door might block airflow over the tail, reducing control. Combining these hazards with slow speed could cause a catastrophic upset that even Pidge could not handle.

Once we found the Remington yacht, we would have just two choices. Call the Coast Guard and circle it until they arrived. Or ditch the Baron in the sea and either get picked up by the yacht or board it by using *the other thing.* I anticipated the latter and carried two BLASTER units for the job.

I made up my mind. If it meant reaching Andy before harm reached her, I would ditch a dozen airplanes in the sea.

Pidge stepped out of the FBO office and marched across the baked ramp to join me. She left her leather jacket and her jeans in her overnight bag. This morning's t-shirt was white with an imprint across her chest that said Born To Fly, worn over tan shorts.

Sight of her made up my mind. I was leaving her here.

As if she read my thoughts, she stopped abruptly. She looked to her left toward midfield. Then she looked at me and gestured.

I stood up on the wing. Heat billowed out the open cockpit door and up my back. I had no idea what she was looking at.

"There." She pointed.

"What?"

She pointed emphatically. I hopped off the wing and hurried around the wingtip. She changed course and headed in the direction she had been pointing. She slipped through a line of parked private jets. For a split second the irrational idea that she had spotted Andy crossed my mind.

"What?" I joined her.

"That."

She pointed at an ungainly aircraft resting on the edge of the flight line. Half boat, half airplane, the amphibious plane sat on retractable wheels. The wings extended from the fuselage at shoulder height behind a forward cockpit. The single engine sat on a pylon above the center section with a pusher prop. Bulbous floats hung down from the wings.

I'd seen Lake Amphibians before. A model identical to this one operated from Leander Lake during the summer, occasionally stopping at Essex County Airport for fuel. I never took enough interest in the water lander to steal a closer look, but I remembered that the pilot had offered rides, and that Pidge had been one of the airport regulars to go for a splash landing.

"That's what we need. Because there's no way you're getting out of the Baron."

"All well and good, but unless the owner strolls out of the FBO and offers us a ride, we're SOL."

"Bullshit. I can fly it." She leaned over the amphibian's cockpit for a look. She tested the pilot's door. Locked.

The fuel truck crossed the ramp and parked in front of our airplane. I walked back to meet the lineman and think about how I would tell Pidge she wasn't coming along.

"Fill all four," I told the lineman. He gave me a cheerful thumbs-up. "What's the deal with the Lake Amphib?"

"That? Belongs to Captain Blackbeard." The lineman laughed. I glanced at the parked seaplane and got the joke. A white skull and crossbones had been painted on the all-black tail.

"Is he around?" I asked.

"Oh, no, he's dead." The lineman tugged a ground line from the back of the fuel truck and clamped it to the Baron's nose gear. I read the name stitched on his shirt. Adrian. Adrian was in his early twenties, generously tanned in accordance with his job, and prone to casting glances at the cute blonde poking around the aircraft in question.

"The original? Or the owner of that seaplane?"

"Both." Adrian grabbed his fuel slip pad and strolled toward the wing tip to see and record the registration number on the fuselage. "That Lake belonged to Captain Don Blakeman, retired American pilot. He kept it here, winters. I think he took it to a lake up in Minnesota during the summer. Called himself Captain Blackbeard, you know. With the tail painted up like that."

"He died?"

"About ten feet from where he parked last November when he came back down for the winter. Parked the airplane. Got out. Walked ten feet and —poof! Gone. Heart attack."

Adrian pulled the fuel hose from the reel and walked out enough length to service all four tanks on the Baron. He started with the right outboard.

"Damn good thing it didn't happen while he was in the air," Adrian said.

"And the plane's been sitting there ever since?"

"Hasn't moved. A lot of people ask about it. There's a guy up in Kissimmee runs a maintenance operation and a school for those things. I heard he was interested."

"Who owns it now? And do they plan to fly it?" I asked. Adrian finished the auxiliary tank, sealed it, and moved to the right main.

"Captain Blackbeard's son owns it. And no, he doesn't fly. He's a lawyer in Palm Beach. He's got it on the market, but he wants like a quarter million for it. Insane. You can pick up one of those for under a hundred. He thinks he can sell it to Jimmy Buffett."

"Jimmy Buffett flies a Grumman Albatross," I muttered.

"Used to. That's retired. Been flying a Caravan on floats lately."

I wasn't the least bit interested in the singer's latest aviation toys. My focus was on something Pidge said.

"Is there somebody around with a set of keys? Maybe let us take a look? My sister over there has her seaplane ticket."

Adrian finished filling the right main tank. He capped the fuel hose so it wouldn't drip on the wing, then sealed the tank.

"I think Lee Flanders has the keys. He runs the maintenance shop," Adrian jerked a thumb in the direction of the large hangar beside the Signature office building. "I'm sure he'd let you look it over. Want me to get the keys for you?"

"No. We have a couple things to take care of before we go. Just wanted to come out and get this topped off. Maybe we'll stop and see him on the way out."

Adrian finished fueling the Baron.

TEN MINUTES after Adrian drove the fuel truck away from the Baron, Pidge and I walked across the ramp to the large hangar adjacent to the FBO. Used more for parking and storage than maintenance, the interior featured a spotless white floor and a long, narrow workshop at the back of a building large enough to house a passenger jet.

"Set your phone alarm to go off in forty-five seconds," I told Pidge, adding instructions for what to do.

I knocked on the door to a small office. A bald man with a Quaker beard looked up from reading a binder with pages of dense numbers and graphs marred by greasy fingerprints at the edges.

"Hi," I said. "Are you Lee? Adrian said to come and see you. We were hoping to look inside that Lake Amphib outside."

Lee's face broke into a smile. "Ah! Captain Blackbeard's pirate ship. Sure. I got the keys here…uh…somewhere." He diverted his attention to the top center drawer of his desk. He stabbed his hand in and began shoving and shuffling a clutter of pens, paper clips, keys, and key chains. "Here they are!" Lee slipped one finger in a ring and twirled a set of keys several times before slapping them into his palm. A fat yellow float dangled from the keyring. "I can show you around. It's a nice bird. Clean. No corrosion. ADs are all up to snuff. Runs good. You talk to the son?"

"From Palm Beach. Yeah. I think he's a little unrealistic about the price, but—"

Pidge's phone dinged and jingled an annoying tune. She pulled it from her shorts, hit a screen button to stop the noise, then lifted it to her ear.

"Hi!...Now?...Where?...Okay, we'll be right there." Pidge shoved the phone back in her pocket. "That was Auntie Andrea, Uncle Will. She says she's done, and we have to pick her up now if we're going to be back in time for the...that thing."

"Really? Now?" I turned to Lee. "Sorry, for the bother. Maybe we can pop in next week before we head back."

Lee dropped the keys back in the drawer and sat down. "I'll be here."

THE HARDEST THING about stealing the keys from the man's desk was quelling the tension gnawing my nerves. In my head, bad outcomes for Andy multiplied with every minute that Remington's yacht sailed away from the island. I had an idea where the ship might be headed, but if it proved wrong, the Gulf of Mexico was far too large to make finding my wife anything but a long shot. Last resort would be returning to the police department to persuade the authorities. I saw little profit in that. Fennick, if he was on that yacht, would simply repeat his denial of any passengers onboard—and he would make damn sure of it before inviting the police or Coast Guard to search the ship.

I saw getting to the yacht rapidly as the only avenue to Andy's safety.

We made a show of leaving the Signature office. Pidge waited by the door, then called out to me that our taxi had arrived. I asked exaggerated questions about their hours on the coming weekend, then wished the attendant behind the desk a good day.

Outside, we stepped clear of the attendant's line of sight, found a secluded spot at the side of the building, hooked arms, and vanished. Using one of the two BLASTER units I pocketed on our rush from the Hampton Inn, I maneuvered around the building and back inside the cavernous maintenance hangar. I had worked out a scheme to knock over a ladder outside the supervisor's office as a means of getting him out from behind his desk, but by the time we arrived, he was gone. His office door stood open. The keys, with a gaudy yellow float attached, were easy to find. I dropped them in my pants pocket to make them vanish.

We pushed back into the hangar and launched.

"How do you plan to do this?" Pidge asked when we cleared the hangar door and performed a low glide across the ramp.

I maneuvered us to the Lake. We touched down near the left outboard float where the tiedown secured the wing to the ramp.

"Without being seen. Let's get this bird untied."

69

"You see a POH anywhere?" Pidge asked after she settled in.

She took the pilot's seat. I loaded her in by swinging her into a horizontal position, then floating her into the cabin feet-first from the passenger side. The Lake windscreen hinged at the center and opened upward, giving plenty of clearance. Someone watching might have wondered why one half of the clamshell doors had opened. We stayed lucky. No one watched.

I maintained a grip on Pidge's upper arm. She strapped in to avoid floating. She lifted a pair of Lightspeed headsets off the passenger seat and stowed them on the rear seat beside a second pair. I levered myself over the side and into the passenger seat. I belted in and pulled the door down and latched it.

To free my right hand and keep Pidge in the vanished state, I switched to a left-handed grip on her thigh.

"Watch it."

"Here." I pulled the Pilot Operating Handbook—a small ringed binder— from a pocket below my door. "Figure out how to fly this thing. For starters, pop the master switch and see if we have battery and gas. Kill the beacon first."

A silver toggle at the bottom of the panel snapped down. Another on the far left snapped up. Electric gyros began to whine.

"We got battery," Pidge reported.

I found the fuel gauge. One tank. The needle lifted and swung narrowly past the halfway mark. Pidge switched the battery off to save power, then lifted the binder out of my hand. She spread it open on her lap and flipped pages.

"You realize there's a shit ton of airspace out here where we could get our asses handed to us by a couple of F-18s from the Naval Air Station," she said.

"They're F-35s. Stealth fighters. Maybe I can make this whole plane disappear and show 'em how it's done."

"If you don't, they will."

"We'll be fine."

"Okay. Here it is." She read off critical airspeeds. I read them back to her. Stall speed. Flap and gear operating speeds. Never exceed speed. "Huh. Full flaps for landing and takeoff. This thing isn't exactly a speed demon."

"It'll do."

"How do you want to handle the tower?"

"I don't."

In the time since we arrived at Key West International, half a dozen aircraft had landed or had taken off. The mix favored air carriers. At least two of the operations were regional passenger jets.

I checked the windsock. "Winds favor 27. The runway's kinda busy. How do you feel about departing from the taxiway?"

"I don't think they'll give us permission for that."

"I don't plan to ask. We can have either of our voices on the tower recording."

The gravity of what we were about to do might have hit me if not for the knot in my chest at the thought of Andy in Fennick's hands. I fought off relentless attempts by my imagination to suggest the worst.

"Are you going to just sit here groping me or what?"

"Look," I warned Pidge, "cards on the table. Now's the time to bail. We're stealing an aircraft. We're busting half a dozen regs, any of which could cost our licenses or land us in prison. This won't be pretty."

"Jesus, Stewart." She broke out a devilish grin. "Don't oversell the fun here. Let's do this."

"I don't think Andy's going to be very happy about it."

She laughed. "Oh, Lord, no. Your wife is going to kill you."

"If that's all she does, I like your optimism."

Pidge returned to flipping pages in the POH.

I found a folded sectional chart in my seatback pocket. I spread it on my lap.

"Here." I pointed. We're going to Marquesas Keys."

"Why?"

"Because it's the tenth key west of Key West." I tapped the map and counted them off. "If I read this right."

"Why ten?"

"It was on the treasure map."

"The treasure map. Of course."

The Pilot Operating Handbook came up off her lap and floated over to my side of the cockpit.

"Put away your treasure map and read the startup checklist to me and let's see if we can crank this baby."

70

E ngine start became a matter of timing.

The parking ramp stretched a third of the length of the five-thousand-foot runway. Half belonged to sterile airline operations under the iron eye of the TSA. The other half, nearer to the center of the runway, served general aviation aircraft. A parallel taxiway accessed the runway at three points; one at each end, and a mid-field turnoff. Half a dozen evenly spaced short taxiways joined the main taxiway to the ramp, one of which—B7—lay just off the right wing of the Lake Amphibian.

Starting the engine meant drawing attention. I told Pidge we would fire up and immediately roll. A one hundred eighty degree turn to the right and a short run across the B7 taxiway took us to the Alpha taxiway that paralleled the runway. Normally, a right turn would take us to the end of the runway for a standard departure on Runway 27. Our plan was to turn left and aim the seaplane down the long, straight taxiway. I estimated that would give us three thousand feet.

Easily enough to get in the air.

The trick would be timing. Aircraft departing were not an issue. Landing aircraft rolled out to the end of Runway 27, turned left, and taxied to the ramp on the Alpha taxiway—our makeshift runway—blocking our takeoff. We needed to start the engine and roll when the path was clear.

I watched the approach path to Runway 27. Landing lights from a large jet hung in the eastern sky, roughly three miles out. A Cessna Caravan turboprop flared out and touched down on the runway. I crossed my fingers that the pilot would make the mid-field turnoff. He didn't. He spared the brakes and let the high-wing airplane roll to the end.

"Here." Pidge reached behind the seat and grabbed the headsets. "We may not want to chat with the tower, but I'd like to hear them freaking out."

I watched her headset rise, then settle in position where her head was. She adjusted the top band and positioned the boom mic. I did the same. To anyone watching, the headsets floated in empty air. Pidge flipped on the battery master switch and the avionics master switch. The radio stack lit up and showed the number one Comm tuned to 118.2. I suddenly realized I had no idea what frequency served Key West Tower. There hadn't been time to fetch my flight bag and iPad from the hotel.

A voice spoke through the headset.

"Caravan Eight Yankee Charlie, turn left at the end, taxi via Alpha, then your choice Bravo Five through Eight to the ramp, remain this frequency. American 4555, cleared to land Runway 27."

"4555, cleared to land."

"Come on, dude," I urged the pilot of the Caravan, who seemed to be taking his sweet time taxiing to the ramp. "Get ready, Pidge. As soon as that Caravan clears, we go."

"Think this thing will start?"

"Positive thoughts, Cap'n."

Looking as if they acted on their own, the mixture control slid to the full rich position, the throttle cracked open, and the key ticked over and held just short of the start position.

We waited. I looked over my shoulder. The American Airlines regional jet dipped through thermals on short final, closer than I had anticipated. I had misjudged the jet's size.

"Jesus Christ, are you looking for a meter with time on it?" Pidge spoke my thoughts aloud as the Cessna Caravan rolled slowly toward the ramp.

The American Airlines jet flared out and bumped purposefully down onto the runway. Smoke puffed from the tires. The jet's nose settled quickly. At five thousand feet, the runway tested the skill of pilots flying regional and full-size commercial jets into Key West. This one wasted no time deploying his spoilers, his thrust reversers and, I'm sure, his brakes.

Blowing aggressive reverse thrust, the jet thundered toward the end of the runway. The Caravan rolled past the first of the short taxiways joining the ramp.

"Turn, dammit!" I muttered.

He rolled past the second turnoff. At the far end of Runway 27, the pilots of decelerating American Flight 4555 pulled in the thrust reversers and finished braking.

"Oh, for fuck's sake!" Pidge cried out when the Caravan finally turned—onto the B7 taxiway we intended to use.

"Crank it!"

Pidge pumped the throttle twice, then turned the key. Behind and above us, the metallic grind of the starter motor woke up the prop. I had no time to utter a prayer. The engine fired immediately.

Pidge didn't wait. She advanced the throttle. The plane surged forward. She hit the right rudder and brake combination and swung the seaplane around. The Lake's nose passed under the wingtip of the Caravan. The seaplane wing passed within inches of the Caravan's tail. The big turboprop cleared as Pidge turned into the B7 taxiway.

"Tower, Eight Yankee Charlie, I can't be sure, but we just had a near miss with that seaplane taxiing out—and from where I sat, um, I don't think there's anyone in the cockpit."

"Yankee Charlie, stand by." The tower controller sounded startled. A few seconds passed. He spoke up. "Lake Amphibian on Bravo 7, hold position and identify yourself."

Pidge let loose a nervous laugh through the intercom. "I guess they're on to us."

The jet rolled to the end of the runway. Pidge reached the Alpha taxiway and turned left. She aligned the nose of the aircraft on the yellow taxiway stripe. Simultaneously the nosewheel of the jet turned and swung the long, sleek body away from the runway centerline.

"Go! Go!" Pidge shoved the throttle to the stops. The boat-like fuselage of the Lake, surprisingly low to the ground, issued empty-sounding metallic thumping as the seaplane surged forward on its wheels. The nose bobbed and reared up.

The American jet turned and presented its full profile.

"Lake Amphibian, hold position! Hold position!" the towner controller called out.

"Shit!" Pidge jerked the throttle back to idle. The seaplane's tail dropped toward the pavement. "This is not right!"

Pidge fought the controls. Almost too late, I realized what was happening. I yanked my hand from Pidge's thigh and pulled back the levers in my head.

FWOOOMP!

We reappeared and sank into the seats. The nose dropped and bounced. Pidge stabilized the controls.

"Sorry!" I spoke into the intercom. "Weight and balance." The absence of weight in the front two seats of the plane put the center of gravity too far aft. Had we lifted off, we would likely have exceeded the flyable angle of attack, stalled, and dropped out of control.

"I got this." Pidge tracked the taxiway line and advanced the throttle again. We resumed the takeoff roll. "Power check. Airspeed's alive."

We accelerated. I estimated that we had wasted a quarter of our available runway.

The nosewheel on the American jet turned. The long, sleek airliner nose entered the taxiway dead in our path.

"LAKE AMPHIB, APORT! ABORT! ABORT!" The tower controller's voice jumped an octave.

I hit the push-to-talk button and mustered a deep, gravel-laden voice.

"American 4555, avast ye scurvy dogs and hold position! Hold position!"

The American pilots hit the brakes. The nose of the jet bobbed sharply. Somebody in the cabin got a face full of seatback.

We lifted off. Pidge grabbed the gear handle and flipped it up. I heard electric whine. The seaplane wiggled and wallowed as the wheels found their hiding places.

The American jet, its nose protruding into our path, swept by two dozen feet below us. Pale pilot faces glared up at us through the windshield. I leaned away from the cockpit window to avoid being seen.

"Tower, confirm an aircraft just took off on taxiway Alpha," the irate airline captain snapped.

"Lake Amphib, this is Key West Tower. Identify yourself and return immediately for landing. Repeat. Return immediately for landing."

Pidge grinned at me.

"Lake Amphib, Key West, identify yourself! Now!"

Mischief sparkled in Pidge's eyes. "Do it."

I touched the push-to-talk button on my side and reprised the deep growl.

"Aye, Key West...ye be talkin' to Blackbeard's ghost."

71

"Do you think they'll send someone after us? Go all Homeland Security on us?"

I shrugged. Key West slipped under the right wing, taking with it the big plaza at the cruise docks. I caught a glimpse of Calbert's truck, still sitting on the brick street in Old Town, now busy with tourists and trams. The pickup eased out of sight before I could determine if the police were nearby. The open, largely empty Gulf of Mexico spread out beyond the top of the instrument panel and on both sides of the cockpit. Stark empty sky hung above us, an inverted blue bowl, vacant of clouds. Overhead and aft, the Lake's trusty Lycoming engine hummed as if it appreciated the chance to see the last of a ramp where it had been collecting dust and rust for the past five months.

I checked the fuel gauge. The needle dipped below the half tank mark. I hoped it would be enough.

"Maybe. I don't know. We'll bust into the ADIZ eventually. I'd be willing to bet they have us on radar right now. Tower's probably up somebody's ass about us. Let's just find that goddamned yacht and deal with one problem at a time. If a couple F-35s show up, we'll do as we're told, okay?" I reached for the radio and switched the frequency to 121.5, the international emergency frequency.

"How far to those islands?"

"Just guessing…twenty, maybe thirty nautical miles. A couple hours for that yacht, unless they have some reason to put the pedal to the metal, which I doubt."

"Tell me again…what's Andy doing on this boat?"

"I don't think she ever intended to board the damned thing. I think Calbert gave her no choice. He had an AR in his possession last time I saw him. What scares me is the crew change."

"Why?"

"A ship that big, they hire pros. But if you're putting out to sea to commit a crime, you probably don't want honest professionals onboard as witnesses. You want some hired hands you can trust to get the job done."

"Aren't you the optimist."

"We're operating on the assumption that the girl was taken from that hospice in Mountain Home, driven to New Orleans, and then put on this boat."

"Because she thinks she's going on a pirate cruise. Really?"

I shrugged. "You had to be there, Pidge. You had to see her drawings. Concocting a story like that gets cooperation from her and her mother. The girl wants to find pirate treasure. Newell arranges a 'pirate treasure hunt' for the dying child—what better way to get them aboard? A Make-A-Wish-type deal. The mom's all googly-eyed over this televangelist. A regular crew picks up the girl and her mother in New Orleans. But they need to remove that crew before…you know."

Pidge threw me a sharp glance. "You think *that's* what they're about?"

"Yeah. I do. That's why the crew onboard now lied to the cops and said there were no passengers. Bullshit."

"So why let Andy on board?"

"I'm not sure. Target of opportunity, perhaps. I think by crashing the party with a nosy off-duty cop, Calbert inadvertently walked right into their hands. More loose ends tied up."

"They could be going anywhere out here." Pidge waved at the windshield. "They could be on their way to South America."

"Let's hope not. Let's hope they plan to carry out the charade for the sick child, at least for a little while. There's a lot of boating and fishing in these waters. Let's hope they don't want to do anything within sight of Key West."

MARQUESAS KEYS APPEARED as a dark streak near the western horizon while Key West and several smaller Keys still lay in sight behind us. Pidge cruised at twenty-five hundred feet, clocking a blistering 125 miles per hour. I watched the water in all directions for the white yacht or its wake. Several wake lines crisscrossed, but I could not detect their origin. Small fishing charters and a single sailboat dotted the waters between Key West and the first of the tiny Keys on our path. No yachts.

I ticked them off on the map as we flew.

Mule Key. Crawfish Key. Archer Key. Joe Ingram Key. I wondered who he was and how he got his own Key. Barracouta Keys. Man Key. Ballast Key. The tiny Woman Key and the large and aptly named Boca Grande Key.

And number ten. Marquesas Keys, a collection of small islets.

We approached the cluster from due east. As we drew closer, I made out turquoise shallows surrounding dark green mangroves. At the fringes of the dark green, white-topped waves broke against the stripe of beach edging most of the island. Slowly, the shape of the key revealed itself. Marquesas Keys consisted of a manatee-shaped blob on the north side, and a string of small islets swinging down and then west to create a natural harbor. The harbor looked shallow, too shallow for a ship the size of Remington's yacht.

"There!" Pidge cried out. "See it?"

First a spec, then a sliver, the white superstructure of the *Amphitrite* rose into sight on the far side of Marquesas Keys. The ship was several hundred yards offshore over darker, deeper water. I did not detect a wake.

"They're not moving," Pidge observed. "How do you want to do this?"

"I want a close look, but I don't want to give them time to get their act together. Take us down on this side of the main island. We'll get below their line of sight and come around the right side of the island for a pass."

Pidge throttled back and let the nose fall. "How low?"

"Low enough to grab a fish for dinner."

Pidge grinned. She rolled the seaplane into a right bank and pulled the carburetor heat on and the throttle to idle. As if she'd flown this airplane all her life, she smoothly executed a dive that lifted me off the seat. Blue water raced up to meet us. Still several miles from the islands, Pidge leveled the wings and brought the nose back up as the horizon flattened all around us. Less than twenty feet above the waves, she leveled off and returned the throttle to cruise. Then she dipped lower, lower, until I thought the hull would smack wavetops racing beneath us.

The yacht disappeared from our line of sight, and us from theirs. We flew a course tangent to the north side of the island. Pidge hugged the shoreline. At times our left wing skimmed above dry white sand. Above the beach, low grass and scrub merged with mangrove forest that shielded us from the *Amphitrite*. Pidge tweaked the yoke with a light touch, keeping us over shallow waves that washed ashore. In a few places, human tracks testified to visitors. We saw no one as we streaked past at a little over a hundred miles per hour.

We flew the length of the main island. A small gap appeared, water delineating a smaller island. Pidge crossed the channel and picked up the next curved shoreline. She banked to follow it.

Amphitrite swept into view. She appeared stationary on the surface, several hundred yards from the small island.

Pidge leveled the wings and placed the yacht dead center in the windscreen. If we had been a World War II era torpedo bomber, we would have pickled our fish with certainty of a strike. The waves raced under us. The yacht grew in the windscreen.

I didn't say a word to Pidge. She knew exactly what to do. Just when our trajectory would plow us into the rear deck of the luxury yacht, she skidded the seaplane to the left, changing our course from collision to low pass. As the stern of the ship raced to meet us, she tipped the seaplane into a steep bank, giving me a perfect view through the cockpit's dome of Plexiglas.

"What the hell?" I muttered.

An unexpected tableau raced past on my left.

Above the transom, on a salon deck, three white clad crewmen stood at attention with their hands clasped. They appeared respectful, formal.

At the rear of the ship below the salon, Reuben Calbert stood at the edge of the transom. He held what at first glance appeared to be an infant in his arms, but then I realized that his bulk contrasted with the frail body of his daughter, creating the illusion of a small child.

Gabby Calbert, wrapped in a white blanket, her bald head bound in a black bandana, lay in her father's arms. She leaned out over the water. She held a cup, a container. A stream of gray ash fell from the cup. Little of the ash reached the water. Most scattered in a strong breeze. Gray liberated ghosts raced away.

Beside Calbert, a small woman wore a broad brimmed hat and dark sunglasses and hooked one arm around Calbert's back. She rested her free hand on the bundle in his arms. Gabby's mother.

At the far edge of the transom, a man in a suit held up a cell phone. Opposite him…Andy.

She stood at the edge of the deck overseeing this somber scene. She looked up to see me flash by. Our eyes met.

Our *What the hell?* expressions matched.

72

What the hell?

Andy told me later the words came into her head in my voice, as if spoken directly to her through the Plexiglas canopy of an unexplained seaplane.

ANDY ADMITTED that when she left Pidge and me at the Hampton Inn, she powered though an exoskeleton of sheer exhaustion. The morning of her second sleepless day dawned when a Ford Explorer in Key West Police Department colors arrived at the hotel. A pair of patrol officers she described as looking like teenagers—this from a grizzled veteran not yet twenty-eight —greeted her with perfect by-the-book demeanor. Andy insists that skepticism goes on over the ballistic vest, but an officer's public face, even at zero-dark-thirty, must remain friendly and open to whatever tale he or she is about to hear.

She expected nothing less from the KWPD.

Andy covered the basics for the officers calmly. Identification came first. She showed the officers her badge. She handed the senior of the two her bag to search for and find the service weapon she advised him that she carried. She offered no opposition when he stepped away from her and placed the bag on the front seat of his cruiser, well out of reach.

From that carefully choreographed introduction, she persuaded the pair to take her to the Key West Police Department building. Entrance through the sally port and an escort into the part of the building where new arrests are processed was to be expected. Courtesy came in the form of not being given handcuffs to wear while her identity took fifteen minutes to be confirmed.

Andy spent the time on a hard bench in a sterile holding zone adjacent to empty cells where drunks puke—one hopes—near the floor drain.

"So sorry for the holdup." A sergeant opened a heavy door and poked his head in. "Would a cup of coffee make up for it?" He added a smile that Andy considered genuine.

"I would have deducted points if you hadn't checked me out." She detached herself from a bench rapidly revealing itself as a torture device. He held the door open for her, and this part she did not tell me, but I knew it to be true. He ran his eyes up and down her as quickly as decorum would allow, hoping she would not notice, though she always does. Some of the genuine in his smile came from the perk of interviewing such an attractive woman. She gets that a lot.

She offered him a professional handshake. "Detective Andrea Stewart."

He took it and shook it. "Bill Merton. I'm the night supervisor. Call me Bill. May I call you Andrea?"

"Please."

He led her to a comfortable break room. She half expected to be placed in an interview room, but the station was empty, the night quiet, and she had that attractive woman thing going on. He offered her access to the coffee station, an extravaganza of brewing equipment Andy compared to Bean Brew, the best coffee shop in Essex. Andy helped herself to something hot, fresh, and nicely roasted.

"You live well here in the tropics." She followed his polite gesture to a comfortable seat at a small table. A nearby window overlooked manicured palms and tropical garden plants. Andy contrasted it to the view from the Essex PD break room, a vista that featured the oil recycling tank in the back lot of the police department.

"I'd join you, but I cut myself off after two a.m. or else I never get to sleep during the day. So…now that you've interrupted Bingo night, what can I do for the Essex Police Department?"

"Bingo night?"

The smile returned. It hooked higher on one side, giving this sergeant a boyish countenance, even though Andy described him to me as being her father's age.

"Two bucks a card. Everybody gets a card. We take the first letter and first two numbers from the license plate of each traffic stop during the shift. Seventy-four dollars on the line and I'm feeling lucky."

"I'll have to remember that one." Andy jumped straight to business. "I'm here to brief you on a fugitive I have reason to believe is coming to Key West, and on the case to which he is connected. Possible child abduction. Likely connected to two bodies that should have been found by now in Mountain Home, Arkansas. I don't believe the fugitive owns the abduction or the murders. I should be clear on that. Consider him a material witness. That said, he is possibly armed, possibly violent."

"And he's coming here?"

Andy sipped her coffee and nodded.

"And you're working this case? Officially?"

"No. I'm here on vacation." This added wry doubt to the smile. "Or else my department would have followed notification protocols. I will say, however, that after dropping my husband at the hotel, this was my first stop."

"Appreciated. Okay. Lay it on me."

Andy explained everything in her concise way. I've listened to countless versions of the same presentation late at night, after a shift, when her energy ran too high for bed and the need to expel the day's stories bubbled over. Her presentation to Merton matched her professional bearing. Her thoroughness left him with few questions, which prompted him to action precisely as she intended.

"Let me make a few calls." Merton rose when she finished. "Enjoy the coffee."

"I'm sorry about the hour. I would have come sooner but we were delayed getting out of Mountain Home. I didn't think this could wait."

"No worries. Nice thing about this hour is I usually get straight through to the person that matters. I'll be back."

Merton's trip to the phone was a short one. Andy knew he could have placed his call to the Florida Highway Patrol from his mobile while they sat in the break room, but she guessed that he preferred to handle the call out of her earshot in case FSP had a different version of the story and her involvement. When he returned, he showed no sign of distrust.

"FSP got the alert from your friend at the FBI, but they have nothing to report. Doesn't mean Calbert hasn't slipped through. Just means they know about him."

"In other words, they'll trip over him if he decides to come down the Florida Turnpike at ninety miles per hour."

Merton didn't disagree. "They get a lot of red flags from the feds."

That's when Andy texted me. *No sign of Calbert.*

Merton's next call went to the Sector Key West Coast Guard Station. This time he stayed with Andy in the break room. He traded sports talk with someone who clearly knew him, lamenting the quarterback situation with the Dolphins before asking to be connected to the Command Master Chief. While on hold, Merton shifted his cell phone aside and said, "Always go to the Master Chief. That's who really runs things."

Andy thought this conversation might be terse, anticipating that a Coast Guard Master Chief about to be rolled out of bed before 4 a.m. would be less than cordial, but the flip side of Merton's aphorism was that supervising sergeants really run the police department, and the two men were not only acquainted, but seemed to be friends.

She learned from the Coast Guard through Merton that the floating Babylon called *Amphitrite* had arrived from New Orleans. Merton pulled out his notebook and scribbled a few lines while he alternated between listening and chatting. Merton ended the call after wishing the Command Master Chief's wife success with her pregnancy.

"Your boat's too big for any of the marinas," Merton told her. "She's anchored offshore at Sunset Pier Marina. USCG sends a few swabbies over to the marina regularly to keep an eye on the weekend admirals and their overpriced tubs. Check registrations. Cite safety violations. Sniff out the drunks. You know. The CMC asked his boys to have a chat with the folks at the dock. He'll call me back."

"They need to get on board. Find out if the girl and her mother are aboard."

"Easier said than done. We have a large maritime community here. A lot of floating money. I don't need to tell you what that means. We tread lightly when we can. Let's see what the CMC says first."

That was at three-forty-eight a.m. Andy texted me, *Boat in KW*

A little more than an hour passed before Merton took a call from his Coast Guard friend. The call was brief. The tone was muted. At the end, the news was not what Andy wanted to hear.

"They spoke to the acting captain. He said the ship is being renovated, the owner is in New York, and they stopped here to rotate out the overwater crew. A refit crew boarded to take it to Galveston for machinery overhaul."

"Do they have passengers on board?"

"The captain said company policy prohibits him from discussing passenger occupancy."

Andy frowned. Merton beat her to the punch and said, "I know, that sounds like some BS, but it's SOP around here for the big money boats.

They're intensely private. He did tell the CMC to draw his own conclusions about the fact that they were a maintenance crew, had no galley crew, and were going for overhaul with most of the staterooms torn apart."

"In other words, no guests. Did they look?"

"That's a big ask. USCG can board, but they need a reason or else they need permission, and just asking generates paperwork. He said the conversation was friendly. Poking around someone's boat is certainly legal, but it becomes something more involved. Unless you can give me something more than wanting to know the passenger list, they're not inclined to push it."

That's when Andy texted me to say, *CG and PD won't search. No PC.*

No probable cause.

Merton, no dummy, knew that wasn't the answer she was looking for.

"Tell you what, Detective. My tour ends at seven. You're free to hang around here and when I'm done, I'll drive you over to the marina and we'll see if we can talk to the acting captain. If we ask nicely, he'll let us onboard."

"Tempting." Andy told me later that she saw zero chance of the captain welcoming a uniformed cop on board for a search. I read the subtext. Andy doesn't admit to using it, but she knows when the attractive woman thing works to her benefit. "You've been more than kind. I'm dead on my feet. I appreciate your time and help." She gave the sergeant her cell number and asked to be kept informed if Calbert showed up.

He retrieved her bag and returned it suggesting that while on vacation it might be better to leave her weapon in her suitcase. Or at home.

"I can have a unit drive you back to the hotel."

"That's very kind of you, but I haven't eaten since yesterday morning." Andy asked for and received a tip on a good 24-hour diner. She tapped her phone for an Uber. Merton gave her a skeptical look. Andy knew that he knew that she had no intention of going to a hotel or a diner.

She left, she hoped, on good terms with Sergeant Merton.

At five-twenty-seven a.m. Andy arrived dockside at the Opal Key Resort in Old Town Key West. With sunrise still more than an hour away, stars flooded the warm night sky. She texted, *Opal Key Marina. Call you soon.*

After hitting send, she went to the waterfront and studied the swept curves and dark tinted windows of the yacht parked offshore. Despite the darkness, only the ship's navigation lights reflected on the nearly calm water. No lights shined from the concealed cabins or luxurious afterdecks. A few expensive cabin cruisers occupied spaces along the boardwalk pier, drawing power through umbilical lines attached to the dock. She checked the time on her phone, then looked for the marina office, set within the resort building that surrounded three sides of the small-boat harbor.

The marina office proved closed, but the resort front desk, taking her for a guest, was only too happy to handle her request. They told her where to wait. A water taxi would be along in the next twenty minutes to take her out to the *Amphitrite*.

Dockside, waiting for her ride, she spotted Reuben Calbert. The big man emerged from the resort building clutching a long canvas carryall. Less than twenty yards from where Andy stood, with no one else up and around at this predawn hour, it took barely a heartbeat for their eyes to meet.

Phone in hand, Andy hit the text function and began a message. *Ru*

"Put it down," Calbert ordered her. He shifted the handles of the bag at his side into his left hand, but then plunged his right hand into the bag which he purposefully aimed at Andy.

Andy froze.

"Put it down, please. Over there. Trash bin. Please. You know what I have in this bag."

Andy didn't have to guess. She made no move.

"I meant what I said. I will go through anyone who tries to keep me from Gabby. That includes you. Don't touch the screen. Drop it in the trash. Now."

Andy held the phone carefully in her thumb and forefinger. She walked to the cement bin and made a show of placing the device over the opening. Just as she let it slip from her fingers, she slid her thumb across the *Send* icon.

"Reuben, this is not the way to go about this. You want to reach your daughter. I can help you. But if you go down this path, you're going to pay a terrible price. You're going to wind up away from your little girl for a very long time."

"As if she has time. I'm a realist. I know the score. If I can get Remington to do the right thing and give Gabby what she needs, then I don't care how much time I spend away from her. She'll be alive. That's all I care about. And if I can't, I want as much time with her as God will give us. At gunpoint, if that's my only option."

"It isn't your only option."

"Really? If you haul my ass off to jail, even if it's for a bunch of bullshit charges for the weapon or Remington's airplane, I'm still tied up for the last days of her life. I'd rather see her now and spend the rest of my life in jail." He looked at the calm water. "They said at the front desk that a water taxi is already on its way. Was that for you?"

"Yes. I'm going out to the yacht. Come with me. But not like this." Andy pointed at the threatening bag.

"And what makes you think they'll let you aboard just by asking nicely? You stay. I'll go. The crew of Mr. Remington's yacht will take orders from the other Mr. Remington." He lifted the bag.

"That's how you want your daughter to see you? At gunpoint?"

"Lady, I still don't know why you're here. I don't really care. Just stay out of my way." He turned his gaze at the edge of the small harbor where a motor launch cut the glassy surface. "My ride's here. I suggest you stay on land."

"If I stay on land, I'm pulling my phone out of that trash can and calling the cops and the Coast Guard. They'll be hauling you off that boat before you have a chance to hug your little girl. Your only play is to take me with you."

"Or kill you where you stand."

"Really? And how's that going to play out? You're going to shoot me and then stand here over my body while a water taxi pulls up and says, 'Where to, mister?' Don't be ridiculous. Take me with you."

"And then what?" He waved to attract the crewman of the motor launch.

"Then I talk you into turning yourself in for Gabby's sake."

"Yeah, good luck with that."

The boat driver's practiced hand showed. He approached the dock, swung around, and tapped the side of the launch lightly against the wooden pier.

"Two for the *Amphitrite*?"

Andy didn't wait for permission. She climbed down into the boat and took a seat. Calbert followed, his weight causing the small craft to dip as he boarded.

"Cash or credit card?" the young mariner asked with a smile.

73

A crewman, one of the three I would later see standing at attention on the deck behind Andy, descended a stairway and met the launch at the yacht's transom. His demeanor was not welcoming.

"State your business."

"I have two passengers for you," the boat driver said, cheerfully thinking the challenge had been issued to him.

"No, you don't. We're not expecting anyone."

Calbert stood up. "I'm Gabby Calbert's father. I'm coming aboard."

The crewman threw up a stop sign gesture with one hand. It managed to hold Calbert in position on the unsteady launch while the crewman pulled a small radio from his pocket. "This guy says he's Gabby Calbert's father."

The small radio responded. "Who's the woman?"

"Detective Andrea Stewart," Andy answered, guessing that the unidentified voice on the radio—watching from somewhere, possibly via a closed-circuit camera she spotted—already knew.

"Detective Andrea Stewart," the crewman relayed.

"Stand by."

Andy told me that during the five or six minutes that followed, an eternity during which Calbert, with his hand still gripping the rifle in his bag, did not move, she seriously considered drawing her weapon and declaring she had authority to board. What stopped her made her laugh.

"Piracy," she told me later. "If I forced my way onto that ship at gunpoint, I wondered if I could be charged with piracy."

74

Permission to board did not come by radio. The lower salon at the rear of the yacht lit up and a man in a crisp white uniform with three epaulet stripes decorating his shoulders hurried to the rear of the ship. He dropped expertly down the steps to the transom where his crewman held Andy and Calbert at bay. He pulled a phone from his pocket and swiped the screen until he found what he wanted. He held the phone up to compare an image to Calbert.

With a simple gesture he brushed the crewman aside.

"Please forgive the delay. We're running a minimal crew. Welcome aboard the *Amphitrite*. I'm First Officer Warren Keiffer. Your bag please, sir." Keiffer reached for Calbert's duffle bag.

Andy tensed and slipped her hand around the grip of the weapon in her shoulder satchel in case Calbert decided this was his moment to make a stand.

Calbert pulled his right hand out of the bag and swung it up into the officer's waiting grip. First Officer Keiffer quickly unzipped the bag and reached in. He pulled out a long, thin leather-bound case with a handle. Curious, Keiffer released the snaps on the case and opened it.

"Do you play pool, Mr. Calbert?"

Calbert threw Andy a wink. "I heard you had a table on board."

Keiffer closed the case and the bag. "We did, but that part of the ship is being renovated. I'm sorry, but the table has been removed."

"S'alright. I didn't think there would be time anyway." Calbert hopped from the launch to the transom.

Keiffer extended a hand to Andy, who accepted the lift.

"Your bag, please." Keiffer reached.

"I'm a police officer. My badge and weapon are inside."

"Are you here on official business?"

"She's with me," Calbert said. Keiffer held his gaze on Andy.

"It becomes official if you refuse me access to the child you have on board," she said.

Keiffer held out his hand. "I still need to inspect your bag. We don't allow weapons on board. You can turn over your bag and I will see that it is kept on the bridge until you leave. Or you can choose not to come aboard. I'm sure this launch will return you to the dock."

Andy slid the bag off her shoulder and handed it to Keiffer.

"You're going to show me where you lock this."

"I can't do that, but I can assure you that it will be on the bridge." He gestured for her to ascend to the salon deck. "Welcome aboard."

Andy climbed a curved staircase to the salon deck. Behind her, the driver of the motor launch called out a thank you and pulled away, steering back toward the lights of the Opal Resort and Marina. A thin pink line kissed the rooftops of Old Town Key West forecasting the abrupt transition from night to daylight.

Keiffer followed Calbert and Andy into the broad, artfully furnished salon deck. A platform made up of six queen-sized mattresses occupied the rear of the space, overlooking the transom. Striped pillows and lamps looking like accessories in a rich widow's parlor accented the giant sunbather's bed. Beyond that, the salon contained plush furniture and a dining table with seating for ten. A marble bar accented with gold fronted the space. Rows of bottles on glass shelves testified to the variety available.

"Please make yourselves comfortable," Keiffer waved an arm. "This is one of the last spaces to be stripped. As I said, we have a minimal crew and the galley is closed, but we have some cold sandwiches and fresh fruit. We'll set a light breakfast for you shortly after we get underway."

"Underway?" Andy asked.

"I want to see my daughter. Now. Where is she?" Calbert demanded.

"Sleeping, Mr. Calbert, but I'll let your wife know you're here. When she wakes, we will help bring your daughter on deck. She'll want to be here for the ceremony, and we will make sure she's comfortable. Please." Keiffer gestured at the furniture. "Make yourselves at home."

"What do you mean underway? What ceremony?" Andy asked.

"Apologies, ma'am. I assumed you knew."

"Knew what?"

Keiffer hesitated. "I think Mrs. Calbert is better able to explain."

"Why don't you give it a shot?" Calbert took a step toward the first officer. The implication of menace was not lost on Keiffer, who took a corresponding step backward. "What ceremony?"

"We're honoring your daughter's request, sir."

"What request?"

"For her friend Sonjay. Mr. Remington has granted use of this ship to the Newell Ministry, who has made it available to your daughter, sir. I understand she and a dear friend of hers, who passed just this week, were enthralled with pirates. Reverend Newell is making it possible for the children—for Gabby—to take her little friend's ashes to Marquesas Keys. She calls it Pirate Island."

"That's it?" Andy asked. "That's what all this has been about?"

"What else would it have been about? The ship picked up the girl and her mother in New Orleans. I took over with the crew change here in Key West, and this morning we're taking her out for the ceremony. We'll have her back by midday, and then we're taking the ship to Galveston. Again, my apologies. I assumed Mr. Jardeen would have provided all the details."

"Who?" Andy asked.

"Mr. Jardeen. From the Newell Ministry. He will be live streaming the ceremony to coordinate with a memorial service being held for the child's family by Reverend Newell at his cathedral."

"I want to see Gabby." Calbert took a step toward Keiffer.

Keiffer, unfazed by the threat, glanced at his watch. "Sir, from what I've seen, your daughter doesn't get much sleep. I'll go and check. If she's awake, I'm sure she will be excited to see you."

"What about after?" Andy asked. "What's the plan for after the ceremony?"

"I believe medical transport has been arranged, but I can check to confirm that. The round trip should only last about seven hours."

"Mr. Keiffer, why the stonewalling? I know that you spoke to the Coast Guard. You lied about having passengers."

"Ma'am, I adhered to company policy, which mandates privacy."

"Why?"

"What Mr. Remington is doing for this family is not something he wishes to share with the media. You may have noticed that he is the subject of a great deal of public attention right now."

"That's not a reason to lie to the authorities."

Keiffer gestured for Andy to step with him to the other side of the deck, away from Calbert. He leaned close and spoke just above a whisper.

"Ma'am, the child is dying. Mr. Remington is granting what is essentially a last wish. Can you imagine the media frenzy if word of this gets out? We're trying to conduct this mission quietly and with respect. I'm sure you understand."

"I need to make a phone call," Andy said.

"We don't allow cell phones aboard. They interfere with our navigation equipment. And frankly," he gestured at the water around us, "you won't get good reception beyond sight of land."

"You have radios. Take me to your bridge. I want to speak to someone on shore."

"I apologize, but I can't. As I said. Renovations. Our insurance prohibits non-crew from areas of the ship that are under construction. There's exposed wiring. Dangerous materials. In some places we have ladders replacing stairs. I'm sure you understand. Tell me who you wish to reach and what message to convey, and I will personally see that it's transmitted as long as your message doesn't breach what I just told you. Frankly, in seven hours you will be back ashore, and you can say whatever you like."

Keiffer pulled a small notepad from his pocket and offered it, with a pen, to Andy. She wrote out a message to Merton at Key West PD and handed it back.

"That's just asking to inform my husband of my whereabouts, and when I will return. Acceptable?"

Keiffer read the message. "I'll bring you the reply." He turned away from Andy. "Mr. Chou here will offer you a beverage. As I said, please make yourself comfortable. We'll be on our way soon."

With that, the first officer departed by climbing a stairway at the forward limit of the long, luxurious salon.

Andy turned and scowled at Calbert.

"What?"

"A pool cue? Where's the rifle?"

"Someone smarter than me suggested I best not be caught with that thing. It's long gone."

75

Gabby Calbert did to Andy what a few dozen children have done to me during after-midnight visits to hospital rooms in multiple cities. She greeted her with a child's bright face that somehow denied existence of the war being lost to disease within her body. She was carried into the salon, and although sunlight now flooded the space, the girl's glittering eyes and beaming smile brightened the entire deck.

A small woman with dark hair and youthful features entered ahead of Gabby, who rode in the arms of a middle-aged man absurdly wearing a business suit, the first Andy had seen in the Florida Keys. Reuben Calbert's wife instantly spotted her ex-husband and her features darkened.

"You're violating the restraining order!"

"And I'm a police officer," Andy intervened. "I have your former husband's word of honor that he will conduct himself properly. He's just here to visit his—"

"Daddy!" The girl stretched out tiny, thin arms. Black and blue stained the skin of her arms. Tape held IV needles in place on both.

When Andy described this to me, she stopped. I knew why. I knew how words sometimes jam up in a sour knot in the back of the throat. I've never described the condition of children I've seen, just as Andy doesn't share the grim details of hurt or abused kids she has seen in her work. Neither of us wish those images on the other.

Andy didn't need a medical degree to see that Gabby was close to the end. Her skin did its best to contain the bones within, but they were embossed against it. Her eyes were huge within her face because the sweet insulation of baby fat normally resident in an eight-year-old was largely gone. She wore a black silk bandana on her smooth bald head. A skull and crossbones patch had been sewed on. Andy noted pierced ears bearing diamond stud earrings—a grownup girl affectation for a girl who would not grow up.

Despite her appearance, Gabby's voice was strong. Her outcry to her father uprooted him from the chair in which he had been brooding since a tremor in the deck announced the ship getting underway. He bounded across the carpet to the man holding his daughter. Almost afraid to lift her body from him, he had no choice when the girl threw her arms around Calbert's thick neck. The girl pressed a kiss against her father's beard. Calbert's huge hands gently cupped his daughter against his chest; his bulging arms folded lightly around her.

"Baby girl." He tucked his huge head gently against hers. "Sweet, sweet baby girl."

"I didn't know you were coming!" She kissed him again and again.

Andy shifted a glance to Shelly Calbert. The woman stood aside, watching her daughter embrace her ex-husband. She wore a broad-brimmed hat and a pair of oversized sunglasses which she lifted off with one hand while she wiped her eyes with the other. Catching Andy appraising her, she quickly replaced the sunglasses.

"It was a surprise, honey," Shelly Calbert said. "Your daddy wanted to surprise you."

"This is the best surprise!"

Andy introduced herself. She shook hands with Shelly Calbert, then turned to the man in the suit.

"Deacon Willis Jardeen." He extended a hand. "Citadel of God Ministry."

Andy described his suit to me as something off the Goodwill rack. He wore a tie that might have been in fashion when Ronald Reagan presided over the Oval Office. She noted a shirt stain hiding under one edge of the tie. His shoes looked like hiking boots.

"I understand there's a service this morning." Andy shook his hand. "A memorial."

"Yes. I'll be live streaming to the cathedral."

"And this is for the boy?"

Gabby turned around quickly. "For Sonjay. For my friend, Sonjay."

"Hi, sweetie." Andy held out a hand, which Gabby shook under Andy's gentle grip. "I'm Andy."

"Are you a real policeman?"

Andy smiled at the gender bend. "I am a detective."

"Do you solve crimes? Do they let ladies solve crimes?"

"Yes. We're usually better at it. And I understand you're going to be a pirate?"

"No." She shook her head sadly and Andy briefly feared she had touched the mortality nerve, but Gabby said somberly, "There are no pirates anymore. I want to be a chef. But I would be a detective, too."

"Well, I am certain you will be a wonderful chef, but if you choose to be a detective, you will have to come and see me."

First Officer Keiffer appeared ahead of Crewman Chou who carried a huge tray full of fruit and finger sandwiches.

"Good morning, everyone. We apologize again for the galley being closed, but we hope this selection will suffice." Keiffer directed Chou to slide the tray onto a heavy wooden dining table centered in the forward half of the salon. The chairs around the table had been removed. "Please, help yourself and enjoy. We anticipate arriving at Pirate Island—" he shot a wink at Gabby "—in a little under two hours. "There's coffee in the urns on the sideboard, and fruit juices in the cooler." He pointed. "It's a beautiful morning and you're free to enjoy this salon, but please do not leave this area unescorted. There are restrooms just through that door."

Keiffer pointed, then began to make his exit. Andy called after him.

"Mr. Keiffer, were you successful? My message?"

"Oh! Thank you for reminding me. Yes. Just a few minutes ago. Your message was received by radio at the Key West Police Department. They said they would reach out to your husband."

"Do you know who you spoke to?"

Keiffer shrugged. "I'm sorry. I'm not sure."

"Merton? Sergeant Merton? He's the night supervisor."

"Yes. That's it. I'm not good with names, but that's right. The shift supervisor."

Andy watched him go, then checked her watch.

Seven-twenty-four.

76

"It's time." Deacon Jardeen used a paper napkin to dab the sweat off his forehead and neck. The natural breeze generated during the ship's three-hour journey ceased when the ship came to a gentle halt and hovered immobile on a sea of light, choppy waves. Jardeen had been careful to sit in the salon's shade, but now he stepped into sunlight. A comfortable shaded temperature in the mid-eighties leaped to triple digits in direct sunlight. Andy imagined him to be dripping inside his suit.

Several hundred yards away, a sandy beach fronted a shelf of grass that quickly blended into a forest of mangrove trees. This, they had been told, was as close to the island as the ship dared approach.

Shelly Calbert disappeared into the forward spaces for a minute or two. When she returned, she carried a bronze container the size of a small teapot. She held it with both hands.

Andy rose as Shelly Calbert passed her. Together with her ex-husband, in whose lap Gabby had dozed during the morning cruise, and who now carried his daughter in his arms, Shelly descended the staircase to the broad wood-decked transom. The family stood together. Andy gave credit to the woman for knowing when to set aside animosities. Shelly Calbert placed one arm around Reuben Calbert's back and the other on their child.

Andy looked on from a respectful distance at the base of the staircase. Jardeen moved to the same position on the opposite side of the deck. He lifted an iPhone and fussed with the screen. After a moment he said, "Okay. We're on." He aimed the phone at the trio on the transom.

Gabby lifted her face to her father. "Daddy, will you recite something for Sonjay? Something from your stories?"

Andy expected the big man to fumble and demur, but he squared himself and cleared his throat.

"Wait!" Gabby twisted against her father. "Mommy! Where's Sonjay?"

"Right here, baby." Gabby reached. Her mother passed the urn into her daughter's open hands. "Hold on tight, sweetie, until it's time."

Gabby clutched the bronze container against the blanket wrapped around her. She spoke somberly.

"Okay, now, Daddy."

Calbert cleared his throat.

"Against the waves, against the wind, against Her Majesty's ships of the Royal Navy, hear ye all now of our brave shipmate Sonjay. No buccaneer ever wielded a sword with greater skill nor fired a cannon with a sharper eye. Nor was there ever a more loyal shipmate. Bow ye heads, ye pirates, ye thieves and scoundrels, in memory of the greatest of them all, the fierce and feared scourge of the seas, our true friend…Sonjay."

Gabby twisted the cap from the container and handed it to her mother. Reuben took a step closer to the transom edge.

"In the name of the Father, the Son, and the Holy Spirit," Jardeen chanted from his corner of the deck. "Amen." He aimed his iPhone at Gabby.

"Amen," Shelly Calbert whispered.

Gabby reached out with both arms.

"Avast, ye Sonjay." She tipped the urn. A stream of gray ash began to flow.

Andy told me later that she thought the hum she heard magically came from the open urn—that a breeze crossing the opening created a harmonic sound. The notion evaporated when she saw the seaplane swing around the nearby island. At first a distraction, then an annoyance, she watched, hoping the flying fools didn't steal from Sonjay's memorial moment.

Gabby shook free the ash remnants. Wisps of Sonjay's pirate ghost raced away on the breeze.

The airplane intruding on the somber ceremony grew annoying.

Unwillingly, all eyes shifted to the plane on a collision course with the ship. Everyone except Andy ducked instinctively when at the last second, the aircraft swung left and tipped into a steep bank.

That's when Andy looked up at me.

What the hell?

77

"Take us back across the stern again. Low." I twisted in my seat, but the structure of the yacht blocked my view. The picture of Andy's bewildered expression froze in my mind's eye.

Pidge steered away from the island. She let the nose swing through ninety degrees, then leveled to put some space between us and the yacht.

"That was Andy. Right?"

"Yeah."

"Uh…not to be a party pooper, but did she look like she was just sort of standing around? I mean, like not in any danger at all?"

"Kinda."

"And were those people dumping somebody's ashes?"

"Looks like."

"So did we totally steal an airplane and bust a dozen regs for no good reason?"

I didn't answer.

"I mean, not that this hasn't been fun."

She added bank to the steep right turn. I marveled that the right wing didn't trace a line in the waves. We pulled a two-G turn and rolled out on a line that would cross the ship's stern with a perfect view of the transom and the luxury deck just above it.

We raced past the *Amphitrite* stern at what should have been eye level with Calbert.

Empty. The transom lay empty. The salon deck, vacant.

"What the fuck?" Pidge craned her neck.

There was no sign of anyone aboard the vessel.

Pidge pulled up and away. "Uh, okay…did we see what we saw?" She initiated a gradual climb and a right turn that would bring us around for another pass. "You saw people, right? Andy? People doing the ash thing? Some guy in a suit? You saw them, right?"

As crazy as it seemed in my head, a split second of uncertainty crossed my mind. I fought it off. Andy was there. Calbert was there. The child. I whipped my head around and looked at the open sea behind the boat, thinking for a horrible moment I might see people struggling in the water.

Wisps of gray ash floated on the wind.

"Yeah. Absolutely." I pressed the push-to-talk button. "Vessel *Amphitrite*, this is seaplane Bravo Bravo transmitting on Guard, please respond."

No answer.

I repeated the call.

No answer.

"Do you think they're not listening?"

"No idea," I replied through the intercom. "Go left and come around it again on the same line as before."

As Pidge executed a wide left turn, I watched the ship. White water roiled at the rear. The yacht surged forward.

I pressed transmit. "Vessel *Amphitrite,* cut your engines and stop. Repeat. Cut your engines and stop. This is Coast Guard seaplane Bravo Bravo. You are ordered to stop."

"Coast Guard *Bravo Bravo?*" Pidge questioned.

"Blackbeard. We have a pirate flag on our tail."

Water churned up at the back of the ship. The bow knifed through the waves. A wake formed.

Pidge completed a teardrop course reversal and made another pass across the stern close enough that I could have leaped onto the deck. Once more, everyone we had seen on the first pass was gone. Even the surface of a large wooden table had been cleared. I could have sworn, in the corner of my eye, that I'd seen food on that table on our first pass.

"We're going in."

Pidge glanced at me. "Landing? Like…on the water?"

"I want to get on that ship." I twisted in my seat. The yacht plowed forward, slicing and spreading the sea in its path. I studied the waves. "What do you think? Winds out of the southwest?"

"Something like that, You want me to land this thing on the water?"

"You're the one that picked out the seaplane. How hard can it be? Line up. Pull the power. Set up a glide. The manual says full flaps. Make sure the gear is up. Flare it onto the water. See if you can put us about a hundred yards ahead of the boat."

Pidge rolled her eyes at me.

"Sure. Why not right alongside? You can step right onto the damned yacht."

I gave her a mirthless grin. "You got this. Once we're down, I'm bailing out." I glanced up at the spinning prop overhead. "I'd rather not be chewed to pieces, so cut the engine for me to get out. When I'm gone, fire it up and take this thing back to Key West. I don't recommend landing at the airport. Beach it somewhere and beat feet before anyone asks questions. In other words, don't get caught."

"Right." She wiggled in her seat. "Here we go."

78

———————

P idge climbed the LA4-200 on a path that matched the sailing course of the *Amphitrite*. Six hundred feet above and a mile ahead of the yacht, she turned ninety degrees to the right, then another ninety degrees. We flew directly opposite the ship on the downwind leg of a landing pattern. As soon as we were adjacent to where the stern of the ship generated a growing wake, she pulled the carburetor heat and reduced power. Our airspeed decayed. She dropped the flaps.

"Flaps down, gear up," she called out. I grabbed the POH binder and flipped pages until I found the landing checklist. I read off each item.

"Fuel pump on." Pidge flicked the toggle.

"Hydraulic pump on." Pidge confirmed.

"Carb heat on." Pidge tapped the already pulled control.

"Water rudder up." Pidge shrugged. We hadn't used it, so it seemed safe to assume.

Pidge executed a smooth ninety-degree turn to the right, placing the ship at our two o'clock position. We descended through five hundred feet. She turned right and set up a final approach course parallel to the ship.

"Gimme seventy on final," I said. She nailed the airspeed at seventy.

"Final gear check. I really don't want to face plant in this thing."

"Gear is up," I confirmed, assuring us that a smooth hull would touch the water instead of wheels that would bury themselves and flip the airplane.

The yacht passed us in reverse a hundred yards off to our right. I estimated our touchdown spot ahead, easily within reach of the ship. I pulled a power unit and prop from my pocket and snapped the blade in place. A quick test of the slide control switch spun the prop. A second set remained snug in my pocket.

We settled toward the vast blue plateau that is the Gulf of Mexico. I briefly understood one of the challenges of landing a seaplane as the distance between us and the water became weirdly unreadable. My ordinarily reliable peripheral vision and sense of perspective wavered.

Hold the glide, Pidge.

She held a steady three hundred foot per minute descent. The seaplane approached the water. Pidge tugged the control and flared. Waves raced toward us, looking rougher now than I had expected. From the sky, the surface looked smooth and inviting. Now it felt like trying to land on a plowed field.

Something smacked the hull. Pidge jittered on the controls. Another smack. Then another and another. Then a succession of them, like tires on a washboard road. Everything merged into a whooshing roar. Water splashed up around us. A few drops spattered the windscreen. Pidge cut the throttle to idle, then pulled the mixture control. The engine fell silent. The prop stopped. The seaplane settled and rocked in the waves.

We were down.

Pidge grinned. "Shit, nothing to it. I could get used to that."

I shook myself out of a self-congratulatory reverie and reached for the door latch. "Okay, I'm outta here. Keep flaps down for takeoff."

"Got it."

"Try to get it up on the step on your run."

"I got it! I got it! Get your ass outta here."

I flipped the door up. Seatbelt off, BLASTER in hand, I threw the levers in my mind's eye full forward.

Fwooomp!

I vanished.

"Fucking weird-ass shit," Pidge muttered. "Hurry up. I'm getting seasick here."

I heaved myself up and sideways. My legs bumped awkwardly against the seat, the instrument panel, and then the door, but my push-off angle was good, sending me sideways along the leading edge of the seaplane's wing.

"Clear!" I shouted back at Pidge. I heard the door swing down and latch.

I sailed out past the wingtip, leaving the bobbing seaplane behind. Quartering behind the plane, the yacht cut through the waves at what looked like full speed. We had landed on a parallel course. Pidge neatly placed me ahead of the ship. A short flight across the water would place me on a tidy intercept course with Remington's big boat.

I reached my right arm out and aimed the BLASTER, calculating the best speed for a quick rendezvous. Too fast, and I would shoot through the ship's projected course. Too slow, and I would play catch-up. Neither presented an insurmountable problem.

Just as I was about to give the handheld unit power to pull me forward, I saw the ship change course. The bow of the yacht shifted to its left, toward me, toward the airplane. For an instant, I thought it was an illusion brought on by my glide away from the plane.

It was no illusion. The ship turned.

Closing fast, the ship cut into the waves on a line directly aimed at the bobbing seaplane. In the cockpit, Pidge bowed her head over the POH, reading through the startup checklist.

"PIDGE! GO! GO!" She lifted her head in my direction. I senselessly waved my vanished arm at her. "GO!"

She couldn't see the ship bearing down on her. The engine pod and cockpit structure above and behind her obscured her view.

"CRANK IT!" I shouted.

A hundred yards away, the yacht's bow cut through wave after wave. Spray flew on both sides of the ship. There was no mistaking the intent.

I rotated my body and hit the power control slide. I shot forward. Too fast, too much. I slapped up against the side of the seaplane. Pidge startled.

I banged on the Plexiglas. "Go! They're trying to run you down. Hit it!"

Pidge threw a look over her shoulder, but it was futile. Her view of the collision bearing down on her was blocked. She spun her head back and slapped the mixture control full forward. She grabbed the key. The prop spun. I pushed away and shot backward along the leading edge of the wing.

Last time the prop had barely swung through a full turn before the engine fired. I expected the lively engine to fire quickly and Pidge to hit the throttle and be long gone ahead of the yacht.

The starter cranked.

The prop turned.

The engine remained silent.

Seventy yards away, the swept lines of the yacht grew larger.

I drifted off the tip of the wing, rising slowly. Pidge released the starter and pumped the throttle to prime the engine.

No! Don't prime it! Hot start, Pidge!

I feared the worst. Instead of priming, she flooded the cylinders.

She hit the starter again. The battery remained strong. The electric starter bit. Blade by blade, the prop turned. The starter motor sounded like someone rapidly gasping for air.

Not even a pop.

"Flooded!" I shouted. "Mixture closed! Throttle open! Hit it until it pops!"

Her hands flew to adjust the controls. She hit the starter again. The prop turned, the engine turned, and then—

Pop-pop!

The motor fired twice, briefly accelerating the prop and starter. In the cockpit, Pidge raced to push the mixture forward, while she held the starter open. Too slow. The pops from the engine ceased. The starter returned to a frustrating, slow cadence.

Fifty yards.

An impulse to charge the yacht crossed my mind. If I could reach the bridge in time, I might be able to throw it off course.

The idea was insane. There was no time.

Pidge cranked the starter. The engine offered no sign of life.

Thirty yards.

Only one other option now.

Ignoring the spinning prop or the possibility that it might fire and pull me up into its arc, I shoved the power forward and dove toward the seaplane. I hit the side of the fuselage hard, bashing my legs against aluminum and splashing my feet into the water. The noise shocked Pidge, who let go of the starter. She looked wild-eyed over her shoulder. The seaplane had weather vaned into the wind. She had a clear line of sight over the right wing.

Twenty yards and bearing down fast.

I threw open the passenger-side hatch.

"I'm here! Get out!"

Pidge threw the POH binder off her lap and jerked the headset from her skull. She snapped open her seatbelt.

Fifteen.

She threw the belts aside and grabbed the edge of the door on my side of the cockpit. I reached in and closed a grip on her upper arm.

Ten. Five.

The violence of the ship's hull hitting the tail of the seaplane blinded me and broke my grip. Something stabbed me in the left leg. Aluminum knocked me aside, then kicked me skyward. Metal screamed. Pidge screamed. Saltwater stung my eyes.

The plane flipped, driven forward by the relentless steel hull striking the tail. I twisted to see the horror from above. Completely inverted, the seaplane crunched under the passing hull. The right wing was gone, sliced through. Torn aluminum scraped the ship. As if dunked by a giant hand, the fuselage dove into the sea, taking Pidge with it. Bumping and hammering, the steel ship and foaming wake passed over the wrecked seaplane.

"PIDGE!" I shouted.

Beneath roiling water and foam, I saw a fading flash of white. Tail. Severed wing. I couldn't tell. It didn't matter. The open cockpit had flooded. The weight of the top-mounted engine anchored the wreckage and pulled it down.

I jammed the BLASTER into my shirt. I rotated and—

FWOOOMP!

—appeared and plunged, headfirst, into the water. No sooner had I hit water, than I hit aluminum. My outstretched arms glanced off something flat and white. The airplane's horizontal stabilizer. I found an edge, pulled, and heaved myself downward, aiming for what I hoped was the wing, a white shape ahead. I kicked the leading edge of the tail to dive deeper.

The seaplane sank. Pressure stabbed my ears. The water grew darker, but my aim held. I felt the underside of the remaining left wing, the tucked landing gear, and the wing's leading edge. I grabbed and pulled myself toward where I thought I'd find the cockpit, only to be smacked on the side of the head on the same bruise Andy had created during her nightmare. Pain flared up the side of my face. Stars accented my vision. I wasn't sure what hit me until it hit me again, and again. Blows came out of the darkness, flailing and fighting.

Pidge!

She had extracted herself from the inverted cockpit and now tried to fight her way past me toward the fading light above us. The sinking plane had taken us deep. My lungs wanted to burst. Neither of us had enough air to reach the surface.

I threw a grip around whatever I could and—

FWOOOMP!

—vanished.

We became weightless empty space that displaced water, the next best thing to a sunken balloon. Instant buoyance shot us in the only direction a bubble will go.

Up.

Water rushed past us.

We burst from the surface gasping. My ears popped. I tightened my grip around what turned out to be Pidge's thin torso. With her back to me, she spit water and gasped, but at least she stopped fighting.

The speed of our submerged ascent transitioned into a rapid climb above the surface. The sea spread around us, marred by a fresh wake. The vicious architect of the seaplane's destruction plowed forward toward an empty horizon, southwestward, away from Pirate Island, away from the Florida Keys.

I shoved my hand down into the soaked front of my shirt and groped around until my fingers closed on the power unit, still attached to the prop. After tangling with the shirt, I pulled it free. Uttering a quick prayer, I tried the slide control. The prop whirred and answered. I arrested our ascent.

Pidge heaved and coughed. She spit again. She gasped and tamed her breathing. I waited for the inevitable curses to fly. Perhaps for the first time since I've known Pidge, she said nothing.

It worried me.

79

On a dreary fall day after a particularly frustrating Packer loss, I muttered something about making myself useful and I wandered out to my garage workbench with a handful of the flashlight cases I use in the small power units I've built. I spent the next two hours carefully sealing the cases with silicone. I remember thinking I might end up in water with one of them.

I gave myself a healthy pat on the back when the unit in my hand buzzed to life despite the seawater dunking it had been given. A second unit in a cargo pocket bumped reassuringly against my thigh.

The yacht that had murdered the little seaplane and tried to murder Pidge sailed toward an empty horizon at the head of a frothy wake. Her captain had commanded full speed ahead.

I brewed something dark and murderous in my heart, something I've touched before. It found fresh power in the fact that Andy and Calbert and his family were nowhere to be seen.

The ship's transom lay bare. The salon deck above that showed no sign of life. Another salon above that appeared empty. Dark tinted windows in other parts of the ship kept her secrets from outside eyes.

I guessed the ship's speed at somewhere between fifteen and twenty knots. Not exactly blowing the doors off, but the distance between the yacht and where Pidge and I hung in the air grew quickly.

I put out my arm and slid the power control forward. The unseen prop spun and pulled us against a brisk relative wind. The cool sensation that envelops me when I vanish insulated my skin. I could only assume that the warm wind began to dry our clothing.

I searched the waters below and behind us.

Seeing Andy, Calbert, and his family casually aboard the yacht had been jarring. The girl had been dumping ashes into the sea. Her friend Sonjay, I assumed. A ceremony. Nothing nefarious about it, except that someone felt compelled to murder two people at the hospice and point a finger at Calbert for the deed. The two scenes did not mesh.

And then suddenly, everyone was gone.

A buzz job by a crazy seaplane pilot didn't warrant a mass evacuation of the deck. I worried that the crew felt they'd been spotted, and that Andy and everyone else had been sent into the sea.

The ship's wake began where the yacht floated when we arrived. I searched the surface but saw nothing, no color, no splashing, no bobbing heads, to confirm my worst fears.

If not in the water, then on the ship.

I pushed the power control slide to the stop. The BLASTER buzzed in my hand, throwing prop wash up my arm.

Pidge continued coughing and spitting, but in between she managed a few choice words. Eventually, she asked, "Where are we going?"

"Blackbeard is boarding that son of a bitch."

"Good." She added a few more words.

80

The yacht had plowed almost half a mile ahead before I began a tail chase that left Pirate Island behind. Backlit sunshine turned the Gulf waters a stark sapphire blue. The emptiness of the flat seascape made me nervous about having nothing but a pair of C-cell batteries for propulsion. I felt a degree of relief when we caught up to the fleeing ship.

My initial impulse had been to approach the lower salon—the space where I'd seen Andy and the others—from behind, but the salon stretched into the ship and hid spaces from view. And I had a passenger. I decided that exploring the ship with my arm around Pidge was impractical.

I veered to the right and climbed. The superstructure passed by until I was even with the broad, tinted, and curved windows of the ship's bridge. Above the bridge, a white deck with a single white leather sofa overlooked the entire bow below a trio of high radar domes and multiple antennas.

I matched the ship's speed. Pacing the superstructure, I gradually angled closer until we passed over a clear glass rail that guarded the high observation deck. I dropped in behind the waist-high glass. My feet touched the deck. I killed the BLASTER power and grabbed the rail to prevent the wind from throwing us aft.

I checked for cameras mounted on the radar mast. Seeing none, I warned Pidge.

"Feet on the deck?"

"Aye, captain."

Fwooomp!

We reappeared and settled. Our clothing dripped on the wooden deck. Pidge staggered, then pushed away from me and dropped on the leather sofa.

"Fuck, this does not look good." She stared down at her left forearm.

Midway between the elbow and the wrist, her arm had an angle that did not belong. She turned pale.

"Nope. That is not right." She tried to rise, but I landed a hand on her shoulder.

"Sit. Stay. Keep that thing immobile."

"It gets better." She cradled her left arm in her lap and pointed with her right. "One of us is bleeding."

Spatters of red painted the deck.

Crap! I quickly looked her over.

"Where are you hurt? Besides that." I searched her skin, her clothes.

"Back off, dude." She pushed me. "It's not me."

"What?"

"It's you. Look." She pointed at my left leg.

Blood ran down my thigh. I traced it back to a tear in my pants. Inside the tear, I found a ragged slash in my skin. I quickly sat down beside Pidge for a closer look.

"You musta caught some sharp aluminum." She batted my hands aside. "Move! Lemme look at it."

One-handed, she spread the torn fabric of my pants leg. "Doesn't look like it caught an artery, but you're going to need a couple dozen stitches. Meanwhile, you're bleeding all over this fucking boat. We gotta wrap this. Pull my shirt off."

"Who made you Nurse Ratchet?"

"Just do it." She raised her right arm. "Pull it up on this side, then over my head."

I followed orders. With her right arm and head freed, I carefully tugged the t-shirt off her broken left arm.

"Does that hurt?"

"Not yet. Does that mean I'm in shock?"

I sat down beside her and twisted the shirt to wring the seawater out of it.

"Maybe. Holy crap, Pidge." I blinked.

"What?" She glanced down at the searing hot pink bra she wore. "This old thing?"

"At least now I'll know the cause if Arun shows up at work blind." I wrapped the shirt around my thigh and joined the ends in a knot. I tugged it tight but still didn't feel the cut. Blood spotted the white shirt, but the spot didn't spread. Pressure on the wound seemed to staunch the flow.

"Tight," she ordered.

"I got this."

I finished the job with a half-assed double knot and decided it would hold until I found something better. There had to be medical supplies on this boat somewhere.

It would have to wait. I had more pressing matters at hand.

"I'm going to find Andy. You're going to stay here. Lie down on this sofa. Less chance of anyone seeing you."

"What, right out here in the open?"

"This is one of those cool spots on a ship like this that no one ever visits. You'll be fine up here. Keep that arm from moving."

She leaned back against a gaudy striped pillow, cradled her arm across her stomach, and lifted her legs onto the sofa. Despite the rough edges she wears like armor, the girl looked small and vulnerable.

"Get me some fucking sunscreen while you're poking around."

Maybe not that vulnerable.

I gave the makeshift bandage another tug, then stood up to test it. It would not do to leave a blood trail all over. I had to assume it would still drip and become visible even if I wasn't.

"Don't go anywhere."

"And a beer. Sunscreen and a beer."

A STAIRWAY LED AFT from the high sundeck. The next level down had a white cloth canopy over yet another seating area that flowed into a paneled parlor space fronted by an expanse of windows. This part of the ship had been stripped of furniture and furnishings. I guessed this deck to be above the ship's bridge.

I eased down another stairway to yet another huge salon—this one also stripped of furniture and decor. Tarps covered the floor. At the forward end, a solid wall separated the living space from the ship's operational bridge. Doors on both sides accessed the command spaces. I heard urgent voices. Movement at the door on the left side caught my eye.

Fwooomp!

I vanished just as two crewmen appeared. Both wore white. Both may have been part of the cadre overlooking Gabby's solemn sendoff of Sonjay. Both now carried backpacks and seemed in a hurry to get below. They jogged through the space and disappeared down another stairway.

I grabbed the stair rail and heaved myself over. The movement sent a jolt of sharp pain up from my thigh.

Ah. There it is.

I checked the deck below. No blood drops. Good enough for now.

I pulled on the stair rail and sent myself across the empty deck to the passage on the right that led to the bridge. Careful to clear it and ensure that no one came from the opposite direction, I pulled myself along a handrail until the passageway opened on the bridge.

Every bit as luxurious as the rest of the ship in its prime, the bridge featured matching pairs of plush leather seats for visitors, an equally plush set of chairs for a captain and first officer, and a bank of computer monitors. Most of the monitors displayed readings from the ship's systems. One showed a moving map as the *Amphitrite* sailed west from Marquesas Keys into open water. One screen showed rows of closed-circuit TV images in high-definition color. I quickly scanned the images to make sure none of them showed Pidge.

A man in a white officer's uniform with shoulder epaulets moved from one station to the next, checking the ship's systems. He made an adjustment to controls, but for the most part touched nothing. Satisfied with his work, he departed the bridge, following the crewman who left ahead of him.

Except for me, the ship's bridge was empty. Automation is one thing, but I had a feeling that leaving the bridge unattended was far from normal.

I shoved off and glided to the nearest officer's chair, then to the row of controls and monitors. A few of the controls made sense to me. Some would need further study. The ship had a wheel, but it looked a lot more like a plush golf cart steering wheel than a ship's wheel. I saw it twitch.

Autopilot.

On the map display, a magenta line lay vertically down the center of the screen. A blue dot rode the line. Boxes above and below the main portion of the map screen read out course, track, speed, and more. Given a few minutes, I felt sure I would be able to decipher all the information.

I didn't have a few minutes.

I shifted sideways to examine the screen with all the camera boxes. The officer who just left hurried through one box after another. The only other movement came from what looked like a boat deck. Somewhere below, a utility compartment contained a pair of jet skis and a small zodiac-style craft with an outboard engine. I looked closer. A crewman loaded a carryall and several smaller packs into the rigid inflatable zodiac. Another connected hoist lines to the boat. Off to the side, a third crewman operated a small panel set in a wall that suddenly moved outward and upward. The side of the ship opened, exposing the passing sea. Part of the wall that opened outward contained two channels that held the mechanism that would lift and extend the zodiac to a position over the water, then lower it for release.

The crew was leaving.

Autopilot. The ship was on autopilot and the crew was leaving.

This could not be good.

Fwooomp!

I appeared and settled on my feet, taking another jolt up the left leg. Ignoring the pain, I started to leave the bridge. On my way out, I saw Andy's satchel laying in one of the two plush command chairs. I picked it up and checked inside. Badge. Weapon. A spare magazine. Her wallet. It appeared intact. I flipped the strap over my head so that the bag hung on my right side, away from the wounded thigh.

I hurried off the bridge and looked for a ladder or stairway. Andy and the rest had to be here, but I had a dark feeling that I wouldn't find them lounging in a plush stateroom.

If this crew—a reduced crew on a ship that might normally carry ten or twenty cooks, stewards, officers and sea crew—was leaving, it meant they were leaving no witnesses.

The message from the KWPD officer, echoed in my head.

They say they did not take on any passengers in Key West.

Like hell they didn't.

81

Everything below the two main salon decks had been stripped clean. The walls were bare steel. Electrical lines hung from above. Plumbing pipes stuck out of the deck. A litter of torn insulation lay on top of canvas tarps dropped to protect expensive teak floors. The mess told a tale—a project interrupted, or perhaps halted for want of payment. People with stratospheric bank accounts go to remarkable lengths to hide their losses, or their bad judgment. Somehow, it's far easier for a billionaire to fail to pay his bills than a single mother. I wondered, as I navigated deeper into the ship, how this floating money pit fit into Terrance Remington's financial picture. To all accounts, the man's wealth would soon eclipse that of the richest man in the world. It looked like he was already spending that wealth.

I buried my curiosity about the condition of the ship. I was far more concerned about my wife.

Our seaplane buzz job cleared the decks. In under a minute, everyone had been ushered out of sight. That could only mean one thing. They had been caught in a lie. Someone could now contradict their claim that the ship carried no passengers.

Pidge and I solved that problem by landing. Running down the seaplane eliminated the witnesses. But what about the witnesses on board?

Dammit, Dee! What were you thinking?

I found a ladder that descended deeper into the yacht.

Fwooomp!

I vanished and took the easy way down, which also dealt with the possi-

305

bility of running into a member of the crew, although by now, having met none of them, I became convinced that they were all on the boat deck preparing their departure.

The zodiac had enough range to reach Marquesas Keys. Was it capable of reaching Key West? Or did they plan to rendezvous with another boat?

Either way, the abandoned *Amphitrite* would sail deeper into the open Gulf of Mexico. I had no illusions about that one-way journey. Something was going to happen to this ship out in the open water. A terrible accident. Lost at sea. Thank heaven, Remington's PR hacks would declare, there were no passengers aboard.

The crew leaving the ship had faith that its destruction would take place uninterrupted. That meant the crew had taken steps to ensure that Andy, Calbert, and his family would not interfere.

Locked up. Or worse.

I picked up the pace. Maybe running into a crewman wouldn't be the worst idea.

I dropped into a passageway marked Crew Only Beyond This Point. Basic tile floor. Painted steel walls. No carpets, no frills. In the direction of the bow, the passage accessed a series of compartments. Storage. A pantry. A chart locker. In the other direction, aft, I heard voices and the whir of machinery. The boat deck. Launch of the escape boat continued.

Something smelled. Metallic. Burning. Familiar. I noticed a slight haze in the air, perceptible as a thin halo around the passage lights.

Fire? Did they light a fire?

The impulse to go aft and rain destruction on the escaping crew tugged hard. Maybe I could disable their escape boat. Enough damage would force them to remain on the ship and reveal what they had done with the passengers.

Or it might get me disabled or killed, and in either case I would be of little use to Andy.

I chose the opposite direction. I used a rail to pull myself past two storage rooms, a room full of office supplies, an empty compartment, and a closet full of pipes and valves. An intersection joined a passage across the midsection of the ship. The smell grew stronger.

Fwooomp!

I reappeared. I moved faster on my feet. I jogged down the center passage, then took a left. Faint smoke hung in the air.

I recognized the scent.

Welding.

Proof of my assumption lay ahead. An acetylene bottle and welding tools had been left in the passage, leaning against a steel door. Dark burn marks in two spots where the door met the jamb revealed spot welding.

I waved my hand over the scorched area, then tapped it. Hot. Not searing, but hot enough that the work had been recent.

The steel door had a handle without a lock. How do you lock a door without a lock? Weld it.

I balled a fist and pounded on the door. Gently. Soft thudding I hoped would not carry to the boat deck. I reasoned that a light touch would bring the answer I needed without bringing someone from the crew.

I paused.

Voices.

Thump! Thump! Thump! Someone inside banged on the door. The voices grew louder. Someone inside grabbed the door handle and worked it. The handle wiggled to no avail. The voices grew louder but remained incomprehensible. The hammering on the inside continued. I waited, thinking hard.

When the noise inside ceased, I pounded out a rapid cadence.

Shave and a haircut...

I waited. The answer came quickly. My heart leaped.

Thump! Thump!

Andy. Who else would know that her childish husband would pound out a joke bit in a life-or-death circumstance? Who else but Andy would know how to answer it?

Now all I needed was a way to cut through a door that had been welded shut. My only problem was that I knew nothing about welding or cutting torches. The rig left in the hallway had been used to spot-weld the door, but it seemed unlikely that the same device could be used as a cutting torch. Worse, if I started using a torch on the door, what would it do inside? Heat? Fire? I had no idea how big the compartment was or what it contained.

Another notion sprang to mind. I thought about it for a moment and then decided I needed some help. I looked up and down the passageway. At the end, where the corridor split left and right, I spotted a red box mounted on the wall. A fire ax hung inside.

No fire ax would cut through the weld on a steel door, but that's not what I needed it for. I jogged to the box, jerked it open and grabbed the ax.

Back in position, I leaned the ax against the door. The voices inside had gone silent. I forced myself to believe that Andy had taken charge and had assured the others that help was on the other side of the steel.

If this worked...

Fwooomp!

I vanished and immediately lost contact with the deck. I reached down with my right hand and picked up the heavy ax, which remained visible. The weight of the ax drove my feet back down on the deck. I split my stance and wedged one foot against the door and the other against the base of the wall opposite the door.

The first spot weld had been applied sixteen inches above the door handle. I laid my unseen left hand on the door beside the weld and *pushed* the levers in my head.

I've become adept at extending *the other thing* into people and objects beyond myself. The levers I imagine accept added pressure when I need it.

I pushed. The effect radiated outward. The steel under my hand began to vanish. *The other thing* spread on the door like spilled water. A hole the size of a silver dollar appeared. Through it, I saw movement. I saw rich auburn hair. The hair moved and I saw the most beautiful gold-flecked green eye in the world. Andy looked through the expanding void. She spoke. The steel may have vanished, but the door wasn't gone. Her words remained muted.

The hole expanded. It reached the seam where the door had been welded to the jamb. I raised the ax and reversed it so that the sharp edge faced me. I waved it over the hole. Andy's eyes, both now visible, transitioned from curious to blossoming awareness. She moved back.

The other thing spread the visual hole in the door. The edges blurred. The steel looked frayed. I pushed until the hole consumed the spot weld. At that instant, I drew back the ax and slammed it into the void in the door. The ax clanged against unseen steel. I felt something give. At the circular border between *the other thing* and visible steel, the metal fractured. The hole in the door flashed back into solid steel, a severed disk that fell and clattered on the deck. Through the new opening, Andy called to me.

"Will!"

"I'm here. One more to go."

I heard Reuben Calbert mutter something Pidge might say.

The second spot weld had been placed below the door handle. To reach it I had to crouch, a contortionist's feat that involved wedging my feet and bending my knees. Pressure on the wound on my thigh increased because of the muscle flexing in my thigh. Spots of blood appeared on the deck below me.

Wiggling and twisting, I struggled into position and repeated the trick. A fresh disk of steel broke from the door, taking the second spot weld with it. I stood up again and—

Fwooomp!

—reappeared holding the ax in one hand and flipping the door handle with the other. The compartment door latch released. The door swung open.

82

Andy hurried past me. She jogged to the intersection of the main fore-aft passageway and searched. When she returned, she led me back into the small engineering compartment. Pipes ran through the space, some with control valves. A huge electrical panel occupied most of one wall. A small desk faced a bookshelf full of manuals. One or two of the manuals had been pulled down and spread on the desk. I made a quick guess that Andy had been searching for a way out.

Shelly Calbert sat in the desk chair. She held her daughter in her arms.

My first closeup glimpse of the girl that had driven Andy to the southernmost tip of the United States met every one of my expectations, and worse. I wondered when she had stopped eating. Pale, emaciated, hairless and at the fringes of life, the girl lay with her head against her mother's shoulder. She was wrapped in a white blanket, but her bony ankles extended. A thin hand clutched a corner of the blanket. Reuben Calbert stood beside his wife and daughter. Save one salient thing, nothing about the man looked any less intimidating. But that one thing told me that, as big as he was, he had been torn down.

Reuben cupped his daughter's hand in his own as if mere touch might shatter it. Tears flooded his eyes. He saw me but said nothing.

Andy spotted Pidge's t-shirt wrapped around my leg. Blood soaked through the shirt. "What happened?"

"It's nothing. Just a flesh wound. Damn. I've always wanted to say that."

Her expression mixed reproach with concern. "Tell you later. Listen, the ship is on autopilot and the crew is abandoning ship."

The news did not surprise my wife. "On autopilot going where?"

"How the hell would I know?" I replied, wondering what difference it made. Then I understood her question. "Oh. Southwest. Open water."

Andy crouched and plucked away the bandage on my leg. "We need to get this wrapped. That's deep." She pushed the soaked t-shirt back in place and then spent a moment retying the knot, tighter. I winced but held my tongue. She stood up. "That airplane you came in? Was that Pidge? Can she pick us up?"

I gave her the bad news.

"Makes sense," Andy said. "After you passed, they hustled us down here. We heard noises. Must have been the collision."

Calbert found his voice. "What about that makes sense?"

"All of it. Letting us come aboard. Conducting the ceremony." Andy looked down at the girl. "I'm sorry, but that was just to keep us occupied until we got far enough out." To me, she said, "As soon as you showed up, they dropped the pretense and sealed us in here. You said the ship is on autopilot. It's on its way into open water. If they're leaving, that means they left behind something that's going to sink this boat."

"A bomb?" I asked. Shelly Calbert's eyes went wide.

"I don't think so." Andy stole another look down the passage. "A bomb would leave obvious evidence of a crime. This needs to look like an accident. They're leaving now because it's close enough to Key West that they can take a small boat back without being noticed. But they put the ship on autopilot so it can go deeper into the Gulf. That way, whatever happens won't be witnessed. They've done something to cause fatal but explainable damage. My guess would be fire."

"If that's true, it means we have time to find it," I said.

"Wait." Andy stared at me.

"What?"

She said nothing. She shifted a glance toward Gabby.

The tiny, frail girl did not have far to go.

"You have to try." The look on Andy's face, in her eyes, spoke volumes. Everything that had happened since a twisted mind thrust a shotgun in Andy's face came to this moment. I wished with all my heart that Andy's obsession hadn't fallen on the shoulders of a dying girl. I knew only too well that this might fail. That I might be too late. Or just ineffective. And then what? What would that mean to Andy? How would that exorcise the demon vision that haunted her? Even if I succeeded, I wasn't sure it would change things for Andy.

Either way, one thing was certain. I could not refuse the woman I love or a child dying in her mother's arms.

"Yeah. How do you want to do this?"

83

____

It came down to trust. Andy stepped up to a man who could swat her aside with one hand if he chose to. She laid her hand on Calbert's chest and looked up at him.

"Reuben. You asked what I was doing here. I came for Gabby. We came to help her. Now I need you to do as I ask."

He swallowed, tried to speak, and swallowed again. "What are you talking about?"

"I need you to give me your daughter—"

"No!" Shelly Calbert snapped. "You keep your hands off!"

I feared Calbert might side with his wife, violently. I stepped closer, ready to pull Andy out of harm's way. The big man fixed his jaw and hardened his eyes—or tried to. He faltered. He attempted to speak, but words failed to form.

"YOU STAY AWAY FROM MY BABY GIRL!" Shelly Calbert tightened her grip on the child.

Andy did not waver. She spoke scarcely above a whisper.

"We came to help. Let us help. Please."

I closed my hand around Andy's arm, ready to pull her clear.

Reuben Calbert didn't swing at Andy. Instead, he carefully tucked his daughter's hand inside the blanket. The girl stirred. Even in sleep, pain wrote its relentless message across her brow. Calbert leaned down and put his face directly in front of his terrified wife. The reservoir of agony building in his eyes spilled down his cheeks.

"Shel…" Reuben whispered.

"No!" Shelly uttered weakly. "No…no…" The words sank into sobs. She leaned down and pressed her cheek against her dying daughter's bare head. "No…"

Andy turned to me and gestured at the girl.

Are you serious?

"Reuben, step aside," Andy touched his arm. He moved.

I drew a deep breath and reached for Gabby.

Shelly Calbert tightened her grip, but her resistance faltered when Reuben carefully unwrapped his wife's hands from their child. I slid one hand under Gabby's legs and the other around her back. I expected a fight. An absurd tug of war over a fragile little girl. Whatever fight Shelly Calbert had left visibly drained. Deep sobs broke from her chest. I lifted Gabby free —there was so little to lift. Shelly rose and fell into her ex-husband's arms. She buried her face against his chest.

Calbert found a way to stare bullets at me through the tears pumped from his eyes. His expression needed no interpretation. *Hurt my girl and I will hurt you.*

Andy closed a grip on Reuben's arm. "Please. Give us a few minutes. We can help. I promise we will not harm her. Please." She tugged Reuben and his wife through the open door. She pressed them into the passageway saying, "Just a few minutes. And I'll be right here. Just a few minutes."

I have no idea how Andy does that. If I could put into words the persuasive connection she made with two grieving parents in that moment, it would be the dictionary definition of Trust.

Andy glanced back at me and nodded.

Fwooomp!

I vanished, taking the tiny bundle with me.

My feet lost touch with the deck. I felt no impulse to launch or fly. The confines of the engineering compartment offered nowhere near enough space to go zooming about. I simply floated.

Matter in an altered state.

I called it Boyd's Revelation. An autistic child's genius expressed it between giggles while I cavorted above a stand of dead trees in a winter landscape. Boyd's words echoed in my mind, but at that moment a new voice intruded.

Stephenson's voice.

"I want to know if by altering the state of matter, Will is altering the cancerous cells."

Gabby stirred.

Or if he's altering the repair limits, accelerating the repair function within the strands.

The girl moved like someone experiencing a dream. Not a nightmare. A benign dream expressed in the waking world by gentle involuntary muscle movements. She twitched and shuddered.

I don't know how many times I've done this. I understand nothing about it. Not one single thing. Stephenson can try to explain, or experiment, or theorize. All I know is that sometimes, it works. I do it for that reason alone. Sometimes it works.

Time was short.

Reuben and Shelly Calbert were going to come to their senses at any moment. Trusting a stranger—someone they both just met—only went so far.

I reached for the wall and used a grip on an equipment panel to shove myself back down until my feet touched the floor.

I saw movement at the door just as—

Fwooomp!

—I reappeared. My weight settled.

Reuben Calbert pushed past Andy.

Shelly followed her ex-husband through the door. She reached for Gabby. Andy's influence over the Calberts had expired. I had reason to resist. I prepared to hand Gabby over.

Reuben and Shelly stopped cold.

Gabby moved in my arms. Not the twitch of a dream state. She lifted her head. I looked down to see what had her parents enthralled.

She met my gaze with shining eyes and a smile, and she spoke in a voice that sounded like song.

"Do it again!"

84

"Take her," Andy ordered Calbert. "Go up to the deck we were on, the one just above where we had the ceremony."

I handed Gabby over to her stunned mother. The girl was awake and alert and wore a trace of disappointment on her face, the child who had just been told, *No, you can't have one more turn.*

I don't stick around to see results when I've done this trick in a hospital full of doctors, nurses, and security guards. I don't know how long it takes to work. The patients I visit tend to sleep through our brief encounter, sometimes stirring when I release them back into gravity's embrace. I've often wondered if the sensation causes them to dream of falling.

Gabby remained pale and frail, but the veneer of pain had lifted. Not in the way drugs mask pain. The way a sky clears after rain. I wasn't the only one who saw it. Her mother gaped at the girl, then at me.

Calbert stood rooted to the deck like most men in an emotionally charged moment. Dumbstruck.

"Reuben!" Andy snapped. "Go! Use the stairs and passages at the front of the ship. Stay away from that boat deck. We can't be sure they're gone."

I handed Reuben the ax. "You know how to use one of these, right?"

He gave me a look well earned by the bad joke. Then the menace he had shown from the moment I met the man returned. The ax looked small and deadly in his hands. The jet he pummeled in Wichita never had a chance.

"Nobody on this ship is your friend, Reuben—oh, wait! There's an obnoxiously cute little blonde up there somewhere. Don't hurt her. She's with us. Nobody else."

Reuben took his wife by the upper arm. They stepped into the corridor. He stopped and sniffed.

"Smell that?"

I joined him and took a whiff. "From the welding?"

He shook his head. "It's something else. Something is burning."

"Go!" Andy repeated. "Will and I will conduct a search."

The sound of a passing motorboat performed a doppler shift alongside the hull.

"Sounds like our crew has abandoned ship," I said. To Reuben I added, "Just the same, keep an eye out."

He nodded and tugged his family forward.

Andy led me on a zigzag path in the opposite direction. After a few minutes of traversing pristine white corridors lined with utilitarian spaces, we emerged on the boat deck. The big bay door I'd seen on CCTV on the bridge was now closed. The zodiac was gone. Two racy-looking jet skis remained. I checked. No keys.

"Any idea how to jumpstart one of these?"

Andy shrugged. A strange look overcame her. She extended her hands at her sides and glanced at me.

"Feel that?"

I sensed motion underfoot. The Gulf waters were relatively smooth, and the big yacht had been built with stabilizers to prevent the paying customers from puking. For the most part, up to that moment, I had felt nothing.

"Are we turning?" Andy pointed at a porthole and the sunbeam streaming through it. The bright spot cast on the deck moved slowly across the woodwork.

"We should get up to the bridge. Maybe see if the autopilot is misbehaving."

"First things first. Reuben is right. Something is burning."

Andy led us back through the engineering corridors. We passed the compartment where Andy and the others had been locked. We jogged forward. Andy touched each closed door as we hurried by.

At one door, she stopped suddenly.

"Hot?" I asked after she stroked her hand lightly across the metal. She shook her head and pointed.

DANGER – HIGH VOLTAGE

She carefully opened the door. Reaching in, she flipped the light switch to On. Overhead LEDs lit up the room.

Racks of electrical equipment, conduits and power panels lined the walls. Out of place, however, was the waist-deep pile dominating the floor. Carpeting. Foam padding. Tarps. Pillows. Bits of wallpaper. Debris from the remodeling project had been dumped here.

"Seems a bit careless."

"Not at all. Look." Andy pointed. "Those are lithium-ion batteries. Lots of them." Slim black and gray slabs lined an entire wall. "Some of these ships have been deploying solar panels and installing lightweight storage batteries."

"How green of them."

"Will, this is all here to fuel a fire. And when those batteries go, there's no putting it out. West Bend FD had a Tesla catch fire down in Washington County last summer. Unstoppable. And this is ten times as many batteries. Maybe more."

I pulled on the slabs of carpeting, digging into the pile.

"What are you doing?"

"Looking for the trigger. They built a bonfire here, but they need to get it started. It's probably at the bottom of the pile."

"I don't think so." Andy leaned back into the corridor. "I think it's already started, and it's meant to spread to this compartment. Leave it."

I followed Andy back into the passageway. She sealed the door behind us.

The scent Reuben had detected grew stronger. Andy's touch test on the wall and each door grew more cautious. Almost immediately, we came to a door that she barely waved her hand over before pulling it back sharply.

"Don't open it."

More substantial than most of the other doors, this one had the nautical appearance of a watertight door, a door that could be locked and latched against forces greater than a person could bring to bear.

I didn't have to touch the steel to feel heat. I looked up, then searched the corridor.

"Where's the smoke going?"

Andy did a similar search. "Not sure. Might be trapped. Possibly into the ventilation system. Or out the side. We'll have to get up on deck to see if we're sending up a cloud of smoke. Did you see those pipes and conduits in that battery room? Along the wall?"

"Sure," I lied. "No."

"They join to this space. That's your trigger. I'd be willing to bet you there's a similar pile of carpeting and carpet padding, which is nothing but solid fuel, in there and it's cooking off. When it gets up to speed it's going to share the fire with that battery compartment—either through the ventilation system or those conduits. There might even be a fuel line. I've read about fires like this, Will. In ship compartments, they can smolder for hours before they break free. This ship is meant to be fifty, maybe a hundred miles from the Keys, out in the Gulf, when things really got going."

I pointed at a pipe with nozzles hanging from the ceiling. "That's a fire suppression system."

"Yes. Probably disabled. This needs to look like an accident, in case someone comes along, or if somebody tries to examine the sunken wreckage. I'd be willing to bet the autopilot is taking it to deep water where it's not meant to be found, not the ship or the four bodies inside a compartment that was welded shut."

"I'm really starting to dislike this Remington guy. So, what do we do?"

Andy didn't answer. She lifted her eyes toward the ceiling and against all common sense, dimples peeked from the smooth skin bracketing her lips.

"I think we're already doing it. Come on."

85

"You need to ask for permission to come on my bridge." Pidge sat in the captain's chair with her feet up on the console. A gaudy sling, fashioned from one of the pillowcases that had been on the observation deck sofa, hung from her neck. The fabric cradled her left arm. She wore a pair of Ray Ban Aviators she found somewhere. Hers had gone down with the seaplane.

"My God, Pidge! Are you okay?" Andy studied her arm.

"Fuckin' arm's busted. And starting to hurt like a sonofabitch."

I studied the navigation screens. What I saw prompted me to look outside. Little had changed about the surface of the Gulf waters, but the shift in light was obvious.

"Did you turn us around?" I asked.

"Seemed like the right thing to do after those assholes abandoned ship. I saw them take off, so I came down here to see what's what."

"How did you know what to do?" Andy asked.

"Please," Pidge scoffed. "It's all Garmin. Not that much different from what we use. Don't ask me how to operate the engines, though. I think that's a throttle control there, but I'm not going to touch it."

"Good call. Leave it."

"Hold still." Andy gingerly separated the panels of Pidge's sling. "Uh-huh. That's a break. You're doing the right thing to keep it immobilized, but we need to get you to a hospital and get it properly set."

"I put us on a course back to Key West, but it's going to take a few hours to get there."

"We don't have a few hours," I said. "The ship's on fire."

Pidge glared at me. "Seriously? You got any other wonderful news?"

"I think we're out of Cap'n Crunch."

Andy stepped forward and studied the control panel screens.

I stared out the sloped bridge windows. The long sleek bow of the *Amphitrite* raced over light Gulf chop. Nothing of the waves or swells transmitted through the deck to our feet. The yacht rode as smoothly as an airplane in an early morning, thermal-free sky.

"Hey…Pidge…" I said slowly "…which way did the assholes go?"

"I'm gonna say east. Most likely back to Key West, or one of the other damned keys. There's like a zillion of them, aren't there?"

"And which way did you turn us? We were down below and couldn't feel it."

"Left. Starboard, matey."

"That's port," Andy said.

I'm no mariner, but it made sense to me that lifelong sailors had the ability to read the surface of water like a book. For example, the thin line, barely a tracing, that angled away ahead of us. I'd seen something like it on our way out to Pirate Island in the stolen seaplane. A wake. In a steadfast sea like the one beneath us, a wake lives a long time.

Like the wake spreading across our new course.

Far ahead, perched on the horizon, I found the spec that caused that wake. Dark, tiny. Nearly imperceptible.

"Do you see any binoculars?" I asked without taking my eyes from the spec for fear I might lose it.

"Like these?" Pidge lifted an expensive-looking pair from a pocket on the side of her chair. She handed them to me.

"What is it?" Andy asked.

I lifted the binoculars to my eyes and made the necessary adjustments. It took a little searching, and for a worried moment I feared I'd lost sight of the spec. The binoculars were powerful, however, and when the lens trapped the object, it was clear as day.

"Pirates. Prepare to be boarded."

86

"What's going on?" Calbert wanted to know.

Andy and I joined him on the lower salon deck, the one that overlooked the transom. He still carried the ax. I noticed that he had found the food tray and returned it to the long, empty table in the salon. Shelly Calbert cradled her daughter on her lap in a fat recliner. The woman could not take her eyes off Gabby any more than she could peel the look of sheer wonder from her face.

Gabby nestled against her mother and munched cubes of cantaloupe from a dish in her lap. She looked up at me and smiled under her jaunty pirate badge kerchief.

Andy gestured for Reuben and me to follow her. The three of us walked forward.

We passed through an elegant bathroom, untouched by the renovation, into what might have been a bedroom suite. A sweeping curved staircase took us up to the next deck, the one directly below the bridge. We moved through another salon, another bathroom—this one massive—into what was probably the master bedroom suite. A wall of floor-to-ceiling power windows provided the billion-dollar view over the bow.

Andy handed Calbert the binoculars and pointed. I held the ax while he fixed the image in his sight.

"They're coming back," Andy said. "They must have seen the ship turn around, and that throws a wrench in their scheme. They may think it's a

321

navigation system glitch, or autopilot glitch—or they may have reasoned that we found a way out of the compartment."

"Suits me," Calbert said. "I'd like a word with these assholes."

"Reuben," she said, "this ship is on fire. It was supposed to sail out into the open Gulf of Mexico and burn and sink. Us with it."

"On fire?" We explained. When we finished, he asked, "Did you guys turn us around?"

"No," I said. "It was that little blonde I mentioned. She's a wiz with things that fly or, I guess, float. Plus, the navigation system isn't much different than what we use in airplanes."

Reuben exchanged the binoculars for the ax. I took another look and estimated our guests to be roughly two miles out. Our combined closing speed gave us two minutes. Reuben slapped the handle of the ax against his palm.

"Like I said, suits me. Those fuckers tried twice to kill my baby girl. My turn."

Andy shook her head. "No. That's not the plan."

"There's a plan?" I asked.

87

To save BLASTER battery power, I fixed a grip on one rung of the ladder welded to the yacht's top mast, just below a steel spar holding three radar domes. I had vanished and used the power unit to pull me up to this high perch. The ship's forward speed generated a twenty-knot wind that swept me back like a flag.

Four stories above the sea, I had an unrestricted view in every direction. Dead ahead, the zodiac closed the distance quickly. Spray spreading on both sides of the craft attested to its speed. They would not be long. I made out five individual heads. The man I'd seen wearing a suit—Jardeen, Andy told me—and the three crewmen who had attended Sonjay's ceremony sat in the well of the boat on canvas bench seats. The one Andy called Keiffer operated the boat's controls at a stand-up pedestal. She told me he introduced himself as the First Officer, however he seemed to be in charge. The existence of a captain had been a fiction. I had my doubts that any of the men were professional seafarers.

Andy's plan counted on our adversaries acting predictably. I hoped she wasn't wrong.

Three issues would drive them, she explained. First, why was the ship heading in the wrong direction? Second, were the captives still sealed in? And third, was the fire progressing as planned?

For the first issue, Keiffer would hurry to the bridge. For the second and third issues one or two of the crew would be sent forward through the boat deck to check on the sealed compartment and the status of the brewing fire. I crossed my fingers that two men would get the job, leaving only two in the zodiac.

It would take the men searching the ship less than a minute to reach the welded compartment and discover that the captives had escaped. Keiffer would reach the bridge in less time.

The boat deck joined the corridor leading to the bow where the fire had been set. Andy picked a storage locker just inside the main passageway as a hiding place. After the search party passed, she and Calbert planned to hurry to the transom with Shelly and Gabby where, fingers crossed, I would have played my part.

I tried to ignore the many ways this was about to go wrong.

The inflatable craft bounded past the bow. Keiffer showed an experienced hand. He cut a sharp turn and skidded the vessel around, jolting over the yacht's churning wake.

Keiffer nudged the bow of the zodiac against the transom and used power to hold it stationary. The crewman called Chou crouched at the ready with a line. He leaped onto the transom and secured the line on a cleat. Keiffer throttled back. The zodiac remained in place, towed by the yacht, rocking in the wake. Keiffer followed Chou aboard.

I released my grip on the mast and immediately sailed backward in the wind generated by the ship's forward motion. BLASTER in hand, I added power as I approached the stern until I kept pace directly above the zodiac.

My prayer paid off. A second crewman crawled forward and leaped onto the yacht's transom. Keiffer issued commands then darted up the stairs to the first salon level. He jogged forward and disappeared. The two crewmen ducked through the door set in the slanted wall, the door that gained access to the boat deck.

Go time.

I angled the power unit and dove toward the zodiac. Of the two men still aboard, the one in crew whites looked more formidable. The one Andy called Jardeen had changed out of his suit into a flowered shirt and tan shorts that exposed white, hairy legs. He sat on a canvas bench seat with a duffle bag between his shins. His hands gripped the lines that ran along the rim of the zodiac's inflatable hull. He looked pale and pained each time the boat bobbed.

The man in crew whites stood behind the zodiac's wheel.

Holding my position over the moving boat required power. The BLASTER's prop buzzed. Jardeen lifted and cocked his head.

I angled in from his right. Holding the power unit in my right hand, I reached for his wrist with my left. I closed a vice grip on his clammy skin and pushed the levers in my head against the stops.

FWOOOMP!

The sound thundered between my ears. *The other thing* spread to the man in the zodiac. Jardeen vanished. The shock of something grabbing his wrist caused him to release his hold on the boat. He tried to snatch his hand away. I anticipated the move. The instant I grabbed his wrist, I angled the power unit straight up. He had no chance. Jerking his hand away only brought him toward me, over the water.

Jardeen cried out incoherently.

The man at the wheel turned his head to find an empty boat.

Surprise!

I cut the power. Relative wind instantly threw me and my cargo backward over the zodiac's engine, over the yacht's foaming wake.

I released my grip. An electric snap coursed through my hand.

Jardeen reappeared, still in a sitting posture. Gravity grabbed him and he cannonballed into the roiling water twenty feet behind the zodiac. By the time his head popped back up, he had fallen forty feet behind. He bobbed away rapidly, shouting, coughing, and splashing his arms. From the look of it, he wasn't a good swimmer.

The man at the controls stared, astonished.

"What the—?"

I didn't wait. I aimed for a spot beside the crewman.

The door to the boat deck popped opened and our party of five streamed onto the transom. Calbert carried his ax. Shelly Calbert carried Gabby wrapped in blankets for protection against the sun and water on the rough voyage to come. Pidge followed. Andy brought up the rear. She spotted the crewman still aboard the zodiac and solved a problem for me.

I had been unsure as to how to grab the man. He gripped the sides of the zodiac control pedestal. Snatching his arm may have caused him to tighten his grip, igniting a battle I was not likely to win.

Andy jabbed her hand in her bag and came up armed and dangerous.

"Let me see your hands!" she snapped. "Hands! Up! Now!"

Wide-eyed and caught in the sights of her Glock, the third crewman braced against the rocking motion of the inflatable boat and lifted his hands from the pedestal.

I didn't wait. I angled in from the side and grabbed his upraised right wrist.

FWOOOMP!

He vanished. I veered sharply right.

A split second later I let go.

Fwooomp!

He reappeared halfway over the side of the zodiac. Arms flailing, he tumbled into the water. His legs pivoted over the side, flipping him. Seconds later, he bobbed in the wake, rapidly receding and gasping for air.

Calbert and the others stared.

"What just happened?" he asked.

Andy secured her weapon and shook him from his bewilderment. "Get them in!"

She hurried to where the bow of the zodiac thumped against the transom. Calbert laid the ax on the deck beside the line that secured the zodiac. Without asking, he hooked his huge hands under Andy's armpits and lifted her over the zodiac's bow. He dared not reach too far and her landing was unceremonious, but she recovered. She unhooked her bag and tossed it to the foot of the command pedestal, then turned around and reached as Calbert performed the same boarding trick with Pidge.

Andy helped Pidge find a seat, mindful of the sling across her torso. She hurried back. Calbert lowered his ex-wife and daughter into the boat and released them to Andy. She helped them get seated. Calbert kneeled to take up the line holding the boat.

"That's enough!" Keiffer burst through the door to the boat deck. He held a semi-automatic pistol at the end of his outstretched arm, aimed at the most immediate threat. Calbert.

"Everybody out of the boat!"

Calbert froze. Andy faced Keiffer, carefully moving between him and the three people seated on the zodiac.

I paced the craft, badly out of position. I had Andy and then Calbert between me and Keiffer. My move was obvious. I angled higher and accelerated.

"Let it go," Keiffer ordered Calbert, who dropped the line from his hand. "And now everyone, get out of the fucking boat. Now."

Nobody moved.

Except me. I gained speed, enough to pace the transom. I calculated my options. Sweep in and knock the gun aside? Problem. In the vanished state I have no mass, or so Lane Franklin tells me. Grab Keiffer? Problem. If I made him vanish with the gun still in his hand, and he fired, I was screwed. Discharge of a weapon inside *the other thing* has the effect of electrocuting me. Almost nothing could persuade me to go through that again.

Almost nothing.

"Are you deaf?" Keiffer glared. No one moved. "Fine." He swept the gun to his right and adjusted his aim. "First shot goes through the little girl's skull. I'm not even going to count. Either you get moving or she dies."

I didn't have a choice.

Calbert moved faster than me. He grabbed the ax and stood up.

Keiffer reversed his move—aimed the pistol at Calbert—and fired.

"DADDY!" Gabby shrieked. Shelly screamed.

Calbert dropped to his knees. For a split second I marveled that a single shot had taken down the big man, but Calbert's move had purpose. As he dropped, he drove the ax through the rope holding the zodiac and into the deck. The released inflatable shot backward.

"NO!" Keiffer cried out. The distraction drew his aim away from Calbert. He raised the gun in the direction of the boat.

Pidge threw herself to the zodiac's deck. Andy swept down on Shelly and Gabby and pulled them behind the command console. The boat rapidly dropped away from the yacht's transom.

"Bring it back!" Keiffer shouted. He fired three rapid shots over their heads. "Bring it back, God dammit!"

Calbert pumped himself upright. Keiffer reversed his aim a second time toward Calbert. I angled the BLASTER sharply left to dive down on Keiffer, thinking the impact might at least knock his aim off target. I was too late.

Calbert jerked the ax out of the deck and swung it with his entire body. The blow hit Keiffer somewhere in the ribcage. Blood blossomed on the crisp white uniform shirt. Keiffer instantly folded and lost his grip on the weapon. The gun clattered on the deck, then into the sea. Keiffer tumbled overboard after it, driven by the ax buried in his side.

Calbert, off balance, staggered through his own ax swing and followed Keiffer over the edge of the transom into the water. Both men vanished in the frothing ship's wake.

"DADDY! DADDY!" Gabby screamed from the zodiac bobbing fifty yards back. She had pulled herself from her mother's arms. She gripped the side of the inflatable.

I slid the power unit control to neutral and ceased pacing the yacht. The billionaire's toy surged away trailing a thin line of smoke from the left side of the ship. Late to the party, the two crewmen who had been sent forward burst through the boat deck door and onto the transom. They could do nothing as they saw their lifeboat grow distant in the ship's wake, which had begun to curve again. The *Amphitrite* eased into a wide turn to her right to resume whatever course Keiffer had reprogrammed, rushing at the maximum speed her designers intended.

I reversed course. I searched the wake's foam and bubbles for Calbert.

Unlike the seaplane sinking in pristine water, the bodies below the wake were impossible to see.

"Crap," I shut down the power unit and pushed it into my shirt, still not dry from the last dunking.

I rotated to a head-down position.

Fwooomp! I flashed into sight and instantly plunged into the warm Gulf water. The dive was clean. It took me down quickly. I searched for Calbert thinking the big man should be easy to find.

The turquoise water revealed nothing. Shafts of light penetrating the disturbed wake acted as a curtain.

I stroked deeper. The water grew darker. The surface above me glittered. Nothing.

My lungs sent alarm bells to my head. I realized I'd gone in too fast. I hadn't taken cleansing breaths. I had no reserve.

In my head Gabby's desperate scream joined the oxygen deprivation alarm bells.

"DADDY!"

I have no clinical way of assessing Gabby's condition, but my heart told me that the girl munching cantaloupe was in remission. The strength of her piercing girl-scream measured as strong and certain as any blood test result.

"DADDY!"

It pissed me off. Gabby got her life and her father back, only to see him taken away. I stroked furiously deeper. Metallic motorboat sound circled above me. The zodiac hull cast a shadow in the water.

Calbert had to have sunk. The man had no body fat. He would go down like a rock. I pulled hard with my arms and kicked with my legs.

Nothing.

Dammit.

Out of air.

Fwooomp!

I vanished and shot upward. It took forever to reach the surface. My vision tunneled. I broke through the yacht wake gasping and choking. The sun blinded me. I sucked water into my windpipe. A sharp cough interrupted the desperate flow of air into my lungs. My chest hurt. My leg sent a signal that salt water was not welcome in the wound on my thigh.

Clear of the surface, I drifted higher. There wasn't time to waste. I needed to dive in again.

I tried to suck in air but continued coughing. Regardless, I rotated for another plunge. Deep breath. Cough. Deep breath again. I pulled in as much air as I thought possible and—

Stopped.

A hair's breadth from jerking back the levers in my head to reappear and plunge into the sea, I saw the zodiac maneuver to a halt twenty yards away. Shelly Calbert and Andy leaned over the side. They jerked and pulled and struggled to heave Reuben over the inflatable's hull. He flopped into the boat like an absurdly large sport fishing catch.

He coughed and gasped. That didn't stop his daughter. Gabby dove onto Reuben's chest and threw her arms around his head.

Andy dropped beside him and began a methodical search for wounds. She found a hole at the side of his chest. The hole oozed blood. Calbert didn't seem terribly concerned. His attention was on Gabby. He held her gently, stroking her back. Andy tore away most of Calbert's t-shirt, balled it, and pressed it over the hole.

"Hold this." She grabbed Shelly's hand and guided it onto the wound. "He'll be fine. Just keep pressure on it."

Andy rolled the big man far enough to check for an exit wound. She probed his back with her hand, which came away bloodless. She slid away from Calbert to catch her breath.

My lungs heaved air in and out. I untangled my BLASTER from inside a sopping wet shirt. My hands shook. I used both to handle the device, worried that I might drop it. Aiming carefully, I maneuvered alongside the zodiac near the stern. I extended myself prone against the outside of the hull near Andy and grabbed a line.

Fwooomp!

I reappeared and slipped into the water where no one could see me. A few seconds later I heaved myself aboard.

My arrival startled Shelly Calbert. Pidge, sitting on the deck with her back against the inflatable hull, looked calmly at me. "Nice of you to show up."

I dropped in beside her. Andy threw me a grateful glance and slid close.

"You okay?" She looked me over, including a quick examination of the bloody rag around my thigh.

"Yeah. You?"

Our eyes met. Across a short gaze, we conducted an intimate system check, a self-examination that went beyond skin deep. In my wife, I saw exhaustion, triumph, relief. I searched for ghost images of an over-under shotgun. Andy let me probe. After a long moment, she shifted her gaze from me to Gabby.

"I think she's going to be okay."

She meant Gabby. Mostly.

"Yeah."

I reached for the woman I love and rewarded us both with a long kiss, a kiss I needed the way I always need it. Evidence that the connection is real, that the moment is real.

The zodiac engine revved, then roared. Andy and I parted and braced against acceleration. We looked at Pidge behind the wheel.

One-handed, she spun us around and set off in the direction opposite of the yacht. Black smoke, growing thicker, trailed from the departing ship.

"Don't go anywhere," Andy instructed me. She touched my cheek.

She found her feet and relieved Pidge of command. Andy reversed our course and for a moment Pidge and I wondered why.

Andy aimed for the two men splashing desperately in the water.

I would have left them.

88

A ndy picked up Jardeen and the third crewman and set a course for Key West. She handed me her weapon to encourage compliance. Neither man seemed inclined to resist, perhaps because I informed them that I had been driven into a pirate frame of mind and making them walk the plank would top off my day. Having already enjoyed a swim in the Gulf with no reason to expect rescue, they elected to remain docile.

Amphitrite headed southwest, taking with her the two men who had gone into the ship's bowels. I prepared an argument against returning to rescue them, but Andy made no move in that direction. Clouds of black smoke obscured the yacht's rear decks as she probed the horizon.

The Calberts handled the rough open-water trip well. Reuben winced when the zodiac jolted. Gabby seemed to enjoy the ride. Her mother tried to cuddle her in blankets, but Gabby held her head up to let the wind stroke her cheeks and the sun warm her skin. I feared she would wind up with a burn on the bald dome of her head.

Reuben probably could have taken half a dozen bullets and still walked to an ER. That big sonofabitch was tough. I was sure I'd seen the last of him when he went into the water with Keiffer hooked on the end of the ax. No one was more grateful than me to watch him in the bottom of the boat with his wife beside him holding a bandage over the hole in his lower chest.

Halfway to Key West, Reuben gestured for me to come close. I'll admit to hesitation, but I had Andy's gun. He lifted his slab-sided head to my ear.

"What did you do?"

I leaned back. He tipped his head toward his bright-eyed daughter. He repeated the question by knitting together his substantial black brows.

I delivered the answer to his ear.

"It's like they say about yachts. If you have to ask, you can't afford it."

I resumed my pirate watch over our captives. When I looked back at Calbert, he mouthed two silent words.

Thank you.

When Key West rose on the horizon, Andy alerted the Coast Guard. This was accomplished using Andy's phone. Pidge had been carrying the phone in her shorts ever since she retrieved it from the trash. My wife, the ever-efficient police officer, had long ago taken steps to waterproof the device, which survived the sinking of the seaplane.

After Andy made the call, I took leave of my guard post and joined her at the wheel. She maintained a steady thirty-knot speed. The relative wind roared past us. We huddled. I spoke into her ear.

"You're going to have to drop off me and Pidge before you take this lot to the Coast Guard."

She made a face and shook her head. I leaned in to hear her refusal.

"No. You need stitches." She pointed at my thigh. "Pidge has to get that arm taken care of."

She wasn't wrong.

"Yes, but there's a problem. We were never out there. We were never on that boat."

Andy's expression suggested I had spoken gibberish. I tried again.

"The problem is the seaplane. We kinda stole it. And broke a lot of regs in the process. A lot."

Her eyes flared. I shrugged, pretending innocence. It didn't help.

"What am I supposed to tell the authorities?" She pointed at Jardeen and the crewman. "They both saw you. They know you were there."

"They're a couple of hired would-be murderers. Obvious liars. Talk to Calbert. Get your story straight. We were never out there. Drop us at the marina. It's near the Coast Guard station. And be prepared. You'll get plenty of attention when you pull up to a restricted military dock."

Andy huffed at me, pretending anger.

I smiled. "You know this cop thing of yours really gets in the way of my grand larceny."

She was not amused.

. . .

THE DROP-OFF at the marina went smoothly. Andy picked the empty end of a long dock devoid of casual observers. Anyone watching from a distance saw just another boat dropping off a couple of tourists.

Before jumping ship, I returned Andy's Glock. Shelly Calbert volunteered to guard the two men huddled in the back by the engine. Andy handed her the weapon and asked if she knew how to use it. Shelly dropped the magazine into her hand to check the load, then slapped it home. She pulled the slide to confirm a round in the chamber.

"I grew up in Georgia."

Andy smiled. "Try not to kill them out of spite."

Pidge and I watched Andy navigate the zodiac away from the marina dock on a course that would take her around the western point of Old Key West to the Coast Guard station.

A taxi delivered Pidge and me from the marina across Key West to the Lower Keys Medical Center. Without much fuss, the Foundation credit card bought me twenty-seven stitches and Pidge an X-ray of her broken arm and painful setting of the bones. She received a temporary cast to be replaced after a consultation with an orthopedic surgeon. Questions about pins and screws and surgical repair remained open. After four long hours, Pidge walked away with a new sling, some happy pills, and a t-shirt that covered her fluorescent bra and which declared her a citizen of the Conch Republic.

My watch showed just shy of eight p.m. when we stepped out the front entrance of the medical center. Pidge wore a narcotic smile. I contemplated my dead phone, and how it wasn't going to help me arrange an Uber. A timely taxi making a drop at the medical center entrance solved the transportation problem, but we still had the problem of where to stay. I asked the driver for a recommendation. He made a call to the Hyatt Centric Key West and landed us two rooms because he heard of a big wedding party trapped by a freak spring snowstorm in Boston, the result of which created unexpected vacancies at an otherwise booked hotel. After a stop at the Hampton Inn for our stored luggage, and a dash into a grocery store to buy a bag of rice for my dead, soaked phone, Pidge and I ended the day exhausted in separate rooms. Pidge issued a terse death threat against waking her…ever.

Andy slipped into my room sometime after midnight. She did not turn on a light. I heard clothing fall to the floor. I felt her slide under the sheets beside me. She forgot about the gash in my leg when she laid her bare leg over mine and settled herself under my arm. I ignored the throbbing pain. Neither of us spoke.

Sleep took us.

89

Andy rose early, showered, and checked her phone every ten minutes. I dragged myself through a shower and shave, then persuaded my anxious wife she could just as easily fret over her phone at the hotel's waterfront restaurant. We ordered a hearty brunch. We'd been a little lax with meals lately. While we waited to be served, I asked about Reuben and family. Andy explained that she persuaded the Coast Guard to keep them overnight at their infirmary.

"I let them know that the Florida Highway Patrol might have an interest in Reuben, but not to be hasty because recent events changed the situation. I suggested they keep the family together. Lots of what happened took place at sea and that raises a question of jurisdiction. To my mind, everything I saw out there vindicates Reuben."

"Including the airplane ax murder thing?"

"Something to be dealt with, of course. But I don't plan to leave Terrance Remington room to make a case."

"What about the hospice?"

"I spoke to the police in Mountain Home last night. They were not happy. I detected a little bias favoring Reverend Newell and the local industry he represents. In their minds, Reuben frames up nicely for those two murders."

"But you think it was Fennick, or someone working on Remington's behalf."

"I do, but I didn't feel it was the right moment to try and explain all that to the Mountain Home officers. It's going to take some work to resolve that."

"You could have told them about Fennick."

"Possibly," Andy said. "But Fennick is probably with his boss in New York, getting ready for their big stock price reveal party. Remington will alibi his man for everything that's happened."

"And tell me again why Remington isn't in custody?"

Andy's phone rang. She waved the screen at me—Key West Police— then took the call. The Coast Guard had asked KWPD to take custody of Jardeen and Chou and the police wanted to know why. Detective Stewart, they were told, had all the pertinent details. Andy asked if they wanted her to come in and make a statement, but no one seemed inclined to conduct business on a Sunday. Andy asked to visit the station in the morning. She was told they were open for business every day.

Being fingered as the cause of an interagency turf scuffle did nothing to settle Andy's growing agitation. I suggested that since our Sunday afternoon had been cast adrift, we sample the Key West sunshine on the Hyatt's sand beach. Andy protested and said something about trying to reach the Key West District Attorney or the U.S. Attorney. I reminded her it was Sunday and if I knew process and procedure at all, she needed to talk to the police first. I argued for the beach and pointed out that I had shorts. Andy protested that she did not bring a bathing suit. I told her the hotel had a gift shop, and if she didn't find something, every other shop in Old Town sold beachwear.

HALF AN HOUR later a reluctant Andy and a welcome second umbrella drink arrived at two beach chairs I had staked out. Andy approached with her phone to her ear. She wore a robe taken from our room and a pair of over-sized plastic sunglasses I'd never seen before. Her hair gathered at the back of her head in a high ponytail.

"Thank you, Master Chief. I appreciate the update." She ended the call. "That was the Command Master Chief at the Coast Guard station."

"They say he's the man."

"Seems like he runs the show." The call seemed to have settled Andy, if only slightly. She laid down her phone and faced me. "Okay. Are you ready?"

"Ready for what?"

She slipped off the robe to reveal a white two-piece bathing suit that looked luminous against the light caramel color of her skin.

"Like it?" She modeled it for me. I stared. She smiled.

"Oh, dear Lord. Will you marry me and have lots of sex with me?" She handed back my credit card and the receipt. I glanced at the slip. "Wow. That's worth more than my car."

"I can see if they'll take it back."

"Don't you dare. Seriously. Lots and lots."

"Let me think about it. Meanwhile, I'll tell you what the Command Master Chief said." She stretched out on the beach chair and began applying lotion to her skin from a small copper-colored bottle. I watched the way the sheen made her glow.

"And lots," I muttered.

"Hush. Listen. He told me the fire disabled the *Amphitrite's* engine about twenty-five miles from where we last saw it. They sent a cutter out. The ship burned all night. Intensely. Those batteries, you know—plus the fuel tanks."

"Nothing like gas to assist with the arson and murder portion of the cruise itinerary."

"The Coast Guard rescued two men from the ship and immediately took them into custody thanks to what I told them last night. The two men claimed to know nothing about the Calberts or me. They swear there were no passengers onboard. They claim they stayed on the ship to fight the fire— they say they have no idea how it started—after everyone else bailed. Obvious crap. Anyway, around four a.m. the fuel tanks blew up and the ship sank. The Coast Guard was able to reach the owner in New York. He expressed shock and outrage, of course."

"Of course."

"The owner claimed to know nothing about the Calberts, or a ceremony for Sonjay, or even the identity of the shipyard crew hired to take the boat to Galveston. He said he never heard of Jardeen or knew about any passengers, but if there were any, they were trespassing, and he was outraged."

"Of course."

"He's angling to hang those guys on the crew with the attempted murder charges I see coming. I'll let KWPD know and maybe they can get one of them to flip on Remington. Or at least Fennick."

Andy handed me the lotion bottle and rolled onto her stomach. I went to work on her back. "You know, you haven't thanked me for busting you out of that engineering compartment."

"Really? Huh. I was wondering how to punish you for putting me there in the first place."

"Excuse me? What?"

"I had everything under control until some maniac in an airplane almost crashed into the yacht."

"First off, that maniac was Pidge, so…not my fault. Second, we came to the rescue."

"I didn't need a rescue. Keiffer and his crew were immersed in their Make-A-Wish charade for Gabby. I let it play out. I was prepared to shut the whole thing down as soon as it was over. But when you showed up, Keiffer dropped all pretense and threw us in the brig."

"You didn't know it was a pretense."

"Yes, I did."

"How?"

Andy propped herself up on her elbow. She slowly lifted her sunglasses onto the crown of her head and gave me her *I'm being patient with you* look. I tried hard to meet her gaze at the eyes, but, damn, that bathing suit…

"Because Keiffer said he spoke to Sergeant Merton at seven twenty-four."

"I know. I got the message. He told me the crew reported no passengers. Only it wasn't a guy named Merton. Ellis. Or Ellison. Or something like that."

"I know it wasn't Merton."

"How?"

"Merton's shift ended at seven. Which is how I knew Keiffer was lying. He lied to your man Ellison, and he lied to me. I also knew the ceremony was a charade because there's no cell service out near Pirate Island, yet that doofus Jardeen pretended to live-stream the ceremony back to the Citadel of God."

"Why didn't you call them on it?"

"Gabby. For her. Sonjay was important to her. That ceremony was important to her. Remember, that girl at that moment was fully aware that she was following her friend in death. She needed that ceremony. Plus, I had to get my weapon back."

"You *gave them* your gun?"

"It was the only way to get on the boat. Not my best judgment, but a tradeoff had to be made. I decided to wait, get the weapon, and then make them return to Key West. Once we got back, we would find a way for you to do *the other thing* with Gabby because…"

Andy drifted away. Right in front of me, her focus on me departed as if a switch had been thrown.

She sat for a long minute in a trance.

I was about to ask when she abruptly sat up and swung her legs off the beach chair. She reached into her bag for her phone.

"What?" I asked.

Andy ignored me. She tapped the phone screen, found something, opened a new screen, and then scrolled.

"Oh…my…God…"

"Jesus, Dee, what?" I sat up and leaned close to her. The scent of coconut flavored sunscreen radiated from her skin. I tried to read the email on her screen.

"Amphitriton's cancer treatment. They gave it to Gabby."

"I thought they didn't. I thought that was the reason for Calbert's anti-aircraft crusade."

"No, we talked about this. Remember? The reason they took Gabby to the hospice, and then to the boat, was to hide her away because they gave the treatment to her, and it didn't work. Failure like that throws a billion-dollar wrench in the IPO. They hid her by listing her as having dropped out of the program, remember? But they needed to make her disappear. Permanently."

"Okay…" I knew all that but still didn't get the clue. "They gave it to her. It didn't work. They tried to kill a child and a handful of other people to cover up a failure. We were there for that last part."

Andy handed me the phone. "Read this."

"What is it?"

"The email from Dr. Maxwell. I forgot she promised to send that to me. Read it."

I scanned and scrolled the screen. Maxwell's email contained the promised shipping list—the list of facilities that received the drug trial medication. I read Maxwell's preamble expecting to find Andy's eureka moment in Maxwell's brief message. I didn't.

"I don't get it."

"Read the list."

I scrolled.

"Sonofabitch."

"We have a whole new problem. We need to go to New York."

PART IV

90

"I can't believe you picked up." I sat on one of the queen beds in the Hyatt room. Andy sat facing me on the other bed. I held my phone between us. The device miraculously functioned after spending the night in a bag of rice. The charging cord, still connected to a wall socket, dangled from the phone. Our packed bags waited by the door.

The voice on the line reminded me of a wine review.

Arrogant, with a hint of narcissist.

Spiro Lewko said, "I can't believe you called. I assumed you were screwing me out of what you owe me."

"Well, today is your lucky day. I'm delivering everything I promised. Full access. With some conditions, of course, but nothing too restrictive."

Lewko went silent. I recognized the trick for making other people speak first. I outwaited him.

"Access to what? From what I hear, you have nothing to offer me."

I smiled at Andy. I did not have the phone on speaker, but I had turned the volume all the way up. She had no trouble hearing the call.

"Dr. Farris did her bit," I said.

"Are you saying she lied to me?"

"I'm saying I lied to her. I would have lied to you, but I'm a lousy liar— so I'm told. Lillian didn't believe a word of it, but—and I don't mean to throw her under the bus—she's not a fan. Polishing up my lie and delivering it to you kinda made her day."

"And the object? Was that a lie, too?"

341

"Nope. The pieces you have are real. The object I collided with was real. Sift past all the comic book crap and fanboy UFO conspiracies, and that site in Wisconsin is real. It's where the object ended up. The site is still there—at least the gash in the woods is still there. It's the back end of the accident that put me in the hospital. I'm ready to share that whole story with you. But I want something."

"Everybody wants something."

Jesus, I thought, *it's not always about you being a billionaire. Get over yourself.*

It turned out I said that out loud. Andy frowned to remind me, *We need him.*

"What do you want?" Lewko asked.

"Terrance Remington is about to take a run at knocking you down a peg on the Forbes list. You've heard about that?"

"I have. I wish him luck. Especially if what he's pitching isn't more of his snake oil. A genuine treatment could help a lot of people."

"It won't."

"You know something?"

"I do. I also know he committed murder on the way to the bank."

"Most people have."

"How would you like to help me sink him?"

"I'm more interested in you holding up your end of our bargain. If you're serious about that, then flicking a wannabe like Remington off the ladder is just frosting on the cake. What do you want from me?"

"Meet me in New York and bring the pieces. I want you to attend Remington's big stock price party."

"I have no intention of attending his event."

"Change your mind. I hear it's an open bar."

Lewko dealt out another moment of silence. I wondered why he pretended to think this over because I already knew the answer. So did he.

"Am I supposed to get you in? Because this is an E-ticket ride."

"Nope. I have my own ticket." *I hope.* "But I need you there."

"When and where?"

"The Ritz Carlton, of course. Meet us there tomorrow. Oh, and use your influence to get a couple rooms—no, make that three rooms."

91

———————

I put Pidge on an airline flight that would take her, eventually, to Milwaukee via Miami and Atlanta. Rosemary II promised to send one of the Essex Air Service pilots to General Mitchell International Airport to pick her up. Her travel day would be long but she had a sufficient supply of pain pills to tolerate the trip. After seeing her off at the terminal, I walked outside and strolled through the sunlight to the Signature Flight Services office next door. I wore my Ray Bans and an Essex County Air Service ball cap, but to no avail. The young man behind the counter recognized me. Adrian. I remembered him even before spotting the embroidery on his shirt.

"Hey! You're back! You were the guy asking about that Lake Amphib, right?"

Right to the point. I wondered if answering was about to buy me a visit with the police, the FBI, and the FAA. I counted a small blessing that Andy was not present. She would have declared this a teaching moment.

"That's right. Any chance of getting Lee to show it to me before I leave? Is he here today?"

Adrian laughed. "You're not going to believe it. Like, right after you were here that day, somebody stole it. Broad daylight. Right off the ramp."

"Get outta here. Seriously?"

"That's not the best part." Adrian grinned. "It almost rammed a Cessna Caravan, and the pilot swears there was no one at the controls."

"What?"

"He swears he saw an empty cockpit."

"How is that even possible?"

"Oh, it gets better." Adrian breathlessly told the tale. At the end, he added, "I heard from the tower guys the Lake transmitted a warning to an American jet to hold short of the taxiway—and claimed to be Blackbeard's Ghost. Crazy, right?"

I tried hard to be both awed and skeptical. "That would never work. Do the weight and balance. A plane like that? With an empty cockpit? It would be way out of C.G. I doubt it would fly, even if someone rigged it with servos and used remote control, they would need ballast."

"Oh, it totally flew. Took off on the taxiway and almost clipped an airliner. Unbelievable, right?"

"Totally. Did they find the airplane?"

"Not yet."

"That's too bad. I was really thinking about making an offer. It would be fun to fly out to the islands around here."

"Ah," Adrian shrugged, "they're not really that good at sea. They need inland water, a river, or at least a decent harbor. Open water can be tricky. But talk about crazy! So…you heading out?"

"Uh, no. The Baron stays here for a few more days. I'm waiting for the rest of my party and then catching a ride." I checked the ramp. No sign yet of the airplane I hoped to see.

Adrian pointed at the front door.

"Is that your party?"

A private ambulance pulled up in front of the building. The rear doors opened and Reuben and Shelly Calbert climbed out. I watched the big man move like nothing had happened. Andy appeared. She must have been riding shotgun.

Calbert and the attending EMT disembarked Gabby. The girl sat in a wheelchair. The moment the wheels hit the ground Gabby insisted on walking under her own power. Reuben and his wife shepherded their daughter toward the door as if her steps were her first. Gabby wore a flowered sundress that might have been the smallest size available, yet it still hung loosely. Pastels and tropical blossoms contrasted starkly with her black bandana and pirate insignia.

Andy hurried ahead. I met her at the door.

"Any trouble?" I asked Andy quietly.

"Not until the Key West police call the Coast Guard to ask where we are. I'd say we have an hour or two."

Gabby hobbled into the FBO lobby and threw an unexpected hug around my waist.

"Oof! Careful. You'll break me." I might have imagined it, but her embrace showed some strength.

She let go and looked up at me.

"We're gonna go on an airplane!" She beamed a smile.

"Ever been on one before?"

She solemnly shook her head

"Then this will be the best day ever." I looked at her father. "I can't believe you're on your feet."

He glanced at his left side. His loose shirt covered whatever bandage wrap he wore. "Didn't hit anything vital, I guess."

Shelly Calbert instantly disagreed. Her argument lacked the venom I expected from an ex-wife. Something had changed between the couple. "They scolded him for wanting to leave, but after he spoke to your wife, there would have been no stopping him."

Andy approached and overheard the comment. She chimed in. "I'm so sorry to ask this of you."

"Screw that," Calbert growled. "If you're right, I plan to have a few words with Mr. Remington."

"Reuben, that's not what this is about. We're not doing this so you can take matters into your own hands."

"Listen to the woman, Ben," his wife said. "Running around like a bull in a china shop hasn't worked yet."

The look on Reuben's face said, *Yes, ma'am* to a woman less than half his size.

I remained amazed to see him upright and said so. "You see nonsense in the movies where the guy gets shot, and then he's running around and fighting and making love in the next scene. Completely bogus."

"He will not be doing any running around or fighting," Shelly warned. Then she smiled. "Or the other thing. He's going to sit. And rest. And take the antibiotics they gave him. And if there's any bleeding or sign of infection, he's going straight to an ER."

"You're not wrong to want justice, Reuben," Andy said. "But this is about a lot more than that. Stay focused, and let's make sure that Gabby's daddy doesn't wind up in the hospital...or jail. Do we have an understanding?"

"We most certainly do," Shelly answered for him, fully in command. I looked away. Men don't like other men watching that sort of thing.

I searched the runway and sky and muttered to myself, "Assuming our ride shows up before the cops."

92

To avoid pacing the FBO office, I walked across the ramp to where the Baron remained tied down. I had no need to get into the cockpit, but I opened the door just the same. I crouched on the wing, letting heat billow out. The familiar instruments and controls offered comfort.

Andy followed me. She had dressed up. She said it was to look official for the Coast Guard when she went to the sector station and arranged for the ambulance to pick up Gabby and her parents. I thought there was more to it. I've seen her command abundant authority in jeans and a t-shirt. On this sunlit morning, she wore white sandals, white slacks and a turquoise blouse that opened low enough at the neck to distract me. She did her hair up in a complex braid that lifted her auburn locks off her neck and shoulders. A gold chain and diamond dangled above the open upper buttons of her silk blouse, drawing my eye for more reasons than one.

Her attire had less to do with looking official and more to do with our ride.

"Are you worried she's not coming?" Andy leaned against the leading edge of the wing just outside the right engine, careful not to let silk brush the bug spattered deicing boots.

"Nope," I lied. "I have all the faith in the world."

"Right."

I closed and locked the Baron's cabin door and hopped off the back of the wing. I strolled around the wingtip and gathered Andy in a light embrace. I tipped my forehead down until mine touched hers.

"Have I told you I love you? And that I'm glad we found Gabby."

"She's changed. I think it worked."

"Yeah. I feel that, too. What about you?"

Andy did not move or speak.

I rested my hands on the backside of her hips. She pressed her hands against my back. I tried to detect change in Andy the way she detected change in Gabby. I probed for the presence or absence of twin shotgun barrels staring her in her face. She felt calm despite renewed urgency. I leaned toward absence, which gave me hope.

Andy drew a breath to speak. I held mine, anticipating something deep, something drawn from soul-searching and, I hoped, the self-affirming insight she uncovered.

"Will," she said softly, "are you looking down my shirt?"

"Yes. Yes, I am."

She reached up and touched my cheek, then turned my head. "Well, maybe you should look at the runway. Is that her?"

On whispering, idling Rolls Royce engines, the sleek white Gulfstream 650 settled onto her wheels. The pilots quickly deployed thrust reversers and deftly handled a runway considered short for the high-end executive jet.

"I do believe it is."

A few minutes later, the jet rolled onto VIP parking in front of the Signature Flight Services building. A lineman in a reflective vest snagged the attention of the flight crew and waved them to a halt with orange wands. The crew quickly shut down the engines. The airstair door opened and unfolded its steps. A uniformed steward hurried down to take up a position at the bottom.

A woman with short blonde hair emerged from the cabin wearing jeans and a sleeveless white top. Ramp breeze sent her hair swirling around her head. The effect caught sunlight and infused gold in her locks.

Andy and I walked toward the jet. Even at a distance, her face and figure were instantly recognizable. I'd seen that face up close, in tears, even bruised, but nothing extinguished the radiant extra *something* she possessed and projected.

Lonnie Penn stopped at the foot of the stairs to her personal jet as if a director had taped a mark for her on the sunlit ramp.

"Andrea!" The A-list actor held out her arms for my wife.

"Hi, Lonnie." Andy traded a hug, tentative at first, but firm once Lonnie demonstrated that her end of the deal was genuine. When they parted, Lonnie turned to face me.

"Hello, Will." She wore a sly smile I'd seen on forty-foot-tall movie screens. "One of these days you're going to have to tell me what you have on my daughter." The smile adopted a wry twist at the corners.

"That's for her to decide. But it was good of Gloria to get you to come."

Lonnie positioned herself between Andy and me and hooked our arms.

"You could have called me directly, you know. I would have come. For you. Both of you. You know that."

"Thank you." Andy said it simply and sincerely.

"As it happens, I have a score to settle with Mr. Terrance Remington."

"Gloria told you that part?" I asked.

"She did."

The fuel truck started up and shuddered toward the parked jet. One of the pilots descended the stairs to meet it.

Andy said, "Come inside. There's someone we want you to meet."

93

———————

S helly Calbert's utter bewilderment affirmed that she recognized Lonnie as we came through the FBO doors. She had the presence of mind, however, to bark at Reuben when he tried to take to his feet.

"Don't you move."

Lonnie caught the exchange.

"He got shot," I explained.

"I bet that hurt." Lonnie held out her hand to Shelly. "I'm Lonnie."

"I'm…amazed. Uh. Shelly. And this is my husband, Reuben."

Lonnie shook hands with Reuben, hesitant when his big paw came out, but none the worse for wear when it was over.

"And who is this little pirate?" Lonnie dropped to a knee in front of Gabby.

"That's Gabby," Shelly said. "Honey, do you know who this is?"

Gabby gave the stranger an unabashed examination. She smiled. "You look like Captain Marvel."

"That is so kind of you, Gabby." Lonnie beamed. "I would have killed for that part. I'm Lonnie. Pleased to meet you."

"Is that your airplane?"

"Uh-huh. And I'm told I get to take you and your mom and dad for a ride."

"It's my first time! Best day ever!"

Lonnie threw me a glance. "I guess she's been talking to the pilot in the crowd." I didn't deny it. "Would you excuse me? I need to talk to that pilot myself."

Gabby threw a hug around Lonnie's neck, which prompted a startled look on Lonnie's face. She gently placed her hands on the child's back and returned the gesture. Sadness, like distant lightning, flashed through Lonnie's smile.

"We'll, uh, we'll stay right here." Shelly sat down again, unable to stop staring. As soon as Lonnie turned away, she threw both hands up to her cheeks as if that might help keep her eyes from bulging out of her head.

Andy, Lonnie, and I strolled into the pilot's lounge.

"How are Gloria and Oscar?" Andy and I settled in the fat leather recliners such lounges favor.

Lonnie went for coffee.

"My daughter and I are still getting acquainted. There's a lot of me in Gloria, so…she can be a bitch. But I love her. We're finding our way with each other. Oscar? That child owns my heart. He is the sun rising and setting every day." Lonnie leveled a hard look at me. "I meant what I said, Will. You should have called me. I would have come. I owe you. Both of you."

Andy answered for me. "It's not something we would ask lightly. You said you have history with Terrance Remington?"

Lonnie joined us and sat down. "Someone in my position…we leave a trail of embarrassing moments in our wake."

"Embarrassing for you?" I asked, drawing a flash of reproach from Andy.

Lonnie laughed. "Heavens, no. For men like Remington. I meet them all the time. They think they can—well, you know, Will. You've seen it firsthand."

I had. I told Andy how Lonnie had been assaulted, although now I wasn't sure Lonnie would be pleased that I had shared, even with Andy.

Lonnie read my discomfort. "You two! You look so serious! It wasn't a Harvey Weinstein moment. Just a blunder at some party. He was probably too drunk to remember. Tell me. Is this about the Amphitriton IPO?"

"You know about that?" I asked.

"Lord, my brokers have been begging me to get them a ticket to the ball for weeks. It's a public offering in name only, you know. The top brokerage firms all have their claws on block allocations."

We must have looked stumped. I know I was.

"You do know how these things work, don't you?"

"I am as dumb as a box of rocks about the stock market," I said quickly.

"Here's the primer. Rare air IPOs like this are opened only to the cream of brokerage firms. And this one is as rare as it gets. You'll only see Goldman Sachs, Merrill Lynch, JP Morgan—maybe some behemoths from overseas—getting allocations. Golden packages of stock they can offer to their cream-of-the-crop clients. They'll all be at his debutant ball tomorrow night. My guys thought I could leverage my name to get them in. It was tempting, but..." She sat back and looked at the two of us. The sly grin returned. "That's why I'm here, isn't it?"

"Full disclosure, yes. But not for the reason you think," Andy said. "We don't need you to get us in the door so we can grab shares like everyone else. We need you to help us get in the door to sink the whole enterprise."

Lonnie Penn turned her head slightly and tightened the corners of her lips. The expression belonged to a scene from one of her movies. The instant when something audacious hatches.

"I'm listening."

94

The Gulfstream G650 carried us from Key West to Ithaca in a little under two hours, thanks to what the two pilots called a "slight tail-wind" of around seventy knots. I live my pilot life in the lower altitudes and thrill to going just over two hundred knots. Dashing around the country at close to .90 Mach just didn't connect to me.

During the flight, Lonnie waved Andy to sit beside her and fill her in on the details. They spoke for the better part of the first hour. I sat facing Gabby, who pressed her face to the window from the moment we began to taxi. She reminded me of my niece Harriet, whose chief fascination with jet travel was the idea that we were higher than Mt. Everest. I pointed out Pirate Island, which appeared briefly after takeoff. Then showed her the Gulf of Mexico and eventually the curve of shoreline where Florida joined its panhandle. Rising through the clouds brought a look of such wonder to her face that I thought she might burst. She impulsively pressed her hand to the window to find out how they feel.

The world becomes a little less fascinating to a child once you get to what pilots call "the flight levels" above 18,000 feet. She watched for a while, then enjoyed a snack served by the steward—who was called back several times for replenishments. After devouring a third round of fruit and nuts, Gabby's eyelids abruptly gained weight and before too long she curled up on a sofa in the plush executive cabin, sound asleep.

I caught Lonnie glancing back at the child, enchanted by a face even I thought of as angelic.

Reuben nodded off as well. By the time we boarded, he looked pale. He waved off the snack and reclined his seat. For most of the flight, he kept his eyes closed, sleeping or not.

Shelly Calbert would have worried and fussed over Reuben if she were not starstruck by Lonnie Penn sitting less than ten feet away. Andy consumed much of the flight time with an extensive briefing, but eventually Lonnie applied what I could only imagine had become a professional sixth sense. After snack service concluded, Lonnie excused herself from Andy's company and moved to sit with Shelly Calbert, smiling and trading stories. Lonnie showed off pictures of her grandson Oscar. Like her daughter soaring through clouds for the first time, Shelly looked about to burst.

Arriving in Ithaca, Lonnie arranged for ground transportation. I expected a cab or an Uber but wasn't shocked when a Lincoln Town Car driven by a uniformed chauffeur waited for us outside the terminal. He greeted us by name. Lonnie must have texted our photos. In short order we were seated and on our way to Belling Shore University. The driver needed no instructions.

"Does she know we're coming?" I asked Andy.

She answered by hold her phone to display a text message exchange.

Where are you?

Work.

Need your help. Coming to pick you up.

Stay away.

Can't.

Locked down. Insane security until it's over. Stay away.

Right. See you in 30.

"Do you think she'll refuse to come with us?" I asked.

Andy shrugged. "I'm not sure how she can refuse."

"But you still don't want to tell her everything."

Andy gave that some thought. Again. We'd been over this several times.

"We will. When the time is right. But I worry that if we do it too soon, A, she won't believe us, and B, she'll freak out and blow the whole thing. We only have one shot at getting this right."

I agreed. "What do you suppose 'locked down' means?"

"I guess we're about to find out."

95

Locked down meant twice the number of uniformed guards at the university's gated entrance. The uniforms were private security, but they had been enhanced. Each man wore a holstered handgun on his belt. Jack, the young guard who had confronted Andy on our first trip to the site, stepped directly in front of the Town Car and folded his arms.

Tolkien fan, I randomly thought.

An older, more senior guard walked to the driver's side of the car and gestured for the window to be rolled down. Before the chauffeur could respond, Andy opened her door and stepped out of the car.

"Good afternoon." Her greeting lacked warmth. "We're here to pick up Dr. Bailey Maxwell."

"Sorry you wasted the trip."

"I doubt that."

"That you wasted the trip?"

"That you're sorry." She took a step closer to the man who was trying hard to suck in a gut that ordinarily hung over his belt. "Listen to me very carefully, Officer Dayton." Andy tapped the name tag pinned above his shirt pocket with a fingernail that I belatedly noticed she had found the time to paint. "If you take your paycheck, after taxes, and deposit it whole—without lifting a red cent for food or rent or a car payment—into an account every two weeks for the next five years you still will not have enough saved up to hire the kind of attorney you will need to defend yourself against the list of charges I will bring if Dr. Maxwell is not in this car in the next fifteen minutes. Obstruction under section 195.05 is just the start. Kidnapping. Unlawful detention. Threatening an officer of the law with a firearm." Andy glanced at his hip.

"And you are?" I gave him points for standing his ground, even though that ground was crumbling under his feet.

"She's that fake cop!" the kid in front of the car called out.

Andy tightened her lips, further chilling her smile. "And now you have a chance to top the list with listening to an idiot rookie when you damn well should have known better. I'm going to guess that you're doing this gig after a solid career behind a badge, so you know better."

I thought the guard would hold things up for a minute or two, at least pretending to exercise control over the decision. He didn't.

"Screw it," he shrugged. "The boss said to keep everyone out. He didn't say anything about keeping people in." He turned around and performed a circular gesture for the rookie with the folded arms. "Open it up!"

Andy climbed back in. The driver raised his window.

"195.05?" I asked my wife. "Is that real?"

"Look it up."

96

Andy told me to stay in the car. I hopped out behind her. She turned to scold me, but I gave her my best look of little boy innocence. She tried to rouse anger in the face of it but ended up rolling her eyes.

"Dammit. You're stupid cute sometimes."

"It's my superpower."

We blew into the research building like we owned the place.

"I'm sorry, you're not permitted—" The third-floor gatekeeper shot to her feet. We ignored her.

The cubicle farm was all but empty under a sea of fluorescent lights and for a moment I feared Maxwell's absence. Scavenger hunting her on a campus full of uncooperative people had the hallmarks of a giant waste of time. My watch confirmed what the low-hanging sun said. Time was short and we had one more travel leg ahead.

"Dr. Maxwell!" Andy called out.

Bailey Maxwell's spiked hairdo bobbed up from the other side of her cubicle divider. We left the gatekeeper in our wake.

"You people are insane." She did not rise from her chair.

Andy placed both hands on the low cubicle wall.

"You need to come with us to New York."

Maxwell blinked surprise. "To the gala? Absolutely not. We're on lockdown here. They have the entire staff staying at the dormitory until the stock price is announced tomorrow night. I'm not breaking the seal on this, Detective. I have colleagues here who are going to bed tonight buried in credit card bills, who will wake up millionaires on Wednesday morning. How do you think they're going to react if I mess this up?"

"I thought you wanted to help."

"What I want…is for good work and true science to succeed, despite all the Wall Street BS and the money and the political backstabbing. We are *so* close! If I go with you and throw a wrench in the works, it won't matter what's true or how many children have been saved—or how *near perfect* the med is. All that will matter is the headlines, and the doubt, and it will set us back *years*. No. I'm staying put. I gave you all the help I could, but I won't be party to you sabotaging things you don't understand."

Andy lowered her chin in a contemplative nod.

"Gabrielle Calbert didn't drop out of the program for tangential reasons. She was on the treatment, but she didn't respond, so she was dropped. And when her father nearly turned her story into a national headline, Terrance Remington—with the collusion of Jim Newell—kidnapped and attempted to murder her, and her mother and father. Now how do you think your science —no matter how good it is—will play in paragraph thirteen under that head-line in the *New York Post*?"

Maxwell sat staring. Andy leaned into it.

"I need you to come with me to New York and walk into that gala tomorrow to tell the correct story. If you want to protect the science, *then protect it*."

Maxwell shook her head. "No. No, I can't. I have nothing to support that story. Sure, her data was scrubbed from the study. Sure, I can make scrub-bing the data look suspicious, but they can easily shoot me down—exactly the way they did it to my stepmother. At best, I'd be presenting a negative, a void, as evidence. I have nothing, no data, to walk in with."

Andy smiled, a distant relative of the cold smile she had given the gate guards. This had warmth, even with a dash of the Devil.

"You won't need data. You will walk in with Gabby Calbert."

97

———————

Maxwell took to Gabby like a baby sister. The two were chattering before the Gulfstream's wheels came up. I saw in the doctor an almost overwhelming urge to reach out and touch the girl, to stroke the paper-thin skin and test the contours of her bony joints—not in a clinical way, but in the same wonderous way Gabby had tried to touch clouds. I wondered how close, if ever, Maxwell had been to the humans whose life signs were dissected on her graphs and charts and spreadsheets.

A few minutes after the jet leveled off to cruise, Maxwell slipped out of her seat and knelt beside Andy.

"Now I'm confused. She looks like she's responding."

"You're going to have to trust us. She is responding, but there's something at work here that needs to be handled carefully. She is getting better. And you're going to be a part of that. A part of the science, just like you said."

Maxwell shifted her gaze to me. "Does this have anything to do with the absolute impossible, which I honestly don't know if I even believe, that you did to me in that bar? Because maybe I should just refuse to help until I get an explanation."

"Yeah," I said, "you wouldn't want to do that. Because we'd have to drop you off and you'd never find out. Stay with us on this, Doc, and you'll get your answer."

Maxwell did not reply. She returned to her seat. I looked at Andy and crossed my fingers.

Lonnie's jet provided excellent cell service. Halfway from Ithaca to LaGuardia Airport in New York—barely enough time to get the gear and flaps up before starting a descent—my phone surprised me by vibrating in my pocket.

"Leslie." I held up the phone for Andy when her raised eyebrows asked the question. I took the call.

"You kids leave a trail of debris," Leslie said.

"Hello to you, too."

"Is your wife with you?"

"She is."

"And what about Thor, the God of smashing jet airplanes?"

"He's taking a nap." Reuben had been asleep when we returned to the jet with Bailey Maxwell in tow. He stirred briefly during the takeoff, then resumed dozing. I thought he might be on a downturn from his wound until I remembered that he had driven from Arkansas to Key West without stopping or sleeping, and probably hadn't slept much in the days before that. Having his daughter and wife back under his wing and allowing himself to feel hope for his little girl's life for the first time in weeks took the stuffing right out of the big man.

"They have a warrant out for his arrest in Arkansas, you know. For murder."

"I think it's safe to say that he didn't do it."

"If you say so. I found that boat you were looking for. It's at the bottom of the Gulf of Mexico. But, of course, you know all about that."

"Did you learn anything about the boy? Sonjay?"

"Don't rush me. Also, um, I found out about the boy. Sonjay."

"And?"

"Sonjay Singh is—or was—the son of an elementary school teacher and a maintenance supervisor at a water treatment plant in Huntsville. He was laid to rest at a ceremony in his hometown two days ago. The ceremony was conducted by an adjunct pastor from the Citadel of God. Apparently, the Reverend Newell wasn't available. There was no cremation."

"So, the whole thing was a fraud," I said aloud what Andy and I already knew. "Spreading ashes from somebody's barbecue pit, I guess."

"What?"

"Sorry." I realized I'd been thinking out loud. "It's been a little crazy."

"Crazy? Would that be why you're going five hundred miles per hour across Upstate New York in Lonnie Penn's private jet?"

"I think that qualifies. Jesus. You have some nice tech."

"Only the best at the Friendly Branch of Insanity. We'll circle back to young Master Singh. Care to tell me how Ms. Penn figures into all of this?"

Leslie already knew the story of how I met Lonnie Penn, how that meeting led me to her daughter Gloria, and her grandson Oscar. She knew in deep detail the role of Sergei Roan, Gloria's husband and Oscar's father, in a scheme that nearly assassinated the entire United States Supreme Court in one stroke. I could not be certain Leslie didn't suspect that Gloria had murdered her cartel chieftain husband in a Boston hospital—with my help—but I understood her question.

"Ms. Penn is our ticket into the Amphitriton gala at the Met tomorrow night. I think the less you know about that in advance, the better, Leslie."

"That seems to be a theme with you, Will. Fine. One more question. Does this have anything to do with Spiro Lewko's private jet landing at LaGuardia an hour ago? Because I know you two have history. In New York, as a matter of fact."

"Yes. Yes, it does. I can't say more than that, but can I ask you to keep your phone handy tomorrow night? Don't change into your jammies too early."

"Sure. That's our deal, isn't it? Listen. I have something else for you, and this concerns us both."

"Lemme guess. It's about those five dead assholes in Louisiana, and your murdered agent."

"And the answer is, 'What is Company W?' for five hundred. Yes. You left a trail of debris, like I said. That includes a rash of smashed pickup trucks in Mountain Home, remember?"

"Like it was yesterday."

"You tipped me that Remington's gofer, Fennick, tapped into local resources in Arkansas. That on short notice, a bunch of Company W heroes came out in the night for target practice. It seemed like a stretch when you told me, but I found something."

"Do tell."

"The day after you ran into Company W in Mountain Home, a subsidiary buried in Remington's portfolio made a quarter-million-dollar donation to the Men's Choir Foundation at Jim Newell's Citadel of God. This is less than twenty-four hours after the same company donated fifty thousand dollars to the same singing outfit."

Andy, who sat facing me in Lonnie's luxurious jet cabin, did not move to join me on the call, but she watched me with growing curiosity. I flared my eyes to let her know that I had something juicy to share.

"First," I said, "holy crap, are your financial guys camping in the colons of these extremist assholes?"

"They are. The Director wasn't kidding. This is one of the biggest investigations in the Bureau's history. We're monitoring the accounts of scores of organizations."

"Second, a men's choir? Has it come to this? They're going to kill us all with pastoral hymns? Because I attended church as a kid, and some of those hymns are just plain deadly. People went comatose standing up."

"The Citadel of God Men's Choir Foundation has a sketchy history of funneling money into the hands of its Company W members. Picture getting cash from some rich conservative who divides their time between Palm Beach and The Hamptons, into the hands of some Confederate flag-waving twenty-something who makes his own ammunition in Mountain Home, Arkansas. You need a channel."

"What does this mean?"

"What? You're not seeing it? Will, think about it. On the front end, fifty K changes hands. On the back end, the payment bumps up to a quarter mil."

"Fifty K to get them out in a field to finish off the infamous Andrea Stewart. A quarter mil to compensate them when they wind up with five demolished pickup trucks and a seriously bruised ego."

"Good. Keep going."

"Which means that Desmond Fennick's casual call out to Company W wasn't entirely opportunistic. They have a history."

"Better. Bring it home."

"Which means there is every possibility that the private security for tomorrow night's big event has Company W DNA embedded. Is that where you're going with this?"

"Will," Leslie lowered her voice. I didn't think she would make this call from her office, but I did accept the heightened seriousness her vocal change implied. "Did you know that there is a vein of special agents in the FBI who have been grumbling about prejudicial treatment because they hold deeply conservative political beliefs? And that vein can be found in police departments, and at Homeland Security, and in the military?"

"You're scaring me, Leslie."

"It scares me, too. Amphitriton's stock price announcement is all over the news. And I don't just mean Bloomberg. It's tearing up the front pages. Security at the gala tomorrow night will be through the roof. At the perimeters, it's NYPD. Inside, it's all private. Are you getting my drift?"

"I am. Why are you telling me this?"

"Because you've got something up your sleeve and because your wife, whom I'm very fond of, is likely to be neck deep in it with you."

"It's that obvious?"

"It has been since you two hopped off to Ithaca. I'm watching it streak across my computer screen at five hundred miles per hour the entire time we're having this conversation."

"Are you calling to tell us to back off?"

She laughed. "Yes. And right after this, I will call and tell Tom Brady to retire. No, Will. I'm calling to prevent you from getting target fixation. Do you know what that is?"

"Funny, but yes I do."

"Good. I know you and Andy won't be stopped—whatever it is you're doing. But you need to watch your six. And your three and your nine. Got it?"

"Got it."

"I mean it, Will. Don't get so hung up on Terrance Remington and Amphitriton that you get blind-sided. Remington's and Fennick's connection to Company W may be incidental, but Company W's connection to you and Andy is all too real. Call me if you need me. I'm here in New York. Call me in if shit and fan collide."

"Good to know."

"Love to Andy." Leslie ended the call. Andy leaned closer.

"So?"

"She said to avoid the canapes at the gala."

98

L onnie's Gulfstream touched down at LaGuardia just after twilight gave way to full dark night, roughly an hour after official sunset. I understood Reuben's fatigue; it took a substantial effort to rouse him after landing. One of the many beauties of private aviation is the short walk from the plane to the open door of a shuttle van that took us to the FBO where Lonnie's crew had town cars waiting.

On the short walk from the Gulfstream to the Modern Aviation shuttle van, I spotted a Cessna Citation in a line of executive jets. I pointed.

"Look at the nose. That's Remington's. He's here."

A fresh, unpainted aluminum patch covered the gashes cut into the jet's nose by Reuben's fire ax.

Andy gazed out the window. "We knew he would be."

True to his word, Spiro Lewko had three rooms waiting for us at the Ritz Carlton. If Andy and I had half a minute to stop and breathe, we would have marveled at the company we were keeping and the venue in which we kept it. Instead, we hustled our inadequate bags through check-in and into our room after a hasty goodnight to the small Calbert family who staggered wide-eyed through the whole experience.

Bailey Maxwell's presence at the Ritz Carlton front desk meant we were one room short. The desk clerk expressed half-hearted apologies and said there was nothing to be done. I nearly suggested a roll-away bed be sent to the room Andy and I occupied when Lonnie saved me from myself. She walked behind the desk as if she owned the hotel and whispered in the ear of a mildly stunned night manager. Moments later, Maxwell carried Lonnie's key card to the elevator while the bell captain directed that Miss Penn's luggage be sent to something called the Premier Park View Suite.

The bed beckoned, but our night wasn't over yet. At ten-thirty, Andy and I left the room and rode the elevator down to the narrow but elegant first-floor bar. A row of leather-backed stools lined up in front of the marble bar surface, all empty. A black wall backing the bar matched a black ceiling, both decorated with random white streaks that looked like someone playing with the paint before getting serious. I am no judge of art.

The absence of patrons prompted me to ask the bartender if they were open.

"Ordinarily, yes," she replied, "but the bar is closed tonight for a special party." I was about to turn away when she asked, "Are you with Mr. Stewart?"

"He is Mr. Stewart." Andy smiled and took me by the arm.

"Lucky you," I told her. We found a seat midway down the bar. Andy hooked her satchel on one of the evenly spaced hangers, which I considered terribly clever. After preliminaries with the young woman, a glass filled with Corona landed in front of me. Andy ordered iced tea.

Andy turned on her stool so that her knees pressed my thighs warmly. She lifted her glass.

"To you, my love." She used a voice that melted something in me. "For Gabby."

"Cheers." We touched glasses and drank. "Do you think we can count on Dr. Maxwell?"

"Her heart is in the right place. When the dust settles, if we get what we want, we will need someone who understands the Belling Shore research, and Lewko will need someone like her. It will be a lot for her to process, but I really think she will see the opportunity."

I wished I had Andy's optimism.

"Is this a private party?" Lonnie asked from the end of the bar.

Without looking up, the bartender said, "I'm afraid it is. If you—"

"No, it's okay," I waved at the bartender. "She looks, I don't know, somehow familiar."

The tease sailed right past the young woman who had already realized her mistake and now showed signs of having an aneurism. Lonnie slid onto the bar stool on my right. I wished for a mirror behind the bar. Andy on my left. Lonnie Penn on my right. I wanted to take a photo and send it back in time to my eighth-grade class.

"Tonic and lime, please."

"I'm so sorry!" The bartender hustled to work.

"Don't worry about it," I said to the young woman. "People mistake her for Captain Marvel all the time."

Lonnie landed a grip on my forearm and gushed. "Ohmigod! That little girl is the absolute most darling thing. *Please* tell me she's recovering."

"We think so," Andy said.

Lonnie's drink arrived. She sipped and forgave the bartender a second time.

"Thank God. In which case I must ask…are we here to sabotage Terrance Remington by discrediting his new cancer medicine? Because if that little girl is the reason Amphitriton is about to make Wall Street history, I'm not sure I'm on board."

"It's not," Andy said. "That's why we asked you to join us here. In a few minutes, you will understand everything."

"Is Dr. Maxwell coming?"

"No," I said. "Her part in this comes tomorrow. Also, she doesn't know your part and I'd like to keep it that way."

"And what is her role?"

"When the time comes, she will escort Gabby and her parents into the Main Gallery at the Met. You and I will be inside with our final guest."

"Who is?"

"Late," I said. "But I think that's on time for him."

Lonnie didn't press. "Do I have a speaking role in this movie?"

"It's one of the reasons we thought of you, Lonnie," I said. "I hope you don't mind, but we needed someone who could get to a microphone, take control of it, and make a short speech without getting thrown out on her ass."

"Oh, I make no guarantees about that last part. Will I have a chance to memorize this speech?"

"Yes," Andy promised. She fidgeted with her iced tea for a moment. "There's, uh, one more thing. I'm so sorry to ask this…" Andy nervously stroked a hair behind one ear.

I dove to her rescue. "We've been on the road living out of roller bags for about a week. Tomorrow is not quite the Gala at the Met, but it is at the Met, and it is a gala, and my wife is trying to ask if you might have some old rag from, oh, I dunno, maybe one of your Oscar red carpet walks that she could borrow."

Andy slapped me on the arm. I took it for the team.

"Oh, darling!" Lonnie leaned across me and took Andy by the hand. "It is done. Done and done."

A rare bit of blush flooded Andy's cheeks. She fumbled through a thank you while I watched a man enter the bar at the far end. The bartender moved with more caution this time and informed the visitor that the bar was closed. He said nothing. Bald, dressed in a suit with a bulge under one arm, and looking like someone who scarcely allows water to pass his lips when on duty, he assessed the dimensions of the bar, examined the three patrons, and then turned without a word and left.

While Lonnie bubbled up exciting shopping plans for Andy and her, I debated the meaning of the visitor's short assessment of us. I thought about it in the context of Leslie's warning. Not good. Remington had to know we were here.

I made up my mind to sign for the bill and suggest we bug out when another man appeared. This one wore a black crew neck sweater over jeans and shabby blown out sneakers without socks. His shoulder-length brown hair looked freshly washed. His wide face gave the impression he was thinking of something mildly amusing, probably at someone's expense. He lifted his gaze from one to the next of us. His appraisal landed on Lonnie just as she turned and registered his presence.

"Are you…?"

"Are you…?"

"Spiro, Lonnie. Lonnie, Spiro," I jumped in, "but don't call him that. He goes by Lewko."

"A pleasure, Mr. Lewko," Lonnie traded handshakes with the forty-something billionaire.

"The same. Just Lewko, please. My parents' decision to name me after a convicted criminal keeps them off my Christmas card list. Detective Stewart, it's nice to see you when you're not holding a gun in my face."

Andy reached across me for the handshake. "Everybody calls me Andy."

"I hold it against you that you saved that fat fuck in the White House. I can only hope his cholesterol will do for him what the inventive Mrs. Palmer failed to do." Lewko made a quick study of the dimensions of the small bar. "I've arranged for a conference suite. One without cameras." He gestured at a ceiling-mounted black half sphere. To the bartender he said, "May I have a glass of water, sparkling, please?"

"I had no idea you swung Democrat," I said.

"I don't. I am saddled with deep grade school faith in law and justice and democracy that this country stands for, which seems lost on politicians from both sides these days." The bartender placed his water on the bar. "Shall we?"

99

———

A ripple passed through me, through my center, a vibration, as if the core muscle that I feel inside *the other thing* were the plucked D string of an upright bass.

It's here.

We approached a double door. Above it, in gold inlaid lettering, *The Central Park Suite.* The bald man I had seen earlier stood outside the door with his hands folded, the pose of a minister greeting the flock on Sunday morning. Just ahead of Lewko's arrival, he opened the door to the suite and stepped out of Lewko's path.

It's inside.

Once before, in Spiro Lewko's Bond Villain laboratory in North Carolina, I had been close to a piece of debris from my aerial collision. At that time, the artifact had been in the vanished state, and it nearly pulled me into the same. I fought it and won. Instead of vanishing, I forced the piece to reappear. In doing so, gravity took hold of it and the chunk of debris dropped and shattered. Since then, it remained visible and proved to be, as Lewko described it to me during an unannounced visit to my home, *Nothing special. A variation on the same stuff that made the tiles for the space shuttle. Any half-assed lab with a dozen MIT grads could create it.*

Except that it did not come from any half-assed lab. It came from an object that knocked me out of the sky but apparently had enough of a conscience that it deployed what an eight-year-old autistic genius called *a life support system* to save me. That life support system stayed with me. Dr.

Doug Stephenson found it on medical scans that gave it the appearance of car stereo wiring down the back of my brain and spine.

Wiring that hits a *twang!* note whenever I get near its origin.

As we entered an executive suite overlooking Central Park, I felt it. Exactly as I hoped I would.

Lewko ushered us into a softly lit open layout sitting room. Dual picture windows overlooked Central Park from the twenty-second floor. Dark for the most part, the park showed puddles of delicate lighting on its iconic trails and avenues. A frame of lights joined the park's borders where the vibrant city reached into the night sky.

Every furnishing and fixture in the room screamed wealth. I might have been distracted by it except for the silver case resting on a polished coffee table. A sofa and several plush chairs faced the table, waiting for us.

Within a minute of our arrival, the young woman from the first-floor bar swept in the room with our unfinished drinks on a silver tray, paired with duplicate seconds. She landed the tray on a dining table in an adjoining room. The bald man from the door watched her every move, then escorted her out, fishing her gratuity from a pocket before closing the suite door from the outside.

"What?" I asked. "The Presidential Suite wasn't available?"

"In point of fact, it wasn't. I asked," Lonnie said.

Lewko ignored me. He selected a chair facing the coffee table and gestured for the rest of us to do the same. As the ladies sat, he sat. For someone I considered the poster child of self-centered, he surprised me by playing the gentleman.

"Does she know?" Lewko gestured at Lonnie, who selected a matching armchair.

"No." I said.

"Know what?" Lonnie asked.

Andy, who sat beside me on the sofa, looked at me and we traded a silent transmission of approval. This had to happen.

I took a deep breath. "Okay. There's something we haven't shared with you, Lonnie. Something that's going to shed a new light on what you and I experienced together when we rescued Gloria and Oscar. It's…unusual."

Lonnie casually placed her hands on the plush arms of her chair. The soft lamps in the room gilded her golden blonde hair. The regal expression on a face people paid tens of millions to put on a screen belied what felt to me like an electric tension beneath her flawless skin. Blue eyes laden with crystal fixed a gaze on me, unblinking.

She may have come to Key West out of friendship, but more likely out of obligation, and at that moment I understood that her guard never dropped. Ever.

I shifted my attention to Lewko.

"There's also something you don't know. You've seen this...*the other thing*...in action, but there's an aspect of it that you're not aware of."

"I assume it has something to do with Remington's wonder drug."

"Yes," Andy said.

"Let me guess. What you're going to reveal proves that Remington is a fraud. And you need the artifact to make that happen."

I glanced at Andy. She said, "Yes, but not quite the way you might imagine."

I said, "I need to tell you about something that happened two Christmases ago. Are you familiar with the concept of an Angel Flight?"

Lewko nodded.

"I've donated my plane a few times," Lonnie said.

I stood to take the floor. "That's good of you. I'm going to tell you about one particular Angel Flight, but before I do...Lonnie, there's something you need to see."

I stepped around the coffee table and faced the chair Lonnie occupied.

"Andrea, please tell me your husband is not going to expose himself." Lonnie forced a laugh.

Lewko's already broad mouth widened into the kind of grin that harbors a private joke. He leveled expectant scrutiny on Lonnie, who looked up at me.

"Don't scream," I said.

Fwooomp!

100

onnie Penn's reaction to watching me vanish fell along the lines I expected. Brief exposure of unguarded shock was followed by automatic regaining of control, followed by disbelief. I repeated the maneuver, which induced speechlessness. She looked to Andy and Lewko for confirmation. My favorite part, however, is making someone disappear with me and inducing weightless flight. I can't see the person's face, but their grip on me transmits their shock. Responses ranging from giddy laughter to tense shrieks always tickle me. Lonnie went with the giddy laughter after I took her off her feet and we bumped into the ceiling.

When I returned her to the carpet and the visible spectrum, Lonnie stood frozen, almost afraid to move. As if the carpet had the surface rigidity of a waterbed.

Andy served the drinks to bleed the tension out of the moment. She took Lonnie by the arm and guided her back to her chair. I caught Lewko looking a bit jealous and realized that although he has known about *the other thing* since a dramatic rooftop encounter with a mass murderer, he was like the last child who didn't get a ride before the park closed. A part of me liked denying him, but another part of me looked forward to scaring the crap out of him, maybe by leaping together off a building.

My reveal to Lonnie wasn't the only reveal. As promised, I told the story of the Angel Flight and the start of a path that ultimately connected me to Gabby Calbert and Amphitriton. Lewko listened without expression. I didn't need to read his biography to understand that his mind churned upon learning how *the other thing* affected sick children.

It was a critical point. A moment Andy and I had discussed, and one in which we both crossed our fingers. A lot depended on him accepting the plan as we laid it out.

For the next few minutes, alternating between Andy and I, we explained our proposal for infiltrating and disrupting Remington's stock price gala.

Lewko listened without objection or amendment.

"And when this is done, it falls into my hands?" he asked.

"We're hoping Dr. Maxwell will join you," Andy said. "Once we ease her into the truth."

"One more thing," I said. "The case stays with me."

"This isn't some elaborate ruse to steal that artifact back from me, is it Will? Because I didn't bring all the pieces."

"I didn't think you would, and no, it's not. You can't take it through security tomorrow night. I can. I'll be bringing in the case and will deliver it to you once you're inside."

"Okay. Works for me."

I studied the Cheshire Cat face he wore. The ease of his agreement caused me to worry that Andy and I were missing something.

On cue, we shifted our attention to Lonnie, who gripped the arms of her chair a little more than necessary and stared directly at me.

"My father warned me that this day would come," she said.

"What day?" I asked.

"The day when I would no longer be the most interesting person in the room."

<h1 style="text-align:center">101</h1>

———————

We wrapped up the meeting and left the executive suite a little before eleven-thirty. I carried the aluminum case. A steady vibration ran down my center. Unnerving, but not entirely unpleasant. I remembered the effect the parent object had on me when we found it in the forest in northern Wisconsin. It let me move and manipulate myself in ways I had been unable to master before. How much of that, I wondered, might I be able to do with a small piece of the object in proximity? The question needed exploring.

On the way back to our room, I made Andy a gentlemanly offer of romance, in case she felt a need to relieve tension. She politely declined and we slept like rocks until light from an open curtain stabbed me in the eye and Andy shook my shoulder.

"Wake up, lover. He's on the *Today Show.*" Andy dropped the TV remote on my chest. I heard voices in the room.

Terrance Remington laughed and sparred with Hoda Kotb and Savannah Guthrie, and playfully evaded their questions about a breakthrough in cancer treatment, refusing to confirm or deny a medical miracle while winking and nodding that it was all true. The co-hosts probed the planned Initial Public Offering and its Wall Street buzz. Many financial experts, they said, anticipated that the Amphitriton IPO would eclipse Aramco and Alibaba, the top two IPOs in the history of public offerings, generating more than the record twenty-six billion dollars that Aramco had garnered. Shouldn't something like this, a touchstone for all of humanity, be less focused on how much money it can generate and more focused on getting medicine into the hands of people in need? Remington, sporting a three-figure haircut and wearing a four-, or possibly five-figure suit, wholeheartedly agreed. His company planned to expand avenues of distribution to as many world markets as possible, he said, as soon as FDA approval opened the doors. Markets, Savannah Guthrie pressed, means profits. What about simply making the Amphitriton treatment—a potential cure for cancer—part of the public domain? Remington leaned into the answer, resting his hands on the studio's glass table, and revealing a watch I guessed cost him tens of thousands of dollars (I was wrong by a factor of ten). Nothing would make him happier, he declared, than to make this technology a gift to humanity, but such a gift needs support and infrastructure and ongoing research, and all of that needs funding which, he was pleased to say, the coming IPO promised to provide. Also important, he insisted, was the need to protect the technology from charlatans and frauds who might exploit the science. He added that this is a public offering, which meant that ownership of this promising technology and treatment would be, in fact, in the hands of the public.

"My ass," I muttered, hitting the Off button on the remote. "Stock in the hands of select clients as doled out by only the wealthiest brokerage firms in the country."

"Are you talking to the TV?" Andy's voice came from the bathroom.

"Getting ready to throw things at it."

"Please don't." She hurried out of the bathroom and retrieved something from her suitcase before hurrying back in again. "Turn it back on. I want to see if they ask him about his yacht."

I complied, reluctantly. They didn't. Conversation turned to the gala at The Met. The co-hosts compared it to the annual fundraiser thrown by the Metropolitan Museum of Art's Costume Institute and attended by the social and celebrity elite. Remington made an *aw-shucks* show of surprise that the stock price announcement had turned into a social event. It is, he claimed, merely a formality, the final formality in a long road of boring paperwork and filings. Instead of being attended by rappers and celebrity artists, this event invited bankers, lawyers, and brokers who—although exciting in their own fields—hardly hold a candle to socialites and movie stars. On that note, he suddenly chimed in, he did hear a rumor that Lonnie Penn may be attending.

Andy poked her head out of the bathroom.

"What did he say?"

The excited conversation onscreen answered her question.

"How the hell did he find out about that?" I asked.

Andy stared at the screen for a minute. The interview gave way to a weather report that described millions at risk. Andy's unfocused gaze said she was thinking, not listening. Eventually, she speculated that, "People pay hotel staff for intel. Lonnie's arrival would not have gone unnoticed."

"Is this a problem?"

"I don't think so. It may be a good thing. It means there's zero chance of being turned away at the door."

"Okay…that's putting an optimistic spin on bad news. You look good."

"Ugh! My clothes have been in a suitcase for a week. I don't have anything decent. All I wanted to do is borrow a dress, but Lonnie has the day blocked out for shopping. It's a nightmare."

"Tell me about it. My day is a disaster. Room service lunch. A nap. Sixty channels on the high-def TV, not to mention trying to sort out which movies to rent. What on earth am I going to do with myself? I was thinking about taking a stroll in Central Park."

"Absolutely not. That smug son of a bitch knows we're here. He just told us so on national television. This is the man who tried to kill us twice. We're on lockdown until tonight."

"Except for shopping?"

"Lonnie has private security. She's also got a car service on call for all our needs today and tonight. The gala starts at six-thirty and ends at eight-thirty. The price reveal is at seven-thirty. Lewko, Lonnie, and I will ride over at seven. The car will turn right around and pick up Reuben, Shelly, Maxwell, and Gabby. They'll come in at seven-ten. You'll be there ahead of us with the package, of course."

"We went over all this last night."

"And I'm sure you memorized every detail, love." She knew I hadn't.

"We're cutting it a little close to the price reveal, don't you think?"

Andy made another round trip between bathroom and suitcase. This trip had something to do with earrings, which she fiddled with enroute.

"Once we do our bit, the stock price reveal becomes irrelevant. Gabby will steal the show." Andy presented herself. "How do I look?"

"Fabulous. You're going to make Lonnie Penn angry. As a rule, she does not travel in public with people who are more beautiful."

"Aw. You're right. You can lie."

No, I can't.

I checked my watch. Just short of ten. "What time are you meeting?"

"Eleven. Brunch somewhere fancy." Andy turned and confronted herself in the mirror, a critical self-appraisal that said she lent zero credence to my opinion. "I'm changing my blouse."

102

My phone rang. I had programmed the contact, so seeing Bailey Maxwell's name onscreen did not surprise me. I automatically read the time. Five-forty. Almost showtime. Andy had been gone all day, apparently choosing to dress for the evening in Lonnie's suite. Alone in the room, I hit the Mute button on the TV and shot a glance at the aluminum case sitting on the dresser.

"What's up, Dr. Maxwell?"

"You need to come right away!" Raw panic flooded her voice. "The Calberts' room. Get down here. I don't know what to do. Hurry!"

I rolled off the bed and all but jumped into the sneakers that replaced the western-style boots that had been soaked with seawater and ruined during my dive for Pidge and later for Reuben. I grabbed a fleece vest from my suitcase. I tapped the zippered pocket to confirm the presence of two BLASTER power units and a pair of carbon-fiber propellers. I slapped the room key in my hip pocket as I ducked out the door and locked it in my wake.

I stopped.

I thought dark thoughts for one second, then pulled out my room access card and opened the door. I grabbed the case, reawakening the plucked string vibration, and left the room a second time.

. . .

The Calberts roomed two floors down. I took the stairs rather than wait for an elevator. I jogged the short hallway to the correct room and knocked.

Maxwell jerked the door open. Over a nice black evening dress, her face wore the panic I heard on the phone. From somewhere in the room, Gabby cried. On the way down the stairs, I let my imagination torture me with suggestions that *the other thing* had failed, that Gabby had relapsed, and that I would find her in her father's arms fading fast, heart stopping, breath wheezing into silence.

The bawling in the other room came from healthy lungs.

"What the—?"

"The cops came and arrested Reuben," Maxwell blurted.

"When?"

"Ten—twenty minutes ago. I don't know. I was here. Gabby asked if I could come and play cards. They knocked on the door. They had a warrant. They put him in handcuffs and took him. Just like that! Right in front of us."

"Where are they taking him?"

"How would I know? They didn't explain squat."

Maxwell led me into the room where Gabby lay crying on one of the two queen beds. She curled in a fetal position and clutched one of the bed pillows to her chest.

"Where's Shelly?"

"She took off after them. She left me here to take care of Gabby." Maxwell threw her hands out at her sides. "What do I do?"

The crying intruded on a jumble of thoughts. I could not settle on any one of them. Call Leslie? Call Andy? I had no idea, save the obvious.

"Stick to the plan."

"What? Are you serious? First of all, no. I don't know what to do with a child. Second, the plan is out the window. This—God, I don't even know what this means.'" She pushed her fingers into the black spikes of her hair.

"It means you stick to the plan," I took her by the arm and pulled her into the bathroom. She looked ready to join Gabby in tears. "Listen to me. Bailey, listen. This happened because Remington orchestrated it."

"Reuben was arrested for murder! *Murder!*"

"Keep your voice down." I stole a glance at Gabby, who remained fetal. "I know. Andy and I knew about the murder charges. We were there—and he didn't kill anyone." Discussing murder did not help. Terror joined the mix on Maxwell's face. "It was a frame-up. They were doing anything they could to take Reuben and his family off the board."

She stared.

Andy and I had agreed that telling Maxwell everything would only muddy things. The woman had been prepared to think Fennick and Remington capable of bureaucratic evil, but not this. Her reaction validated the decision.

"Look, there's a lot here you don't know. We didn't have time, okay? We still don't have time."

"I don't believe you. God. This isn't happening."

"Really? Not happening? At quarter to six when the show starts in forty-five minutes, you think this isn't happening. Do you think any of this is coincidence? Remington knows we're here. He said so on national television this morning." This news drew a questioning look. I skipped past it. "Remington set this up to throw a wrench in our plans. We're the wild card he cannot allow to be played tonight."

"I don't believe it…"

"Bailey, Remington tried to drop Gabby from the study. He hid her at a hospice in Mountain Home, Arkansas along with Sonjay Singh. When we got too close, he put her on a boat and tried to murder her in the Gulf of Mexico in a way that would take weeks, if ever, to be revealed."

Horror blossomed on Maxwell's face. A voice in my head said, *You're not helping, Will!*

"Andy and I stopped him at each turn." I took Maxwell by the shoulders and leaned in. "*You must get her to that gala on time.* You can't let anything stop you. Not this arrest. Not anything. Do you understand? If she's not there tonight, everything you think you're so close to falls apart."

Gabby's crying died down and shifted to uncontrolled sobbing. Maxwell turned her head at the change in sound.

"Do this for her. Do this for the science you believe in. You're the only one who can get her there tonight."

"Why not you?"

"I can't. I need to be in position already. Same with Andy. But we'll be waiting. At exactly seven-ten you've got to walk that little girl into the gallery. Andy will meet you and take over."

Maxwell tipped her head back and took a deep breath.

"Remington did this," I said.

She closed her eyes.

"Fuck."

103

I stepped out of the Ritz Carlton and paused under the overhang with a serrated fringe. The aluminum case in my right hand sang to me. I'd grown comfortable with its steady note. Blue half shell awnings hung over the windows to my left and right. Traffic jammed Central Park South yet moved with startling speed. Horses stood placidly in carriage harnesses at the side of the road, oblivious to tons of moving metal just feet away.

Nearly as busy as the street, the sidewalk carried enough foot traffic to make me hang back against the stone building façade while I assessed the situation.

I needed to vanish. I felt tempted to just wink out of sight in front of anyone and everyone in front of the hotel. Let them try to explain it.

DURING MY IDLE AFTERNOON, while Andy shopped with Lonnie Penn, I experimented in the hotel room. The first test was easy. I picked up the case and pushed the levers in my head to the wall.

Fwooomp!

The cool sensation flooded my skin. My feet lost touch with the carpet. I looked down and felt some satisfaction in seeing that the case was gone without extra effort. I drew back the levers and reappeared, as did the case.

I laid the case on the room desk and rolled in the combination Lewko had provided. The latches released.

Two unremarkable pieces of the object I had seen in Lewko's lab lay in a

378

form-fit velvet mold. Nothing special. Dull gray, not glowing or flashing. Broken Styrofoam packing. Junk that would have passed unnoticed if it were found on the side of a highway.

The note that vibrated down my center cranked up to a five on the rock band amplifier. I reached for and touched the dull surface. The note cranked up to an eight. I thought about—

FWOOOMP!

I vanished. Without picturing the levers in my head. Without pushing those levers. Scarcely thinking about making the move, the result had been instantaneous and powerful.

"Whoa."

I tested the rev—

FWOOOMP!

—erse.

"Holy crap!"

Both ways, the action responded to the slightest subconscious thought. Which prompted me to consider the next experiment.

I closed the case and stepped back. The vibration that had become white background noise in my center weakened but did not disconnect.

This time I carefully imagined the levers in my head and my hand upon them. I flexed and felt the familiar ball atop each lever. I tightened my grip. I narrowed my concentration to the vibration, to the note it sang to me.

FWOOOMP!

I vanished.

The case vanished. Without contact.

"Holy mother of God..." I whispered.

For a long minute, I hung in the air and stared at the empty space on the desktop. Long enough that I failed to realize that I had not begun to float toward the ceiling. Any time I vanish with my feet pressed into a floor or carpet by gravity, the natural release of the pressure causes me to rise.

I remained fixed on the spot I had occupied. My body had gone weight-less, adopting the many sensations that result from organs not pressed against bones and blood not having to be pumped uphill. But my feet remained firm on the carpet.

I lifted one foot and moved it to the side and set it down again. My body adjusted slightly to one side.

I lifted the other foot and joined it with the first.

I took a step forward. I moved. I took a step back and moved again.

I turned and performed a slow walk across the carpet and nearly broke into giddy laughter when I realized that I was walking. The sensation of my body having no mass made the enterprise nothing short of goofy. My feet acted as if gravity remained in force.

This led to the third experiment.

Up.

I fired the thought off as close to my subconscious as I could.

My feet broke contact with the carpet and I rose to a midpoint between the floor and the ceiling. I laughed out loud.

Okay. *There.*

I focused on the door to the room. Something tugged that upright bass string muscle in my center. I swept toward the door.

Stop.

No such luck. I smacked into the door.

"Ouch!"

Fwooomp!

I reappeared a foot too high in the air and dropped, bumped my knees on the door, and staggered backward, nearly falling on my ass.

"And we're going to pretend that never happened."

I walked back over to the case on the desk and stood over it, staring at it for long enough that I lost track of time.

Thinking hard about what this meant.

SEVERAL HOURS and a dozen more experiments later I contemplated some of my findings as I stood streetside in front of the Ritz Carlton hotel. I was tempted to try a few new tricks, but it is never a good idea to send an airplane fresh out of maintenance off on a mission. Applying that logic, I set aside the afternoon's revelations and dealt with the pressing matter at hand.

From the second zippered pocket of the fleece vest, I pulled out a Bluetooth earpiece. I wiggled it into a comfortable fit in my right ear, then extracted my phone, found Andy on the contact list, and dialed.

"Are you on your way?" Andy spoke in my right ear. I carefully tucked away the phone.

"We have a problem. The cops grabbed Reuben."

"When?"

"Fifteen, twenty minutes ago. Maxwell called me in a panic. Shelly took off after them and left Gabby with Maxwell."

Andy didn't speak for a moment. I chose not to interrupt her thoughts. When she had processed the new information, she spoke decisively.

"You have to get Dr. Maxwell to bring Gabby."

"Already on it. She freaked and almost backed out. I think I got her back on board. What do we do about Reuben?"

"Nothing. There's nothing we can do and nothing we do helps us in the next two hours. Even if we could find out where they took him, he's probably in a holding cell and we'd have no chance of getting anywhere near him. Anything we try would be a waste of time we don't have."

"We stick to the plan. That's what I told Maxwell. I have my earpiece in, so call me when you get there."

Moltke the Elder knew from whence he spoke when he said, *No plan survives contact with the enemy.* I wondered if it helped that what we had was barely a plan.

"Love you," Andy said.

"For which you should be committed."

104

An angled crosswalk at the corner eventually granted passage across Central Park South. I couldn't help but feel, as I crossed, that the drivers held up by the light resented me for the delay. Being from out of town, I cared. No one else hustling across the street to and from the park noticed.

I contemplated sneaking behind the marble pedestal beneath the statue of Simon Bolivar to vanish but decided the act of sneaking was as attention-grabbing as simply winking out of sight on a sidewalk. Jumping the low fence behind the statue also seemed too flamboyant. The fence guarded a steep drop, which meant someone going over it might attract concerned citizens, or at least someone wanting video of the mangled body.

I veered left, past another equestrian statue, this one of Jose Marti, whose horse looked hellbent on throwing his rider. At the entrance to Center Drive I found a set of steps that descended to a narrow path skirting the Central Park Pond.

Fewer people strolled or jogged this path. I went right, past a bench with a young woman working hard to ignore the park's beauty in favor of something on her phone. A jogger approached, dangling wires from her ears. She invested serious effort in avoiding eye contact with me. A quick glance backward after she passed confirmed she was the only person in sight.

Fwooomp!

I vanished along with the case in hand.

Not yet ready to trust the new sensations I discovered in the hotel room I pulled a BLASTER from my pocket. With the prop fixed in place and the motor responding eagerly to the fresh battery charge, I kicked off the ground and aimed the power unit over the placid pond waters.

A few seconds later I reached treetop height. I steered a path parallel to 5th Avenue which bordered the park's east side. Passing over the Central Park Zoo, I glanced down to see if any of the residents alerted to something in the sky. I found no open-air habitats, no curious upturned animal eyes.

105

The flight to the Metropolitan Museum of Art took longer than I anticipated. I underestimated the size of Central Park. The museum, located off 5th Avenue near the north end of the park, stood as one of the few structures within the park rectangle. I learned this only after a Google map study of the terrain.

I approached from the south over the famous avenue, then eased left over a square pool just short of the pyramidal steps leading up to the entrance. A red carpet had been laid, not just to the door, but carefully tucked in place all the way down the steps to where a line of limousines disembarked tuxedo- and evening-gown-clad patrons of the stock market.

I timed my arrival to be at the entrance at precisely six-thirty, when the doors opened. I figured that would give me a chance to get in ahead of the crowd. I was wrong, perhaps because of the limits set by the museum. Special events open at six-thirty and close at eight-thirty. For an extra fee, an event can become an "after hours" event, which Remington had elected to add. I thought the ticket holders tonight would clamor to be fashionably late. Instead, the line of people entering formed ahead of my arrival.

Six pillars fronted the museum, paired in twos to create three sections defined by high arched windows. The sections on the left and right hung huge banners advertising prominent exhibits. Only the center section offered entrance. The evening remained well lit by a sun that would linger another hour above the horizon. Despite an overcast sky, the day had been warm. The museum doors were propped open, solving one problem for me.

The standard door height put patron's heads just one or two feet below the top of the frame. Not enough for me to squeeze through while hugging an attaché case to my chest.

I eased down behind the open door to the right. People gripped and touched the door edge, which eliminated using the door to slip into a gap. Worse, there were no gaps. Security just inside the entrance called for bag checks. Since the bags being checked were tiny evening purses carried by the women, the process went quickly, yet the brief delay solidified the line outside.

I needed a distraction, a gap.

I saw my chance. As a stout man in an ill-fitting tux approached beside an equally stout woman, I reached past the door, unsnapped her handbag, and upended it. The contents clicked and scattered on the concrete.

"Oh!" The woman startled.

The line stopped. The man took a second to comprehend what had happened. He held up the line and bent to retrieve her possessions. People behind the woman captured escaped lipstick tubes, tissues, a silver compact, a cell phone.

I slid around the door and pushed myself forward until I captured a grip on the inner door in time to stop before colliding with the people who had been just ahead of my victim. For a second, I thought the last man through might blow the whole gambit. He turned around and saw a plastic Tic Tac box on the floor. He hinted at backing into me to retrieve it, but a tug from his date beckoned the couple forward to an available open bag inspection station. My path cleared.

I pushed through and upward and entered the museum's impressive Great Hall.

Holy crap.

106

The Great Hall stretched from my left to right under three saucer-shaped domes supported by dramatic arches. Guests mingled on a mosaic marble floor. A continuous balcony marked by ornate stone rails under a vaulted ceiling lined the entire space. At each end and in the center, colonnades guarded access to the galleries. The massive stone space had been darkened, then painted with light. Colors moved and flowed on the walls and ceiling like something from a vintage lava lamp. Electric candles by the hundreds lined the balcony rails above and dotted stand-up cocktail tables on the main floor. At the center, the octagonal information desk had been converted into…I wasn't quite sure. A self-serve bar? Scores of tiny medicine bottles covered the marble counter, interspersed with tall bottles of golden liquid. Scotch. I recognized the label as I ascended. My father-in-law's favorite. Macallan 25. It only took me a second to realize that the small bottles were marked with Amphitriton's product label, the miracle medicine that made this evening financially possible. Each vial contained a gift sample of the expensive scotch.

A stage had been set up under the colonnades opposite the entrance, jutting into the hall at the midpoint. On the balcony railing above the stage, four wide-screen monitors were mounted side by side. A computer scroll bar worked its way across the joined screens with a countdown timer at the end of the bar. The timer represented the moment the stock price reveal would, no doubt, appear on these screens in two-foot-tall digits.

On the stage below the screens, a DJ worked his defibrillator beat. A microphone stand waited to one side of the audio panel. Speakers set up around the hall conspired with the limestone and marble acoustics to fill the air with impenetrable sound. The audio synchronized with the light show. A few people nodded and bobbed to the music, but no one danced. Not yet. Perhaps after some of the medicinal scotch warmed them up. To be heard, guests leaned into each other, mouth to ear.

Tuxedos and evening gowns stretched to both ends of the room. A few people raised phones to capture images and selfies. Others posed to be captured in the self-agrandizing antics.

I drifted fifteen feet above the milling heads, roughly even with balconies which were crowded with guests, tables, and electric candles. The men were handsome, well-groomed, perfectly tailored. The women on their arms were a mix of sophisticated, powerful, or candy for the arms of the wealthy. A few men in their sixties or seventies made no pretense regarding their companionship. The girls tucked in close were a fraction of their age and dressed to expose as much charm as tastefully possible.

Someone with social or financial knowledge of the upper strata in Manhattan probably could have narrated a list of who's who to me. I had no idea. I was interested in only three faces in the milling, mingling crowd and I saw none of them.

Nor could I find a clock.

I powered up the BLASTER and flew a circuit around the great hall at balcony height. The scenery didn't change much. Black tie. Low-cut dresses. Drinks in hand served either from tiny medicine bottles or by the army of young waiters who navigated the crowd with trays of champagne.

Near the south end of the hall, I navigated close to the balcony rail. A man leaned on it, working his charm on a young woman with high blonde curls above a luminous green velvet gown. I had no interest in their conversation, but I grabbed the ornate balcony rail and pulled myself close to read his watch.

6:51.

I pushed off and completed my circuit, returning to take up station above the flower arrangement at the center of the information desk. From there I watched the entrance. The stream of invitees dried up to a trickle. Most of the uniformed security inspectors at the bag check tables stood idle. The open outer doors had been closed.

On the monitors above the stage, the scroll bar crept toward the halfway mark.

107

———————

"We're here."

Andy's voice broke through the steady techno beat bouncing off the Great Hall walls.

"Where?"

"Front steps. We'll be inside in thirty."

I rotated and squared up to the entrance.

Lonnie Penn, followed by Spiro Lewko, followed by Andy passed through the entrance. The women made a brief stop at the bag inspection table. Lonnie passed over a clutch the size of a sandwich. Andy carried something larger, but which surprised the inspector by being nearly empty. The inspections were brief. The trio turned and formed a line with Lewko at the center.

I wasn't the only one watching. Most attendees kept a wary eye on the door, curious to see who else landed a ticket—surveillance that tried to appear casual. It turned into unabashed staring.

The music faded to silence. Crowd babble dropped to a low hum.

A spotlight, not overly bright, landed on the trio.

Lonnie stood out in white. Her dress relied on a single delicate strap, a strand almost, that swept up from her left breast and over her shoulder. Like liquid flowing in diverse currents, shimmering fabric streamed down across her bosoms, tightened at the waist, then embraced her hips. The waters parted high on her left thigh, revealing ample leg while fabric swept around, dipping behind her knees before rising again to rejoin the flow. At her neck,

388

something massive glittered above the swell of her cleavage. Diamonds. A cluster suspended by a chain of sparkling stones that disappeared behind her slim, bare neck. Despite the jewels and the million-dollar body encased in a gown worth the mortgage on a modest home, it was the face that sucked the attention from both levels of the room.

She was Lonnie Penn, every commanding bit of her.

Andy, opposite Lonnie with Lewko between them, was all of that and more in black. I could not find a seam or wrinkle on the gown she wore. I had no idea what held it up on her breasts. There were no straps over her bare shoulders. Nor could I see what prevented the shimmering materials from simply sliding to the floor. I know the compound curves of my wife's body intimately. The dress she wore made them public. A deep slit down the left side exposed one leg all the way to the hip bone, begging the question of what if anything else she wore. I felt pride poisoned by bubbling jealousy knowing that every man in this room laid his eyes on something that belonged to me. My jealousy burst like a child's soap bubble when I saw that at her neck, in contrast to the gross national product of a small country that Lonnie wore in jewelry, Andy wore a simple gold chain that ended in a sculpted silver heart with a single tiny diamond at the center—a gift I had given her. My modest but earnest statement of love. A statement she displayed for every lusting eye in the room.

She left me breathless.

Her lips moved. "You there?"

"Uh…yeah. Just trying to get my heart started again. Wow."

"Christian Dior. Do your job tonight and I'll let you play with it later."

I was glad she didn't require a response. It would be a minute or two before I could speak.

Lewko, who I had barely noticed, anchored himself between the two women in a simple tuxedo, but with a black shirt under his black tie. As much as the women on either side of him commanded the libido of everyone —man or woman—in the room, the presence of Spiro Lewko commanded the financial attention of every broker and lawyer in the room. Exactly as we had hoped.

I glanced at the stage. Two of the three faces I had been looking for filled the space evacuated by the DJ.

Terrance Remington stepped up to the microphone. The Reverend Jim Newell stood upstage under his signature pompadour hair style wearing a deeply satisfied smile. Why not? The flock he looked out on from this pulpit was loaded.

Remington spoke.

"Wow," His voice boomed through the Great Hall. It silenced the remaining rumble of conversation. "Ladies and gentlemen, good evening. I…uh, I honestly did not think tonight's exciting announcement could be upstaged—yet…what can I say? Ladies and gentlemen, Miss Lonnie Penn!"

The guests broke into applause.

Lonnie dipped her chin almost imperceptibly, a gesture of acknowledgment both regal and humble. The applause continued. She repeated the gesture, left and right.

Remington squinted slightly. "And if I'm not mistaken, a gentleman whose riches might just be eclipsed tonight by the beauty of the company he keeps—is that you, sir? Mr. Spiro Lewko."

More applause. Money talks. Lewko painted on a toothless smile.

Remington paused when a man in a suit, not a tuxedo, hurried to him and spoke in his ear. If the bump under his arm didn't give him away as security, the curl of earpiece wiring running down his neck did. The words he spoke to Remington had a sobering effect.

"And my apologies…I, uh…I guess we also have the honor of Ms.—I mean to say—Detective Andrea Stewart. Looking lovely tonight, officer."

The applause faltered slightly, but most gave it an effort even if they had no idea who Andy was. Or worse. If they did.

Remington regained his composure. "Miss Penn, I wonder if I might be so bold as to ask you to join me on stage for tonight's announcement. Please." He held out a hand.

The applause picked up. People shouted her name.

"Won't you please?" Remington implored.

Lonnie played the role perfectly. She summoned a blush beneath her cheeks. She waved away the adulation for just the right amount of time, then lowered her eyelids in acceptance and stepped for the stage. Shouts and whistles joined the applause.

I hit the BLASTER and circled around in front of Andy and Lewko who remained beside the information desk. The spotlight had moved the crowd back far enough to give me the space I needed.

I dropped to my feet directly in front of Lewko. I placed the case at his shoes and released my grip.

It failed to reappear.

Dammit!

The D string note hummed down my center—my connection to the artifacts in the case. I reached out with my imaginary hand and gripped my imaginary levers and tugged, focusing on the connection, careful not to make myself pop into sight.

Fwooomp!

The case appeared on the floor. I remained vanished.

I used the vibrating connection to the artifacts inside the case the way I had used them in the hotel room. I shifted sideways until I faced Andy. I carefully flipped the lid of her handbag open and reached behind my back to where her Glock had been under my shirt and fleece vest, resident in a holster attached to my belt. I snapped the gun free and lifted it, then dropped it into her bag. The instant I released my grip, it snapped into sight inside the bag. An electric sting nipped my fingertips.

The sudden added weight in her bag alerted Andy. She focused on the empty air where I stood in front of her. She glanced down and replaced the flap on her bag, then noted the case.

"Thank you, love," she said.

"I love you, too." I pushed off.

Lonnie stepped onto the platform aided by the gentlemanly hand of Terrance Remington. Playing to the applause, she waved at the crowd on the Grand Hall floor, and to people waving from the balconies.

Remington lifted the wireless microphone from its stand.

"How about it, ladies and gentlemen? Lonnie Penn!"

The adulation continued. Lonnie dipped a polite bow at Remington, then waved at the crowd again. She paused long enough to look up at the screens hung from the balcony above. The scroll bar had edged into the home stretch. She lifted her eyebrows at Remington who clasped his hands together in triumph.

Lonnie reached out. Remington pantomimed asking if she meant the microphone. Lonnie flexed her fingers. He playfully withheld it, then handed it to her.

Lonnie turned to the adoring audience. "Thank you! Thank you so much! Please..." She waited for the applause to die down. "Please. Thank you for that kind greeting. Good evening, everyone. Wow. What a night. There's some genuine excitement in the air, yes?"

Whoops and cheers. I wondered how often stockbrokers got the chance to act like drunken Packer fans.

"This is like the Ball Drop on New Year's in Times Square, without the urination."

Big laugh.

"Listen, I want to call on someone to say a few words, Terry. I hope you don't mind. I know we have a little time." Remington stiffened slightly but Lonnie paid no attention. "Ladies and gentlemen, you all saw him enter. You all recognize him. He never—and I mean *never* steps out in public like this, let alone speaks, so you're all in for a huge treat tonight. Please. Mr. Spiro Lewko. Sir, would you come forward?"

Lewko bent and picked up the case as if it had been there all along. With Andy beside him, he strolled to the foot of the risers. The crowd parted as if Lewko had Moses on the payroll. He stopped short of the stage.

Lonnie played to the crowd. "Now…I know you're all a bunch of children waiting for Santa to give you the best Christmas ever, but I think we have just enough time that we can get Mr. Lewko to say a few words. What do you say, Terry? The chance of a lifetime."

Remington showed signs of wavering—a man who felt the floor tilt. He pasted a grin on his face and held out his hand for the microphone. A bid to regain control. Lonnie returned the grin and began to extend her arm, but in a deft gesture, flipped the microphone over her shoulder.

I would not have believed it if I hadn't seen it, but Lewko calmly put up one arm and snapped the wireless mic out of the air.

The crowd went wild.

Remington, still gluing the grin to his lips, stared hot bullets at Lonnie, who returned a smile that suggested she had just neutered him with a butter knife.

Lewko turned and faced the crowd, still cheering, anticipating his voice, his words. Wisdom. Humor. Insight. It didn't matter what was said as long as it came from one of the world's richest men.

He waited patiently.

He offered no Thank You or You're Too Kind or chatter.

He waited until near silence descended on the huge hall.

He lifted the mic to his lips.

"Tonight, I am announcing my intention to purchase one hundred percent of the proffered Amphitriton public shares that will go on sale tomorrow."

The crowd sucked in a massive gasp in unison.

Lewko waited for the shockwave to reach its terminus. Silence slowly returned.

"I will offer a share price of ten cents. This offer is good for one hour. After that, my price goes to one penny per share."

Silence.

Lewko held out the mic and released.

108

Andy ignored the chaotic conversation that bubbled up all around her. She fished her phone from her purse. She glanced back to search the entrance. At any second, Maxwell and Gabby would be coming through the front door. She tapped her phone. A chirp in my ear indicated she had put me on hold to make a call. I watched her dial and wait. The call connected. Her affect shifted. She spoke as she searched the entrance. Her expression darkened.

On the stage, Lonnie stepped beside Remington and hooked his left arm in a tight embrace. She leaned over and spoke in his ear. Payback for whatever he had done in their mutual past, I had to assume from the look on his face, which went pale.

Andy abruptly tapped her phone again. Her voice returned to my ear.

"Will, I have Dr. Maxwell on the line. She says she's not coming. Doctor, where are you?"

Maxwell sounded distant, panicked. "I can't do this. I'm sorry."

"Bailey, please, tell me where you are."

"I understand what you're trying to do, but it's not fair to sabotage everything just because the treatment isn't perfect and the company is run by assholes. And you're wrong about it not working. Gabby is doing fantastic. How can you not see that?"

"Gabby's condition isn't because of the treatment, Bailey. That's why we need you here."

"You're wrong. And this isn't about the IPO. Or money. Not for me, at least. Honestly, I don't have a dime of stake in this—except my job, and I don't even care about that."

"Doctor, where are you?" I asked. "Are you at the hotel? I can come for you."

"We left the hotel. Gabby is safe. She's with me. I'll keep her safe."

"Left to go where?" Andy asked. "Please."

"Look—I know the treatment isn't perfect. I know I blew the whistle on some of the data practices. But there is still good work here. *We're nearly there!* We can reach perfection—I know it."

"Bailey," Andy said gently, "you're not wrong, but there's something you don't know. The list you sent me. It's proof that the Amphitriton treatment *is not* the cause of the results you're seeing. Documentable proof."

"I can't. I can't let you do this. I'm so sorry …" I feared the connection would break, but Maxwell lingered.

"Bailey, please! Wait! I know you believe in what you're doing. Just tell me one thing. Are you with Mr. Fennick?"

She hesitated. "I know what you think. I don't like him either, but he's not wrong. He told me your plan is to ruin the IPO and destroy our chance to perfect the technology. Gabby proves the treatment works. You're trying to discredit that. He promised to keep us safe."

"He's lying," Andy said.

"And you're not? Please leave us alone. Gabby is safe. We'll be safe at the air—"

Silence.

"Bailey? Bailey?" Andy glanced at her phone screen, which gave the bad news. The connection was gone. "Dammit!"

"The airport," I said. "Fennick is taking her to the airport. Remington's patched up plane is there. If he can get her in the air and away from here for the next twelve hours, they think they can still make their killing." I regretted the choice of word instantly.

"We'll never get there in time. Or find them, let alone get her back here."

"Ten minutes. Give me ten minutes."

"Impossible!"

"Not the way I fly."

109

I knew what Andy didn't. LaGuardia Airport sits on land jutting into the East River in a wide spot dominated by Rikers Island. To the average New York driver, reaching the airport from Central Park might take half an hour to an hour, depending on whether traffic was bad or awful. However, seen on a map, the airport is horizontally even with the Metropolitan Museum of Art at the north end of Central Park. I guessed the linear distance between the two to be less than four miles.

I can crank sixty knots out of my BLASTER. That put the airport just under four minutes away.

I hit it.

My first shot took me to the entrance. I dropped to floor level just past the bag inspection tables. The space between the inner and outer doors was empty. I aimed for one of the doors and grabbed the release bar. I planted my feet on the floor at an angle that gave me leverage and popped the door open. Heads turned at the door opening by itself. I didn't care. I heaved myself through and launched over the broad museum steps.

Full power on the BLASTER. The prop screamed. The wind built up rapidly. I shot over 5th Avenue and angled upward. I soared above the apartment buildings carpeting the Upper East Side.

A mid-height overcast stretched toward a horizon that burned bright orange thanks to the setting sun. The underside of the clouds adopted the appearance of a stove burner, spreading hot color across the sky.

I leveled off a couple hundred feet above the rooftops. Streets full of traffic swept by below; long strands of headlights in one direction, red tail-lights in another. If anyone heard the loud whine of the prop, they passed it off as just another inexplicable sound in a city of endless sound.

Relative wind rippled my clothes. Lacking the handy ski goggles that always seem to be in my flight bag when I need them, I was forced to squint. Tears streamed back from my eyes.

I aimed for LaGuardia. My navigation proved sound when I spotted landing lights in the sky. A light breeze from the northwest told me that the active runway was 31. The string of lights hanging below the clouds confirmed it. A line of jets descended through the overcast.

When Lonnie's jet landed at LaGuardia, I could not help but wear my pilot's hat. I followed the taxi route to general aviation parking at a spot called The Five Towers, a span of ramp on the west side of the airport. Secure access to parking went through authorized shuttles run out of the sole FBO on the field, Modern Aviation. If I had any hope of catching up to Fennick, Maxwell, and Gabby, it would be at the FBO or on the ramp.

The East River swept under me. I crossed the waterway on an angle. The Triborough Bridge bisected my path. I aimed between twin suspension towers topped with red beacon lights. Steady toll traffic connecting Queens to Wards Island and Manhattan beyond traversed the bridge below me.

The airport crept into sight. I automatically checked the traffic flow. The line of arrivals from the southwest extended well into the sky. I noted a departure climbing away to the northeast from the perpendicular runway. Alongside that departure runway, jets crawled down a parallel taxiway. Arrivals on 31. Departures on—I guessed at the runway number—04, still too far out to see it. Nothing unusual, but good to know.

If Fennick planned to load Maxwell and Gabby into Remington's jet and spirit them away until the dust settled on the IPO, he first needed a ride from the FBO to the airplane. Once loaded, he would have a short taxi run from the general aviation ramp to the departure runway.

I prayed that I still had time.

The river fell behind me. Rows of rectangular townhouses, packed shoulder to shoulder, passed below me. I aimed for the red concentric roofs of the Modern Aviation building adjacent to a small man-made bay in the river.

As I passed over the LaGuardia Airport perimeter, I pulled the power slide control back to neutral and let wind resistance reduce my speed. Several hundred yards away, Remington's jet remained parked on the small acreage allocated to non-commercial aircraft. That was the good news. The bad news was that the shuttle van used by Modern Aviation rolled on a path toward the jet.

I slowed. The wind roar died down. I spoke to Andy.

"You there?"

No response. The connection had either ended or dropped. I had no way of dialing Andy. I hoped she would connect to me. A call from her to Leslie to the tower at LaGuardia would end this chase before it started.

I dove toward Remington's parked Citation. It was no contest. I arrived well before the van.

Fwooomp!

I reappeared and dropped to a landing beside the jet. The aluminum patch on the nose caught my eye. Expecting no less, the work looked clean and professional, as it would have to be for the jet to be deemed airworthy. It doesn't take much to render an aircraft unairworthy. Thin slices to the props on the Foundation's Navajo proved that point.

Time to return the favor.

I dug a thin survival knife out of a pocket in my jeans. It only took a minute. One quick slice, and the work was done, well before the van rolled up and stopped.

The driver, a man with a pear-shaped torso, crewcut hair, and a rough beard, gave me a startled look as he hopped out and opened the van doors. He stopped short of asking what the hell I was doing on the ramp, although the question lingered on his tongue.

Maxwell stepped out of the van first. Her face, although pale, carried a fresh red welt on her left cheek. She flashed startled recognition upon seeing me. Her affect mingled defeat and apology.

"I'm sorry," she mouthed the words without sound. It was easy to see why.

Desmond Fennick climbed out behind Maxwell. He held Gabby to his chest like a human shield, using his left arm to cradle the small girl. He hid his right hand in the pocket of his windbreaker. The embossed shape under blue nylon left nothing to the imagination. His gun pressed against Gabby's body. If my presence surprised him, the emotionless expression on his gray bearded face gave no hint.

Gabby looked at me and recognition blossomed over fear. "I wanna go home. I want my daddy." Her plaintive cry was swallowed up by the whine of passing jet turbines. Less than a hundred yards away, a line of aircraft taxied for departure.

"Pretty soon, honey," I said.

"Tip the good man," Fennick said to Maxwell. She fumbled with her purse and produced a bill for the driver who watched all of us suspiciously.

"Thank you, ma'am." He tucked the bill in his shirt pocket. "Anything else I can do for you?"

"We need a ride back," I said.

"We're done here," Fennick countered. "Take off."

"Not so fast," I said, freezing the driver in helpless indecision. "There's a small problem with the airplane. Afraid we're not leaving, Des." I gestured at the nose wheel.

The wheel rim pressed the flat rubber tire against the ramp. The tire stem I had severed lay on the concrete.

Fennick's ruddy face gained a crimson cast. He stared at me just long enough to formulate a new plan. His right hand came out of the windbreaker pocket holding a semi-automatic pistol. I expected him to press it against Gabby but instead he extended his arm and pointed the pistol at the face of the van driver.

"Keys! Put them on the seat!"

The driver wasted no time. He jabbed his hand in his pants pocket and produced a key fob attached to a piece of plastic with the van's license number scrawled in Sharpie. He dropped the key on the driver's seat.

"Now run." Fennick gestured with his weapon.

The driver bolted. I would have picked the nearest fence, but instinct took him in the direction of the terminal, several hundred yards away.

Fennick pressed the pistol against Gabby's back.

"Who the fuck are you?"

"You met my wife, Detective Stewart."

"Your wife is a bitch."

"Yeah, well that bitch is on the phone with federal authorities, the TSA, and the NYPD and in a minute or two all hell is going to rain down on you. You've got nowhere to go, Fennick. Dr. Maxwell, would you step over here by me?"

"Move and I will pull this trigger." Fennick pressed the gun against Gabby again. He said to Maxwell, "Get in the van. You're driving."

"This is the thing I never get about hostage situations, Des. Pull that trigger and you have no more leverage." I strolled forward until I reached Maxwell.

"Get in the fucking van! Now!"

I turned to Maxwell.

"I'm so s-sorry," she stammered. "I was wrong. I was so wrong."

"A minute here, please," I said to Fennick. I held out my hand. "Doctor, I'd just like to shake your hand." Our eyes met. "Again."

Across a locked gaze, Maxwell transmitted startled understanding. She held out her hand. I took it and winked.

Fwooomp!

We vanished. I instantly locked a grip on Maxwell and kicked the pavement. We shot upward. She gasped.

Fennick reacted as I expected.

"Hey! What the—?"

The gun came away from Gabby's back. He aimed it wildly at the spot we had vacated. I feared he might start shooting but he had nothing to shoot at. He waved the gun wildly from side to side, blinking, uncomprehending.

"*Where are you?!*"

I grabbed the BLASTER from my back pocket and fired it. The whine of the prop disappeared beneath the roar of a jet departing runway 04 nearby. Hidden in that thunder, I maneuvered us sharply into a tight turn over Fennick's head. I dove for the pavement at the back of the van. The ramp offered nowhere to hide, but the van blocked Fennick's line of sight. I cut a tight corner at the left rear of the vehicle.

Fwooomp!

I released Maxwell. "Stay quiet!"

She landed hard. She fell flat near the rear wheel of the van. I didn't have time to do more than confirm that she stayed down, out of sight.

I kicked off and added power to fly an arc around the back of the van hoping Fennick had not yet come to his senses.

"Fuck!" Fennick cried out. He whipped the gun around in all directions as if I might sneak up on him.

"Right here, asshole," I called out. It was an arrogant mistake. He followed the sound with the gun and fired. The discharge cracked the air. His aim was close enough to convince me to shut my stupid mouth.

"Show yourself or I will put the next one in the kid!" He pressed the gun to the back of Gabby's head. "Show yourself!"

I aimed for the open driver's door.

Fennick did what I feared he would. He backed toward the van, twisting his head from side to side.

I dropped to the side of the van by the open door and scooped the keys off the seat. They vanished in my hand, setting off an electric tingle in my palm. I jammed them in my pocket.

Fennick backward-walked closer. I considered making both him and Gabby vanish, but the weapon in his hand eliminated that move. If I made him disappear with the weapon and he fired, chances were good we would all end up on the pavement paralyzed. Gabby, frail as she was, might not survive such a potent lightning strike.

Fennick backed right into me. He caught me in the van's open doorway. He felt me and spun around. The gun came away from Gabby and headed in my direction.

Fwooomp!

I flashed into sight, dropped into the grip of gravity, gained weight and mass, and threw my left arm up to fend off the incoming weapon. With my right thumb, I pushed the BLASTER slide control full forward. The prop screamed. I stabbed it at the fingers of Fennick's right hand, wrapped around the gun swinging toward me.

The razor-sharp carbon fiber prop blade sliced into his fingers. The gun fired into the air. The prop shattered. Blood sprayed from his mangled hand. Fennick howled and staggered backward. Defenseless, I feared another shot, but the gun dangled from his wounded hand. He shifted Gabby in his arms and passed the weapon to his left hand.

Fwooomp!

I vanished. Once more, I kicked the pavement and shot upward just as Fennick gained enough control of the weapon to fire five times into the cab of the van. The shots passed just beneath my feet.

"FUCKER! Where are you?" He searched in vain, then realized what I had done. "Gimme the goddamned keys or I swear I will shoot this damned kid!"

My BLASTER lay whining on the ground, the blade gone. I pulled a second from my vest. My hands shook. Thrust took me higher and higher while I struggled to snap the blade in place. It took three tries.

Fennick backed away from the van, still clutching Gabby. Maxwell cowered on the other side of the vehicle, curled beside the rear wheel, hands thrown over her head.

I needed to get Fennick away from the vehicle.

"Fennick!" I called down to him. "Let the kid go and I'll toss you the keys."

"Screw you!" He spun around, hunting the sound of my voice. "The kid stays with me."

"I'll sell you the keys. Ten million."

He staggered in a circle, searching.

"One million. I'll give you one million for the keys."

"No deal. You're in on the whole scheme with Remington. This time tomorrow you'll be worth more than a billion. Ten million for the keys."

"Deal!" he called out. "Throw me the keys and you can have the kid."

I pulsed the BLASTER and maneuvered toward the runway. Another jet roared into its takeoff run.

He had as much intention of giving up Gabby as he did of paying me ten million dollars.

"Throw me the keys!"

Two parallel taxiways lay between the general aviation parking ramp and runway 04. Jets taxied to line up for the runway 04 departure using the second of the two taxiways.

"Over here." He spun around to the sound of my voice. "Put her down."

"No way. The kid stays with me until I have the keys!"

"This way." I drifted across the first of the two taxiways. "Over here." The second taxiway, marked AA, slid beneath me. A Boeing 737 rolled toward me several hundred feet away. I didn't have much time. I lowered myself to the pavement.

"Here!"

Fwooomp!

I dropped into sight and held the keys out. Forty feet away, Fennick spotted me. He clutched Gabby with his bloody right hand and pointed the gun at me with his left.

I dangled the keys for him to see.

"Throw them to me!"

"No way. Ten million. You promised." I lowered the keys to the pavement. "Come and get them."

Fwooomp!

I vanished again before he could draw a bead on me. He hurried forward.

This time, instead of kicking off, I stayed where I was, hanging in the air above the keys. He crossed the BB taxiway and jogged to where I hovered above the AA taxiway. His bloody left hand pressed Gabby to his chest. He aimed the gun at her back with his right.

The Boeing jet rolled steadily down the taxiway centerline.

Come on, guys, get your eyes outside the cockpit! I willed someone in the front seats of the jet to see Fennick. A man running around the airport with a child clutched to his chest and a gun in his hand guaranteed an immediate shutdown. It would bring the whole world down on Fennick.

The jet rolled toward us unabated.

Fennick reached the taxiway and hustled to the centerline where I had dropped the keys on the yellow painted stripe.

Jesus Christ, guys! I implored the crew of the jet. The big engines hanging from the wing spun and sucked in mountains of air.

Fennick needed his good hand to pick up the keys. His gun hand. It meant removing the deadly barrel from Gabby.

The jet bore down on us. Two hundred yards.

Rage painted Fennick's face over pain from his mangled fingers. "Fucker, I don't know how you're doing this, but you're not getting a penny from me. And this kid is dead. Hear me? Dead!"

One hundred yards. In a moment, the air drawn into the jet's engines would pull me in, too.

Fennick crouched and reached for the keys with his gun hand.

Fwooomp!

I reappeared in his face. I jammed the BLASTER to full power and swiped it across his good hand. More blood spattered. The blade sliced his fingers. He screamed. The gun fell from his hand and clattered on the pavement. I jerked the BLASTER back before my last blade sustained damage.

With my free hand, I grabbed his wounded right hand and crushed his fingers in my grip.

Fennick screamed. Gabby tumbled free. I scooped her from his arms before she dropped to the pavement.

FWOOOMP!

Gabby and I vanished. I punched my legs at the pavement.

The nose of the big jet loomed, so close now that even if the pilots stared straight ahead, they would not see us beneath the high instrument pane and nose. Gathering wind swept around us toward the spinning jet engines. In the vanished state, we were nothing to those engines. Dandelion fluffs in the wind. Without weight or mass, we were the equal of the air the engines consumed by the cubic yard.

I threw up my arm and pushed the BLASTER control to full power. The air around me tugged us down, but the BLASTER fought it. We shot toward the blazing orange clouds above.

Below us, Fennick scrambled for his weapon but neither hand worked. I heard him scream. He fumbled for the gun.

The jet didn't stop. The crew never saw the drama on the pavement. It wasn't hard to understand. No crew expects someone to be running around on a taxiway. A crew need only glance out the window between cockpit duties and preparation for takeoff to stay on a taxiway traveled day after day.

Fennick tried to run. Too late. He stumbled out of the nosewheel's path but not out of the engine's reach. The right engine, sucking in huge gulps of air, pulled him off his feet. He flailed and spun in the air. I watched him disappear into the mouth of the engine. Sparks and flame exploded from the engine exhaust.

The crew reacted quickly. The jet stopped.

Smoke boiled from the rear of the engine.

In a few minutes the airport fire brigade would race to the stricken airplane and traffic at LaGuardia would grind to a halt.

I didn't wait to watch.

Fwooomp!

I dropped to the pavement beside the van where Bailey Maxwell crouched, shaking. She looked up to see me with Gabby hanging from my neck, her thin legs wrapped around my waist.

I lowered the girl to the ground. She released me reluctantly, but had no choice when Maxwell swept her up into a desperate embrace.

"I'm so sorry, honey, I'm so sorry!" Maxwell buried her face against the girl's head. "I didn't mean it to be like this!"

"It's okay, Bailey," Gabby stroked the woman's hair. "It's okay."

Maxwell looked at me.

"She's not wrong," I said. "This isn't your fault. You didn't know what we know."

"We're so close."

I shook my head. "Actually…you're not. That list you sent Andy. Those are all hospitals that I've visited. Doing…*this*. With children like Gabby."

Maxwell blinked.

"This *thing* you've seen me do. It has a side effect. A good one. It helps kids like Gabby. Remington's treatment doesn't."

"It was you?"

"Yeah," I said. "I had the dumb luck to be doing my thing in hospitals that were testing Amphitriton's treatment. And where I wasn't doing it, Remington's trick was to drop the kids. Like Gabby. And Sonjay. The miracle results he's pitching tonight to Wall Street are all my work."

"But—how—what—?"

"Not now. We need to go. Come with me. We need you. I'll explain on the way." I held out my hand.

Maxwell stared at it blankly.

"I mean it. We need you."

Maxwell hesitated. Gabby had no such reservations. She flashed a broad smile that burst through the fear and tears she had been shedding.

"Come on, Bailey," she cried. To me she said, "Do it again!"

110

———————

Maxwell cradled Gabby. I hooked arms with Maxwell. I explained what I could between giggles and laughter and cries of wonder as we retraced my flight path across the East River and the Upper East Side of New York, back to Central Park and the Metropolitan Museum of Art. By the time we reached the doors, Maxwell understood what we had intended to be her role all along. I looked back on how we handled things and took some of the blame for what had happened. If we had revealed the truth to her, she would not have lost faith.

At the door, Maxwell passed Gabby to me. I released Maxwell. She landed on her feet but staggered and needed a grip on the door to steady herself. To her credit, she pulled herself upright, gathered her wits, and opened the door for us.

Gabby and I floated into the Great Hall.

Not much had changed. The low rumble of conversation had returned. The atmosphere of revelry and imminent immense wealth seemed undiminished.

Lonnie remained on the stage. Lewko looked like he had not budged since dropping the mic. Andy remained close by. She tapped her phone screen then waited for a call to connect. When it didn't, she flashed frustration.

"Pretty cool place," I said to Gabby who clutched my neck. I could feel her head swinging from side to side, taking it all in.

I used a burst of power to get above the heads of the still mingling crowd. A short glide took us to Andy. I lowered Gabby and me beside her.

"Hey." Andy startled. "We're back. Got Gabby."

"Ohmigod! I've been trying to call you!"

Maxwell hurried through the crowd and bumped into me from behind. I had to grab her to keep from shooting across the floor.

"Sorry!"

Maxwell turned to Andy.

"She knows it all now," I said.

Maxwell nodded. "I'm so sorry. I—"

Andy pulled her into a hug. Nothing more needed to be said. When they parted, Maxwell rubbed tears from her cheeks.

I touched my ear and discovered why Andy's calls had gone unanswered. The Bluetooth earpiece was gone.

"Gabby? Are you there?" Andy reached out. She broke into a smile. Gabby must have touched her hand. "Is this cool or what?"

"Better than an airplane!"

"Alright, we need you to do one more thing, sweetie. Will is going to take you up on the stage with Mr. Lewko. Did Will tell you all this? Did he tell you the most important part? The part about Will?"

"Especially the important part."

"And you can do this? Can you keep a secret? Can you do it to protect Will?"

"You betcha!"

Andy tapped Lewko on the shoulder. "They're here. It's time."

Lewko nodded and picked up the case.

From the stage, Remington took to the microphone again.

"Ladies, gentlemen, everyone else, your attention please!" He laughed at his own joke. He regained some of his polish and composure. Overhead the scroll bar had nearly reached its end point. The stopwatch display beside the bar showed less than thirty seconds. "Mr. Lewko has had his fun, and no, sir, I think we'll pass on your *generous* offer." Laughter, if slightly strained, rippled through the crowd. "It's time. This is it. This is what we've all been waiting for. You've seen the data, the case studies, the research and the market factors, a team of the top investment bankers in the country—you know who you are—has determined the opening bell price for the new public offering. The new publicly traded Amphitriton! Ten! Nine! Eight! This is it, people!"

The crowd joined the countdown.

"FIVE!"

"FOUR!"

Andy took Lewko by the arm and moved him toward the risers. Onstage, Lonnie slid closer to Remington.

"THREE!"

"TWO!"

Remington, Newell, and the entire assembled crowd locked their eyes on the screens. Flashing animated fireworks, a giant number appeared. The crowd exploded.

Remington screamed into the microphone. "EIGHTY-SIX! EIGHTY-SIX dollars a share! Absolutely record-breaking!"

Newall leaped forward and grabbed Remington by the arms, jumping up and down.

"EIGHTY-SIX!" Remington shouted. He pumped his fist in the air. "Do the math, people!" He jabbed the microphone out at the crowd, which shouted an unintelligible number back to him. "How much?" The crowd shouted again. "How much?"

"FIFTY-FOUR BILLION!"

The DJ hit his cue and rock music pounded from the speakers. People jumped and danced with each other.

Gabby and I felt the crowd surge toward us. I pushed off and ascended above the unbridled financial joy on the Great Hall floor.

Lewko, led by Andy, ascended the risers to the stage where Lonnie Penn lent them authority by reaching out and embracing Lewko.

Remington grinned and shouted over the music.

"Yeah!" he shouted. He pointed at people in the crowd. "That's right!"

The celebration raged. Andy passed Lewko off to Lonnie, who maneuvered him to center stage behind Remington. Andy, I noticed, shaded her eyes against the spotlights and studied the spaces around her. Remington's private security had multiplied, apparently in proportion to his wealth. Guards studded all four corners of the stage. I glanced at the room. More guards appeared at the perimeter.

Two uniformed guards stepped up onto the stage and took up positions behind Remington and Newell. One wore a handgun on his hip. The other held a shotgun at port arms. The weapons struck me as out of place. None of the uniformed guards around the room carried weapons.

"When that bell rings tomorrow morning, we will make HISTORY!" Remington shouted. Cheers buried the pounding music.

"It's loud!" Gabby shouted in my ear.

"You got that right! We're going down there and then it's time, okay? Are you ready?"

I felt her nod, not quite fully acclimated to the whole disappearing thing.

Good enough for me.

The celebration roared on. I feared it would be difficult for Andy or Lonnie to gain control, but Remington solved the problem for us.

"Hey!" he shouted. "Hey, Spiro!" I winced at the use of Lewko's hated first name. "Hey!" Remington strutted across the stage, waving for relative quiet. "I got something to say."

Lewko waited, fixing his gaze on the marble floor.

Remington gushed, "I guess, Spiro, that you were a little off on the stock price."

The crowd laughed and cheered.

Lewko stood implacable, wearing his arrogant private joke grin. For once, I thought he wore it well.

"What do you think? Should we sell?" Remington shot his arm out. The crowd shouted.

"NO!"

Lewko held out his hand for the microphone, for a chance to speak.

Remington, awash in his own glory, bowed and handed Lewko the microphone. The cheering crowd settled, expecting the punchline from the billionaire because his comments earlier had to have been a joke.

The Great Hall regained order. The DJ killed the music.

Lewko let the moment hang. His grin remained fixed.

He waited.

He waited.

When he spoke, all other sound ceased.

"You may wonder," he said, "why I made the offer I did, and why, at tomorrow's opening bell, I will be true to my word, and I will buy your stock for one cent a share, Mr. Remington." He gazed out at the audience, then at Remington. "If I may…" Lonnie lifted the aluminum case and held it for Lewko, who opened it. He extracted one of the two pieces of flat gray artifact. He held it up.

Twang! I felt the connection snap down my center.

Lewko continued. "This remarkable piece of material has an origin I will not explain to you tonight. It has properties you will find difficult to comprehend. For example…"

I eased into position on the stage. Andy posted herself to Lewko's left, leaving a gap.

"You're on, Gabby," I whispered. I slid the girl down until I could feel that her feet had found the floor. "Grab it."

The artifact in Lewko's hand wiggled.

Fwooomp! I released Gabby. She snapped into sight.

The crowd gasped. An uproar rippled through the room. Someone shouted out the name of a popular magician. Someone laughed.

Remington stared.

Maxwell stepped up on the stage and put one hand around Gabby's shoulders.

"Ladies and gentlemen, may I introduce you to Gabrielle Calbert," Lewko said. "Gabby was a part of the Amphitriton tests you so thoroughly reviewed, but when she did not respond to the meds, she was dropped from the study and her data was scrubbed—like a dozen other failures. And yet… Gabby has survived cancer thanks to what you just saw."

"This is absurd," Remington reached for the microphone.

"Gabby not only survived cancer thanks to this artifact, she also survived an attempt by Mr. Remington to murder her when she proved that his so-called treatment, his *worthless* treatment, is a fraud."

A gasp rippled through the crowd.

"Bullshit!" Remington shouted. "This is the fraud! This is some kind of fake!"

Remington lunged for the microphone. Lonnie drove an elbow into the man's diaphragm. He doubled over.

Behind Remington the armed security guards jumped forward. The first guard released the security strap on his handgun and began to lift the weapon from its holster. His move jolted me because his focus was on Andy, not Remington or Lonnie or Lewko. The second, also fixed on Andy, shifted the shotgun in his grasp.

Andy moved fast. I didn't see how, but before anyone knew what she had done, the second security guard lay on the stage clutching himself while his shotgun found its way into Andy's hands.

She jacked a round into the chamber and swung the shotgun to her shoulder. The black barrel hole hovered in the first guard's stunned face. His weapon hung at his side, barely clear of the leather holster.

"Drop it."

Andy stared down the steel barrel. Her finger flexed against the trigger. The man stared into a black hole hovering inches from his eyes.

Andy did not waver.

He slowly lowered his gun to the stage. Andy followed the move with the shotgun. The crowd released a collective gasp. Andy kicked the gun aside and ordered the two men to their knees.

"This is an outrage!" Remington huffed. "You will—"

Andy swung the shotgun in the direction of Remington and Newell. "On your knees. Both of you. You're under arrest for the murder of two individuals in Mountain Home, Arkansas, and the attempted murder of Gabrielle, Reuben and Shelly Calbert. Hands on your heads. Knees. Now."

Both men reluctantly obeyed. Remington uttered an unbroken string of threats until Andy placed the barrel of the shotgun on the bridge of his nose and told him to shut the hell up.

Lewko watched the incident without flinching. Andy glanced back at him to signal that he had the floor.

"Tomorrow morning," Lewko's voice, unruffled, filled the silent Great Hall, "I will assume ownership of Amphitriton Pharmaceutical at the price I stated. In the coming days, Dr. Maxwell here will work with me to reveal the fraud perpetrated by Amphitriton, and in turn, the true cause of the remarkable results that have been recorded. What you saw here tonight with young Gabby is real—a tech that is beyond anything previously imagined. Because of that tech, the outcome for this child—who nearly died at the hands of Mr. Remington and Mr. Newell—and for others who regained their health through no fault of the treatment program, is real. Amphitriton's treatment is not. What you saw here was no trick." He turned. "Gabby?"

Gabby placed her hand on the artifact again.

I pushed.

Fwooomp!

From several feet away and without contact—to my amazement—Gabby, Lewko, the artifact, and the case on the floor with the second artifact disappeared.

Fwooomp!

And reappeared.

A tidal gasp flooded the room.

Lewko broke into a grin that looked less like a boardroom shark and more like a boy who just got off the Ferris Wheel.

Dammit, I really wanted to throw you off a building.

The crowd stood silent. Lewko thanked Gabby with a nod and placed the artifact back in the case.

After regarding the sea of faces with a hint of disdain, Lewko resumed. "Dr. Maxwell and I will be sharing these results, and this technology, in the public health domain at no cost. We will make this treatment available to any who seek it…at no cost and without profit."

Maxwell stared at Lewko, stunned.

"It's your program if you want it," Lewko said to Maxwell off mic.

Her eyes glittered. She nodded.

Lewko returned to the microphone. "There will be no stock ownership. For any of you. Now go home."

EPILOGUE I

"Nice of you kids to come up for air." Leslie gestured for us to join her. The Ritz Carlton bar was not closed to the public, but only two other stools held patrons at one-thirty in the afternoon. Leslie sat at a discrete distance from the others. She looked the same as ever in a black blazer over a black tank top, her short dark hair carefully windblown.

"We've been out and about." I hopped on the stool beside her. Andy took a seat on my right. "We had a lovely dinner last night at a restaurant whose name I cannot pronounce eating food I could not identify with someone I can't remember."

Andy bumped me with her elbow. "It was Lonnie. Lonnie took us out last night."

"Were you drunk?" Leslie asked.

"No. I blame Christian Dior."

Andy smiled and stroked my cheek with a kiss.

"Ah. I get it. I saw photos. You were stunning, Andy."

The bartender took our order. Corona with lime for me. Andy opted for lemonade. Leslie nursed what looked like iced tea.

"Well, I wish I had better news for you, but Arkansas is extraditing Reuben Calbert for the murder of the orderly and nurse at Newell's hospice. Remington and Newell were not held."

"That's absurd!" Andy slapped the bar surface. "I gave NYPD a full statement. They said they'd reach out to both the Arkansas authorities and the police in Key West."

"They did. Problem is, after the Arkansas authorities get their heads out of their asses about Reuben, Fennick is likely to get fingered for those killings—and probably for the shenanigans in Key West—and he conveniently shredded himself at the airport. Remington claims he has no idea who Fennick was. Just one of hundreds of employees he never met."

"That's crap," Andy said.

"It is crap. Political crap. This DA has a lot of friends in the community if you get my drift. Friends who are also friends of the Citadel of God, but don't get your undies in a twist. Newell, whether he knows it or not, is circling the drain. The U.S. Attorney has opened an investigation and I expect he'll be taking it to a Grand Jury soon, which will undercut anything the county guy is trying to do to Reuben."

"What *is* he trying to do?" I didn't understand how prosecuting Reuben had any legs.

"He's trying to keep his buddies in the Men's Choir happy, Will. Making a bunch of noise about investigation and prosecution deflects attention from the shitstorm that's coming for Remington and Newell—who were both probably contributing to this DA's political aspirations. I'm told he has his eye on the governor's mansion."

"This absolutely sucks."

"Relax, Will. It's not going anywhere. The DA will drop the charges against Reuben before it ever gets started. Quietly. When people are least likely to notice. For now, he's stoking his constituents with warnings that New York elites are coming after their house of worship and their God and their guns and America and apple pie. He'll stir that soup for as long as it gets his name in the papers."

"Meanwhile, Reuben sits in a cell and spends a small fortune on lawyers. Screw it. I'll bust him out." I glanced at Andy for approval I did not expect. She didn't disappoint.

"That won't help, darling."

"No," Leslie agreed. "It won't. Be patient. Mr. Calbert's legal needs are being underwritten by a certain anonymous billionaire. Seems Lewko took a shine to Reuben's little girl."

"Didn't we all." Mention of Gabby made me smile.

"That county DA is about to be eaten alive with his political aspirations tossed in for dessert." Leslie gazed in the general direction of Arkansas. "I'd almost like to be there to see it."

"I may be." I turned to Andy. "I didn't get to tell you. Earl had Doc order new props for the Navajo. I want to be on hand when they're installed so I can fly her home."

"Just don't take your wife, Will. Sorry, Andy. You're too much of a target in some parts of the country. Those two nerf balls on the stage on Tuesday night were chock full of Company W DNA, just like I said. Newell is denying up and down that he knows them, but CCTV shows them entering with his entourage. When you showed up, I think they decided to 'protect' the good Reverend by shooting you. You were a target of opportunity."

"That sounds like supposition that won't put them in jail."

"Don't be a pessimist, Will." Leslie waved her hand to brush away the notion. "NYPD is not happy about the weapons they carried, and those two are not terribly bright. I hear one of them is chatty, which will make it a contest to see who gets a better cell—although the Company W contingent at Rikers will make them right at home."

Andy stared at her hands, which she had folded together on the bar. "But at the end of the day Remington walks?"

"For the moment," Leslie said. "But…fun stuff. I heard his check to the Met bounced. And he owes a hundred and twelve million dollars for the yacht, plus another thirty million for the partial renovation."

"Small change when you expect to rake in fifty billion," I said.

Leslie laughed. "And we see how that turned out. Apparently the insurance company takes issue with the boat being lit on fire intentionally. They're asking for an investigation. I suspect after they talk to those two pirates in coast guard custody, they will be reluctant to issue a check."

"Ouch." I liked the idea. "Guess Remington owes somebody a bunch of money."

"Not just somebody. He purchased the boat from a Russian gentleman who is currently living in Lisbon. You may infer the obvious."

"That suggests that Mr. Remington may find himself getting tattoos from a welding torch in the cargo hold of a Russian trawler." I lifted my beer to toast the idea. "I can live with that."

"You watch too many movies, Will. Amphitriton and Remington are getting a serious cavity search from the Justice Department and the SEC. They will eventually get him on fraud and potentially murder. He is destined for a federal prison. For one thing, it appears that his in-hospital pharmaceutical reps were bribing admin staff to recruit kids to the treatment program *after* recording positive results. *Your* results, Will. They stacked the deck with kids who suddenly showed mysterious signs of remission."

"I don't know how far you want to pursue that line," Andy said. "It could mean dragging Will into the spotlight, which is what all of this was intended to avoid."

Leslie nodded. "Agreed. Besides…Remington will probably wind up getting tattoos from a welding torch in the hold of a Russian trawler." Leslie winked at me. I sipped my Corona. Andy sipped her lemonade.

"Anything new in Louisiana?" I asked. "I really wouldn't mind hearing that the FBI is throwing a nationwide net around all the Company W assholes once and for all."

"Don't hold your breath," Leslie said. "Sedition is a tough case to prove. For now, all I can tell you is that Louis Blaze is issuing communiques from his cave in Tora Bora denouncing the federal government. He blames the FBI for murdering patriots and beating his daughter nearly to death. Chatter is up in all the wrong places. Extremist threats are up. T-shirt sales on white supremacist websites are up. Business as usual."

"How is she?" Andy asked. "The daughter."

"Alive. Getting put back together by a Beverly Hills plastic surgeon, last I heard. Her jaw is wired shut and she needs new teeth, so she's not making a statement to law enforcement. Not sure she would, anyway. We hope whoever did the job was someone on the inside, someone making a power play."

"You hope?" I asked.

"A betrayal like that has a chance of driving her into the Bureau's loving arms. It's a long shot. Blaze and his minions are saying the FBI did it—or in some of the wilder chatrooms, Andy did it. Either way, she's not talking."

"I feel bad for her." I remembered the sad bride to be. "I mean…after being treated like chattel in a trade with Spellman…and then…"

"Don't worry. We're watching her." Leslie leaned on the bar, trying to look casual. She used the move to confirm that the bartender chatted with the only other remaining patron, well out of earshot. "Meanwhile, there's something I need to share with you."

Andy looked sideways at Leslie. "This is never good."

"You're not wrong. Look. I get what you did. Pretty damned clever if you want my opinion. You couldn't let Remington get away with this, but standing up in front of a bunch of people and telling them that you can make kids disappear and can cure cancer—that would be bad. You put the focus on those chunks of whatever-the-hell they are, and it was genius to bring in Lewko. No one is more opaque than Spiro Lewko. But here's the problem: Gabby and Lewko vanished in front of a thousand people and it wasn't a David Copperfield gimmick. It was a very public event caught on video by just about everyone with a phone."

"That's true. Everyone focused on the rare Spiro Lewko sighting," Andy said. "They got more than they expected."

Leslie pulled her phone from her pocket. She laid it on the bar and tapped it for emphasis. "The whole world did. Dozens of videos have gone viral. Top ten viral. Plus, it's all over the mainstream news outlets. CNN. The networks. Even Fox. There's a raging debate on social media over whether Gabby was real or CGI. Half think the whole thing was faked. The other half think Lewko the boy genius invented a way to vanish and cure cancer. His stock enjoyed a huge bounce overnight. Estimates are that he woke up twenty billion richer this morning."

Unintended consequence, I thought. "He was going to give me one, you know."

"One what?"

"Billion." I grinned at Leslie and watched her expression slip toward shock.

Andy cut off the question rising to Leslie's lips. "Old news, Leslie, and no we did not nor are we ever taking his money."

"You break my heart, Dee. That could have paid for a new weed trimmer." Andy ignored me. I turned to Leslie, who looked relieved. "I think I know where you're going with this."

"And you would be right. There isn't an intelligence agency or law enforcement agency in this country, or around the world for that matter, that did not perk up and go '*What?*' when this went viral. Real or fake, some serious hard-assed people want their hands on those artifacts."

"Won't do them any good," I said.

"Kinda my point, Will." Leslie looked at me sharply.

Andy closed a grip on my arm. "No."

"I'm not suggesting—"

"No," Andy repeated. "The answer is No."

I sat with a dumb look on my face. "I'm sorry. You left me in the dust here. What was the question?"

Leslie flicked a hand gesture at Andy, signaling it was her point to make.

"She's saying that the FBI, the CIA, Homeland Security and a dozen other agencies studying and analyzing those videos will be beating down Lewko's door to get their hands on something they think will let them send agents waltzing into North Korea's nuclear program unseen."

I shrugged. "Like I said…won't do them any good. Those pieces don't work if they're not connected to me."

Andy leveled her gold-flecked green eyes on me like spotlights. "And what happens when those agencies figure that out?"

"Oh."

EPILOGUE II

Lonnie provided one more multi-stop ride in her sleek Gulfstream. She flew Andy and me back to Key West and then delivered Shelly and Gabby Calbert home to Wichita before jetting back to Los Angeles.

Shelly wanted to stay in the city but resolving Reuben's incarceration had accelerated to a snail's pace. Reuben insisted his wife and daughter go home. He was, he claimed, happy to sit in a jail cell knowing that Gabby would live, and that he had a wife and daughter to go home to. I didn't think he had long to sit. Lewko's lawyers descended on the case in a way that made even Shelly stop worrying—or at least pretend to—and agree to leave.

Andy contemplated flying directly back to Wisconsin but decided to accompany me to retrieve the Baron, which remained on the ramp in Key West. It wasn't lost on me that she enjoyed Lonnie's company. I also think part of my wife didn't relish leaving me alone in said company. We disembarked Lonnie's jet in the sunshine in Key West.

Gabby insisted on climbing down the airstair to see us off. She remained fragile but would not be daunted. She wobbled down the steps full of determination while her mother held her breath.

We gathered on the ramp. Lonnie pulled me into a hug while the sea breeze stirred the air around us.

"Do I dare ask Gloria?" She slipped the question in my ear. I gave her a squeeze and whispered my reply.

"I wouldn't. Let it be."

She pulled back and studied me with those jeweled blue eyes, then star-tled me with a kiss on the lips.

"Sorry, Andy," she said after parting. "I had to. I'll never have one of my own."

The hug Andy gave Lonnie forgave the kiss. There may have been a glint of pride on Andy's face, too. I'd like to think so.

Gabby all but leaped into Andy's arms.

"Thank you for coming to Sonjay's ceremony!" she cried. "I just know he's out there now. I just know it." She threw her thin arms around Andy's neck and pressed her hairless head into Andy's long locks. Andy squeezed and struggled to hold back something that stung her eyes. She pressed them shut and held Gabby for a moment, then let the girl slide down. Gabby didn't stay earthbound long. She leaped into my arms on the rebound.

"Can we do it one more time?" she whispered in my ear.

The two of us turned devious grins on Andy and Lonnie and Shelly Calbert.

"What?" Andy asked. "I'm not sure I like that look…"

Gabby giggled. I laughed.

Fwooomp!

EPILOGUE III

"Oh lord," I said. "She let you keep it."

Andy posed.

Christian Dior and my wife sucked the air from the Hyatt beachside room. Andy turned slowly, watching me. I made no effort to meet her eyes. I studied every shimmer, every curve exactly as she intended.

"I told you I'd let you play with it."

"You are a goddess."

"After dinner."

"Okay, I take it back. You are a demon. Dinner, you say? I'm a little underdressed." I gestured at my staple jeans and t-shirt.

"Put on a nice shirt."

I jerked the t-shirt over my head, balled it up and threw it across the room. I started for my roller bag to retrieve the one decent shirt that traveled with me, but Andy stepped in front of me.

"One second." She placed her fingers on my chin, then slid them down my neck, down my chest until they came to rest on my belt buckle. Placing her hand flat against my skin, she slowly retraced the route, stroking indentations and contours along the way. When she finished, she stepped back and released a pent-up breath. "Okay. Now you can get dressed."

I pulled the shirt out and unfolded it. She watched me in a way that I thoroughly enjoyed.

"You know…" I brushed the wrinkles out of the shirt "…Sandy

mentioned something to me that night she came over with Earl. It touched on a subject we haven't talked about for a while."

"What did she say?"

I pulled the shirt on and worked the buttons.

"She said, 'Take her somewhere with sand and palm trees and get her pregnant.' I notice there are palm trees outside. Just saying."

"Won't work." The words flagged a serious downturn in the conversation. Andy stepped close. She pressed herself against me. Her scent cast its spell. She gazed up at me. "But after dinner you can bring me up here and try to make me more pregnant."

DIVISIBLE MAN - TEN KEYS WEST
Thursday, June 23, 2022 to Tuesday, January 03, 2023

If you enjoyed TEN KEYS WEST, please
share your feelings by posting a review.
Reader reviews give an author's work greater visibility
and help propel the book to a wider audience.
Reviews are deeply appreciated.

Post your review with your book's retailer
or at www.GoodReads.com.

Thank you!

PREVIEW THE NEXT DIVISIBLE MAN ADVENTURE

DIVISIBLE MAN - THE ELEVENTH HOURGLASS

A *BookLife from Publishers Weekly* **Editor's Pick**
"A book of outstanding quality."

THE ELEVENTH HOURGLASS
CHAPTER 1

"You need to get your ass over here like *right now*." Pidge delivered the command in a breathless whisper.

"Why?"

"Earl's holding a baby hostage and the cops are here. *I am not shitting you!*"

"What?"

Pidge ended the call.

I rolled the creeper out from under the Piper Navajo wing where I'd been wiping a film of dirt and oil off the bottom side of the flaps.

"Well, that's weird." With no one else in the hangar, I got no argument.

I tossed aside the oily wad of paper towels and levered myself up off the floor. I left the cleaning supplies because, dollars to donuts, this would add up to a waste of my time and I'd be back at this task soon.

The big hangar door hung open, perhaps a little optimistically. Despite the mid-May date on the calendar and a bright sunlit sky, the morning temperature had barely topped 40 degrees. The airport MOS predicted mid-sixties, but it would be afternoon before such glorious warmth crept in.

Still, the air was fresh, and the crystalline sky promised the best a Wisconsin spring had to offer. Lingering traces of what were once snow piles between the hangars melted into the grass. I liked the way the open door caught the sound of student pilot runups or morning charter flights departing. Ordinarily Pidge would have been piloting one of those charters, either in Earl's Piper Mojave or one of the Beechcraft Barons he operated, but she was in the home stretch of having one arm in a cast. The break she suffered during a misadventure in the Florida Keys did not set properly and had been re-broken and reset using an assortment of pins and screws. Being grounded accounted for her presence in the Essex County Air Service office at 9:15 a.m. In lieu of flying, Pidge updated charter records, tutored students studying for written exams, and relieved Rosemary II of some of the scheduling, but mostly she drove everyone from the building or else insane. Thanks to an earthbound Pidge, not much has been seen of Earl Jackson, the operation's owner, and my former boss. Earl either locked himself in his office or found cause to spend long hours in the engine shop arguing with Doc, the chief mechanic. Rosemary II confided in me that despite the way Pidge and Earl mimic a crate of nitroglycerin on a roller coaster, Earl plans to offer her the chief pilot title before some regional airline lures her away. At twenty-four, she has all the ratings and twice the skill.

Earl's holding a baby hostage and the cops are here.

This I had to see.

Earl stood with his feet planted wider than his bowlegged usual. His stance suggested a linebacker ready for the snap of a football. His elbows rode high and away from his fireplug frame. In the scarred and gnarled claws he calls hands, sure as hell, he clutched an infant at arm's length. The bald-headed pair stared at each other.

"Hey, Will." Del Sims, the smallest cop on the Essex Police Department patrol roster, stirred coffee in a mug a few feet from Earl and his hostage. The scent of Rosemary II's mysteriously delicious blend warmed my senses.

"Del." I stopped inside the tinted glass doors to the Essex County Air Service office where, until just short of two years ago, I had been chief pilot. "What's up?"

"Not much. You?"

I shot a look down the hallway. Pidge's mop of short blonde hair poked out of the second office door. She fought to keep a full-blown laugh from slipping through the devilish grin on her face.

"Hey, Earl." I pointed at the bundle in a tiny blue onesie. "Who's your dance partner?"

Earl said nothing. Despite the permanent expression of rage on his aged yet ageless face, I got the distinct impression that the infant was winning the staring contest. I got an equally distinct impression that Del, in full uniform and armed per department policy, was more interested in his coffee than the child. A second glance at Pidge's grin confirmed I'd been had. Still, I wasn't sorry for getting suckered. I wouldn't have wanted to miss this scene.

I contemplated grabbing a photo.

I was about to question Del when the doors behind me swung open and Rosemary II struggled into the office with an armload of grocery bags. I grabbed the door for her. She shoved one of the bags into my hands.

"Uh!" She adjusted the load. "Thank you, Will. I—" She stopped. Her deep brown eyes darted from me to Earl to the baby to Del then back to me, returning laden with questions.

"Beats me." I shrugged before she could ask.

"Earl Jackson, what on earth are you doing?" Rosemary II lowered two loaded paper grocery bags to the floor and darted forward. Before Earl could answer, she swept the child out of his grip. "That's no way to hold a baby!"

I swear the child giggled. Earl remained rooted to the floor with his eyes locked on the kid. Rosemary II cuddled the infant against her chest. Like dawn, a bright smile spread and creased the smooth milk chocolate skin on her face. "And who are you, little one?"

Rosemary II is not much older than me, but she is everyone's mother at the airport. Radiant in that role, she instantly communicated to the infant that its fortunes had changed for the better. It grinned up at her adoring face.

"He's mine. I'm sorry." A meek voice came from the hallway leading to the restrooms. "I'm so sorry. I really, *really* had to go. It's been hours."

A wild shock of long red hair atop a girl with a slender physique emerged from the hallway. The hair framed a face pale enough to have been rendered in marble, with skin as smooth. Shy but piercing blue eyes warily regarded the fresh assembly of strangers.

I knew that face. So did Pidge.

"Kelly?" Pidge hurried up behind me. She looked astonished. "Jesus, Kelly, why did you come back here? Are you under arrest?"

Kelly Pratt darted a glance at her friend Pidge, then at me, then at the woman holding her child. Her expression betrayed the same undertow of ingrained fear I had seen the first time I met her and the last time I saw her, yet she seemed different.

Pidge ducked past me and took her friend in a hug, then sternly gripped her arms. As if Del wasn't standing three feet away, she whispered, "You can't be here. You can't be back here."

The Police stoically sipped his coffee. Something told me he had no idea who Kelly Pratt was or why her presence in Essex might have just blown up an elaborate and somewhat illegal plan executed for the young woman's own protection.

"I had to come." Kelly turned to face Earl's withering glare. "Mr. Jackson, I had to come. It's your wife. I think someone wants to hurt her."

THE ELEVENTH HOURGLASS
CHAPTER 2

"Kelly Pratt." I repeated the name into the phone for Andy. I strolled down the hall, past Earl's closed office door.

"Back up the truck, Will. What do you mean a hostage situation?"

"Oh, yeah, that. Pidge walked in and saw Earl holding a baby and Del standing there in his gear and she swears she heard Earl tell Del not to get any closer, but in retrospect, I think Earl was talking to the baby."

"Why was Earl holding Kelly's baby?"

"Kelly had to go potty. Bad. She was on a bus all night. And then she hitchhiked from the stop on 34."

"She hitchhiked?"

"Or tried, until Del picked her up. What else are you going to do when you see a girl hitchhiking with a baby? Kelly begged Del to take her to the airport."

"I'm sorry, Will. I'm trying to get up to speed here. Why was she hitchhiking? More importantly, why did she come back to Essex? Did she come looking for Pidge?" Andy knew the story of Pidge's friendship with the girl, and of how Pidge had come to Kelly's rescue.

"Actually, she came for Earl." I explained Kelly's message about Earl's wife—his ex-wife—Candice.

Candice Hammond Stubowsky Day Jackson O'Connor Thorpe. I don't know why, but the laundry list of Earl's ex-wife's married names stuck in my head like lyrics looking for a song. Candice owned Renell Lodge in northern Minnesota, a rustic dream she inherited from one of the husbands—

I forget which—where Kelly had been hiding since Pidge persuaded me and Earl to help the girl and child escape an abusive boyfriend. Andy knew the story of what happened at Halloween, a story I liked to entitle *Attack of the Killer Zombie*. Andy's title of *Criminal Child Abduction by Three Idiots* carried less appeal but landed more on point. The abusive baby daddy could have proven a genuine problem if he had not sacrificed his custody standing by being sentenced to state prison, thanks to the stash of drugs found by the cops after he crashed his pickup truck.

After the Killer Zombie made him crash his truck.

"Hurt Candice how? Who?"

"Dee, I have no idea. The baby started fussing and Kelly went to feed it—"

"Him. If I remember correctly, the baby is a boy. Seth, I think."

"Right. Anyway, Kelly set up in the pilot's lounge to—you know—hook the kid up."

"Breastfeed, Will. It's called breastfeeding and you need to get a little more comfortable with the concept." A lot of new concepts introduced themselves since Andy let me know she was pregnant.

"I know what it's called. And I am perfectly comfortable with the concept. And totally respectful." It was half true. My mind wandered a bit when thinking about Andy in that way. "Anyway, Kelly's feeding the baby. Rosemary II is making Kelly something to eat. Earl locked himself in his office. Del is finishing his coffee. And I called you because—"

"You want to know if Kelly is in any legal jeopardy over the abduction."

"Bingo. I don't think Del knows who she is, but he will certainly remember what happened last Halloween. He was there. I was hoping to head off trouble."

"Off the top of my head, no, there shouldn't be any trouble. Technically Kelly committed an unlawful abduction of a child subject to shared custody, but the ex-boyfriend hadn't filed anything. Lucky for her, we got him on the drug charges before we knew she had fled the state. But if the boyfriend hadn't been in prison he could have filed for custody, and she'd be subject to an open fugitive warrant."

"Can you let Del know? Right now, he's hanging around to drink Rosemary II's coffee, but he says he wants to talk to the girl."

"I'll call him. Please call me when you find out what's going on. Please?"

"Will do. Love you."

"Will."

"What?"

"Don't get tangled up in something here. You have that thing coming up. On Thursday. With Lewko."

"Me? Never."

"I mean it. You know how important it is."

"Love you, too."

THE ELEVENTH HOURGLASS
CHAPTER 3

I joined Pidge behind the front counter. We watched Del answer Andy's phone call. He listened for a moment, then waved at us and pointed at the door. He tucked his phone between his ear and shoulder, freed up his hands to pour himself a to-go cup of Rosemary II's coffee, then slipped out the front door still chatting with Detective Andrea Stewart, my wife.

"Was that Andy?"

"Yeah." I sent Pidge a look that attempted to scold. "Hostage situation?"

"How was I supposed to know it was Kelly? I walked in and saw a cop and Earl holding a baby." She poked my arm. "Come on—you gotta admit. That was priceless. You had to see that." She wasn't wrong.

"Looked to me like Earl was the hostage."

"What did Andy say?"

I explained Andy's assessment of Kelly's standing with the law. Pidge blew out a sigh of relief and chased it with a few choice words for the still-incarcerated ex-boyfriend.

"How did Earl wind up with the baby?" I asked.

"I wasn't here for that part. Rosemary II ran over to the Piggly Wiggly. I was in the back. Earl must have been the only one in the office when she came in. When a girl's gotta go, she's gotta go. I guess she handed the kid off to the only warm body in sight." Pidge gestured at the closed pilot lounge door. "How long does it take to feed one of those?"

"Beats me. I suppose I better learn—" I caught myself before I let

Andy's pregnancy slip. Andy and I had decided to hold back any announcement until her condition approached obvious.

"Better learn what?"

"Um…I suppose I better hang around and learn what's going on. Being a co-conspirator and all."

"Do you think?"

"He's such a beautiful child." Rosemary II sat on the floor beside the cushy leather sofa with her legs curled under her body. She gently stroked the back of the blue onesie. The baby lay belly down on a faded yellow and blue blanket, sound asleep.

He seemed cute enough. He had no hair to speak of. His fair skin reflected that of his mother. For his sake, I hoped his genes favored her. His biological father was hawk-faced and mean looking.

I dropped into one of the fat recliners. Pidge sat on the sofa beside Kelly who threw her arm around her friend and issued a deep squeeze mindful of the cast on Pidge's left forearm.

"Kel, what the fuck? Why did you come back here? You could've gotten in a lot of trouble."

"I need to talk to Mr. Jackson." Kelly looked for Earl in the empty front office outside the pilot lounge door. Pidge glanced at Rosemary II. Kelly followed the glance. "Is he coming back?"

Rosemary II gave the sleeping infant one more gentle stroke, then leaned close to breathe in the scent of his bald scalp.

"Heavens, it's like a drug." She pushed herself upright. "Of course, dear, but best not to talk in here. It might get loud. Let's all step out and let this little one sleep. Will, push that coffee table up against the sofa in case he rolls, would you?"

"On it."

After moving the furniture, I joined Pidge and Kelly at the office front counter. Rosemary II went to fetch Earl. When she returned alone, she carefully pulled the door to the pilot's lounge closed.

"He's making some calls. How long does the child usually nap?" Rosemary II asked Kelly.

"He's a sleeper. He'll be down for at least two hours." Kelly suddenly lifted her arms and pressed her wrists against her shirt. "Oh, gosh. Sometimes they just don't want to shut off. I'll be right back!" She scooped up the baby bag that had not left her side and hurried toward the restroom.

Earl stomped down the hall and joined us. He cast a sharp eye around the office and the lobby.

"Where is it?"

"*He*, Earl, is sleeping." Rosemary II gestured at the pilot's lounge. "So, keep your voice down. Is someone going to explain to me what this is all about?"

Earl looked at Pidge, who looked at me.

"What?" I frowned. I waited. No one relented. "Fine."

I told Rosemary II the story of how Kelly was on the verge of letting herself be enslaved by an abuser, trapped by their shared child, and how Pidge brought the problem to me, and I engaged Earl in a conspiracy to separate Kelly from her dangerous ex-boyfriend on the opening night of the Essex Fall Festival—on Halloween night. I left out the part about how I made Kelly and the baby vanish inside a dark funhouse ride. And the part about how Pidge took off with Kelly and the baby, pursued by the enraged ex-boyfriend. And how I chased the boyfriend's pickup truck and made myself reappear on the truck's hood, scaring the bejesus out of the shithead because of the zombie makeup I wore for my role in the haunted funhouse. The ploy caused Kelly's pursuer to lose control and roll his truck. Pidge delivered Kelly to the airport and Earl flew her and her baby to Minnesota and into the care of Earl's ex-wife, Candice. The cops scooped up the ex-boyfriend along with possession with intent.

I was about to explain Andy's assessment that violating the law by abducting her own son was a near miss for Kelly—that she was safe—when Kelly returned from the restroom. Earl lifted an accusing finger in her direction.

"I warned you about getting your panties all wet for your ex and coming back here." I thought he might scare the girl into the kind of helpless catatonic state he had induced in her when they met last fall.

She surprised me and, I think, everyone.

"Don't you snap at me, Mr. Jackson. You're going to listen to what I have to say. Candice always told me not to let you scare me. So...just you *don't*. Scare me, I mean." She swallowed hard and stared at Earl who tucked away his finger. "I've had a lot of time to think about this, Mr. Jackson, and you're probably not going to want to hear it, but if I live a thousand lifetimes, I don't think I can ever thank you enough for what you did for me and Seth. You and Candice. You took me to her, and she didn't just take me in, she gave me life. Neither of you have ever asked anything in return, but if you did, I would give you anything, so just you don't...yell...at...me." The last few words escaped a quivering lower lip. Kelly rubbed tears from her eyes.

Rosemary II made a move toward hugging the girl, but I closed a grip on her arm. Kelly wasn't finished.

"Now you *listen to me*." She rubbed her face again. "Two nights ago Candice came into my room and told me to pack whatever I could carry and get the baby ready. She said there was no time to explain. I didn't know what to think, but I did as I was told. She said someone was coming for us. I don't know, but it was super scary. I put what I could in this bag. Mostly it's baby stuff. And then she rushed us out of the lodge and into her Jeep and she drove us into Big Fork and made me get out in front of the courthouse and she told me to stay there out of sight until the pharmacy across the street opened. She said that's where the bus stops. She gave me a bunch of money to buy a ticket and she told me not to come back and not to tell anyone where I was going. Just go somewhere safe, she said. You know how she is. She's always so strong and tough. I didn't know where to go, so I bought a ticket to Minneapolis and when I got there, I bought a ticket here to Essex because I had to see you, Mr. Jackson. Something is wrong. Something bad has happened. Candice needs help and you're the only person I could think of who can help her."

Earl curled his claws into fists and mounted them on his hips. He stared at Kelly for a long minute, then lowered his gaze to his shoes. The modulated low rumble of his voice had nothing to do with a sleeping baby in the next room.

"She tell you to come get me?"

"No, sir. The opposite. She said I shouldn't tell anyone. She said I should stay away."

"And you came straight here?"

"Yes, sir. The bus to Minneapolis yesterday morning—then we had to wait all day for a late bus last night to get here. We got off out at the highway stop this morning and hitched here—at least until the policeman picked me up. I told him your name and got him to bring me to you."

Earl showed Kelly the leathery top of his bald skull while he locked his gaze on his steel-toed work boots.

"And she didn't say nothing about nothing?"

"No, sir. She wouldn't hardly talk to me." Kelly waited. None of the rest of us dared move. "I think she was scared, Mr. Jackson. I never seen Candice scared of anything, but I think she was scared and not just for herself. I think she was scared for me and Seth. Whatever it was that was coming, I think it was coming for her, but she was afraid it might come for me and the baby, too."

Earl's head bobbed once. He lifted his face at the girl. She flinched.

Beneath Earl's crags and creases, I saw his judgment of Kelly shift. A curt nod paid her the compliment of both belief and gratitude.

Earl turned to me. "I tried calling. She ain't answering her cell and the line for the business says it's out of service."

"That makes no sense," Kelly said. "The summer season is starting in a couple weeks. She told me she was booked through October."

"Boss, you don't think this is blowback for that old Queen Air you and I pulled outta there. I mean—that outcome was pretty damned public. Anybody with an interest in the airplane and its cargo saw it spread all over cable news."

"What Queen Air?" Pidge asked.

"Tell you later." I watched Earl think about it for a moment. He didn't take long.

"Pidge, get 619 out and gas her up. Will?" He paused. "You in?"

Worst idea ever. In just two days I needed to be in Memphis, and the day after that in Evermore, North Carolina to connect with Spiro Lewko and engage in what might be the biggest test of *the other thing* yet. There was no way I could just charge off on a mission with no plan, no schedule, no idea of duration. Too much had gone into preparing for Evermore. The stage had been set recently in New York City where the world watched Lewko and a child vanish in front of dozens of phone cameras. In a single stroke, Lewko became the focus of a worldwide media frenzy that might otherwise have landed on me. More importantly, the scheme made it possible to organize the still mysterious curative aspect of *the other thing*. In a few days, in Evermore, it would be tested on two dozen eager, desperate children.

Andy would kill me.

"Lemme grab my overnight kit."

I started for the door when Kelly hooked a gentle grasp on my arm.

"I'm coming, too."

"The hell you are." Earl's growl left no room for negotiation.

Kelly's voice gained strength I didn't think she had. "I am, Mr. Jackson. I'm coming, too. You can't say no. You saved me. You and Cassidy and Will saved me, but Candice changed my life. What she's done for me made me know I am a person, *a real person*. What I was before would have run and hid. But a real person helps someone who needs help. I won't go back to being a non-person. *I won't*. I'm coming, too."

Earl stepped directly in front of Kelly. This time she did not flinch.

"I am not taking no baby. That's that."

"The baby can stay with me." Rosemary II put her arm around Kelly.

"He's been taking formula," Kelly said. "I started him…"

Earl looked into the eyes of one of the few forces of nature that he could not overcome. Rosemary II stared right back at him.

"You heard the young lady."

Earl turned and marched toward his office. "Wheels up in twenty, Will. Anybody else wants a ride, they best not dawdle."

ABOUT THE AUTHOR

HOWARD SEABORNE is the author of the DIVISIBLE MAN™ series as well as a collection of short stories featuring the same cast of characters. He began writing novels in spiral notebooks at age ten. He began flying airplanes at age sixteen. He is a former flight instructor and commercial charter pilot licensed in single- and multi-engine airplanes as well as helicopters. Today he flies a twin-engine Beechcraft Baron, a single-engine Beechcraft Bonanza, and a Rotorway A-600 Talon experimental helicopter he built from a kit in his garage. He lives with his wife and writes and flies during all four seasons in Wisconsin, never far from Essex County Airport.

Visit www.HowardSeaborne.com to join the Email List
and get a FREE DOWNLOAD.

DIVISIBLE MAN

The media calls it a "miracle" when air charter pilot Will Stewart survives an aircraft in-flight breakup, but Will's miracle pales beside the stunning aftereffect of the crash. Barely on his feet again, Will and his police sergeant wife Andy race to rescue an innocent child from a heinous abduction. *Will's new ability might make the difference between life and death…if it doesn't kill him first.*

Available in print, digital, and audio.

Search: "DIVISIBLE MAN Howard Seaborne"

Join our Reader Email list at **HowardSeaborne.com**

DIVISIBLE MAN - THE SIXTH PAWN

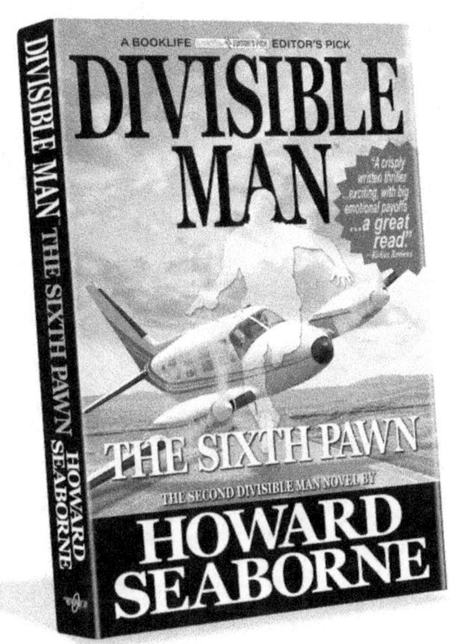

A *BookLife from Publishers Weekly* Editor's Pick.

"A book of outstanding quality."

When the Essex County "Wedding of the Century" erupts in gunfire, Will and Andy Stewart confront a criminal element no one could have foreseen. Will tests the extraordinary after-effect of surviving a devastating airplane crash while Andy works a case obstructed by powerful people wielding the sinister influence of unlimited money in politics.

Available in print, digital, and audio.

Search: "DIVISIBLE MAN Howard Seaborne"

Join our Reader Email list at **HowardSeaborne.com**

DIVISIBLE MAN - THE SECOND GHOST

Tormented by a cyber stalker, Lane Franklin's best friend turns to suicide. Lane's frantic call launches Will and Andy Stewart on a desperate rescue mission. When it all goes bad, Will must adapt his extraordinary ability to survive the dangerous high steel and glass of Chicago as Andy and Pidge confront the edge of disaster. **Includes the short story, "Angel Flight," a bridge to the fourth DIVISIBLE MAN novel that follows.**

Available in print, digital, and audio.

Search: "DIVISIBLE MAN Howard Seaborne"

Join our Reader Email list at **HowardSeaborne.com**

DIVISIBLE MAN - THE SEVENTH STAR

A horrifying message turns a holiday gathering tragic. An unsolved murder hangs a death threat over Detective Andy Stewart's head. And internet-fueled hatred targets Will and Andy's friend Lane. Will and Andy struggle to keep the ones they love safe, while hunting a murderer who is supposed to be dead. As the tension tightens, Will confronts a troubling revelation about the extraordinary after-effect of his midair collision.

Available in print, digital, and audio.

Search: "DIVISIBLE MAN Howard Seaborne"

Join our Reader Email list at **HowardSeaborne.com**

DIVISIBLE MAN - TEN MAN CREW

An unexpected visit from the FBI threatens Will Stewart's secret and sends Detective Andy Stewart on a collision course with her darkest impulses. A twisted road reveals how a long-buried Cold War secret has been weaponized. And Pidge shows a daring side of herself that could cost her dearly.

Available in print and digital.

Search: "DIVISIBLE MAN Howard Seaborne"

Join our Reader Email list at **HowardSeaborne.com**

DIVISIBLE MAN - THE THIRD LIE

Caught up in a series of hideous crimes that generate national headlines, Will faces the critical question of whether to reveal himself or allow innocent lives to be lost. The stakes go higher than ever when Andy uncovers the real reason behind a celebrity athlete's assault on an underaged girl. And Will discovers that the limits of his ability can lead to disaster.

A Kirkus Starred Review.

A Kirkus Star is awarded to "books of exceptional merit."

Available in print and digital.

Search: "DIVISIBLE MAN Howard Seaborne"

Join our Reader Email list at **HowardSeaborne.com**

DIVISIBLE MAN - THREE NINES FINE

A mysterious mission request from Earl Jackson sends Will into the sphere of a troubled celebrity. A meeting with the Deputy Director of the FBI that goes terribly wrong. Will and Andy find themselves on the run from Federal authorities, infiltrating a notorious cartel, and racing to prevent what might prove to be the crime of the century.

Available in print and digital.

Search: "DIVISIBLE MAN Howard Seaborne"

Join our Reader Email list at **HowardSeaborne.com**

DIVISIBLE MAN - EIGHT BALL

Will's encounter with a deadly sniper on a serial killing rampage sends him deeper into the FBI's hands with costly consequences for Andy. And when billionaire Spiro Lewko makes an appearance, Will and Andy's future takes a dark turn. The stakes could not be higher when the sniper's ultimate target is revealed.

Available in print and digital.

Search: "DIVISIBLE MAN Howard Seaborne"

Join our Reader Email list at **HowardSeaborne.com**

ENGINE OUT AND OTHER SHORT FLIGHTS

Things just have a way of happening around Will and Andy Stewart. In this collection of twelve tales from Essex County, boy meets girl, a mercy flight goes badly wrong, and Will crashes and burns when he tries dating again. Engines fail. Shots are fired. A rash of the unexpected breaks loose—from bank jobs to zombies.

Available in print and digital.

Search: "DIVISIBLE MAN Howard Seaborne"

Join our Reader Email list at **HowardSeaborne.com**

DIVISIBLE MAN - NINE LIVES LOST

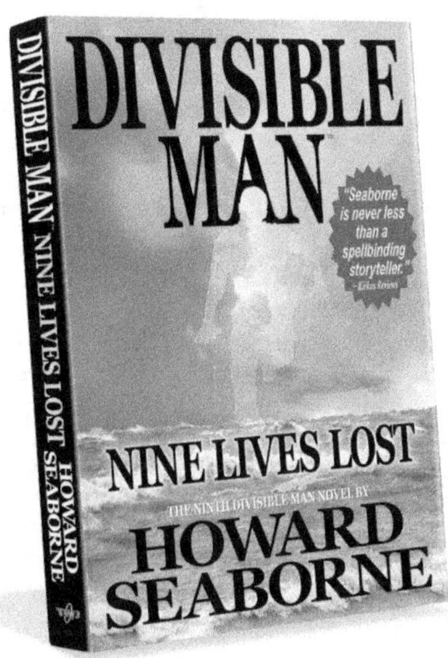

A simple request from Earl Jackson sends Will on a cross-country chase. A threat to Andy's career takes a deadly turn. And a mystery literally lands at Will and Andy's mailbox. Before it all ends, Will confronts a deep, dark place he never imagined.

Available in print and digital.

Search: "DIVISIBLE MAN Howard Seaborne"

Join our Reader Email list at **HowardSeaborne.com**

DIVISIBLE MAN - THE ELEVENTH HOURGLASS

A *BookLife from Publishers Weekly* Editor's Pick.

"A book of outstanding quality."

Will joins Pidge and Earl on a rescue mission that encounters a scene of unimaginable violence. The obvious explanation is impossible but grows equally impossible to ignore as the body count rises. Tensions spiral as billionaire Spiro Lewko, old secrets, and criminal lies push will to a breaking point.

Available in print and digital.

Search: "DIVISIBLE MAN Howard Seaborne"

Join our Reader Email list at **HowardSeaborne.com**